DOCTOR
TO DUCHESS

BY
ANNIE O'NEIL

Married to the man she met at eighteen, **Susanne Hampton** is the mother of two adult daughters—one a musician and the other an artist. The family also extends to a slightly irritable Maltese shih-tzu, a neurotic poodle, three elderly ducks and four hens that only very occasionally bother to lay eggs. Susanne loves everything romantic and pretty, so her home is brimming with romance novels, movies and shoes. With her interest in all things medical, her career has been in the dental field and the medical world in different roles, and now Susanne has taken that love into writing Mills & Boon® Medical Romance™.

Annie O'Neil spent most of her childhood with a leg draped over the family rocking chair and a book in her hand. Novels, baking, and writing too much teenage angst poetry ate up most of her youth. Now, quite a few years on from those fevered daydreams of being a poet, Annie splits her time between corralling her husband (and real-life Scottish hero) into helping her with their cows or scratching the backs of their rare breed pigs, and spending some very happy hours at her computer, writing. Find out more about Annie at her website: annieoneilbooks.com

A BABY
TO BIND THEM

BY
SUSANNE HAMPTON

Published in Great Britain 2015
by Mills & Boon, an imprint of Harlequin (UK) Limited,
Eton House, 18-24 Paradise Road, Richmond, Surrey, TW9 1SR

© 2015 Susanne Panagaris

ISBN: 978-0-263-24727-5

Printed and bound in Spain
by CPI, Barcelona

Dear Reader,

When planning this book, set in the neonatal intensive care unit of a large teaching hospital in Adelaide, I drew on the experience of my youngest daughter's premature arrival into this world almost thirty years ago. While neonatal medicine has changed so much over the years since Tina entered the world, the roller coaster of emotions experienced by parents has not changed at all.

The joy of holding our baby, prevented by the sea of wires needed to monitor her fragile life, the worry, the prayers for her survival and the elation at each tiny milestone during those first few days and weeks is what I hoped to capture in this book.

And just as the range of emotions for new parents has not changed over the years nor has the empathy and love shown by the dedicated doctors and nurses of the NICU. I wanted my hero and heroine's love story to unfold in this setting, where emotions run high and the greatest gift is finally to cradle your tiny newborn in your arms.

My hero, Mitchell Forrester, is the ridiculously handsome neonatology consultant at the Eastern Memorial Hospital. He has spent his life avoiding commitment by never staying in one place for too long—and then he meets Jade Grant. Jade has seen tragedy in her life, and has lost those she loved dearest, but still she finds a way through, driven by her love for the little girl who needs her most.

Although Mitchell and Jade share a bond—their niece Amber, who was orphaned at birth—they have never met until Jade and Amber visit Adelaide from Los Angeles to meet Amber's grandparents and celebrate her third birthday. Their visit, and the baby that binds them, opens their eyes to a different way to see life…and finally find love.

I hope you enjoy Mitchell and Jade's story.

Susanne Hampton

Dedication

Thank you to Orianthi and Tina for being the most
wonderful daughters in the world. You are amazing
young women who appreciate your God-given gifts
and every day bring joy to those around you.
I am so proud of all that you have accomplished
and all that still lies ahead.

And once again thank you to Charlotte…
who always brings out the best in my writing…
and ensures I finish on time!

Books by Susanne Hampton

Mills & Boon® Medical Romance™

Unlocking the Doctor's Heart
Back in Her Husband's Arms
Falling for Dr December
Midwife's Baby Bump

**Visit the author profile page at
millsandboon.co.uk for more titles**

Praise for Susanne Hampton

'From the first turbulent beginning until the final
climactic ending, an entire range of emotions has been
used to write a story of two people travelling the rocky
road to love…an excellent story. I would recommend
this story to all romance readers.'
—*Contemporary Romance Reviews* on
Unlocking the Doctor's Heart

'I recommend this read for all fans of medical romance.
It's the perfect balance: spunky, emotional, heartfelt—
a very sweet and tender romance with a great message!'
—*Contemporary Romance Reviews* on
Unlocking the Doctor's Heart

PROLOGUE

JADE GRANT HUMMED along to the radio as she prepared dinner for one. The music was loud, just the way she liked it when there was no one around to complain about the volume. Occasionally she sang a few words, but remembering words to songs was not her strength, and neither, according to her sister, was her pitch, so mostly she stuck to humming.

Her bare feet danced a few steps on the way to the refrigerator. Her slim hips, dressed in faded denim shorts, swayed, and she managed a spontaneous spin in time to the music. While her voice left more than a little to be desired, dancing was something she was good at.

Opening the door on the beat, she bent down to peer inside then pulled some fresh broccoli and carrots from the crisper before she closed the door on the next beat and headed to the chopping board. Her new favourite song was blaring from the portable radio on the windowsill. A smile dressed her face and she felt good about life. It hadn't always been that way but finally she was in a happy place. Her career as a neonatal nurse was on track, she loved working at Los Angeles District Hospital and, although she wasn't dating anyone, there were more than a few residents paying her attention.

She wiped some tiny specks of broccoli from her cotton tank top before she glanced up at the clock on the wall and smiled. Her sister and brother-in-law would have arrived in Palm Springs and be in their happy place for the long weekend.

The hotel looked so luxurious online and the reviews were all good. Jade hoped that it would live up to the hype and Ruby and David would have a wonderful few days relaxing before their baby arrived. Ruby was just over six months pregnant and Jade wanted to give the pair a second honeymoon as she knew that once they were new parents their focus would be their baby. The way Ruby struggled with her pregnancy, and morning sickness that still hadn't abated, Jade wasn't sure how much of a honeymoon it would be, but it would at least be a getaway.

Ruby and David had taken Jade into their home after her ground-floor apartment had been flooded by a burst water main the previous month, and this was her small way to show appreciation. She planned on moving back in to her beach-side home as soon as repairs were completed but the insurance company was still arguing with the landlords so no date had been confirmed. Jade hadn't lost any personal belongings to the murky water, as she leased the apartment furnished, so it wasn't devastating, just inconvenient.

She finished chopping the vegetables and put them on to steam before she turned off the radio and went into the sitting room. While it was only temporary, it was still wonderful having a big house to herself for a few days, she thought as she sat down on the sofa. Her place in Santa Monica was quite small and the paper-thin walls allowed her to know far too much about her neighbours. Some mornings she found it difficult to look them in the eye in the car park. There were some things she just didn't want to know and some she found hard to forget. So Jade was enjoying everything about being in her big sister's house.

Collapsing back into the huge armchair, she threw her legs over the padded arms and reached for the remote control. It had been a long day on her feet at the hospital and she decided that after watching the six o'clock news and eating her dinner she would soak in the tub, read a book and turn in early.

Switching on the television, her mood abruptly fell as she saw the horrific footage of an eight-car pile-up on the Pacific Coast Highway that afternoon. Her stomach turned and heart fell with the sight of wreckage. Jade was carefree about a lot in life but not when it came to tragedies like the one playing out on the screen. It wasn't only the victims she thought about. Her prayers went out to the families whose lives would never be the same.

She and her sister had been one of those families. They had been left to pick up the pieces of their shattered lives when their mother and father had died in a road accident when Jade and Ruby had been in their late teens. It had been a turning point for both of them. Ruby, being the elder sister and feeling the need to take control, had changed almost overnight. She had become more cautious and wanted stability, while Jade had steered her life in the opposite direction. She had decided to make the most of every moment with the mantra that *life was short*.

The television showed the lights of the LAPD patrol cars flashing and ambulances parked randomly across the freeway near the mangled metal that trapped the victims against the cement pylons. Traffic was built up for miles in both directions. Every detail of the horror was being captured by the news helicopters hovering in the air above. Watching with a heavy heart, Jade assumed with dread that there would have been fatalities. With no dance in her step now, she returned to the stove and turned off the heat under the saucepan, just as she heard her telephone ringing inside her bag. There was no caller ID, she noticed, before she answered.

'Jade Grant?' the sombre female voice asked.

'Yes, speaking.'

'I'm Sergeant Meg Dunbar from the LAPD. I'm afraid there's been an accident on the Pacific Coast Highway. Your sister's been taken to Los Angeles District Hospital.'

Jade felt her head spin and her heart race with panic. 'No, it can't be. There's been a mistake. She's in Palm Springs with her husband.'

'I'm afraid she and her husband were involved in an accident on the PCH just over two hours ago. They finally cut your sister from the wreckage and she was transported here. She is still unconscious but I was able to get your details from her cell phone. Please come immediately, she's heading for the operating theatre. Her injuries are critical.'

'What about the baby?'

'Miss Grant, I'm sorry, I can't give you any further information about your sister's condition. I've told you everything I know. The doctors will tell you more when you get here.'

'And David, her husband, is he there with her?'

There was a moment's silence. 'I'm afraid, Miss Grant, your sister's husband didn't survive the accident.'

The phone crashed to the floor. Jade froze with her hands limp by her sides, her body trembling before she cried out loud and fell against the cold wall. The officer's words were ringing in her head, not unlike a siren. She could still see the footage of the accident on the screen and she realised David was lying there in the carnage. He had never reached Palm Springs. She couldn't speak or even find a logical thought at that moment. A numb feeling engulfed almost all of her body. Only her heart could feel anything, and that was unrelenting stabs of pain that threatened her breathing.

Eight years disappeared and suddenly Jade was the eighteen-year-old girl who had been told by the social worker that her parents had been killed. A heavily laden lorry had run a red light on the corner of Fairfax and Wilshire and they'd both died on impact. Jade remembered the distressed expression on the woman's face as she'd delivered the devastating news. She felt certain the policewoman on the other end of the phone had the same poignant expression. She didn't think that life could be so cruel and deliver her family the same overwhelming sadness twice. It was too much for one lifetime.

For a moment, she stared blankly at the wall, seeing nothing through the blur of her tears. But Jade couldn't fall to pieces the way she had all those years ago. Back then she'd had Ruby to tell her that everything would be all right and that they would always have each other. Reassuring Jade that she would always have someone to lean on through the hard times. Now Jade needed to hold herself together enough to stand strong beside her sister when she found out she had lost David. She had to be Ruby's pillar of strength this time.

Jade reached for her bag and keys as she brought herself back to reality, and to what remained of her shattered senses. She needed to get to the hospital. Ruby had just lost the love of her life and the father of her unborn child.

With tears running down her face, Jade ran for the door, and taking deep breaths she focused on the task of getting safely to the hospital. Their home was barely ten minutes from the Los Angeles District Hospital but it felt more like a lifetime away as she was stalled by the heavy evening traffic on Wilshire Boulevard. Every minute she sat there her heart was pounding in her chest and her stomach was churning with the reality of the crash that had claimed David's life.

Only a few hours before they had been in the kitchen together, talking about the wonderful few days ahead and thanking Jade for arranging their short holiday. David had planned on painting the nursery when they returned and Ruby was already filling the cupboards with baby clothes in preparation for the birth of their first child. They had been overjoyed when they'd been told it would be a little girl, just as they would have been overjoyed if they'd been told they were having a son. They had been so thrilled to be starting their family. She would be the first of four children, David had lovingly teased his wife as he'd patted her already rotund belly.

Finally Jade pulled into the hospital car park. Her tears had dried and she was steeling herself to be strong for Ruby as she stepped from the car. She had no idea that that was the same moment Ruby's heart stopped. Her sister had died on the operating table only minutes after having an emergency Caesarean to save the baby daughter she and David had already named Amber.

* * *

Jade wept openly and uncontrollably when she was told. Nothing the nurses or police could say would stop her tears. There was no amount of compassion or understanding that could stop her sobbing. She doubted the tears would ever cease and she knew her heart would never be whole again. This time she had no one to lean on.

'Will she live?' Jade asked, scared of the answer but still needing to know. She had kept vigil beside her tiny niece for every waking hour of the two days since her birth. She had dozed sitting upright.

'Jade,' the neonatologist said with an equal mix of warmth and authority tempering her voice, 'you know that Amber's having the very best care with the finest facilities.'

Jade sat in silence for a moment, gathering her thoughts before the shaky response slipped from her lips. 'I know, Dr Greaves, and I don't mean to be abrupt, but I don't want you to sugar-coat anything. I've been working here in the neonatal ICU for over two years now, so please just be honest with me about her prognosis.'

Jade watched the neonatologist as she cast her eyes down and her lips formed a hard line in her somewhat tired face. She knew that the paediatric specialist had been attending Amber all night and the toll of her dedication showed in the morning light. Her naturally thin features were further drawn. But Jade was as tired as the attending physician and that brought her close to becoming a victim of her emotions. She would rather appear forthright and detached at that moment than risk her arm reaching around her in a comforting way and reducing her to a useless, snivelling heap of guilt. Melissa Greaves was that type of doctor. Professional but also motherly. Jade made a space between them to make it difficult for Melissa to reach for her. She had to do this alone.

The doctor's hesitation in answering confirmed Jade's fears, and her stomach tensed with a hollow cramp. Her composed veneer of bravado was close to shattering.

Melissa turned to her with a look that signalled she was about to deliver the harsh reality. 'If complete honesty is to be the call then I have grave concerns for your niece. She's dropped below her very low birth weight of two pounds, only marginally, but every ounce is critical, as you know, Jade, with VLBW patients.' She paused for a moment as she slipped her pen inside her coat pocket.

'Amber's a little fighter but since you don't want me to lie to you, *if*, and that's a big *if*, she makes it through the day, I'd still only give her a fifty percent chance of survival. Her gestational age was twenty-nine weeks, so it was always going to be a struggle, but with the compromised maternal metabolic and cardiovascular factors brought about by the accident there are additional complications. With her mother trapped in the vehicle for almost two hours, there was decreased uterine blood flow and abnormal placental conditions prior to the emergency Caesarean, and she is a tiny baby, so Amber has a fight ahead if she is to survive.'

Anxiously, Jade turned to the tiny figure lying behind sterile glass walls. A sea of wires, all linked to monitors, supported her fragile life. Jade gently reached her hand through the porthole door of the incubator and gently stroked Amber's warm, wrinkled skin. She was like a tiny china doll. Despairingly, Jade looked at her tiny niece's beautiful face through the transparent head box that was supplying a constant stream of oxygen to make her breathing less difficult. All the while a drip was feeding nutrients through the sole of her swollen foot as the veins in her spindly arms had collapsed and had ceased being of any use for intravenous nourishment. The innocent child was fighting to survive, unaware that her parents' lives had been taken by the cruel hand of fate.

'You know, if there's a glimmer of light in all of this,' Melissa added, and crossed to Jade and gently placed a hand on her shoulder, 'Amber isn't suffering respiratory distress and her tiny lungs appear to be coping so she didn't need a ventilator. I am amazed and a little bewildered by this and it does give me reason to give you the fifty-fifty chance ratio. Without that, her survival would be much lower than fifty per cent. At birth, I placed her survival at less than twenty per cent.'

Jade took another deep breath. The odds were improving. However, the slight degree of optimism the doctor had imparted didn't bring her peace of mind. Jade wanted the one hundred per cent guarantee that she knew in reality no one could provide.

This environment was second nature to her, yet now being in neonatal ICU made her fearful. Every day, as a neonatal nurse, she cared for premature infants, yet seeing Amber needing the same level of intense assistance made her feel vulnerable. She had to pull herself together. Not for her sake but for Amber's. She had to be able to process what was happening and, if called upon, make the right and informed decisions regarding her niece's care.

'And you moved her from the open radiant warmer

last night?' Jade asked, appreciating and finding a level of comfort in the compassion she had tried to deflect.

'Yes. When you fell asleep for a few minutes in the early hours I decided that the increased stimulation from light and noise and the associated risk of decreased growth and weight gain was greater than the disadvantages of the incubator. She is just too tiny to lose any further body mass. The next twenty-four hours will be critical.'

'Then it looks like we're here together for another long day, Amber, but you will get through this,' Jade promised aloud to the sleeping infant, before adding silently, *And I will never leave your side. Never.* Trying unsuccessfully to quash her unshed tears, she turned away before Melissa witnessed her breakdown. Through a watery blur, she watched the shaky breathing of her niece's tiny body and felt so helpless it was overwhelming.

She had never felt so totally powerless before in her life. She wished she had saved every forgotten wish from each birthday cake over the past twenty-six years and could tie them together to wish for the one thing she wanted with all her heart. If only she could gently lift the spindly bundle from her tiny glass crib and softly whisper that everything would be all right. But she couldn't. There was no guarantee that everything would be all right. There were no promises of a future for this little girl clinging tenaciously to life. And if she did have a future it would be one without her mother and father.

The days passed slowly, but each hour that Amber lived gave Jade hope. The hospital granted her compassionate leave to focus on Amber. The baby's weight was stabilis-

ing and the doctors looked less worried, as did the neonatal nurses, who were all friends as well as colleagues.
None of them provided false hope but neither did they
talk about the possibility that Amber might not survive.

Her heart ached for the baby she had been with for
four days. A baby as wanted and loved as any child
could be. She was the daughter that Ruby and David
had dreamed of and planned for so many years. It made
the bleakness of the prognosis so much harder to handle. She worried that not having her mother's love and
natural bonding could add to the complications of Amber's early entry into the world. Although Jade wasn't
her mother, she swore to herself she would be the next
best thing and do everything in her power for the little
girl at that moment and for the rest of her life. Amber
had lost the mother she had never known but she would
never lose Jade.

She would spend her life making it up to her niece for
sending her parents on the holiday that had claimed their
lives. And she would spend her life being the woman
that Ruby and David would want raising their little girl.

But Jade was also struggling with her own grief. Grief
the little girl knew nothing about. Over those first few
days it was almost too much to bear. Not only was she
close to crippled with worry about her niece, but she
had also lost her sister. A sister she'd loved with all of
her heart.

Ruby and Jade had been close all their lives and even
more so after the loss of their parents. Ruby had been,
in Jade's mind, the most wonderful sister in the world.
She had been kind, and funny and nurturing. It was as
if half of Jade was gone. Ripped from her life without
warning. No chance to say goodbye. No opportunity to

thank her sister for everything she had done. All the big sister advice she had given over the years. The advice that Jade had always appreciated but mostly ignored. The tears they had shed over boys who hadn't been worth it. The late-night calls to chat about nothing much but which had somehow lasted for hours.

It was all gone. She would never laugh with her sister again. She would never watch David look lovingly at his wife and hear them make plans and talk about their daughter's education. How Ruby would tell him that the little girl would be brighter than anyone else in the class because he was the father, and how he would say she would be without doubt the prettiest because she would look like her mother.

At times, Jade would tell them they sounded like a bad midday movie but their love for each other had been undeniable and real.

With that in mind, Jade held herself together. She owed it to Ruby and David to be there for their daughter and surround her with the love they would have lavished on her.

And then there was the added burden of guilt that sat heavily on her shoulders. No matter which way Jade looked at the situation, she felt responsible for Amber's early entry into this world. She had played the scene over and over in her mind since the accident. Why had she booked the holiday for them? If only she hadn't given them the present of a few days away in Palm Springs, they wouldn't have been a part of that terrible accident. And Amber would still be safely inside her mother with another ten weeks until her much-anticipated birth.

But instead, Jade was arranging the funeral of Amber's parents and staying strong for the tiny daughter they would never be able to love. She knew they both had a battle ahead but they would face it together. All they had now in the world was each other.

CHAPTER ONE

'WE ARE NOW commencing our descent into Adelaide. Please ensure your tray table is secured and your seat is in the upright position. We will be landing in fifteen minutes and you will be disembarking at gate twenty-three. Current time in Adelaide is eleven-thirty. Your luggage will be available for collection on Carousel Five. On behalf of the cabin crew, we hope you enjoyed your flight and will fly again with us in the future.'

Jade wound up the cord of her headset before she tucked it away after the flight attendant's announcement, then, smiling, she looked over at her niece, still sleeping soundly. She looked like a tiny angel. Her little round face was resting in the pillow, her tight, strawberry-blonde curls a little messy, her arm tightly holding her rag doll and her bright blue eyes still hidden from the world. It was the second leg of their travel. The fifteen-hour-long haul from Los Angeles to Sydney had been followed by a shorter flight to Adelaide.

The trip to Australia was not a journey that Jade had wanted to make initially and one that she had been delaying, but she had known it was the right thing to do. David's mother, Maureen, and stepfather, Arthur, had wanted so much for their granddaughter to spend some time in the town where their son, Amber's father, had grown up. So here they both were, about to touch down in a city that she remembered from David's conversations but a place she knew nothing about. Her stomach was churning nervously.

The last time she had seen Maureen and Arthur had been at the funeral almost three years before. It had been a time that Jade would never forget. Despite the overwhelming grief that no one had tried to mask, they'd shown great kindness in allowing David to be buried in Los Angeles with his wife. Jade knew that it would have been reasonable for them to want their son to be buried near them in his home town, but they had all known that David would want to be laid to rest with the woman he'd loved.

And so it was that they'd left their son for ever in a city eight thousand miles from them. It displayed a generosity of spirit, and Jade knew in her heart why David had been such a loving and considerate man. He had been his parents' son.

They had not visited Los Angeles again after the funeral, but Jade had accepted it would have been too sad to return to the place where their son had died. They had kept in contact with calls and emails and gifts for Amber's birthday and Christmas. Amber's birthdays were a bitter-sweet time for everyone as she had been born on the day her parents had both died. An unspoken agreement made them all try to celebrate the beautiful gift they had been given on that fateful day.

Jade felt an empty ache inside for what everyone had lost. Some nights she lay awake with her memories and overwhelming sadness. A trigger such as Amber's first step, first word, first anything reminded Jade of how

Ruby and David should be there to witness their daughter's milestones. And they weren't.

Amber never cried; she was too young to know what she was missing, and Jade was determined to devote her life to filling any gaps. Amber would never want for anything in her life. She would never be alone in the world.

As they walked across the air bridge, Jade spied David's mother and stepfather. Maureen was beaming with excitement, her smile so wide that Jade could see it before she entered the arrival lounge. Arthur's expression was more stoic, almost stern, but she knew he was a good man and a generous one. Maureen was dressed in a pastel floral summer dress and wore flat gold sandals, her blonde hair cut in a short, modern style. Arthur wore long beige trousers with a navy and cream checked shirt, his hair silver grey. They were a stylishly conservative couple, sharing David's dress sense, Jade thought.

Holding Amber's tiny hand in hers, Jade walked up the carpeted incline to where the couple were waiting. Still a little drowsy, Amber was struggling to hold on to her ragdoll, and the soft legs dragged behind them into the terminal.

'Hello, Maureen,' Jade said, and kissed the woman's cheek lightly. Then she greeted Arthur with a kiss to his sun-wrinkled cheek. Jade wondered if it was tennis or golf that had weathered his happy face. Now retired, he had spent his working life as a surgeon so she knew it wasn't from toiling in the midday sun.

'Amber, sweetheart, this is Grandma and Grandpa.'

'Hello, Amber, I hope you both had a good trip,' Maureen said, directing her comment to Jade as she wrapped her arms around Amber and kissed her ruddy, warm cheek.

'Hello,' came Amber's shy, almost muttered reply. Jade noticed her niece flinch and wriggle before she leant back, wanting to be in her arms. Understanding the little girl's reticence at being embraced by a woman she didn't know, Jade gently reached for her.

'She's a bit tired,' she said apologetically, and she lifted the child, who was now looking quite worried, almost teary, into her arms 'It was a long flight, but I certainly couldn't complain. It was very generous of you to fly us here first class.'

'Nonsense, we wouldn't have it any other way,' Maureen announced, still stroking the little girl's arm, and to Jade's relief not offended by the child's reaction. 'Nothing is too good for either of you. You are family and our home is your home for as long as you can stay. I'm hoping you love Adelaide so much you won't ever leave. We have such a big house all to ourselves.'

Smiling, Arthur rolled his eyes at the complete lack of subtlety in his wife's announcement, took hold of Jade's carry-on luggage, and together, the four of them made their way to collect the checked-in luggage.

Jade smiled at the warmth and genuine sentiment in Maureen's words. But it would never happen. Their lives were in Los Angeles and they were in Adelaide for one month. It was all the leave she could take from Cedars Sinai, where she still worked but now part time. Jade had thought about leaving when Amber had been discharged to her care. She had wondered how she would pull into the car park of the hospital where her sister had passed away. But over time it gave her comfort to know she was where Ruby had spent her last moments of life. And where Amber had taken her first breath.

But now they were in Adelaide and, despite being a

little weary, Jade was happy she had made the trip. Maureen and Arthur had lost their son and they deserved to spend time with their granddaughter. It would be Amber's third birthday while they were together and the third anniversary of Ruby and David's death. They could both console each other and celebrate together.

As they all headed down the escalators, Arthur insisted on collecting their bags from the luggage carousel so Jade and Amber could enjoy the sun outside.

'Go on, head outside and stretch your legs,' he told Jade.

'Amber's case is bright pink with yellow polka dots,' Jade replied as she scooped up the rag doll, now a little grubby from being dragged through the airport, and put it in her oversized handbag. 'Mine's a little less embarrassing for you. It's a silver hard-shell suitcase with a red luggage tag.'

Arthur smiled, handed Maureen Jade's carry-on and headed over to wait with the other passengers and families for the luggage to arrive.

Slipping on her sunglasses, Jade stepped out under the brilliant blue sky with Amber stuck by her side like a magnet. The sun felt good on her face. Perhaps a break like this was just what they both needed.

'We can't tell you how excited we both are to have you and Amber here, Jade.'

Jade turned and smiled at Amber's grandmother. The joy in Maureen's face made the long flight worthwhile to Jade. 'We're very happy to be here.'

It wasn't long before Arthur reappeared with the two large suitcases and they were on their way to the high-rise airport car park.

'Uncle Mitchell might be there when we get home,'

Maureen said to Amber, who in turn showed little reaction to the words of the nice older lady she didn't know.

Jade was momentarily confused. *Uncle Mitchell?* Then quickly the fog of the long flight lifted and she remembered David's brother. Although last she'd heard he was still living in some remote part of the world. He was the older but immature brother who never settled down but instead travelled widely and lived his life as one great big adventure. Like a nomad who pitched a tent wherever the mood took him.

'Isn't Mitchell living overseas?'

Maureen ran her fingers gently through Amber's mess of curls that Jade realised badly needed a brush. This time Amber didn't flinch, and Jade surmised that her niece had worked out that Maureen posed no threat. Jade hoped the two would grow close quite quickly, as their time together would be limited and precious.

'No, Mitchell's here in Adelaide at the moment. He's been in Africa for over four years but he came home a few months ago. Not long after he heard you were planning on visiting. Quite a coincidence really.' She raised her gaze to meet Jade's and with a knowing look added, 'I think he knew we needed him. Although he'll never admit it. He's quite the independent type but I think he was worried about all of us. Not sure how long he'll stay, though, as he's not one to lay down any roots. But still, he's here and he has the opportunity to meet you and celebrate his niece's birthday and that is all that matters.'

Jade didn't give it much thought. Her focus was to repay Arthur and Maureen for their kindness in the only way she could—by allowing them to spend time with Amber. Uncle Mitchell could waltz in and out as he pleased, which, from everything she had heard, was his style. No fixed address for any extended period appeared to be his way of life and it didn't look as if it had changed.

Mitchell's devil-may-care way of life was not her concern. She had met men like him before and had dated a few of them but that was in her past. And she had no intention of treading in that territory again. When it came to men Jade was numb. She didn't hate men, but she certainly didn't need a man in her life any more. Her priorities had changed the night of the accident. She didn't have time to think about men or relationships. They no longer factored into her life.

Now her focus was Amber, her work at the hospital and building a happy, secure life for the two of them. Men were a distraction and she didn't have room in her life for any distractions. She owed her sister and David her undivided attention to their daughter. She had promised them both that in her prayers the night Amber had been born.

'So how is little Amber doing?' Arthur asked matter-of-factly, as he inserted his validated parking ticket into the machine and waited for the arm to rise and release them. 'I know she's had a number of medical issues but she's a far cry from the infant we saw in ICU. She looks the picture of health now.' As he spoke, the automated arm lifted, and they left the car park and headed in the direction of the main road that would lead to their beachside residence.

Jade looked down at Amber, who was still drowsy and now sucking her thumb. The last time she'd seen Maureen and David had been at the funeral and when they'd visited Amber in hospital. She had been less than a week old and a little over two pounds by then. The little girl had been through so much over the years and there were still potential medical hurdles ahead, but Jade tried not to dwell on them. She was also aware that Arthur was a retired orthopaedic surgeon so he had the understanding and ability to process the medical details.

'As I said in my emails, Amber was diagnosed with dysplasia in her right kidney.'

'What's kidney dysplasia and is it serious?' Maureen interrupted.

'It means, darling,' Arthur began to explain as he watched the lights change at the intersection, 'that one of little Amber's kidneys didn't develop properly before she was born and she has fluid-filled sacs instead of healthy tissue in one kidney, but the other one is perfectly fine and doing the work of both.'

'Can that go on indefinitely or will the good kidney be overworked?' Maureen's question was directed at both Jade and Arthur.

Arthur looked over at his wife with a knowing expression. She had no medical knowledge but she was an intelligent and inquisitive woman and they were two of the many reasons he had married her. He knew she would have excelled in any field she had chosen so he did not need to over-simplify his medical terminology around her.

'A baby or, in Amber's case, a young child with one working kidney can grow normally without too many health problems. Babies with kidney dysplasia affecting both kidneys generally do not survive pregnancy, and those who do survive need dialysis and a kidney transplant very early in life.'

'How dreadful for the child and the parents.'

Jade stroked Amber's forehead gently and watched

her precious niece holding on tightly to the favourite rag doll she had pulled from Jade's bag.

'We are fortunate, but Amber is still being closely monitored back in LA,' Jade added.

'How did it happen?' Maureen asked as they left the highway.

'Kidney dysplasia can have genetic causes,' Jade replied, imparting the information as if she were back at the hospital, rather than talking about the little girl dozing by her side. It was easier that way. 'It appears to be a dominant trait, which means one parent may pass the trait to a child. Normally, when this is discovered, the child's parents undergo an ultrasound to confirm if either have the condition but this wasn't possible for Amber so we will never know if it was Ruby or David. And really it's a moot point,' she said as the car headed over a small bridge. Jade could see the shimmering ocean ahead and she looked forward to spending a few weeks by the beach, not overthinking what might lie ahead. She knew what she might face in the future with Amber's condition and, as always, it was upsetting just to think about it.

'But the important thing is our granddaughter is healthy and that makes me happy.'

'Amber is healthy now,' Jade confirmed, then paused for a moment to gather her thoughts and not become emotional. She was tired from the flight and she tried not the think about the potentially life-threatening condition that Amber could face if her functioning kidney were to fail. 'She's monitored closely and I suppose that's why it took so long for us to get here. I wanted to make sure she was well enough to fly and not compromise or exacerbate her condition.'

'So she got the all-clear to be here from her paediatric nephrologist in LA?' Arthur asked as he indicated and turned into their street.

'Yes, Dr Mulligan said it would be fine but he gave me the details for the renal unit at the Eastern Memorial Hospital should there be any issues.'

'That's my old stomping ground. I only retired last year,' Arthur responded with a touch of melancholy colouring his voice.

'Yes, I remember that from one of your emails, so it's comforting that you know the hospital well,' she returned. 'But let's hope we won't need to visit there as she had an examination with Dr Mulligan only two days before we left and he said that she is progressing well and may travel through life with no other issues. That's the best-case scenario, but if we aren't that fortunate, I hope treatment is many years away and she is old enough to understand it. Although she will need genetic counselling when, and if, she wants children of her own one day.'

'Goodness, children of her own. That's such a very long time away. Let's not rush the poor child.' Maureen turned around and once again looked proudly at her only grandchild. Her happiness was contagious and lifted Jade's spirits again.

'So there's no need to think she'll be anything other than fine and she can look forward to spending four lovely weeks with us,' Arthur retorted, purposely lifting the tone of his voice.

'And her Uncle Mitchell,' Maureen added, happiness evident in her voice.

Uncle Mitchell. Jade was taken aback yet again at hearing his name. Although she was far from curious about the elusive Mitchell, apparently she was finally going to meet him and so was Amber. The seemingly irresponsible brother with wanderlust. Ruby and David had eloped so there had never been a wedding to allow the families to meet. Although it wouldn't have been a huge gathering as there had not been much of a family on Ruby's side. There had only been Jade and Ruby.

Jade suspected that was why David had suggested eloping. The idea of David's family filling one side of the church and their side empty but for their friends would have made the day bitter-sweet and that was why she assumed he'd arranged an impromptu sunset wedding in Maui. He had been a considerate and devoted man. And from what she had heard completely at odds with his brother.

Mitchell hadn't travelled over for the funeral but Jade had been dealing with her own insurmountable sadness so she hadn't been too aware of anyone else and their presence or lack thereof then. It had been a sad time that she wanted to both forget and remember. Remember because it had been her last connection to the sister she'd loved completely, and forget because she hadn't thought she would survive the sense of loss that had threatened her sanity during those weeks and months that had followed the accident.

But apart from his lack of interest in his brother's funeral, Jade knew little about Mitchell. Over the years postcards and photographs from far-away places had arrived, somewhat battered, and the very occasional email when Mitchell had been somewhere with an internet connection. Jade had seen them pinned to the corkboard in her sister's kitchen when she'd visited. It had been difficult to see what he looked like behind the wraparound sunglasses he'd worn in all the shots. But scruffy and rough around the edges was the lasting impression. His hair was long and wild, almost in dreadlocks, and so, too, was his beard. David, on the other hand, had been clean cut and well mannered. And Mitchell appeared to have a new girlfriend in each photo.

For some reason, David's face would light up when he'd looked at the photographs and the reverence he'd felt for his brother had been clear. He would say proudly that Mitchell was the most selfless person in the world and the best brother, but neither Ruby nor Jade had been able to see any evidence of it.

The brothers had had a bond that had stretched across the continents and oceans that had separated them, and Ruby would often say that she never understood what was so admirable about his carefree, and from the content of the photographs, playboy lifestyle. The bungee jumping, abseiling and mountain climbing all pointed to an adrenalin-driven way of life. He was a nomad and spent a great deal of time in countries on the African continent. Nothing like the life that David had chosen. Ruby and David had been so perfectly suited and Jade had been happy for her sister.

Jade was not like her sister, though. She had never found the man perfectly suited to her. Although she wasn't actively searching, either. Her mantra drove her to live a full life and not rush to settle down. She had dated a few men, including an up-and-coming musician who had left town to make it on the East Coast, then a pro-football player while she'd been at college and a bull rider during her first nursing placement. Jade had liked the idea that she'd been with a man involved in what was called the most dangerous eight seconds in sport but the fascination had quickly faded and Jade had lost interest, just like she had with the others. There had been something missing. They'd had fun times but there had been no real connection. She hadn't been looking for *the one* but even if she had been she hadn't found him.

Ruby had not liked any of Jade's boyfriends. She'd thought her taste had been deteriorating, not improving, and hadn't hidden her aversion to what had appeared to be Jade's less-than-desirable type. She'd worried that the way her sister had dressed might have had something to do with the men she'd attracted and she oftentimes would suggest a more demure style, like her own, but Jade had loved her shorts and T-shirts. Ruby had complained that the men Jade had liked had been too wild and a man who couldn't be tamed would never be for keeps. Jade hadn't been looking for for ever, like her sister; she'd been happy to just enjoy a life without ties. She'd lived for the moment. A serious relationship had held little or no appeal.

She'd just been too busy enjoying life and having fun because *life was short*.

Looking back now, Jade reluctantly admitted to herself that Mitchell's ongoing carefree life was not too far from her former life. Her life before she'd become Amber's guardian. A life that she had almost forgotten. She had been skydiving more than once and had loved it. The rush that had engulfed her mind and her body as she'd been freefalling towards the ground just before the chute had opened had been thrilling. Her heart had raced, and she'd felt alive and exhilarated, but now her feet would be firmly placed on the ground. Now she wouldn't even contemplate a roller-coaster ride at Six Flags, her once favourite theme park and the destination of her former regular weekend trek with friends.

Now there was nothing in the world more important than taking care of her niece and making sure they were both safe at all times. The old free spirited Jade Grant was now very tame and very conservative in every possible way. Her once long blonde hair was now a short pixie cut, her clothes were more in keeping with someone at least ten years older and her make-up non-existent save for some tinted sunscreen and lip gloss. She was doing her best in every way to be exactly the person Amber needed and that Ruby and David would have wanted to be her daughter's guardian. The old Jade had been packed away. She wanted Amber to feel safe and the best way she knew how to do that was to be more like Ruby. Sensible was now her middle name.

'Here we are,' Arthur announced as he pulled the SUV into the driveway of the luxurious three-storey home. The architecture was modern, with a large glass balcony on both upper floors overlooking the beach.

Jade lowered her glasses. The home was palatial and the view as she stepped out of the car and looked around was spectacular.

'It's beautiful. What part of Adelaide is this?'

'Glenelg... North Glenelg, to be exact,' Arthur said with pride as he lifted the cases from the back of the vehicle. 'Just love it here, like an all-year-round holiday but still so close to the city. And you can go surfing if you'd like. Mitchell's renting a condo just down the road, walking distance actually, but it has on-road parking, with no storage space so he leaves his surfboard in our garage. I'm sure he wouldn't mind if you borrowed it. I remember David telling us you were quite a surfer girl.'

Jade froze. *Surfer girl?* That had been a lifetime ago. And it was a pastime that she would never contemplate again. Now that love of riding a wave was tainted by the reality that she could easily be knocked unconscious by her own board and drown at the bottom of the ocean. Surfing was right up there with the all the other activities from her past. Something she'd once done during summer break with her friends at Malibu but something that she would never consider now. With every day she found a greater understanding of how Ruby had seen life. And how that was needed, for Amber's well-being.

'I'm not a surfer any more, or even much of a swimmer, to be honest, but I'm sure Amber will love building sandcastles.'

'I'm sure she will. And the shops are close by, too,' Maureen added, hoping to bond with Jade over a shared love of shopping. Struggling to bring up two sons on her own, before she'd met Arthur much later in life, hadn't allowed her to share too much but now with Jade and Amber she thought they could enjoy some time together and buy lots of pretty things for her granddaughter.

Jade walked around to open the door and reach in for Amber.

'May I?' Maureen asked as she moved towards the car.

Jade wasn't sure how Amber would react but she politely stepped back and was pleasantly surprised when the little girl allowed her grandmother to lift her from the car. Jade stayed close at hand so Amber would stay relaxed. A smile overtook Maureen's pretty face and she carried Amber, and the grubby rag doll, up the steps to the front door.

'Perhaps you and your doll might like a nice bubble bath before lunch,' Maureen said softly, and waited for Arthur to unlock the door to the home that they would all share for the next four weeks.

Jade smiled as she entered the second guest bathroom half an hour later. She knelt down next to Maureen and watched her fuss over Amber as she played in the large white porcelain tub of warm bubbles. Jade had enjoyed a relaxing shower in another marble-tiled bathroom before she'd towel-dried her short hair and changed into an ankle-length cotton sundress. Long showers were a rarity as she didn't like to leave Amber alone for too long, but safe in the knowledge that Maureen had the little girl, and that she seemed content to spend time with her grandmother, Jade had taken her time and let the hot water and steam massage her tired body.

It had been almost three years of being the sole provider and now she knew that Amber was happy spending time with her grandparents Jade was looking forward to a few luxuries, like the occasional long, hot shower, over the next few weeks. But she still wouldn't be too far away.

She had heard laughter as she had approached the bathroom. Amber had a bright pink-and-white floral bath cap perched on her head but more than a few curls had slipped out and were now decorated with bubbles. The bathtub was filled with colourful plastic bath toys that Jade suspected had been purchased just for Amber. There were no other grandchildren and the toys looked far too new to have once belonged to David or Mitchell.

The next four weeks no doubt would be a time for spoiling Amber, and Jade was not about to tell Arthur or Maureen otherwise. Amber had been through so much and she deserved every bit of happiness and love that could be given to her. And equally Arthur and Maureen had suffered a terrible loss and she was happy that they could finally spend time with their only link to their son, their gorgeous granddaughter.

'What about we all head over to the beach to build a sandcastle after you're all clean?'

'Well, that makes no sense at all!' came a deep male voice from behind them.

Jade jumped a little with surprise. It wasn't Arthur's voice and she had not heard any steps, but looking around she immediately knew why. She saw two very tanned bare feet that would have made no noise on the tile corridor leading to the bathroom. Slowly, her gaze rose to equally tanned legs and then low-slung board shorts. When her eyes met the perfectly sculpted abs and chest, she felt her heart race a little underneath her thin cotton dress. It was a feeling she had not experienced in a very long time.

It was a feeling she didn't want or need. And it rattled her usual calm demeanour.

'You wash a child and then take her to roll in the sand. She'll look like a piece of crumbed chicken.'

'Mitchell, don't be awful,' Maureen scolded him light-heartedly without turning around. Her attention didn't waver from her granddaughter in the water. 'Amber has flown for almost twenty hours so she needed to clean up. I'll dry her before we head to the sand and she is much too beautiful to ever look like crumbed poultry.'

Jade started to climb to her feet as the banter continued. Her long dress was caught around her knees and ankles and made it difficult to get up quickly.

'I thought I heard you up here,' Arthur cut in, and patted Mitchell on the shoulder. 'You're in time to meet Jade, Amber's aunt…'

'Oh, I know who Jade is,' Mitchell replied, and put out a hand to help Jade up. 'Pleased to finally meet you.'

Jade felt obliged to accept his hand, but she was pleasantly surprised that it wasn't grubby and in keeping with his jungle appearance in the photos. It was clean and warm and strong. Immediately, she almost wished she had refused. Slowly, she stood to her feet and came face to face with the man she had heard so much about—the wanderer who never stayed anywhere long, the brother whom David had loved and admired, and the man who she now knew enjoyed teasing his mother.

And the man who immediately took her breath away.

He was not scruffy, not even close. His long blond hair, once wild and dirty, was very short and well groomed, his long beard replaced by a fine covering of dark stubble and his eyes, always hidden behind sunglasses in the photos, were the brightest shade of blue. As clear and brilliant as the sky she had seen when she'd arrived a few hours ago.

It couldn't be the same man. This man was gorgeous. And as he gently pulled her to him to softly kiss her cheek, she smelt the fresh overtones of his cologne. Her senses were suddenly overloaded.

'Aunty Jade, catch!'

Jade turned her attention back to her niece to see a soapy plastic duck heading towards her. Instinctively, she moved to catch the airborne object but caught her sandal on the bathmat, losing her footing. She tried to steady herself but was swaying precariously. Suddenly, Mitchell's firm hands reached out and caught her. She fell into his arms and his mouth hovered only inches from hers. His touch was warm on her bare shoulders and his strength kept her upright until she gathered her composure and could do it for herself. Her stomach began to churn nervously. Her reaction and feelings surprised her. No man had affected her that quickly for a very long time. Then she mentally corrected herself. No man had *ever* affected her that quickly.

'Are you all right?' His voice matched his appearance. It was as deep as the tan of his skin and very masculine.

She stepped back and smoothed down her dress. Words had completely escaped her and his nearness made her conscious of his sensuality. Astoundingly, he had managed to remind her of her own. It was ridiculous, she knew it. She had no interest in men. Any men. They were off limits to her. She had signed a deal with herself to forget dating, to forget men in general until Amber was married or at least enrolled in college. And by that time she surmised she would probably have no appeal for them, or them for her. It hadn't been a hard deal to keep. The men she had dated previously, *her type*, no longer appealed. In fact, no man had been appealing since the accident. But somehow Mitchell's touch had left her dizzy.

His expression was serious and his concern seemed genuine but she knew his type, a very handsome drifter with no ties. What she didn't know was why she was reacting this way. There was something about the man, other than his looks, that was attracting her to him. Then she realised that looking into his eyes was like looking into Amber's. The stunning blue eyes staring back at her were the same colour as those of the little girl she had kissed goodnight for almost three years. He was a part of the little girl as much as she was. They both shared a special bond with their beautiful niece.

But looks alone was where his bond ended. The bond of family was one he had chosen not to act on. He had never tried to see Amber. Mitchell had apparently been too busy enjoying life to bother checking in on his niece. He'd left that role to Jade and although she was more than happy to be the sole caregiver, the occasional call might have been nice. It might have shown that he actually had a heart and cared.

Mitchell hadn't displayed any interest in the little girl up to now so she wasn't about to just let him step into Amber's life without any scrutiny. And without a damned good explanation.

He had returned home to spend time with his parents for reasons known only to him and at a strangely coincidental time, but Jade supposed the shine would wear off the situation and he would be riding back into the sunset very soon. His type was nothing new to her.

'I'm fine,' she finally mouthed, still confused by the way he was affecting her, given the situation. Bringing her niece to Australia was not about to change the way she looked at men, or didn't look, as the case had been.

The idea that she could in any way be attracted to Amber's uncle was ludicrous. She snapped her wandering thoughts back to reality. She was beyond angry with him for not investing some time in his niece over the past three years, although she wasn't about to take him to task over it on meeting him. Maureen and Arthur deserved better than that. They were gracious and generous to a fault and she would not show any animosity to their son in front of them. And she also didn't want Amber to feel anything but love when she thought of her family so she wouldn't let on how she really felt about Mitchell when anyone else was around. That was between the two of them.

Jade was aware that Amber might ask questions about Mitchell as she grew up, but she had already planned on being diplomatic about the absent uncle purely out of respect for David. She owed nothing to Mitchell so it was not out of respect for him.

Jade planned on asking the hard questions when they were alone. She deserved to know why he had never bothered to reach out and get to know the little girl who was a living bond to the brother who had adored him. Jade did not understand how he could move on with his life and not want the child to be a part of it. It made no sense at all to her.

Neither had her feelings when he'd touched her. Suddenly, nothing made sense. How could she be attracted to a man she resented? It was ridiculous.

'Are you sure you're okay?' Mitchell gave her a wary look as he studied her. She was pretty, very pretty, he thought, but she appeared quite uptight. Almost like a governess. Her dress was plain, not unlike something a farmer's wife or librarian might have in their closet. It was safe, almost virginal. Then the word came to him. *Prim*. Jade's appearance was the epitome of primness. Proper and nice and completely disguising any sign of her womanly curves. The hem of her sundress was just above her ankles so even her legs were almost hidden from view. Her arms were bare but he suspected she would have a cardigan or shawl close by. Her hair was practical and he saw there was no sign of make-up, although she truly did not need it anyway. She was naturally pretty.

Yet this woman before him did not match the one described by David as Ruby's wild-child sister. The one who lived life like one long party. Mitchell had arrived at his parents' home expecting a fun-loving Daisy Duke and was sadly disappointed. There was no reality he knew in which wild-child and Jade would sit comfortably side by side. They were poles apart—in fact, Mitchell thought there was close to a universe dividing them. He had imagined from his brother's reports that they would have much in common and would enjoy spending time together while she was in town. But as he had no interest in spending time at the local library, it wasn't going to happen. Life was short and he wasn't about to waste any of it.

It was a not a coincidence that he had returned while Jade and Amber were in town. He had wanted to meet her and extend his condolences. Something he hadn't been able to do after the accident. He had been working in a remote village with Doctors Without Borders and he hadn't managed to secure passage home in time for the funeral. There had been no internet or phone coverage and he'd only found out about the accident the day before the service. After that he'd seen no point in going. He hadn't wanted to fly to the US and have expectations and responsibility put upon him the moment he landed. He was not father material and suspected that, however wild, Jade would be a better guardian for Amber. Better by far.

Coming to Australia meant he could meet Jade and Amber and then disappear again back to his own life and leave them to theirs. He'd wanted to meet his niece more than anything and it had torn at him not to have done so before, but he'd been afraid about the damage he might cause by raising expectations he couldn't meet. He hadn't wanted to step into their lives when he had no intention of staying.

But this visit was different. It was a holiday and that in his mind equated to no residual scars for any of them. It was neutral territory for the meeting. Jade and Amber would have Maureen and Arthur to depend on in the future if the need arose. It was a better option all round.

He had, however, imagined he might enjoy his time with Jade. With everyone in holiday mode it might be fun, but looking at her now he felt sure that the word *fun* was not in her dictionary. He wondered how his older brother's idea of wild could be that different from his own.

Or had Jade changed?

Something just didn't add up.

'I'm absolutely fine,' she responded politely, and turned away from what she found to be a scrutinising gaze from an absurdly handsome man whom she wanted to scold for his apathy where his niece was concerned.

'Are you ready to build some sandcastles?' Jade asked Amber to steer her mind and mouth from telling him what she was really thinking.

'Yeth, pleath,' came the lisped reply.

Maureen laughed and reached into the warm water and pulled the bathplug free. 'Grandma will lift you out then, sweetheart,' Maureen began as she pulled the little girl from her watery surroundings and wrapped her in the fluffy white towel.

'Amber, this is your uncle Mitchell.'

Mitchell dropped to his knees and put out his hand. Amber met it with a handshake.

'Very pleased to meet you, Amber,' Mitchell said softly. Then, looking from side to side, he added, 'If you want some fun away from the fuddy-duddies you call me and we'll go pony riding or maybe up to the Monarto Zoo, where they have lions and tigers and bears... Oh, my...'

Amber giggled at him. *The Wizard of Oz* was one of her favourite movies.

'I think that Amber will be just fine building sandcastles,' Jade cut in firmly with an expression of horror. *Lions and horseback riding?* Was he completely mad? Not a word or sight of the man in almost three years and now he wanted to whisk his niece off on a wildlife adventure and call it a fun day out. Hell would freeze over before she would let him take Amber anywhere.

'Then I guess I'll leave you ladies to it,' Mitchell said, climbing back to his feet and stepping back. He tried to mask his confusion and disappointment. He had been looking forward to spending time with the fun-loving Jade he had heard about but this very tame version was definitely giving him the cold shoulder. He got the message loud and clear. They had nothing in common, except their fondness of the little girl now walking like an Egyptian mummy in her oversized towel towards the door.

'There's a great breeze up now so I'm going to spend the afternoon windsurfing.' With that, he disappeared from the doorway.

'Don't forget the sunblock.' His mother's words echoed down the hallway after him.

'I'm thirty-six years of age and I've spent four years

in Africa and two in Saudi Arabia so I think I'll be just fine.' He shook his head and waved goodbye but didn't turn around.

Jade watched his mother's lips curve into a smile. There was clearly something in Mitchell that made his mother happy, but Jade wasn't buying it. To her, he was selfish and self-serving. Extremely handsome, she conceded, but that was not the point, she reminded herself. He was everything she didn't want or need to influence Amber's choices in life.

'Really, Maureen, do you want to scare your son away again?' Arthur asked with a grin as he scratched his shaking head. 'He's an adult, so just do your helicopter mothering with little Amber... And be careful, Jade, she'll have her sights on doing the same to you if you let her.'

Jade knew she had to mask the animosity she felt for Mitchell. She would be happy if he windsurfed for the entire four weeks and left them alone. Or, better yet, a huge gust took him safely back to Africa.

She was unnerved by the man. She didn't like the feeling at all. Although she didn't like simmering anger either, it was preferable to what he was stirring inside her.

Her pulse had slowed after he'd left and that was how it needed to stay, she thought as she followed Amber and Maureen back to the guest room. It was a pretty room, decorated in soft peach hues with two double beds and a view of the beach. The balcony doors were closed, and Jade intended on keeping them that way, even though she knew the high glass-and-chrome balustrade would more than protect Amber. *Better safe than sorry* was her new mantra. *Life is short* had been replaced the day she had held Amber in her arms for the first time.

'There's another guest room but I thought Amber would want you to sleep in the same room as it's a strange house to her.'

'She would, thank you.'

'I bought a few bits and pieces for Amber to wear here and then take back home to America with you,' Maureen announced, and slid open one of the built-in wardrobe doors to reveal clothing fit for a little princess or three. 'I wasn't sure what Amber's favourite colour was—'

'So she bought them in every colour,' Arthur cut in, rolling his eyes before he walked away and left the women to themselves.

'It's too much. It will never fit in her suitcase,' Jade said softly, not wanting to offend Maureen but also aware that Amber shouldn't become accustomed to a lavish lifestyle as she would not be able to keep it up when they returned to Los Angeles.

Amber and Jade were living in the home that David and Ruby had bought. Although it was sad at times, Jade thought that it was important for Amber to grow up surrounded by her parents' belongings. The house had been left to Jade and Mitchell in the will but Mitchell had sent a message through his lawyer that he wanted his share given to Amber. She had sent a letter back to him through the lawyer, showing her gratitude at his generosity, but she'd never received a reply. She didn't know if he hadn't received her thanks or if he'd just chosen to ignore them.

Either way, Jade had left it alone. Whatever his reasons, he had given Amber his share of the property and his actions did allow them to own a house. It was a lovely home in Hancock Park, not too far from the hospital. Her neighbours were an older couple who had never been blessed with children and they were very happy to babysit Amber when Jade was working. They'd told her it was better that she got out of the house and they loved the time they spent with the little girl. She was like the grandchild they'd never had.

But working only part time didn't allow for too many luxuries. Jade had invested the insurance money that David and Ruby had left behind to ensure that Amber had her college education well covered.

'Nonsense,' Maureen replied. 'I will have them shipped back to LA for you. Now, what about shorts and a pretty top for the beach?'

'That would be lovely,' Jade responded, accepting that Maureen had every right to spoil Amber and it would save her buying clothes for at least two years, judging by the number of outfits decorating the brightly coloured hangers. 'Her favourite colour this week is yellow.'

'Yeth, yellow!' Amber said, jumping up and down and losing her towel, which fell to the floor.

Maureen looked up at Jade with a knowing smile. 'Then yellow it is, Missy Amber,' she said, giving the little girl a yellow bikini before she pulled a pair of yellow shorts with daisies embroidered on the pockets and a yellow-and-pink-striped top with pretty capped sleeves.

Jade walked over to the long line of glass doors as Maureen happily helped the little girl into her new outfit. The breeze had picked up, sending white-tipped waves gently rolling into the shore. The huge expanse of sand was dotted with large colourful beach umbrellas. The Australian coastline was even more stunning than she had imagined.

Suddenly, something caught her eye, and she saw a figure crossing the road below. She leant forward against the glass and recognised Mitchell. He was carrying his windsurfing board to the steps that led to the beach. His broad shoulders were tanned and his shorts still hung low on his hips. Her view was spectacular and the ocean had nothing to do with it. The vision of the man made her heart skip a beat involuntarily and stole her breath away yet again. Nervously, she bit her lip and tucked her hair behind her ears. Neither action distracted her. Mitchell had her full attention. And she didn't like it because she didn't want to like Mitchell Forrester.

CHAPTER TWO

'WHY DON'T YOU lot come on in? The water's fine.'

Jade fought her desire to look up, but her eyes had a mind of their own and even convinced her chin to lift in the direction of the voice she knew full well was Mitchell's. It was deep and mellow, not unlike the smooth delivery of a late-night radio host on a programme that played love songs to those people who had no one beside them in bed. Jade knew the tone very well. It was how she fell asleep most nights. She had tried talk-back radio but listening to strangers' intimate thoughts didn't do anything for a good night's sleep, and the news was at times distressing, so late-night love songs became her preferred bedtime companion.

'I'm sure it is…' she started coolly, and paused as she watched through the filter of her sunglasses the water trickle down his sculpted body. She had already witnessed the firmness of the curves when he'd steadied her from tripping, but this close, and with the sun hitting every muscle and the salt water still dripping from his hair, the image was magnified. A life drawing class would not have seen a model more perfect. She tried to blink away the thoughts he was stirring but they were standing their ground and disturbing her equilibrium.

'We're happy here making sandcastles,' she finally managed to mutter with a lack of interest at his proposition she hoped was evident in her tone.

'And it's an awesome castle, but how about you and I hit the shallows?'

Jade was confused. *The shallows? Why would she want to hit the shallows?* It seemed an odd suggestion but he was being persistent and she thought it would give her the opportunity to question him over his lack of contact with his niece out of earshot of his very sweet parents. It wasn't his fault the universe had bestowed a body upon him that was causing her dormant hormones to suddenly feel alive. She would just have to deal with that. Maureen was there to take care of Amber so perhaps a stroll along the shallows would be a nice idea. The rationale for her decision to accept his proposition seemed logical, so she slowly stood to her feet. He had generously given his share of the house to Amber so her line of questioning would be polite but firm. She just had to keep her cool.

'I think that's a lovely idea,' she said, thankful that her voice did not betray her breathlessness. Now she was angry with herself as well as him.

'Great. Amber, let's go. Aunty Jade has given me approval to take you in to get your feet wet.' He stretched his hands down and playfully pulled her to her feet.

'Yippee,' came Amber's excited response, followed by a huge smile.

'Do you want to race me?'

'Yeth, I'll win!'

Jade was speechless. The invitation hadn't been for her. It had been for a splash in the shallows with his niece. Embarrassment brought the colour rushing to her cheeks as the pair took off across the sand.

'Would you like a cool drink?' Maureen asked. 'You look a little flushed. Perhaps you should come back under the umbrella with me.'

Jade nodded sheepishly and, dragging her dress in the sand, walked over to the shade where Maureen was sitting with her legs stretched out. Jade lifted her sun hat off and sat down in the soft sand. Words had escaped her. She felt like a fool but was at least grateful she'd been the only witness. It could have been worse, she thought. At least she hadn't put her hand up to be lifted from her sandy rest, so no one knew she had mistakenly thought Mitchell wanted to spend time with her.

As if he would… And as if she was interested.

It was only ever going to be a chance to hear his reason for being the absent uncle, nothing more. There was no other reason that could possibly make her want to spend time with Mitchell. Now she was doubly angry. With him…and with herself.

'Here, take this.' Maureen handed Jade a cold can of soft drink. 'It might help you to cool down.'

Jade wanted to put the icy metal can against her reddened cheeks but decided against it and drank the sweet fizzy drink instead. It felt good. And it made for a good cover. Maureen would have no idea it was pure embarrassment and not the sun that had made her blush.

'Look over there at the pair of them. Isn't he a natural father?' Maureen proudly stated rather than asked.

Jade raised her brow sceptically as she watched Mitchell and Amber splashing in the shallows. 'They're having fun,' she conceded, but she wouldn't commit to anything more. She wasn't about to agree to his paternal potential. In her eyes, he was a rolling stone who didn't show any interest in anyone but himself. Not even close to the criteria for the title of father.

'So what about you? How have you been?' Maureen asked with genuine concern and interest in her voice. 'Everything has been about Amber but what's happening in your world?'

Jade appreciated the question. It was nice to be asked but not something she had expected. 'I'm fine. Amber keeps me busy and I do part-time nursing in Neonatal ICU… I mean Intensive Care.'

'I know the acronym. Arthur's used the term enough. But it must be hard for you. Taking care of a little one and working.'

'We get by. Amber is a joy and a blessing so you'll not ever hear me complain.'

'Well, we just want you to relax and enjoy your time here. You can do with a break. I'm more than happy to help with Amber. She's so adorable and a credit to you, Jade. You've done a wonderful job, bringing her up.'

'Thank you, but it hasn't been too difficult. She's her parents' daughter and a sweetie, she rarely complains—well, except for her current dislike of broccoli and Brussels sprouts.'

'I'll remember no green vegetables when I put dinner on tonight.'

Jade returned a distracted smile as she looked back at Mitchell and Amber, now lying on the sand and letting the water hit their feet. Amber was doing her best sand angel and Jade knew her niece's toothy grin would be from ear to ear.

'Arthur told me you've applied to do some agency work while you're here. I'm more than happy, as he probably told you, to look after Amber any time. So if you want to do a shift, please, don't hesitate, but…' She paused for a moment and then her perfectly manicured hand patted Jade's, whose hands hadn't had a manicure in years. 'I just think that you, with your role as a single parent for the last three years, could do with spending the summer on the beach with a good book.'

Jade would love to do just that but she needed to work. A month without work could not be accommodated by her tight budget. While there was no mortgage, running the big house meant a lot of bills and Jade would never touch the money put away for Amber. Six months before the planned trip she had applied to the Australian Nursing and Midwifery Board for recognition of her qualification to ensure she met the criteria to allow her to work for a health professionals' agency over the month's holiday.

'I appreciate you taking care of Amber but I will try to fit my work around you and Arthur, I don't want to impose or overstep your kindness…'

'Nonsense,' Maureen countered. 'It's our pleasure and I insist that you spend the next four weeks doing whatever you want. Maybe even fit in a massage at my favourite spa. They have the most serene ambience with scented candles and soft music and I know Enrique's hands could do wonders for you.' Maureen's eyes were closed as she described the sensation.

Jade felt a tingle suddenly run down her spine. She wasn't sure if Mitchell had awakened something in her but suddenly didn't think it would be a good idea after three years of solitude to be in small softly lit room with Enrique, mood music and massage oil.

She drew a deep breath and blinked away the images.

'So…' Maureen dropped her already soft voice and leant in towards Jade '…is there a special man in your life?'

Jade was still pushing unsettling thoughts of the spa from her mind, and was about to answer the personal question diplomatically when she realised Amber was standing in front of her, dripping wet and smiling and looking a little like sand-crumbed chicken. And beside her was her very handsome beach chaperon.

Jade was painfully aware that he might have heard the question his mother had dropped on her without warning. Quickly, he confirmed her suspicions.

'Don't be shy,' Mitchell urged with a smile that showed his perfect white teeth. 'My mother is quite a busybody and if you're single she'll try to matchmake you with an eligible neighbour. So if marriage is on the cards for you and you'd like her to fix you up with an Aussie husband, let her know. Personally I couldn't think of anything worse than being trapped in that institution, but each to his, or her, own.'

Jade wasn't surprised by his views on marriage. To a man with wanderlust surging through his veins marriage would be like a prison. Ruby had been fortunate that she had met David. He had been the staying type and, no matter how short their lives had been cut by fate, they had loved each other completely. It had been a love and commitment that Jade had admired and respected but doubted she would ever find.

'I'm happily single,' she announced, not meeting Mitchell's gaze. 'And not looking for a husband here or in the US.'

Mitchell thought her answer made sense. From the way she was dressed he thought she should be singing on

a hilltop in Austria. It wasn't the way a woman dressed
to get a man's attention, unless he was looking for a reliable nanny for his army of children.

Jade was definitely not his type of woman. It wasn't
her appearance alone that was sending him running, it
was her lack of interest in anything that even slightly
resembled fun. She was more like a retired army colo-
nel than a young woman. Strict and staid.

'Well, now you know, you can leave the poor woman
alone,' he told his mother with a wink that didn't go un-
noticed by Jade. She wasn't sure what to make of it. Was
it a signal that she was indeed a lost cause and Maureen
was off the hook in trying to matchmake?

It didn't matter. Mitchell was a confirmed bachelor
and she was single by choice too.

Later that evening, Mitchell and Jade found themselves
sitting together after dinner on the balcony of the house.
Amber and her grandparents had gone to bed early but
Jade wanted to stay up a little longer to unwind from
the day. Knowing Amber was safely tucked into bed,
she was able to relax for the first time in many years.
Finally, she had the feeling of family support and reassurance that she and Amber were not alone in the
world. She knew they would only be in Adelaide for a
few weeks but the love Maureen and Arthur had shown
in just one day was a gift she had never expected to receive and she felt in her heart that they were forming a
bond that would last a lifetime.

She didn't expect or particularly want Mitchell to stay
but he did of his own choice. Maureen and Arthur had
appeared exhausted from the excitement of the arrival
and, Jade suspected, from the preparations for the visit.

Amber's rag doll had been washed and hung in the sun to dry, so she and her favourite doll were clean between pretty pink sheets.

Mitchell was relaxed as he swung away from the table, stretched out his tanned legs and placed them on the padded footstool. He thought the meeting with Jade and Amber had gone well. They were family and he felt good to have finally met them. Amber was a cutie and would without doubt be a heartbreaker in the future. Jade was not what he had expected but as a caregiver she fitted the bill.

He had no clue that Jade didn't feel the same way. She didn't think he fitted any bill, and she was looking for answers. With the others asleep, she decided that it was as good a time as any to get some.

She wanted Mitchell to explain his absence from Amber's life, particularly if he wanted a place in her future. But she was also mindful that his generosity in forgoing his inheritance from his brother had provided a lovely home for them. It was a little like an emotional landmine, but one she wanted to navigate to a satisfactory conclusion for all of them.

Biting the inside of her lip awkwardly, she tried to find a way to ask without the question escalating to something unpleasant, particularly in Maureen and Arthur's home. She shifted uncomfortably in her seat and drew a few short breaths. She felt a little torn about her line of approach. Gratitude, confusion and anger were all vying to direct the opening line of the conversation.

'What is it?' Mitchell asked, a little confused by her demeanour as he watched her becoming increasingly agitated.

'I just don't…' she stumbled, and paused and looked

away from his intense stare. His deep blue eyes were drawing her in. The softness of his mouth was a stark contrast to the angular lines of his jaw. The same way her demure dress was a stark contrast to the desire he was unwittingly stirring deep inside her.

The old Jade would not have hesitated to see where this infatuation might lead. To flirt a little and find out if it was a two-way street. To see if Mitchell's strong, tanned arms would pull her close and hold her as his sensual mouth claimed hers. She hurriedly blinked away the mental images that were crippling her line of thought. It was crazy. Perhaps that was a side effect of jet-lag, her sensible side suggested. But she knew the change in hemisphere wasn't bringing her to life. That it was Mitchell doing it all on his own. And she had to stop it.

Reminding herself that she didn't even like the man sitting opposite her, let alone desire him, she took a sip of her iced tea. It was old Jade's healthy but unwanted libido rising to the surface again.

'I just don't understand why you never visited Amber. She's your niece. The daughter of the brother you lost, and you didn't want to meet her. I just don't get it.' She blurted the words out at lightning speed to block out everything else she was feeling.

That was exactly the question that Mitchell had hoped to avoid. Not that it wasn't warranted. It just wasn't something he wanted to go into. He wasn't ready to once again be responsible for others. He'd been there and done that. He had hoped his financial contribution would be far more valuable than anything he could offer emotionally.

'I'm not a fan of LA,' he offered up as a reply. It was a half-truth as he didn't like big cities. 'I'm more of an uncharted waters kind of a guy. Not into multi-lane free-ways and high-rise apartments. Frankly, Hollywood just isn't my scene.'

Jade's face contorted at his response, and harshness coloured in her voice. 'She's your niece. It wasn't a sight-seeing trip that I was suggesting.'

'I'm here now,' he retorted with no audible emotion. 'Amber's a sweet little girl and I just want us to enjoy the next few weeks.'

'That still doesn't answer my question. Didn't you want to meet your brother's daughter?' Her brow was lined as she spoke. She was disappointed that he didn't offer a better explanation. She had hoped there was something of substance. Something that could justify why Mitchell had ignored his own flesh and blood for so long. But there wasn't. The long hair was gone, the beard too, but the disinterest in anything other than sat-isfying his wanderlust was still there. Jade realised that Amber would never be able to rely on her uncle and that made her sad.

Mitchell ran his long fingers through his hair ner-vously. It was clear that Jade wanted more of an expla-nation than he'd planned on providing. She would only be in town for a month. He didn't want to open up old wounds about his past and his reasons for not wanting to reach out. There was no point, he reasoned. No good would come of it. He'd been burnt, he knew his limits and that was why he steered his life away from anything that resembled long-term responsibility.

'Jade,' he began, 'I'm sorry that I couldn't be there for Amber but, in all honesty, I didn't think it would have been fair to drop in and disrupt the life she had with you and then hoist sail and take off. You provided stability for Amber. I didn't want to wreck that when I may not have been around for too long. Over the last decade, I've never stayed in one place for any length of time.'

His words were honest but they were not the entire story. He would rather appear shallow and deflect people than try to be something he wasn't and then hurt them in the long run. He just hoped that this explanation would suffice so he could leave that part of his life behind. And that part of his mother's life too. It had been sad for everyone and they were all in a better place now.

Jade wanted to hate him but the look in his eyes was somehow making that difficult. She sensed there was more to his behaviour than that, but taking a deep breath she decided that it was perhaps not the time to dig any deeper. It was late, she was tired and he had apologised. His reasons were flimsy at best but she also had to accept that losing his brother may have affected him differently. Everyone had their own way of dealing with grief. She had changed her life and settled down; Mitchell had done the opposite. Although his life on the run had started long before the accident, whatever affected Mitchell had happened well before he'd lost his brother. He clearly didn't see the world the way she did. It was best, she thought, to let it go for the time being.

Mitchell was nothing like David. And she and Amber both needed someone exactly like David. Dependable and giving with unbreakable ties to family. Mitchell didn't tick even one of those boxes. He was just a handsome drifter, a man with a wandering spirit and more than likely a wandering heart.

The night was warm and the ceiling fan was moving the air above them gently as Jade looked across the black ocean in silence. She had said enough. They both had.

The moon lit the waves as they rolled in to shore and she closed her eyes for a moment. So much had happened over the past three years. So much had changed. Three years ago she would never have thought her life would play out the way it had.

The old Jade's focus had been on living for the moment and the new Jade's was on responsibility. At times she wished her outlook on life wasn't crippled by fear, but that came with the territory of losing Ruby and David. She refused to let anything happen to Amber, ever, even if it meant wrapping her in cotton wool sometimes. It was something that Mitchell would never understand. And something she would not bother even trying to explain.

Mitchell lived in another world. And she remembered for a moment that she had once lived in a similar one. But she didn't miss it. What she had was infinitely better. She had Amber and the little girl filled her life and her heart.

As she slowly opened her eyes she felt her animosity start to lessen and looking across at Mitchell she felt it being replaced with sadness for what he had missed by not being a part of his niece's life. And for what he would miss in the future. Living the life of a rolling stone, he would never experience the joy she had every day waking up to Amber's precious face and the warmth of her cuddle.

'You've done an amazing job raising Amber,' Mitchell said, his voice husky and low and his eyes focused on hers.

Jade was taken aback by his unexpected compliment. She lowered her gaze, a little from feeling self-conscious and a little tired from the toll of a long day of travel, and graciously accepted the olive branch. 'Thank you, Mitchell.'

He poured some more iced water into their glasses and took a sip as he watched Jade sitting in the light of the moon. Unexpectedly for Mitchell, the longer he looked, the more Jade's prettiness became evident, no matter how she tried to hide it. She was cute. But not his type, he reminded himself. She was a little too serious for his liking. She was a combination of mother earth and elementary teacher with a hint of Sunday school thrown in for good measure. But he was still finding himself drawn to her and he had no idea why.

They were opposites of each other on every level. They both wanted only the best for Amber but that connection was as far as it would go. An unspoken truce was created in the warm evening breeze. Jade decided to leave the past where it belonged. And she also made a promise to herself…to leave Mitchell where he also belonged, at arm's length.

CHAPTER THREE

WITHIN MINUTES OF Jade's head resting back into the softness of the pillow in the bed next to Amber's she fell
into a deep sleep. The past twenty-four hours had been
a whirlwind. It had been happy, exhausting and a little
confronting. The happiness exuded by Amber's grandparents was contagious. It was evident to anyone within
a mile that Maureen and Arthur had fallen in love with
Amber on sight.

Amber seemed to be enjoying the attention and being
spoilt by the very kind people she had learned were her
grandma and grandpa. Jade had often spoken of them
over the years, and the cards and presents had arrived in
the mail, but to the three-year-old they hadn't become a
reality until they'd been in the same room.

The long-haul flight had been the tiring element but
to Amber's credit she hadn't complained, although flying first class had made it much more enjoyable, and
Jade was extremely grateful for that.

Then there was Mitchell. Meeting him had been surprisingly unsettling. She had expected so much less than
the dangerously attractive windsurfer. Her mind's image
of Amber's uncle had been of a scruffy, sunburnt wanderer, not unlike the survivor of a shipwreck, with hair

and beard that resembled an unkempt hedge. The reality was so far removed from that. He was gorgeous and as far as she could see he was under Amber's innocent spell. But how long would that last? she wondered. Would the novelty of a niece fade as he realised that it brought with it responsibility? Although her anger was fading, her defences were still high. She accepted that he was equally irresponsible and compassionate. A walking contradiction. But no matter what, his irresponsible side would guarantee that there would be no fun excursions without her consent.

In the moments before sleep claimed her, she admitted to herself that she was suddenly experiencing emotions that she had long since packed away. Her head was spinning madly and she knew the old Jade would have stepped up and enjoyed life the way she'd known how— at full speed with no brakes and no questions. But she couldn't. Not any more. She was Amber's guardian and she knew that it required her to behave as a dependable and controlled adult, like her sister. Providing guidance and being a role model was the job description. The Jade of old had been neither. She would have been more of a warning than a role model to her niece.

Amber had to be her one and only focus. There was no room for a relationship and with a man like Mitchell a relationship would amount to one night of pleasure before he headed off to some remote location on a different continent for an indefinite period. But she dared not imagine what that night of pleasure would be like. His innocent touch sent her spiralling, so a night alone in his bed would no doubt be close to heaven.

But now she had to push those needs aside and think of someone else before herself. In her heart, Jade would always know she was the reason Amber didn't have her parents raising her so she intended to spend her life making it up to Amber.

One day, when Amber was much older, they would have that conversation. Jade hoped Amber would forgive her for sending Ruby and David away on that fateful trip. Maureen and Arthur had pleaded with Jade not to hold on to any blame when they had attended the funeral but that didn't abate the sadness and sense of responsibility she felt. She wondered if Mitchell knew the circumstances of the accident, not that she cared what he thought about her anyway. But judging by his behaviour he was not exactly strolling along any moral high road.

It didn't please Jade that Mitchell's handsome face was the last thing she pictured before she fell asleep and her first vision in the morning.

First vision?

It wasn't a dream. Jade blinked and rubbed her eyes, trying to focus. It was a reality. Mitchell was standing at the end of her bed with a beaming Amber already dressed in yet another yellow outfit, complete with a headband decorated with bumblebees and some strange blue flowers. Maureen had worked overtime in styling her granddaughter.

'Hello, Aunty Jade,' came the sweetest voice in the world. 'Here's breakfatth.'

Jade was so happy to see Amber's smiling face but equally mortified to see Mitchell. She could only guess how dishevelled she looked. Quickly, her fingers ran through her hair to straighten the bed hair catastrophe.

'Good morning, Jade,' came the radio host voice. It

wasn't forced or put on. His velvet-smooth voice was God-given.

'Good…good morning, you two. I must have slept in… What time is it?' Horror still coloured her expression.

'It's barely ten,' Mitchell said as his eyes involuntarily roamed her barely clothed body.

Pulling the bedclothes up to her chin, she sat up. She was wearing a strappy powder-blue camisole and she felt awkward and uncomfortable with Mitchell so close to her.

'I really did sleep in,' she conceded sheepishly. 'Well, I'd better get up and shower and see what Grandpa and Grandma have in mind for us today.'

'It's a pancake. I helped make it.' Her little voice was insistent.

On cue, Mitchell walked around the bed and carefully placed the tray on her lap. He paused for a moment as he looked at her, his eyes intense as they traced the curves of her body, and his mouth curved into a smile.

'Pancakes, juice and a beautiful flower too,' Jade said as she leant forward to smell the rosebud. 'I am spoilt.'

'Grandma thed that you need a retht.'

Jade smiled the most beautiful smile. That's how Mitchell saw it. In the morning light with her bed hair and skimpy nightdress he thought she looked stunning. Not prim at all. She looked naturally sexy in a girl-next-door way. He had recoiled the moment he'd put the tray on her lap. He couldn't take his eyes away from her but he didn't want her to know just how appealing he found her. He didn't want to admit it to himself either. The previous night he had taken the time to really look at Jade and try to find the woman underneath the layers of drab clothing. Now there was nothing to look past. She was in bed in something skimpy and revealing. The messy hair was so much better than the neat, slick bob. He imagined that it would be just as untidy if they had taken a motorcycle ride through the narrow, winding back roads leading through the foothills and he had slipped the passenger helmet slowly from her head before he kissed her...

He shook his head and swallowed. He had no idea what had possessed him to be thinking about the American governess like that.

'Okay, I think I'll leave you to it,' he called as he crossed the room to the doorway, quickly pulling his thoughts in line. 'I'm off to catch some waves. I intend to make the most of my last day off before I'm back at the hospital for a week straight.'

He needed to bring the unexpected images to an end. He disappeared from her sight, knowing he couldn't afford to think that way. She was off limits. Clearly, she was not his type and he was not hers. She was a sensible woman looking for a reliable nine-to-five accountant type. Not the fun-loving, fly-by-the-seat-of-your-pants sort of girl he needed. But damn, she looked so sexy all messed up in the morning.

Jade watched him leave the room, not knowing what he was thinking. But she definitely had unwanted thoughts about the man who had brought her breakfast in bed.

She enjoyed the wonderful spread as she listened to Amber's adventures in the kitchen, cooking pancakes. She felt a little guilty that Amber had never enjoyed time with her extended family before now. But she conceded that it hadn't been possible before. Amber's health had

had to take precedence. Maureen and Arthur had never said the trip would be too difficult emotionally for them but their lack of travel to Los Angeles spelt it out to Jade and she understood. Burying their son was the only memory they had of the city. And Jade had been busy trying to pay the bills and monitoring Amber's medical issues while working part time, so a trip Down Under hadn't been a priority, but she decided, as she was listening to her niece's tales from the morning, that this trip should not be the last.

When her plate and glass were empty, Jade slipped on her long cotton dressing gown and the two of them made their way downstairs so Jade could say good morning and thank Maureen for a delicious breakfast. After a chat over a cup of coffee, Maureen and Arthur offered to take Amber for a stroll along the jetty to see if they could spot any dolphins, have lunch and give Jade some much-needed time to herself. Amber was excited by the idea so Jade agreed. Amber had taken to her grandparents and Jade was very happy.

'I thought we might have a little birthday party dinner for Amber tonight,' Maureen said softly so that Amber couldn't hear.

'But her birthday isn't for three days.'

'I know, but Mitchell will be working all week and he always works late, and I thought it would be lovely for him to be a part of the celebrations.'

'Whatever you would like to do.'

'We can have a little luncheon party on the day at the zoo perhaps but this is a pre-birthday party, and it means Amber will get two cakes this year!'

Again Jade wasn't about to say no. It was Maureen's decision; it made her happy and it appeared to have been made already. Jade was aware that this week would be particularly hard on all of them. It was the third anniversary of the accident. It had been a day that had changed everyone's lives for ever. Those who'd died, the one who had been born and the ones who'd been robbed of loved ones. So a double celebration of Amber's birthday would be a distraction that would be beneficial for everyone.

'There's lots of salad things in the refrigerator and some lovely fresh bread on the bench,' Maureen announced on the way out the door. 'Please, help yourself for lunch, unless, of course, you want to join us. You're most welcome—we don't want you to think we've kidnapped Amber but we do feel that you've being doing it alone for so long that you should have a break.'

'I think I will stay in, but thank you for the invitation. Salad sounds great.'

Alone in the house, Jade decided to enjoy a swim in the pool. The only 'old Jade' outfit she had packed was a nude-coloured string bikini. She never had time to go swimming back home between work and Amber so it was the one piece of clothing she hadn't bothered to replace with something a little more sensible. A little more suitable for her role as Amber's guardian. Knowing that the house was hers, she slipped on the tiny swimsuit and, feeling a little self-conscious, wrapped a towel around herself and made her way to the pool, where she planned on doing laps of the crystal water in solitude.

The solar heating had taken the chill off, rendering it refreshing but not cold. Jade swam the length of the pool on her back, looking at the clear blue sky with not a cloud in sight. The morning sun was warm and the breeze had dropped. It was a perfect day and she was enjoying the feeling of the water against her near-naked body.

The last time she had felt so uninhibited had been on a holiday in Cabo San Lucas almost four years before. It seemed a lifetime ago. Not that she would trade her life or anyone in it but she was relishing a few minutes to herself. She climbed out of the water and, still wet, lay down on the sun lounge. Her skin was a light golden colour courtesy of one of her nurse friends who had insisted on giving Jade a spray tan in her home before she'd left for Australia.

'Don't want the Aussies to tread on you 'cos you match the white sand,' her friend had said with a laugh as she'd refilled the airbrushing machine while Amber had sat giggling as she'd watched. They had covered the room with plastic bags to protect the white tiles from the brown stain. It had been a fun afternoon, and Amber thought they'd been quite silly and very messy.

Mitchell let himself into the house. With the car gone, he assumed his parents and the house guests had headed off somewhere for the day. The beach had been great, not yet hot and with just enough of a breeze for him to enjoy an hour's windsurfing before he dropped his gear back at his house. It had cooled his libido as well.

Seeing Jade in bed, looking so dishevelled, had made him view her differently and that was wrong. He knew when she was put back together the way she apparently liked to dress, she would not be his type. He liked to spend his time with fun-loving, easygoing women who knew the rules. No strings attached and definitely no schoolmarm attire. He just wanted a good time and he never misled a woman about it. He called it as it was and the women he dated knew he was not husband material.

There was no chance of Mitchell Forrester being tied down. Long-term relationships always brought responsibility in buckets and he knew he was certain to fail if he was pushed to travel that road again. There was nothing that would convince him otherwise. He was burnt out on that level. He had been bolting at the first sign of responsibility or commitment in his personal life for more than a decade and he had no intention of changing now. And Jade had commitment written all over her conservative self.

Walking in the front door in his now dry board shorts and sans a top, the house was quiet, just as he'd imagined it would be. Amber was as cute as could be but her high-pitched chatter with a distinct American accent would probably not let him concentrate on the task at hand. He loved children and that was why he had specialised in neonatology and paediatrics but he liked to keep his private life and his professional life separate. He never planned on having children of his own. The title of father did not factor into his future. Uncle was fine but that would be his limit.

He spied the new sound system that Arthur had purchased lying unopened in the box in the living room. Arthur had no idea of how to actually make it work, and Mitchell had offered to connect it. With an empty house, he knew he would have the job finished quickly. With Maureen around, any job he did for them resembled an instructional video on replay as she asked a barrage of questions with each step he took and then asked him to repeat it again later. So this chore would be a pleasant change. He would have it all done and be gone before they came home, and that sat well with him.

Leaving before they pulled into the driveway would be best. It wasn't that he didn't want to see Amber, it was more that he didn't know if he wanted to see Jade. She was a conundrum. The morning before he'd felt positive that he could be around her and not feel at all attracted. But that morning when she'd lain in her crumpled bed, all fresh-faced and messy, she'd suddenly inched a little closer to being his type. And that was a bad thing.

Maybe that was the real Jade. He wondered if the new Jade was an attempt to be more like Ruby. A woman invented to be what Ruby and David would have wanted.

But lying in bed she had been exactly what he wanted. He pushed the image from his mind. There was work to do and daydreaming about Jade would not progress anything except his desire to a level requiring a cold shower.

Mitchell cut open the box and removed the first speaker. All he needed to start was the tool kit from the shed by the pool.

Jade had finished applying the sunscreen to her body. The mid-morning sun probably wouldn't burn but she knew that underneath her man-made tan she was still naturally pale and was aware the Australian sun was quite intense. With her skin now glistening from the lotion, she lay back on the sun lounge to enjoy the warm rays. Her oversized sunglasses protected her eyes and her earphones were plugged in. She didn't have to listen out for Amber for a few hours, so she listened to her favourite southern rock as she lay in the warm sun. She didn't have to hide as there was no one to see her in the private pool area. Her bikini was still wet and her skin tone was now a perfect match. She was completely un-aware that from twenty or more feet away she appeared to be completely naked.

Mitchell spied Jade from the corner of his eye and dropped the entire contents of the tool kit on the ground. His chiselled jaw fell and his eyes widened as he saw the most stunning vision lying naked beside the pool.

Jade?

It couldn't be her…or could it?

He hadn't seen her when he'd walked to the shed and rifled through the contents, looking for a screw-driver and small wrenches. It had been as he'd closed the shed door that he'd seen her body draped across the sun lounge. He had never seen a woman so perfect. And she was naked. That made the vision doubly perfect to him.

He struggled to pull his eyes away. The desire to ad-mire her stunning body was fighting with the shreds of decency that had survived the shock of seeing her like that. Falling to his knees and not allowing himself to look in her direction, he began gathering the tools now strewn across the pavers leading back to the house. It was obvious she hadn't seen him so he decided to exit the back yard and go inside without causing her any em-barrassment. She had obviously decided to skinny-dip while the family were out, he realised as he fumbled to collect the last tool that had rolled onto the lawn.

But Jade skinny-dipping?

That was not in keeping with the persona she was portraying to everyone. She had gone from looking like a missionary to a centrefold. Maybe this was the real Jade. The woman his brother had called the rebel sister was lying naked under the Australian sun. He liked this Jade so much more.

His heart was pulsing blood around his body at an alarming rate. His mind was spinning with the image that he didn't want to blink away. The idea that Jade was prim and uptight no longer had any grounds for existence. Jade was so far from what she hid beneath her dowdy clothing. Clothing that he now suspected was a shield from the world or a reaction to what had happened. When his brother had died, he had run further from responsibility and Jade, he now assumed, had stepped up, left the fun behind and donned the sensible clothing. She had morphed into her sensible sister, Ruby.

Without making another sound or looking back, he left. He had stumbled upon the most beautiful vision but he wasn't about to take advantage of the situation. Jade thought she was alone and he would respect that assumption and leave the house. There was no need for him to let her know that he had accidentally seen what she hid from the rest of the world. The sound system had to wait until another day. Mitchell needed to take a plunge in the ocean to cool off.

Jade lowered her sunglasses. Over the music, she thought she heard a noise. It was like a door was being slammed. She pulled the earphones free, wrapped the towel around her damp bikini and headed inside.

'Anyone home?'

No response came back so, surmising it had probably been a neighbour's door, she headed upstairs for a warm shower. The swim and the sun had been wonderful beyond belief, but she had calls to make. She needed to let the nursing agency know she had arrived and was ready for work as she needed an income while she was in Adelaide. It was obvious that Amber loved being with her grandparents and they adored being with her, so a weight had lifted from her, and Jade knew she wouldn't be putting anyone out by working some shifts at a local hospital.

She was waiting for jet-lag to hit but it hadn't so she suspected she might be one of the few who didn't suffer the effects from long-haul flights. So she was ready to start working whenever they called. Her papers were in order, she had been approved by the statutory body and she was ready to take on whatever temporary nursing was available.

Mitchell dived into the cool waves and intended on swimming until the image of Jade lying naked on the sun lounge began to fade. Around two hundred strokes into his swim he realised that it would never disappear. It was burnt into his memory. And he wasn't entirely sure he wanted to erase it. It was much too stunning a visual to give up that easily. He would just try very hard not to recall it too often.

And particularly not when she was near him.

Jade put her damp swimsuit in the laundry to dry and dressed in a calf-length grey-and-white striped skirt and grey knit top then put a call in to the nursing agency. While she was waiting to hear back, she towel-dried her hair as she wandered around the stunning home. There were pictures of David and Mitchell everywhere. As children, teenagers and also their graduation photos complete with caps, gowns and scrolled parchment.

Maureen was obviously very proud of her sons and

their achievements and Arthur was an equally proud stepfather. Jade didn't know what had happened to their biological father but she did recall David saying that he had been quite young when his parents had divorced and Arthur had married Maureen quite a few years later. Then she spied Maureen and Arthur's wedding photograph. Maureen looked to be in her early forties and Arthur perhaps in his late forties. They were dressed quite simply, both in suits, and the photograph had been taken in a park rotunda with a marriage celebrant.

A photo at the back, almost hidden from view, then took her attention. It was of a very young Mitchell dressed in a work uniform. He looked barely old enough to be in high school but he was in what appeared to be a large warehouse. He appeared far too young to be working. Perhaps it had been work experience, she thought as she put down the photograph.

She noticed there were a few photographs of Mitchell, resembling Tarzan, on his travels, although none with women, as there had been in the photos he had sent David. Instead, they were all solo shots in the wilderness. He had hidden his array of girlfriends from his mother, which did hint at a level of good taste. She quickly blinked away thoughts of his very active love life and continued admiring the collections of photographs.

There were pictures from the beach wedding of David and Ruby. Jade reached down and picked up one of the silver-framed photographs. The happy couple were beaming and the beach at sunset in the background was spectacular. She ran her finger absent-mindedly over the image of her sister. Her long blonde hair was braided with fresh flowers and the hemline of her stunning white lace wedding gown disappeared into the sand. Ruby was a beautiful bride and they looked such a happy couple. Jade put the frame down with a tear threatening to spill onto her cheek.

She noticed pictures of Amber on the sideboard and the sight of them all lifted her mood. So many of the photographs that Jade had sent to them were on display, and each had its own frame.

Maureen and Arthur were doting grandparents.

Jade's mobile phone suddenly rang in the pocket of her skirt.

'Hello, Jade Grant,' she answered, after pulling it free.

'Hi, Jade, this is Susy from the ANR agency. We spoke earlier and I wanted to see if you would consider a three-week placement, starting tomorrow.'

'That's quick, but, yes, I'm sure it will be fine,' Jade responded, immediately recognising the acronym for the Australian Nursing Recruitment Agency. She had thought it would be a few days till she heard anything from them.

'With your experience and your qualifications in neo-natal ICU and midwifery, you were snapped up. I only wish you could stay longer. There would never be a shortage of work for you,' Susy told her. 'I know you only want to work part time during your stay in Adelaide so this placement is three shifts per week. It's to cover holidays and I have another temp neonatal nurse who can job-share with you. What do you think?'

'I think it sounds great. Where will I be working?'

'You'll be at the Eastern Memorial right in the heart of Adelaide, working across paediatrics and neonatal as I know you have experience in both. I think you'll like working there. The nursing staff are second to none, the facilities state of the art.'

'It sounds wonderful.'

After Jade ended the call she turned away from the photos of the family and breathed a sigh of relief. It was hard to admit it, but she had to concede that Mitchell was beyond attractive and he had stirred some feelings she'd forgotten she had ever felt, but now this would not be an issue: she would be busy working three days a week so would not see much of him during her stay.

Despite his obvious masculine appeal, and the way he was making her feel, she tried to convince herself that Mitchell Forrester would not be a threat to her. He was wayward and reckless if his postcards were anything to go by, she told herself just in case her hormones were making their own plans. Reliable, steadfast and sensible would be the prerequisites for any man to be in Amber's life, just the way Ruby had liked her men. And it wouldn't happen for a very long time, if ever. She needed to focus on being the best caregiver to Amber. That was the role she had been given and she intended on doing the very best job.

She had sat Amber down a few months before the trip and tried to explain why her life was different.

'I know that most of your friends at playgroup have mommies and daddies but you have an aunty instead,' Jade began to explain. 'Your mommy and daddy look down from heaven and watch over you every day to make sure you are happy and safe. And I think that I am the luckiest aunty in the world to have you.'

Jade had become Amber's legal guardian with Maureen and Arthur's blessing as they had wanted what was best for their granddaughter. Mitchell had never contested the role, and Jade wasn't surprised. Jade had seen from the moment she'd arrived in Adelaide that nothing had changed. Maureen and Arthur were so supportive and Mitchell was just there for the fun times.

'Ith it my birthday?' Amber squealed her question when she saw her grandfather blowing up balloons and her grandmother putting out pink and yellow napkins and a small stack of brightly wrapped gifts on the table.

'Not for a few days, but this is an early birthday party so that Uncle Mitchell can say happy birthday and watch you blow out the candles,' Maureen told her. 'He has to go to work for the rest of the week so he will miss your real birthday. So you'll have two parties.'

Amber's eyes grew wider. 'Two parties?'

'Yes, Amber,' Jade answered. 'Grandma is spoiling you and you'll be having two parties this year.'

Amber was clapping her hands and laughing as she sat beside her grandfather while he blew up the last of the balloons.

'Don't tell me I'm doing this again in a few days?'

'Darling,' Maureen began, 'there's only a handful of balloons so please just tie the ribbons onto each one and we can put them up before Mitchell arrives.'

'Too late, I'm here.'

Mitchell had initially hesitated to accept the dinner invitation when his mother had called but when he'd discovered it was to celebrate Amber's birthday he agreed immediately. The vision of Jade by the pool had haunted him all day and was the reason he'd hesitated. Something made him want to stay away from Jade but something stronger made him want to spend time with her.

He wanted to find out more about her, and if he was right about her motives. Did she really think that wearing clothes so dour that they were suited to a retired prison warden would make her a better guardian? A blind man could see her devotion and success raising Amber. She didn't need to dress in costume to achieve anything. He would never understand why she covered the body he knew for a fact was amazing. And why she seemed so averse to his light-hearted remarks about life.

It was as if she had nominated herself for the position of moral compass of the family, if not the world. But as he looked at her he had to admit something about her was growing on him. She was cute, a good and devoted woman, and now that he had seen so much more she had also become desirable woman in his eyes. Common sense told him to limit his time around her but something else told him the opposite.

Jade turned around to see Mitchell standing in the doorway with a large white bear in a yellow spotted dress and a very small white box with a silver bow. He was wearing black jeans, black boots and a tight plain white T-shirt that didn't hide his ample chest. She felt her temperature start to rise and her heart flutter. Then she noticed he was avoiding eye contact with her.

She prayed he had not seen her watching him from her balcony as he'd walked to the beach that morning. The swagger in his step and his lean, tanned body barely dressed had had a mind-numbing effect on her the moment she'd seen him and the image was still close to doing the same now. She felt her skin heat up and threaten to flush and she was bewildered by what was happening to her.

Over the past three years on her own she must have seen hundreds of good-looking men walking the streets, having coffee in the hospital cafeteria, in the twenty-four-hour supermarket when she called in after a late shift, but none of them had stirred any interest. Nothing.

She'd walked past them as if they'd been store manne-
quins. But now, looking at Mitchell, she was very aware
of the unsettling attraction she was feeling.

With difficulty, she attempted to drag her thoughts
back to where they belonged and where they needed to
remain for the next few weeks.

'This is for the birthday girl,' Mitchell said, his hands
outstretched to Amber.

Jade could see Amber's face light up as Arthur led
her by the hand over to Mitchell and the presents.

'The teddy is for now,' he began, as he put the bear
into her arms. 'And this present is for when you are
older.' He carefully handed her the small present.

Jade noted the colour of the dress. Mitchell had remembered Amber's favourite colour. Amber took the
presents and gave Mitchell a hug before she returned to
the chair and unwrapped the white bow on the box, her
teddy firmly planted on her little lap.

'It-th's pretty!' she exclaimed, as she pulled a silver
heart-shaped locket from the box. 'Look, Aunty Jade,
it-th's pretty.'

'You can put photos inside so one day when you are
off travelling the world you will always have your family travelling with you,' Mitchell added.

Amber had no idea what he was talking about but
Jade was taken aback and the expression on her face
did not hide it. The teddy was cute and the locket was
lovely but the message behind it didn't sit well with her.
Was this Mitchell's advice to her? Head off, put family in a locket and live your life somewhere else? She
hadn't pictured Amber ever leaving to see the world.
She felt sick at the thought of not being there to protect
her. And upset that Mitchell was using Amber's birth-

day to impart his set of values on niece when she was only three years old.

'That is very pretty' she said, as she sat down and opened the delicate locket. 'It will be lovely to wear to very special *parties*.' Not a trip around the world away from family, she continued in her mind.

'I'm surprised you didn't buy one in green to go with her camouflage outfit for her trip down the Amazon for her sixth birthday,' she said to Mitchell in a lowered voice as she made her way past him to the kitchen. 'Really, a trip around the world? She's three years old and maybe there's the chance she'll be like her father and she won't want to run away from her family.'

Mitchell was stunned into silence. He thought her rebuke was an overreaction. It was a present of his choice with his sentiment. Not everyone saw the world the way Jade obviously did. He noted her dress sense had returned to that of elderly maiden aunt.

'Like me? Is that what you mean? Actually, the message was about the importance of family,' he said in the same low voice with a scowl as he followed her into the kitchen. 'Pity you couldn't see past your own agenda to see I didn't have one.'

'My agenda?'

'Yes. It's pretty obvious you're planning on wrapping Amber in cotton wool for her entire life. Let her build sandcastles but avoid the water. Like a bystander who can watch but not experience life. That's what this is about. It's not healthy to bring up a child with no sense of adventure.'

'How lovely to see you two getting to chat finally,' Maureen said as she entered the kitchen to collect some plates. 'Arthur is putting some prawns on the barbeque to go with the potato bake and salad.'

'That sounds delicious,' Jade said through gritted teeth. She was so angry with Mitchell. She was just protecting her niece the best way she knew how. She suddenly prayed that Mitchell wasn't right. She didn't want to cocoon Amber and not let her take her place in the world or have fun as she grew up. She bit her lip as her eyes darted nervously around the room. His words made her question herself. *Was she at risk of smothering Amber?*

'I'll see what I can do to help outside,' Mitchell said, his eyes narrowing in Jade's direction before he disappeared onto the balcony to help Arthur put up the balloons.

'Such a pretty locket and so sweet of Mitchell to think of something like that. I thought you'd approve of something so delicate and timeless,' Maureen said as she collected the salad from the refrigerator, added some home-made dressing and headed back outside.

'Very pretty,' Jade returned. She couldn't agree with the rest of Maureen's words. She wasn't sure what she thought about Mitchell or herself any more.

Mitchell and Jade chose to sit at opposite ends of the table for dinner. They said nothing to each other and neither made eye contact with the other. Amber didn't appear to have much of an appetite and just played with her food, then lay down on the sofa with her new teddy.

'Are you okay, sweetheart?' Jade asked with a little frown of concern.

'I'm full.'

Maureen looked over at Amber and lowered her voice. 'She didn't want much for lunch today either. I think jet-lag has hit her. It was a long trip for a little girl. And you too, Jade.'

'I'll keep an eye on it,' Jade said. 'You're probably right but if she doesn't pick up I'll take her for a check-up.'

'Do you want me to make an appointment with the nephrologist just for peace of mind?' Arthur asked. 'It's probably not related but it will put your mind at rest.'

'Let's see how she goes,' Jade replied, as she watched Amber play with her yet-to-be named bear. 'The flight probably exhausted her. In a day or so she should pick up.'

'Teddy wants to lie down, he'th tired.' Amber said softly.

The adults all smiled and returned to their dinner, each of them not wanting to appear concerned but still keeping an eye on Amber.

'And what did you get up to today while Amber was showing us the dolphins, Jade?' Maureen finally asked to lift the conversation.

'Nothing much… I just relaxed by the pool.'

Mitchell choked loudly on hearing the words. His drink threatened to spill from his lips and his eyes watered as he valiantly fought to not splutter. *Nothing much* didn't just describe her day…it did, however, describe her outfit, or lack thereof, perfectly. She had been lying naked by the pool. And had looked amazing doing so.

'Are you all right, dear?'

'Uh-huh,' he responded, his lips forming a rueful slant as he tried not to make eye contact with Jade. He wasn't all right. He wanted to be honest and tell her that he had seen her that morning lying sans clothing by the water's edge but he would never embarrass her that way. Also peeping Tom came to mind to describe him and he didn't want that label. It had been an accidental sighting but a very pleasant one.

But the sighting even now, many hours later, was

causing his heart to beat a little faster despite his opinion of her. It was an image at total odds with the role she was playing. Perhaps being the only one at the table who knew the real Jade drew him to her. He had seen the version she was hiding from the world and his parents. And he liked what he'd seen. He suspected why she was behaving that way but he didn't agree with it. Just as she had over-reacted about the locket, Jade was trying to protect her niece from the world and even the real Jade. He just had to find a way to convince her that she didn't need to be anything other than herself.

'I just got a bit of sun…'

'Oh, I'd say you got a whole lot of sun,' he muttered under his breath.

'Is everything okay?' she asked with a curious frown.

'Yes, fine, I'm just saying that you must have enjoyed sunbathing while everyone was out. I guess you just *really* like the sun.'

'What a peculiar thing to say, Mitchell,' Maureen said as she took another mouthful of salad.

Jade shot him a confused glance as she collected the plates.

'Never mind,' Mitchell returned as he stood to take the stack of plates from Jade's hands. His warm skin brushed against hers and the electricity surged despite her anger towards him.

'Forget I said anything. It's just my warped Aussie humour. I'm sorry if the present upset you. There was nothing meant by it. Amber can put anything she wants in the locket. By the time she's sixteen she will probably have a crush on a pop star who can't sing a note but he'll have great hair and perfect teeth and she will put his picture in the locket.'

Jade stepped into the kitchen. 'More than likely.' Her tone was cool but pleasant.

'What about a truce?' he whispered as he followed her. 'For Amber's sake?'

Jade met his glance but wasn't convinced.

'I was out of line,' he apologised. 'I understand you want to keep Amber safe. With what happened to Ruby and David, you have every right. But please trust me, I would never let anything happen to Amber.'

Jade squinted a little as she took his words on board. They did seem heartfelt and she didn't want any animosity ruining what little time they had with Maureen and Arthur.

'Truce.'

'Happy birthday, dear Amber, happy birthday to you.'

Amber was happy to sit back at the table for the arrival of her two-tier princess birthday cake. Her eyes lit up when she saw the iced strawberry sponge cake with tiny wax figurines of her favourite storybook princesses sitting on the top, with three candles burning brightly.

To the sounds of *Hip, hip, hooray*, she blew out the candles, ate half of the slice of cake on her plate and then went back to the sofa with her new teddy and rag doll. The trip had taken its toll, and Jade wasn't surprised that Amber wanted to go to bed early.

On seeing how tired she was, Mitchell scooped her up and carried her to the bathroom, where Jade brushed her teeth then slipped her into her pyjamas before he helped to tuck her into bed.

His assistance with the bedtime preparations was his effort to show he was serious about the truce and helping out, but he was surprised how much he enjoyed being a part of it all. Something deep inside felt good about being able to kiss Amber on the forehead and hear her say goodnight to him. It was a long way from his handshake two days previously. He had never experienced that unconditional affection.

He spent all of his working hours saving the lives of children but he never saw them tucked into their own beds. He experienced gratitude in buckets from the parents, although he never expected it. Ensuring these little patients had the best possible opportunity for healthy, happy lives was just what he did. But as he stood watching Amber drift off to sleep he felt a tug at his heart. Perhaps he was missing out on something after all.

He wondered for a moment if his self-imposed exile from family and commitment was worth it.

Then he shook his head and realised that he was fooling himself.

Despite his feelings towards his niece, he would never be ready for children and a family full time, it wasn't in his genes.

'Are you okay to sleep in here by yourself for a little while?' Jade asked softly. 'I'll leave the door open and you can hear us on the balcony.'

Amber nodded and she went to sleep with her bear and rag doll. She was so tired she didn't need a story. Jade couldn't help but notice the shift in Mitchell and how his face had lit up when Amber had said goodnight to him.

'I've been asked to start tomorrow for the temp agency,' Jade announced on their way back to the dinner table. 'I have a three-week placement.'

'That's great. Which hospital?' Mitchell asked as he tried to process the feelings that still lingered after being a part of Amber's bedtime ritual.

'The Eastern Memorial,' she said, then added, 'Arthur told me it was his old workplace.'

'Yes, it was,' Mitchell replied with a rueful look. But he didn't tell her that it was also his workplace and that he was a consultant neonatologist there.

And that fate had just decreed that he would be her very temporary boss.

CHAPTER FOUR

M<small>ITCHELL WALKED DOWN</small> to the water's edge in the warm night air. He wanted to clear his head before he tried to sleep. This was not how he had seen Jade and Amber's visit playing out. He had pictured a fun-loving, easygoing woman, a kindred spirit of sorts. A Californian beach babe who might like to hang out, enjoy a few drinks at a bar, hit the surf and maybe even enjoy a casual hook-up.

Instead, he had found a woman whose commitment ran so much deeper than that. She had changed everything about her life for her niece. In Mitchell's eyes it wasn't necessary and he doubted he would be able to do the same, but he couldn't help but admire how far she would go to provide the upbringing she believed her niece needed.

The rebel girl was now more at home having a cup of tea and an early night on her own. And she would give her life to protect Amber but he found it such a waste for her to hide behind the image of someone else. He had seen the real woman beside the pool and it had sent his body into overdrive.

She was pretending to be so much less than she was. Looking out over the moonlit water, Mitchell wondered how someone could be so completely selfless. Someone so young and beautiful who would have so many options yet she had obviously turned her back on them all for Amber.

He wanted to know more about her yet he had to prevent this conundrum of a woman from getting under his skin. He didn't want to be involved with a woman that genuine. It would be a disaster for everyone. The idea of being tied to one woman and having a family would never work for him. Or would it? he wondered as he picked up a pebble and cast it into the moonlit ocean. It had felt so good to be in the room with Jade, putting Amber to bed. It had seemed so natural and as if they had done it before…and could do it a thousand times and never tire of it.

But there was doubt weighing heavily in his mind. An uncertainty that he could stay the course. A hesitation in his heart that he could not be relied on in a forever situation. His greatest misgiving would be his ability to last the distance and not break the hearts of those who loved him.

Until now that had never been tested. Until now he had never wanted to really get to know a woman beyond a one-night stand or contemplate being a part of a woman's life.

The feelings that he was experiencing were all new to him. Mitchell was at an unexpected crossroad with no clue how he intended on navigating his future.

He stood in silence alone on the beach more confused than he had ever been.

Jade crossed to the scrub room and slipped on a disposable gown over the white nursing uniform she had pulled from her suitcase and pressed that morning. Morning had come quickly after another good night's sleep. Amber's day had been so filled with fun and adventure with her grandparents and then her early birthday dinner that she had been exhausted and had slept through the night, allowing Jade to do the same.

Jade's shift began at two in the afternoon and she would finish at ten that night. Arthur had offered to drive her but Jade had insisted on catching the tram as the temp agency had advised, since their home was not far from the tram stop on Jetty Road. She really didn't want to impose and it gave her a chance to see more of the city on her walk.

She reached out with her foot to the pedal to turn on the tap and noticed a woman in her late twenties, with a worried expression and dressed in a gown and slippers, drying her hands. Jade gave her an encouraging smile.

'I hope to be going home soon. It's my third day,' the woman said softly, returning a meek smile. 'I so wish I was taking Jasper with me but that will be a while, they say. How long do prem babies usually stay in hospital?'

'It's hard to say because all babies are different,' Jade began to explain. 'It depends on how your baby's progressing. Babies who are smaller and those born earlier sometimes have some medical problems other than just being tiny and so tend to stay longer on the unit. But a premature baby who is otherwise well usually stays in the neonatal unit until around the date he or she was due to be born. If your baby does very well, is eating and gaining weight, then he or she might even be able go home even sooner. How early was Jasper?'

'Ten weeks early. He's on a ventilator because he has a lung problem that I don't really understand,' she returned quietly. 'Hy-mem...something disease. The doctor tried to explain it to me but I didn't really understand. And I didn't want to ask too many questions. I thought he might think I'm being pushy, wanting to know everything medical when I'm not a doctor or even think I'm stupid for not understanding.'

Jade knew from her training and years of neonatal nursing that mothers of premature babies and their families all faced uncertainty and this caused raised levels of anxiety. Visiting their baby in Neonatal Intensive Care was a stressful situation that most knew little or nothing about.

'It's important that you never think of yourself as being difficult. Any questions you might have are valid,' Jade explained, as she turned off the tap with her elbow. She was aware that the exchange of information allowed the nurses to gauge the stress within the family and most particularly the mother's ability to cope. 'Parents need to feel a part of the decisions being made for their baby, and you can't do that if you don't understand what is happening.'

'Really? He won't mind if I keep asking questions, and he won't think they're silly things I'm asking? It's just that you're here every day and it's all so new to me.'

'I promise you that the doctors and the nursing staff would never think of any questions as silly. More than likely the doctor assumed that you knew what he was saying if you didn't ask any questions, and I guarantee he would have been more than happy to explain it to you. You're a mother of a newborn in intensive care and you have every right and need to know what is happening throughout his treatment. Please, never hesitate to ask any of us whatever you want to know.'

The young woman sighed and seemed to lift in confidence a little.

'I just don't know what the disease is and why Jasper has it?'

'Hyaline membrane disease is also called infant respiratory distress syndrome and is suffered by almost half of premature babies under thirty weeks,' Jade offered instinctively as the woman's body language showed she was relaxing. 'It means that every time Jasper breathes in he has to expand his lungs completely. Healthy lungs don't collapse to an airless state, but because of his prematurity Jasper's lungs are deflating totally. It makes breathing very hard work for him.'

The woman dropped the dampened paper towel into the bin and tentatively approached Jade, looking for reassurance. 'So it's common, then?'

'Many premature babies have issues with breathing as a result of their early arrival, and even if they aren't as premature as Jasper they can still have this problem. But your baby is in very good hands here. If you have any questions about Jasper and the doctor isn't available, just ask any of the nurses.'

'I haven't seen you here before. You're American. Have you moved to Adelaide to live?'

'No, I'm on a working holiday. Today is my first shift and I will be here for the next three weeks. So let me know if you have any other questions. I'll be here tonight till late.'

'Thanks so much. I have to express some milk and grab something to eat. The nurse told me that I have to keep up my calories to make sure I can produce enough for Jasper.'

Jade nodded. 'Yes, you do. You have to get sleep and

rest and eat well for both you and Jasper. One of the most important things you and your partner can do for your baby is look after yourselves. Get sleep, eat healthy meals, and take a break from it all. It's exhausting having a baby in the neonatal unit, particularly after a difficult or emergency birth. It's natural to want to put your baby first but you must be good to yourself, too.'

She watched as the woman put a half-smile on her tired face then left the washroom to head back to the ward, hopefully secure in the knowledge that she could ask anything she needed to know without any judgement from the medical staff. Ultimately, she would be her baby's only constant in the multiple care-giving system of neonatal intensive care and she needed to feel confident in that role.

Jade had already been given her patient roster at handover. It wasn't a busy time in the nursery and she only had two infants to monitor. Checking the first infant's chart, she noted that Costa was due for a gavage feed. She crossed slowly to another nurse already on duty. As she drew closer, she noticed she was quite young. She had a friendly face with a smattering of freckles across the bridge of her nose. Her hair was a mass of copper curls kept out of her eyes with a pearly clasp on the top of her head. She wasn't particularly tall, perhaps two or three inches shorter than Jade, and this added to her overall young appearance. She imagined that Amber might look similar when she was older.

'Hi, I'm Jade.'

'I'm Mandy. You're from the agency too, then?'

'Yes, first shift and staying for about three weeks, part time, though.'

'Welcome on board.' Then, distracted by something

or someone in the glass-walled scrub room, she paused and then lowered her voice. 'Scrumptious, isn't he?'

Jade noticed a huge smile spread across the young nurse's face but had no idea why.

'If I wasn't engaged…' Mandy began in a wistful tone, before tilting her head to one side in the direction of the door '… I'd offer him breakfast in bed.'

'Who?' Jade cut in.

'Mitchell Forrester, the dishy doctor just scrubbing in.'

Jade froze. Mitchell worked at the hospital? He hadn't mentioned it the night before. She felt her stomach jump and her heart race. *Why hadn't he told her?* She was suddenly quite confused as she'd thought they were getting on well and if he wanted it to remain that way he certainly should have volunteered that information the previous night.

Perhaps he didn't like the idea of them working together. She couldn't be sure but there were so many things about which she wasn't sure. Including her feelings for the man scrubbing in. She could see exactly why the nurse spoke that way. Mitchell was very handsome and more than likely up for some fun with the right woman, but it wasn't her. She was not in the market for a one-night stand and up until now her resolve to stay single had not been tested.

'I suppose,' Jade replied coldly, not wanting to let on that she had any connection to Mitchell or the fact there was a tiny part of her that agreed.

'It doesn't hurt to have some eye candy in the workplace. I mean, it's a nice distraction from the round-the-clock care we provide for premmies. I think it's the universe rewarding us!'

Jade could not join her enthusiasm. She wanted to be anywhere else but near Mitchell. He was resurrecting needs she had put to rest the moment Amber had arrived in her life. She didn't want or need a distraction from her role. She didn't dare let her eyes rest on him for long. His raw masculinity was reminding her that she was a woman with desires that hadn't been met in a very long time.

'I guess, from what I've heard, the parents can rest assured their babies are in the very best hands. And in Mitchell Forrester's hands is where I'm sure every second nurse in the hospital would like to be,' she added with a laugh.

'Well, there's no accounting for taste,' Jade answered woodenly, making it clear she had no intention of joining the recruitment line for his harem. Then she noticed that a theatre nurse spoke to him briefly and he turned and left the scrub room with her.

She was relieved that he wasn't coming in. It gave her a little longer without him there.

Her attention quickly returned to baby Costa. She began the gavage feed that was due by aspirating the contents of his tiny stomach to assess the quantity of still undigested food, along with the colour and appearance. Satisfied that everything was within normal limits, Jade slowly returned the contents to ensure that valuable electrolytes were not lost. Then, attaching the syringe with the milk, she held it above the baby to allow gravity to control the feed, and began the thirty-minute process.

'I'm Soula, Costa's mum,' came a young female voice as Jade was about twenty minutes into the feed.

Jade raised her eyes only momentarily from her tiny

patient to acknowledge the young woman dressed in her gown and slippers.

'Hello, Soula. I'm Jade, and I'll be looking after Costa this afternoon. He's certainly a handsome young man.'

'He looks like his father,' Soula returned with a nervous smile. 'The same thick black hair. His *yia-yia*, Maria, adores him as he reminds her of Yanni…he's my husband and her eldest son. She had five boys but I think maybe one or two will be more than enough for us.'

Jade monitored the feed as she listened to the young mother talk about the close-knit Greek family.

After the feed was complete, Jade instilled a tiny amount of sterile water to clear the tubing of residual milk before she capped the tube and settled Costa. Suddenly Soula's voice became unsteady. Jade turned to see the young woman's eyes welling with tears.

'If anything happens to Costa I don't know what I'll do. I love him so much already.' Soula broke down and began sobbing. 'I loved him before he was born.'

Jade closed the incubator door and asked Soula to sit down. It was less than twenty-four hours since she had given birth and she was emotionally and physically drained. Jade gently touched Soula's arm as she spoke. 'Since Costa arrived he has had the best medical care. He might be tiny but he's a strong little boy and putting up a big fight. The injection you were given before delivery has stripped the mucous lining of Costa's lungs enough to allow a head box and avoid a ventilator. He's doing very well.'

'Yes, but Dr Forrester said he's still critical.'

'Soula, every baby here in Neonatal ICU is critical, for different medical reasons. Some are tiny, some have complications but we are all doing our very best to ensure they move to the nursery as soon as they are ready. If Dr Forrester gave you a less than rosy picture, it's because he is being sensibly cautious. It's important that you understand what challenges Costa is facing now and those he will face in coming weeks, and Dr Forrester is telling you everything. That is far better than not knowing what lies ahead.' Jade paused. 'But as he's only just arrived, and after reading Costa's notes, it appears that he is doing very well. We will feed him your milk as soon as it comes in and that will help enormously with his immunity.'

'His father just wants to know that Costa is okay,' she said, mopping her tears. 'I promised Yanni that I'd call as soon as I'd visited this morning. He's up in Roxby in the mines. He works two weeks on and two weeks off and he'd arranged to be here for the birth but Costa arrived eight weeks early. They're trying to arrange a flight down here today for Yanni and he's desperate for any news of his son.' Her words arrived at an increasing speed because of her nerves.

'I can imagine he would be,' Jade told her, empathy in her soft voice. 'It must be such a worry for him, being so far away. As you can probably tell by my accent I'm not from here, so I have no idea where Roxby is located. Is it a big mining town?'

Jade decided to engage Soula in a conversation about the man she clearly adored. It was something tangible and positive and would help the young woman to perhaps focus on something to pull her anxiety down to a manageable level. Jade was fully aware that Soula might within a day or so have to deal with symptoms associated with the postpartum blues, such as mood swings, sleep disturbances and tearfulness, and this would add to her already anxious state. She was glad that Yanni would be arriving soon to support his wife. They would be able to face Costa's hurdles together.

'Roxby is a mining town up north. I've never been there but…' Soula began to slow her words and take breaths. 'When we were trying to get pregnant, Yanni said I should make a trip up there with him because the town has one of the highest birth rates in the whole of Australia.' Soula was trying to appear a little braver than she really felt but her shaky sigh betrayed the anxiety still very close to the surface.

'Really,' Jade replied evenly. 'They might have to bring more televisions into the town if it becomes a problem.'

Soula smiled, a meek smile but still a smile. Happy that the new mother was comfortable, keeping her baby company, Jade headed over to see how her other little patient was progressing. It was time to check his vital signs.

'Looks like you've settled in very well.' The voice like molten chocolate came from close behind her and resonated through every part of her body. 'Even have our new mothers swap tears for smiles. I'm impressed, Nurse Grant.'

Jade tugged at her lower lip with her teeth. She didn't want or need to hear that voice. It was inevitable, she admitted silently, as he was her boss and she had seen him scrubbing in earlier, but it was not welcome. Mitchell Forrester was causing her body and mind to react in ways she had forgotten she had ever felt. She swallowed before she turned to him but it wasn't enough to steady her racing heart when she came face to face with him again. It was ridiculous. Only the day before she had been so angry with him, then had agreed to a truce, and now she found it hard to be near him for very different reasons.

She didn't trust herself.

'I like to see parents smile,' she managed as she struggled to level her rapid breathing. 'But I can't stop to chat, I'm super-busy, just about to check Jasper's vitals. I just finished Costa's feed. His mother is quite anxious but he appears to be doing well. He's feeding, vitals are stable and her husband is expected to arrive soon, which I hope will alleviate her distress to some degree. She needs his support. Oh, and you forgot to tell me last night that we'd be working together. Any reason for that?'

'Thought it might be a pleasant surprise,' he replied with a smile. He wasn't entirely sure why he hadn't told her. Perhaps because he was still trying to figure out in his head how he felt about the working arrangement. And how he felt about her.

Jade couldn't believe how he looked so good even in his scrubs. And how nervous he made her feel and how the words were spilling from her lips at lightning speed. It was as if she were a first-year nursing student suddenly and not the confident neonatal nurse with years of experience under her belt and on her résumé. How she wished he had retained the unkempt look of old. Resistance would have been so easy if he looked like a castaway but now he was causing an awareness of needs and desires she had pushed from her mind for so long. She was not about to join the bevy of nurses at the Eastern Memorial who found his charm irresistible.

'So do we operate any differently from over in the US?' Mitchell asked as he observed her taking baby Johnson's temperature.

Jade reminded herself that if she wanted to keep him at arm's length she had to remain aloof and professional at all times. 'Not that I've noticed. Maybe a few different terms like *obs* when I would say *vitals* but it's not going to be a struggle for me to adapt.'

Mitchell smiled. He thought she would fit in very well. Too well, in fact, he thought as he walked away. He didn't want to become accustomed to having her around.

Jade kept her focus on the baby as she finished recording his vitals and then, satisfied he was progressing well, she closed the incubator door. She was relieved Mitchell was assisting with another small patient that had just arrived in NICU.

The afternoon turned to evening, with Jade liking her temporary new workplace. The other nurses were lovely, a little infatuated with Mitchell but other than that Jade enjoyed working with them. Those who didn't want to sleep with him couldn't praise him enough, and Jade had to agree that he was brilliant with the patients and ensured that the parents felt a part of decision-making around their newborn.

She had overheard his conversations with anxious mothers and fathers during her shift and his bedside manner reduced their unfounded fears and allowed them to understand the real hurdles ahead. He answered their questions honestly but with enough compassion not to add to their heightened anxiety. Jade witnessed his skills as a neonatologist and she knew that she would feel safe if she were a parent and he was the attending doctor diagnosing and arranging a treatment plan for a tiny infant.

The shift came to an end at ten in the evening, and Jade knew that Amber would be tucked into bed and sound

asleep. She had called during her late lunch break and
spoken to her niece and discovered to her delight that
she was enjoying her time splashing in a wading pool.
Maureen assured Jade that Amber was wearing sunscreen and inflatable arm bands and that she and Arthur wouldn't take their eyes from her for a second.
During the second call, Jade had found out that Amber
had dried off from the pool and was busy making cup-
cakes. It had been a weight off Jade's mind to hear her
so happy. She had been safely inside the house and Jade
knew that Maureen was very responsible so she had
nothing to worry about. Maureen was nothing like her
elder son, not likely to run off with Amber on an adventure of any sort.

It was late and dark so Jade was going to get a cab
home from the city. She had caught the tram in but, despite the glorious warm evening air, the walk to the tram
stop along the dark city road didn't hold much appeal.

'Need a lift?'

Jade knew it was Mitchell without turning her head.
Her heart annoyingly skipped a beat and confirmed it.
She felt like a teenager the way her body was reacting.

Or overreacting, as she told herself.

'I'm catching a cab, it's a bit late for the tram.'

He walked closer and made Jade very aware of his
presence. The cologne on his clothes was faint but still
enough to stir her senses.

'I'll give you a lift. I live in the same road, remember, so it's not going out of the way.'

Jade drew a deep breath and in silence she turned
around to face the most intense blue eyes. She knew it
would be rude to decline his offer but the alarm bells

in her head were louder than the ambulance siren as it pulled into the nearby A and E bay.

'You're sure?' she asked, hoping against all hope that in the moments since he'd asked he had suddenly remembered somewhere he had to be on the other side of the city. Or that there was a single young nurse in need of his attention. Anything really that would allow her to squirm her way out of sharing the trip home.

'Very sure,' he insisted. 'I'm in the doctors' car park at the side of the building.'

With reservations and a deep breath, Jade followed her handsome chauffeur into the dimly lit car park. She could see a few cars but had no idea which one belonged to Mitchell. There were a four-wheel-drive, three late-model BMWs, a couple of hatchbacks and a motorbike. She felt pretty sure it was the four-wheel drive as it had roof racks that she assumed would be utilised for his surfboards. The hatchbacks would be a squeeze for his six-foot-two frame, but he might have gone the sophisticated route of the imported sedan.

At this time of the night Jade's concern about her mode of transport was close to zero. She just wanted to get home and put her feet up. And do it without being too close to Mitchell.

'Here,' he said as he held out a motorbike helmet and took her bag from her shoulder. 'This one's for you, and I'll take the bag for safekeeping.'

'You can't be serious.'

'Deadly,' he said, raising one dark eyebrow over a twinkling eye.

Her rising anxiety levels began pumping adrenalin around her tired body. 'I'm honestly not comfortable with the whole bike thing. I think I'll catch a cab.' She felt a tension headache coming on.

'And make me ride home alone?' he asked her with a stare so intense it refused to be ignored. 'Come on, keep me company. It's only a twenty-minute trip.'

Jade felt her heart begin to stampede. But this reaction wasn't purely the fear of the bike. It was the man. If only she hadn't looked at him when he'd looked at her that way. It was almost impossible to remain distant but she had to. She couldn't risk getting close to him. She definitely couldn't let him get under her skin.

'It's not a tough decision,' he said. 'I can assure you that in all the time I've been riding bikes I haven't killed, maimed or lost a single passenger.'

'That's supposed to make me feel better?' Jade asked tartly, taking a step backwards to reclaim some distance between them.

'Come on, lassie, take the boy up on his offer and be off with the pair of you,' said a paediatric consultant Jade recognised from NCIU. Her accent was thick and Jade felt certain it was Irish. She was putting her bag in the back seat of one of the BMW sedans that Jade wished with all of her being was Mitchell's mode of transport. Not for the prestige attached to the vehicle, it was the doors and roof that she wanted. And the console between them.

'You're a wise woman, Maggie O'Donnell, to be sure, to be sure,' Mitchell, said mimicking her accent.

Maggie sharply turned her attention to Mitchell. 'Any more from you, Dr Forrester, and I'll convince the poor girl not to take the ride and I won't be talking to you again, to be sure, to be sure!'

Mitchell smiled as he watched Maggie shake her head

of neat grey curls. 'It's been a long day and I'm in need of a cuppa and some kip so you two can do what you please. I'm away.' With that she reversed from the car park and drove off into the dark, leaving Jade alone with Mitchell again. And a problem.

Why couldn't he just drive a regular car like all the other doctors?

Dread filled her thoughts. It wasn't safe.

For two reasons.

It was a motorbike and they could have an accident. They could be sideswiped, hit a pothole or skid in the rain. It wasn't raining, she admitted to herself, but it still was a bad idea.

And secondly, if she were crazy enough to accept a lift, a bike would force her to wrap her arms around Mitchell just to stop her falling off. There was no way she wanted to be that close to him and feel the warmth of his body close to hers.

'It's a straight run down North Terrace then ANZAC Highway to Glenelg,' he said. As if he read her mind he continued, 'It's not raining, the highway's just been resurfaced so there's no potholes along the way and not much traffic so there's negligible risk of being knocked off the bike.'

'I just don't feel good about it.'

'Have you ever been on a motorbike before?'

Jade nodded reluctantly. She had been on so many motorbike rides that she'd lost count. She'd loved to ride around the winding roads to Malibu on the Pacific Coast Highway. Whether she had been the rider or the passenger, she'd loved the feeling when she'd headed out along the beach road, the faster the better as the fresh ocean breeze had hit her face under the helmet.

'Yes, a few times but—'

'And you're here to tell the tale so that makes two of us. So I say let's get going.'

Jade felt she'd be a hypocrite if she refused and walked back to the cab rank when she knew she had ridden a bike in far more dangerous situations than a quick trip home.

Grudgingly, she accepted the helmet and that simple act elicited a huge smile from Mitchell. He knew that underneath Miss Prim was a woman who wanted to let go and lie naked in the sun. He would just have to take small steps to draw out the real Jade and make her feel comfortable to be herself. He wondered how long she had been hiding beneath the maiden aunt façade. Had it been since Amber was born or something more recent? It would be a challenging few weeks but he would do his best to make Amber's aunt fun to be around for Amber.

It wasn't for him, he told himself. He wanted Jade to lighten up and be fun for her niece, that was all.

He slipped on his helmet, put her bag in the storage compartment of the seat and then climbed on the bike and started the engine.

Jade stood frozen to the spot. Her helmet was securely on her head but her mind was fighting her decision.

Mitchell lifted his visor and reached his hand out to her. His eyes told her a story that she didn't want to hear. He was handsome, intelligent and fun. And she was losing the struggle to refuse his invitation.

She relented and, accepting his hand, climbed on the back of the bike.

His warm scent was all around her, and she prayed that once they hit the road the breeze would make it dissipate, along with the feelings he was stirring in her body. Her hands limply held on to the sides of his body until his strong hands suddenly pulled her hands across his waist in a tighter grip. Her body was pulled against his as they hit the road. Together.

CHAPTER FIVE

'HOME IN ONE PIECE, as promised,' Mitchell announced as he stood holding his helmet beside the shiny black motorbike that had been their carriage home.

Jade was already off the bike and in the driveway, putting distance between them quickly. His proximity during the ride home had been unsettling and now his silhouette against the light of the streetlamp was ridiculously appealing. She had to step away and stay away. If things were different she could see this night having a different ending too. Perhaps a kiss and the promise of another bike ride. But it couldn't end any other way than a polite thank you, she thought as she looked wistfully up at the window where Amber was sleeping.

But she wasn't angry with Mitchell any more. That had subsided. He had his reasons and he was clearly smitten by Amber now. She hoped that their relationship would build over the years and deepen. His dedication to the babies in his care at the hospital and the empathy he had for their parents was clear, and it did raise her opinion of him. His absolute determination to see the tiny children survive against the odds was an admirable quality.

And his gift to Amber of the locket to carry with her

on her adventures all over the world was something that Jade had to admit to herself she would have appreciated a few years ago.

Mitchell was not a bad man but he was still the wrong man for her and she couldn't allow their truce to grow into something more. He was suddenly ticking every box. And some she hadn't known had been there to start with.

It was ironic that it scared Jade how safe she'd felt, taking a risk with Mitchell and riding the motorbike. In the past, she would take risks because she wanted to and because she didn't care about the consequences, but with Mitchell it wasn't like that. She felt protected by him. But she had to remember what was at stake. She had Amber to consider. And they would only be in Adelaide for a few weeks and Mitchell might not even stay that long.

It would be over before it began.

'Thank you for the lift.'

'You're most welcome, and if you need a lift in tomorrow morning I'm happy to oblige.'

Mitchell could see that beneath Jade's sensible exterior was a woman who could let her hair down. Tonight had proved it. She knew how to ride a bike. She'd leaned into the turns, she hadn't been afraid. He hadn't been teaching her anything that she hadn't already known and he liked that about her.

She was fun and adventurous but she was playing a safe hand of cards. He liked to shuffle the deck and take his chances and he suspected that once upon a time she had too. He just had to find that woman inside and draw her out so she didn't raise Amber to be scared of her own shadow.

'Thanks, but I'll be fine to tram it in. I'm on an afternoon shift again tomorrow.'

Perhaps she was more like him than she cared to remember. Independent, happy to have a good time and willing to enjoy what the world had to offer. Only time would tell, he thought as he said goodnight and rode off down the street.

Her head felt light as she entered the house. She'd found the ride exhilarating. Mitchell had been in control of the beast of a bike, and she'd loved that. A little too much, she realised when she quietly climbed into her bed next to Amber's and struggled to fall asleep. The feelings he'd unleashed during the ride had been unexpected. Freedom, fun and…desire. Jade had pushed these feelings to a place from where she'd thought they could never escape. And they hadn't, until now. Until Mitchell had threatened to release all of them at once.

Jade heard Mitchell's motorbike roar past her window next morning and felt her stomach churn and chills run down her spine with the sound. Not ominous chills. Just the opposite. She had been so close to the sound only a few hours before and it had made her feel alive. Now she worried that she could grow to like the feelings he was stirring.

She spent the morning with Amber, playing on the beach, trying desperately to push Mitchell from her mind. He was just a man and she had dated her fair share and ignored even more over the years. Yet the scent of his cologne so close to her and the feeling of her arms around his hard body as they'd ridden together were haunting her waking thoughts. He was making her question her safe life choices.

Maureen decided she would take her granddaughter to the shops on Jetty Road to find a few 'sparkly things' when Jade left for work. Jade wasn't entirely sure what 'sparkly things' meant but Amber was excited by the prospect so Jade was happy as she headed off for her second shift at the hospital.

Her shift began at two. There was handover and she was informed of a new airlifted baby from Melbourne who would be in her care. She hadn't been named yet so they referred to her as Baby Morey.

'There was no alternative, considering they were short of incubators in Melbourne. The hospitals over there had a whole run of prem deliveries within a few days. They're grateful the Eastern Memorial could accept her,' Mandy told Jade as they neared the incubator. 'She's tiny but a fighter.'

'Why didn't the parents travel with the infant?'

'The mother delivered her via Caesarean after a car accident,' Mandy told Jade as they neared the incubator. 'I saw the report that arrived. Four-car pile-up on the Tullamarine Freeway near the airport.'

'Are the parents all right? Did they survive?' Jade's voice suddenly became shaky as her hands hovered nervously. She prayed they were both alive, she didn't want to hear anything else. *Déjà vu* instantly made her skin crawl and her stomach knot.

'They're both stable and off the critical list. Her mother has a hairline fracture of her collarbone, a punctured lung and, of course, the postnatal effects of the Caesarean birth, and Cara's father has damage to his vertebrae and a fractured hip. He's in Spinal Injuries.'

Jade swallowed hard. The infant they were attending had entered the world the same way Amber had three years previously. The time peeled away in an instant as she looked at the baby lying innocently in the incubator, completely unaware of what had happened, all the while holding tenuously to her own life. But she did still have her parents. However injured they were, they would pull through and be a part of her life. Jade was happy for the little girl.

Mandy left Jade as she needed to tend to another tiny patient. NICU was at capacity, with all of the nursing staff, including Mandy, rushed off their feet. Jade was grateful the other nurse hadn't had time to notice the tears welling in her eyes. Amber's fight to stay alive and the battle her parents had lost hit home at lightning speed and brought emotions rushing to the surface.

'The paediatrician had noted suspected respiratory distress, causing cyanosis, but I wasn't convinced and I ran some additional tests,' Mitchell told a small group of medical students as he approached the new arrival and Jade. 'The bluish discoloration of the skin and nail beds would indicate respiratory distress but the degree of cyanosis was not proportional to what was shown in the X-rays that accompanied the baby from Melbourne. And it has not been decreasing with increased inspired oxygen and the tests quickly confirmed congestive heart failure.'

He then turned his attention to Jade. 'Nurse Grant, can you move Baby Morey to a radiant heat warmer within the next fifteen minutes so we can maintain her body temperature?'

'Certainly,' Jade replied, trying to blink away the tears before they ran down her cheeks and anyone noticed them.

But Mitchell did. He noticed everything about Jade,

even though he didn't want to. He decided to release the students, who had been with him for most of the morning and were due to end their time in NICU. They looked exhausted and no doubt had information over-load, which he suggested might be abated by a coffee in the cafeteria.

As the students left, he called another nurse to take over. 'I need to speak with Nurse Grant for a moment but in her absence I want both cardiorespiratory and ox-ygen saturation monitoring and I'm prescribing digoxin. Dosages are in the notes and I want close observation until Nurse Grant returns.'

Jade had turned to walk away. She didn't want to be confronted about her reaction. She didn't want or need his concern.

'Nurse Grant, please come with me for a moment.' He kept his professional tone in front of the others then gently took her arm and directed her to a small office nearby used by consultants and residents when they needed to speak with parents in private. He closed the door and turned to her.

'Jade, what's wrong?' he asked, releasing her from his firm hold but not the intensity of his gaze.

'Nothing,' she lied, and blinked even harder as she tried to look anywhere but at Mitchell. 'I'm fine.'

'You're anything but fine.'

'I'll be okay. I don't want special treatment.' She looked up, and his expression wasn't what she had been expecting. It wasn't judgmental. It was empathetic and real and etched into every part of his face. And it suddenly and unexpectedly allowed her to give in to her feelings. Tears that had built up for so long began streaming down her face.

She hadn't cried since the funeral. Her feelings had been bottled up inside. She had been strong because she'd felt she'd had no other choice. There was no one for her to lean on while she was Amber's only support.

'You're so far from okay.' Without hesitation, he reached out, put his arm around her and pulled her into his arms, and she didn't pull away.

'Is it Amber?' He murmured the question as he gently stroked her hair. 'Are you worried about her?'

Jade knew as the moments passed that, as much as it felt good to have a man's arms around her, she couldn't stay there for ever. And particularly not in Mitchell's arms. He wouldn't be there for ever; neither would she. It was crazy to let him into her heart. She slowly moved from his embrace and a place that had made her feel safe, if only for a moment.

'Amber's fine, honestly, Mitchell…' She hesitated for a minute to gather her thoughts and put any growing feelings for him away. 'It was the new arrival in NICU. The baby was delivered by C-section after a motor vehicle accident…and it just brought everything back. I have to toughen up. I'm working on it.'

Mitchell didn't want Jade to toughen up at all. She didn't need additional walls. He wanted more than anything to break down the ones she had. She might not be his usual fun-loving, easygoing type but suddenly he wondered if just a casual good time was enough any more. Being around Jade for the past few days, even putting Amber to bed and all it entailed, had not been the chore he had imagined. He had enjoyed every minute of that special time with his niece and with Jade.

His type was fast becoming a cute Californian girl with a pixie cut and the dress sense of someone's maiden aunt but the soul and depth of no one he had ever met before.

'The best nurses are those with empathy and compassion,' he told her as she turned to face him. 'You have both. Don't hide what is inside you.'

Jade didn't want to meet his gaze. She wanted to pull herself together and face the job outside. 'I need to get back to work. We're short enough on staff, let alone with me sitting in here, snivelling. I'm being self-indulgent and silly.'

'You're not being either, so take a minute,' he continued. 'And when you're ready, head back out. If you prefer, I will switch your patient roster.'

Jade took a deep breath and gently shook her head. 'I want to stay with my patient. I really do.'

'It's your call, if you're up to it.'

'I am,' she said, crossing to the door, feeling the need to put space between them. He was much too appealing on a whole other level now. It wouldn't just be his smouldering looks that would make it difficult. Now that Jade knew he had a heart, and a level of compassion and empathy she hadn't thought he possessed, it would make it that much more difficult to be around him. But that wasn't his problem. It was hers.

Jade walked back into NCIU and straight to her patient. Mitchell followed behind her. He admired her dedication and compassion, and although he wished she had taken some time out, he respected her wishes and acted accordingly.

'I noticed her slow feeding time so I want you to switch to gavage feeding so she's not working hard for the food and can conserve energy. Later we'll try her sucking again but provide higher caloric formula. And I'll see if they've decided on a name yet. I don't want to refer to her by her surname. She needs her own name.'

Mitchell's last few words made her smile. He genuinely cared so much for these babies and it wasn't just his clinical abilities that impressed Jade. He treated the babies as little people with feelings, extending even to having a proper name. She was falling for the man, and there was no way to stop her tumble.

Jade followed Mitchell's instructions, inserted a gavage tube into the tiny stomach and began the slow feed. Aware of the management of babies with congestive heart failure, Jade placed her in a semi-erect position for feeding and burped her every half an ounce to minimise the chance of vomiting after the feed. Jade felt an extra-special bond with this baby, who had a small tuft of blonde hair on her crown. Jade planned on spending additional time with Baby Morey as she didn't have a mother who could visit and she wanted to provide that additional care.

Mitchell returned briefly to give additional instructions regarding the baby's management and feeding but noticed Jade was already implementing those procedures. He was impressed with her abilities and initiative so did not interrupt. He just wanted to share something with her.

'Baby Morey's name is Alina. It apparently means light,' he told her.

Jade lifted her eyes to meet his smile. A rush of warmth flowed over her. Mitchell was so pleased the baby had a name. It seemed to mean something to him. Jade could tell his happiness at bestowing the name on the baby was genuine. He was genuine. He was a good man. And it scared her that she was starting to *only* see the good in him.

Quickly, she averted her eyes and returned her focus to Alina.

He might be a good man but she needed to remind herself that she wasn't looking for a man, good or not. But it was a message that was becoming less audible every minute.

'Another delivery,' Alli announced as she wheeled in another tiny patient and transferred the baby to a radiant heat warmer near Jade. 'This is Liam. Dad's just scrubbing in, Mum's still in Recovery. Caesarean delivery, gestational age twenty-nine weeks.'

A few minutes later a very worried-looking man in his late forties arrived. He was still wearing his blue disposable scrubs from Theatre.

'Over here, Mr Phillips,' Alli called. 'Dr Forrester is on his way. Just take a seat beside your son.'

'Oh, my God, he's so small,' the man said anxiously as he looked at the baby lying on a radiant heat warmer. He looked around at the other babies and then back at his own. Jade could see the concern on his face. He was a big man but his fear was almost palpable.

'Mr Phillips,' Mitchell said as he approached the newborn, 'I'm Mitchell Forrester and I'll be assessing your son.'

Nervously, the man asked, 'Why isn't he inside one of those?' He was pointing to an incubator. 'Don't you have enough of them? Wouldn't that keep him warmer? Shouldn't he at least have a blanket on him?'

'There are different levels of care available in Neonatal and it depends on your baby's needs where he will be placed,' Mitchell began to explain. 'At the moment we need to access Liam, he will need complex care and the incubator limits access for the medical staff. Please don't worry, your son is being kept warm and is in the best place for him at this time.'

'Okay, if you're sure.'

'I am, Mr Phillips.'

The man looked around to see other parents sitting beside their babies so tentatively he sat and began unconsciously wringing his hands. 'How long will he need to stay here in Intensive Care?'

'I can't give you an accurate idea yet. Premature babies need additional help while their bodies catch up on the growth and development they missed in the womb. He'll need assistance to stay warm because he can't control his own body temperature yet. And Liam is just over two pounds, so he's still too immature to feed. He'll need a tube that carries milk into his stomach,' Mitchell told him as he warmed the stethoscope and gently placed it on Liam's tiny chest.'

'But my wife wants to breastfeed. She told me that.'

'She can express milk until Liam's strong enough to feed but we need to get his weight up and feeding is tiring so we need to make it easier for him,' Jade added, aware that Mitchell was listening to Liam's heart.

The man understood and remained silent until Mitchell removed the stethoscope and put it back around his neck.

'How many staff do you have here to take care of the babies?' he asked. 'Will there be enough to look after Liam if more babies arrive?'

'Yes, there are more than enough staff to cover the patients and any unexpected arrivals such as Liam. You will see many different staff providing care to your son over the coming weeks. Neonatal Intensive Care has a number of special nurses like Alli who you just met, and we are very fortunate to have Jade, who is over from the States, bringing her knowledge and expertise from a large teaching hospital is Los Angeles.'

Mitchell spoke with pride about Jade and it wasn't lost on her.

'Then there's Laura, the senior nurse in charge of the unit,' he continued. 'And the neonatologist, who, in Liam's case, is me. I'll be leading your baby's care. On top of that there are other specialist doctors, such as surgeons if the need arises, and physiotherapists to help with your baby's development, radiographers and dieticians, and then there are social workers to help you with family issues and support that might be needed after you take your baby home in a few months' time. There is quite literally a small intensive care army to provide everything that your family will need over the coming weeks and months.'

Jade was still listening as Mitchell handled the barrage of questions with ease. He related so well and wasn't short with his answers. He took his time to quell the man's heightened anxiety and let him catch his breath. And the way he had spoken about her made her feel valued and important and it resonated in her heart.

'It's important that you visit as much as possible and no matter how many staff are attending to Liam, remember first and foremost he needs you and your wife. Having a parent here as much as possible makes such a difference to the child.'

Jade saw the man relax his shoulders into the chair. He had arrived feeling out of his depth and overwhelmed, but Mitchell had given him a sense of purpose and validated his questions.

'I'm just going to continue my examination and you are most welcome to stay, or if you would like to check on your wife and let her know Liam is safe with us, you could come back down together. I'll be here all afternoon and can answer any other questions you have. And there will be new questions every day so don't hesitate to ask anything you're concerned about. This neonatal unit has an open-door policy so parents can visit twenty-four hours a day.'

'I think I might go and see my wife then and let her know everything's under control,' he said, climbing to his feet. 'But if anything changes and you want me back here, call my wife's ward and I'll be straight back down.'

'We'll be sure to let you know, but Liam is stable at the moment. So you come back down when you're both ready.'

Jade watched the man shuffle out of the unit in somewhat of a daze. There was so much to take in and he was clearly also concerned about his wife. They had a long road ahead of them until their son was in the nursery and preparing to go home.

'Have you had dinner yet?' Mitchell asked Jade as she was leaving NICU for her tea break.

'Heading there now. I have an hour, so I intend to put my feet up and grab a wrap or a salad in the cafeteria.'

'I've got a better idea,' Mitchell said as the elevator doors opened and they both stepped inside. 'A little Italian restaurant across the road. They serve the best pasta and they do it quickly. They know we don't have much time. It's delicious and just like being in Italy.'

Jade was surprised by the invitation but it happened so quickly she didn't have time to refuse. Or think it through. Perhaps that was a good thing, she surmised as they stood at the traffic lights a minute later, waiting to cross the main road as darkness was falling.

'I should have asked if you like Italian food,' he said after a minute or two. 'I guess I just assumed everyone does.'

'You guessed right with me, I love Italian.'

The meal came out quickly and they were halfway to finishing their risottos when Mitchell decided to tell her about the pool and what he'd seen. He had been thinking it over since it had happened and had decided that he wanted and needed to be honest with Jade. He had no intention of embarrassing her but he felt she had the right to know.

He just wasn't entirely sure how to raise it.

'You seem quiet suddenly,' Jade commented as she pushed the risotto around with her fork. She was borderline full but searching for more of the tasty grilled chicken pieces. The herbs were amazing and Mitchell was right, the food was great.

'There was something I wanted to tell you,' Mitchell began, and then hesitated. He wasn't sure how Jade would react but he hoped she might see the humorous side of it. He had definitely not taken advantage of the situation by looking back at her after the initial shock sighting.

'Go on,' she urged as she gave up on trying to fit in any more food and just sipped on her iced water.

Mitchell took a nervous sip of his own water. 'The other morning, I came to the house to assemble the sound system. Arthur had no clue how to put it together so he asked me to do it.'

Jade had no idea where the conversation was heading and why Mitchell thought there was a need to tell her about his handyman work. 'Was this when you served me breakfast in bed with Amber?'

'Yes.'

'So did you get it done before I woke up?'

He drew a deep breath and continued. 'No, it was later in the morning.'

'But I was home all morning after Maureen and Arthur took Amber out, and I didn't see you,' she returned with a puzzled look.

'No, you didn't see me, but I saw you sun-baking by the pool.'

Embarrassment hit and Jade put her hand to her mouth and closed her eyes for a moment. 'I thought there was no one home or I would never have gone out in the sun like that.'

'I just wanted to say that I looked away as soon as I realised what you were doing. Your secret's safe with me but I wanted us to have a level of honesty. I didn't want to keep it from you.'

'What I was doing? What are you talking about? I was sun-baking...that's all. You hardly had to avert your eyes, I'm sure you've seen it a million times before.'

Mitchell stared at Jade with a puzzled look. She was so casual about sunbathing naked and it took him by surprise.

'Hardly a million,' he remarked.

'There were so many bikinis on the beach the other day.'

'Yes, there were, but you chose not to wear one and... and that's okay...'

'What on earth are you talking about?' she cut in abruptly. Her eyes were wide and completed her horrified expression. 'I was wearing a bikini.'

'Not by the time I got there,' he told her. 'I walked to the shed to get some tools and when I closed the door I saw you lying there on the sun lounge with nothing on. I dropped the tools, picked them up and left.'

Jade sat up in her chair and wiped the corners of her mouth with the white napkin. 'I don't know whose house you were in, but it couldn't have been the same one as me because I had on a string bikini. I have to admit it isn't something I would parade around Amber but it's all I had and I wanted to enjoy the sun. Clearly, you don't know me very well to think for a moment I sunbathe in the nude.' Jade dropped her voice to barely a whisper. 'It's not what I'd do.'

Jade thought back to her wildest days and even then she would have drawn the line at that.

'Jade, we've only known each other for three days, so I can't say I really know much about you at all. What I do know is that you're a brilliant nurse, amazing with both the parents and the neonates, and you've done an amazing job of bringing up Amber. She's a sweetheart and she adores and depends on you. I'm not about to judge you for skinny-dipping. In fact, quite the opposite,' he said with a twinkle in his eye.

'In your parents' pool…that would be so wrong.'

'My family owes you so much for how you have raised Amber and been there for her every step of the way. Honestly, Jade, after what you've done for our family you can pretty much do anything you want and get away with it.'

'You can stop right there. It's been hard at times but she is a joy and so precious and I couldn't imagine a day without her,' Jade told him. 'But no matter how *grateful* your family might be, I wouldn't overstep the mark and skinny-dip in their pool…ever. Stripping down to a bikini is a stretch for me, let alone running around the pool naked.'

Mitchell smiled but wasn't sure why she wouldn't wear a bikini around Amber. It was Australia and the twenty-first century so there was no reason that she couldn't, and from what he had seen there was absolutely no reason for her not to wear one. Maybe she was telling the truth. Maybe she had been wearing a swimsuit and his eyes had misled him.

'What colour is your bikini?'

'It's kind of skin-coloured Lycra. You could call it nude. Maybe you should check your distance vision.'

'Damn, maybe I should,' Mitchell said, laughing. 'If only I'd known that you were wearing a swimsuit, I would've stopped and focused. But, Jade, I must say from my brief glance you looked stunning.'

Jade felt her cheeks redden with the compliment. She knew Mitchell really had looked away quickly. He was a gentleman. If he had stopped to look at her he would have quickly seen she'd been wearing a bikini so decency really had made him look the other way in a hurry.

Although now she felt quite self-conscious that he had seen her in the skimpy swimsuit and she felt the need to explain why she had been wearing something so at odds with her normal dress code.

'I haven't worn it in years. I don't think it's the right image any more, particularly around a little girl. I think Amber would prefer to see me in something a bit more respectable.'

Mitchell did not break eye contact as he looked at

his dinner companion and the woman who was slowly claiming more than his attention. She was getting closer each day to claiming his heart. 'I would have to disagree with you on that one, Jade. I'm sure Amber would think her aunty looked gorgeous in a bikini. I know I did.'

CHAPTER SIX

THE CALL CAME through from the Royal Flying Doctor Service just as Jade was scrubbing in the next afternoon. It was her last shift for the week, then she would have four days off with Amber to visit the zoo and have a birthday picnic.

'I can leave immediately,' Mitchell said as he saw the paediatric consultant scrubbing in. He knew NICU would be well covered. 'Do you have the gestational age?'

'Around thirty-four weeks.'

'Thirty-four weeks, so not critical, but there are two babies to consider. If you have your flight nurse ready I'll bring a neonatal nurse with midwifery experience.' Mitchell knew exactly whom he would take on the trip. He had spied her scrubbing in for her shift.

'We can transport the three of you.'

'Good, as I said, thirty-four weeks is not critical but twins can mean smaller babies so if there are complications I would prefer to have additional hands on board. Please let the pilot know I will arrange ambulance transportation to the airport straight away. ETA fifteen minutes.'

Mitchell hung up the phone and, looking around the NICU, quickly found Jade. With long, purposeful strides he crossed to her just as she was about to take Costa's obs.

'I need you to come with me. It's urgent.' He signalled Alli to come and take over Costa's care from Jade.

Jade didn't doubt for a second by the tone of Mitchell's voice and the look on his face that it was something serious. His brow was knitted and his jaw rigid as he spoke.

'I need you to walk as we talk,' he said, leading her from NICU. 'I want you to travel with me to the Outback, to near a small town in the central Flinders Ranges. It's called Blinman and it's about an hour's flight from here. We have premature labour with twins and the town has no medical facilities. The woman was on a camping retreat with her husband and friends when her waters broke.'

'Why me?'

'Because you have both neonatal and midwifery skills and you have just scrubbed in, so you are fresh,' he replied matter-of-factly. 'Alli and Laura have some midwifery behind them but they are about an hour from finishing long shifts. They're tired and you're better placed to help.'

They had reached the doors of the hospital and the ambulance bay at a ridiculously fast pace.

'But what about Amber?'

'She won't even know you've gone with me. It will be just over an hour's flight time and by the sound of it the babies are close to being born so we will be back by dinner at the latest and I'll let you knock off and go home the moment we get back. You're not due to finish until late so you'll be home earlier than usual.'

'Isn't there a flight nurse and doctor on board already?'

'No, just a flight nurse. She will meet us at the airport. This is still deemed a high-risk delivery and there is enough room in the emergency retrieval aircraft for a three-person medical team, the mother and two portable cribs According to the RFDS, the mother is not fully dilated but well on the way so I'm thinking maybe four hours all up. Your shift has only just begun so we should return in plenty of time for you to get home to kiss Amber goodnight. I'll text home and let them know we're both in the air and we'll be back in a few hours.'

'Why would an expectant mother head to the bush? What was out in the middle of nowhere?' Jade asked as she and Mitchell climbed into the ambulance.

'Sounds like eastern suburbs hippies, doing yoga and meditation for a week,' he returned with a roll of his eyes. 'Eastern suburbs means nothing to you, I know, but basically they are well educated, financially secure people who head to the bush to centre themselves once or twice a year. I have nothing against it but travelling over rough terrain probably wasn't the best idea. It may or may not have brought about the early labour but it's happened and she's in trouble. Last antenatal check, twin two was still breech.'

'She's definitely going to need our help, then,' Jade replied.

They arrived at the plane fifteen minutes later. The pilot warned them of bad weather rolling in from a tropical storm in the northeast, bringing a high chance of turbulence. He had exchanged intermittent radio contact with the patient's partner, Jeremy, on the ground as his mobile service coverage wasn't great and the storm-clouds were interfering. He would be making his way to the nearest makeshift airstrip. The flight nurse had ascertained that the woman was coping with the pain, she was as comfortable as could be expected in a tent and had another female companion with her. Then radio contact had been lost.

'Emma Kingston,' the flight nurse introduced herself as she boarded and buckled up.

'Mitchell Forrester, neonatologist, Eastern Memorial.'

'Jade Grant, neonatal nurse.'

'And midwife,' Mitchell added, with a sense of pride for the woman sitting beside him.

'Good to have you both on board,' Emma said as she looked over the notes that had been sent to her phone and handed them to Jade and Mitchell to read. 'Twins, one breech, in a bush delivery will be challenging.'

'What are the biggest risks in your opinion?' Mitchell asked Jade as they became airborne.

'I have concerns with the safety of natural breech delivery and we obviously can't perform a C-section. Natural birth requires at least the first foetus to be cephalic, which I'm noting here was the case at the last antenatal visit, but if the first baby is anything but this then a natural delivery is unsafe.'

'The RFDS operator said her obstetrician is confident that hasn't changed,' Mitchell told her.

'Then we just have the normal issues after the first infant is delivered. With the cervix still wide open, the umbilical cord can make its way down and this can be dangerous for the remaining foetus. Then there's the risk that if the uterus shrinks rapidly with the delivery of the first twin, then the placenta can separate. As I said before, there's always a small risk with twin delivery of the need for a C-section for the second twin, and we won't have that option in the bush.'

Mitchell considered Jade's concerns for a moment. 'Then let's hope for everyone's sake that the birth is straightforward as I want both babies out ASAP.'

Emma nodded her reply. She had been a flight nurse for over fifteen years with the RFDS but twins in remote areas was a worry. Not wanting to overthink the situation, she slipped on her headphones, pulled out some reports and began reading and making revisions.

The increasing cloud cover made it a bumpy flight and a little nerve-racking for Jade. Each pocket of air that lifted and dropped the small plane sent Jade's stomach into a tailspin. Her heart was beating at an alarming rate but she did her best to mask her concern.

'Are you okay?' Mitchell asked when he heard the sudden intake of air by Jade. 'I thought this would be a piece of cake compared to the long-haul.'

'Not a huge lover of small aircraft,' she said, still trying to control her emotions.

Emma was engaged in her paperwork and didn't seem perturbed by it at all. But there was more to it for Jade. She really didn't want to discuss her recently acquired fear of nearly everything with a man who had daredevil on his résumé. He would never understand her love of thrills had flown out the window when Amber had arrived. She wasn't scared for her own sake. It was the thought of Amber losing another person from her life that scared Jade to the core. No one deserved to experience loss the way Amber had without even being aware yet of what had been taken. One day she would understand more fully and Jade wanted to be there in one piece to help her though that realisation.

'We'll be fine. This weather might seem frightening to you but not to the pilot, who will be very experienced,' his deep but still silky-smooth voice reassured her. Mitchell looked at Jade and realised that what he had deemed slight turbulence was really unnerving her. His bedside manner kicked in and he changed the subject. 'How about you tell me why you chose the noble profession of neonatal nursing and midwifery and then I will bore you with why I became a neonatologist.'

Jade considered the very handsome passenger beside her and she appreciated he was trying to distract her. She felt she knew him better now after they'd worked together for two days and, of course, the enlightening lunch. It concerned her more that she was increasingly finding him as attractive on the inside as on the outside.

Without warning, the plane dropped, and Mitchell instinctively reached his hand across to Jade's and held it tightly.

She didn't pull away. His skin was so warm. His grip so firm. It wasn't the turbulence that took her breath. She swallowed and tried not to look down to her lap, where his hand was protectively covering hers. His touch was unsettling but she had to admit silently, although it was ridiculous, that she suddenly felt better. Again. This was the second time that Mitchell had made her fears disappear with his touch. It was silly to think that his hand on hers could protect her in an emergency landing. But it felt as if it could. It also felt wonderful to have someone want to reassure her. And hold her.

Jade knew what she had to do. And it was very different from what she wanted to do. She wanted to let him protect her for a few minutes longer. She wanted to relish that feeling of his skin against hers. But she needed to pull away and take care of herself. She had been doing it alone and there was no reason to change that now. She couldn't rely on Mitchell. She couldn't let him in.

'I fell into it literally,' she said, pulling her hand free to supposedly check the time on her wristwatch. 'I was fourteen and I'd been skateboarding and took a tumble down some steps. I was attempting a stupid manoeuvre that didn't pan out and I was admitted to A and E for a broken wrist. Before that I had no idea what I wanted to do but, watching the nurses, I decided that was my career path.'

'So why neo and midwifery after an A and E admission?' he asked, aware that she had strategically withdrawn her hand and set the purely professional boundaries yet again. He wasn't about to push that boundary.

'On student placement I felt at home both in NICU and Obstetrics. I trained to be a midwife but also wanted to work in Neonatal so undertook additional training so I could work across both. What about you?'

'I left school and backpacked around Australia and then headed to Asia and Africa,' he returned quickly, not wanting a lull in conversation that would let Jade think about the size of the plane and the worsening weather outside. 'I saw what was needed in the developing countries that I visited and decided that I needed to qualify to be of any use so I headed home, applied to study medicine at Adelaide Uni and then specialised. It was a long haul but worth it. Once I was qualified and had completed my residency I returned to Africa and signed on with Médecins Sans Frontières. I worked in small villages and two refugee camps. They had squat when it came to medical equipment, but as a team we did save lives and improve the quality of those who may have been handicapped without early intervention.'

Jade had had no idea that he had been providing life-saving medical assistance to people who would otherwise be denied access to even the most basic health care. Suddenly she realised that the man she had judged as irresponsible was, in fact, quite the opposite. He didn't want ties but he certainly wanted to give to those who needed him most. Mitchell was quite complicated and not a man just after a good time.

'But now you're home,' she said, not really sure why she did and even less sure of why she kept going with that line of questioning. 'Will you stay here or head back overseas?' It was none of her business and she wasn't sure why she wanted to know.

Mitchell paused to think. He hadn't made plans, he never really had after his initial decision to study medicine. Everything else had just seemed to happen. He'd gone where opportunities and challenges arose and where he could avoid commitment. Mitchell had lived his adult life with a 'fly by the seat of his pants' attitude to life and he liked it that way.

'I heard that there was an opening they couldn't fill in NICU at the Eastern and thought it would be a good chance to catch up with family. Haven't really thought about how long or what my plan is, I'll just take it as it comes.'

The plane entered heavy grey clouds and rocked from side to side a little.

'I'm afraid the storm front arrived a little early,' the

pilot announced. 'Might get a little rough but shouldn't be too long before we're through to the other side.'

Jade felt her breathing stall as the plane lurched and jolted. She swallowed anxiously but very quickly the plane steadied and so did her breathing. She looked nervously from the window at the solid wall of grey and white fluff surrounding the small plane. She had to be brave, and with Mitchell so close she found it a little easier. It was only slight turbulence and perhaps the worst was already over.

Suddenly the plane dropped about fifty feet from its flight path. Steadiness disappeared as Jade felt her stomach churn and her heart begin to pound. She gripped the armrests, her knuckles quickly turning white. Without thinking, Mitchell's arms held her tightly. He didn't care that she had tried to build a barrier. He ignored what she wanted and gave her what he knew at that moment she needed. Security and a sense that everything would be okay.

Mitchell had travelled in enough light aircraft over the years to know they would be fine but she didn't have that experience. He understood her fear was very real and he didn't hesitate to reach out to her.

Jade didn't pull away, even after the turbulence subsided. She felt like she had found her safe harbour with Mitchell. And this time she wasn't about to tell it any other way, to him or to herself. It was the truth. He made her sense of fear lessen and it was as if she could halve the worry, knowing he was there to lean on. She could not remember the last time she'd felt that she could rely on someone, more particularly a man. She had never let herself feel that way.

As she looked down at the strong hand that was

covering hers so warmly and the arm that was holding her tight, she wondered if Maureen and Arthur had
raised *two* exceptional sons.

CHAPTER SEVEN

THE PLANE LANDED without incident and the medical team quickly unloaded their kits, including two portable incubators, and made their way to the woman's partner, who had been waiting at the makeshift runway with his four-wheel-drive.

'I'm so bloody relieved to see you,' he began as he helped to load the equipment into the back of the vehicle. 'I left Sophie's best friend, Wendy, with her. She's had four kids of her own so I figured she would be more use than me,' he told them as they climbed into the vehicle. 'It's only a ten-minute drive from here but I can get Wendy on the phone for you if you like. My hand-free connection's not good so I'll call before I start out and give you the phone.'

Jade watched as he pulled up the number. His fingers were shaking and beads of perspiration were covering his brow. The sun was warm and the air was dry. It was clearly nerves causing his reaction.

'I have the doctors with me,' he said into the mobile phone then put it on loudspeaker and handed it over.

'Hi, Wendy, this is Jade Grant, I'm a midwife from the Eastern Memorial Hospital and I have with me Mitchell Forrester, a neonatal specialist, and also Emma, the

Royal Flying Doctor Service flight nurse. The plan is
for us to be there to deliver the twins and we are a little under ten minutes away. How far apart are Sophie's
contractions?'

'About three minutes. I really hope you make it here.
I've had four of my own but not in a tent and I had an epi-
dural with all of them so Sophie's doing it the hard way.
She's on a clean sleeping bag on all fours to help with
the pain because I don't have any painkillers to give her.'

'Three minutes should give us time. I'm happy to
hear she's in a clean and dry environment. Can you see
the head of a baby yet?'

'Yes. The top of the first twin's head is crowning and
Sophie's got the urge to bear down but I've told her to
try to hold off until you get here, which I know is easy
for me to say.'

'I'm glad she can see a head,' Mitchell said. 'At least
the first is not breech and maybe there's a chance the
second has turned in utero.'

Jade nodded her agreement with Mitchell's comment
and turned her attention back to the surrogate midwife.
'We are only a few minutes away now, Wendy, and you
are doing a great job. Just keep Sophie calm, discour-
age her from pushing, and if you can massage her back
it might help with the pain.'

Jade kept talking to Wendy as the four-wheel-drive
manoeuvred through the rough terrain to the campsite. It
was obvious to them all why the man had not attempted
to take his wife into town once labour had started. Jade
was surprised, with the way they were all thrown about,
that labour hadn't started when the campers had first arrived. It was not the ideal place for an expectant mother
to holiday only six weeks from delivery of twins but

clearly by the number of tents she could see at the site, this was a majority choice holiday destination.

As they pulled up Mitchell, Jade and Emma hurriedly climbed out with their equipment. Quite a few people had gathered outside the tent that had become the make-shift birthing suite. They were all trying to offer advice and although it was heartfelt, Jade knew that it probably wasn't helping Sophie or Wendy.

'Please make way.' Mitchell's voice was firm and the small crowd parted as the medical team approached. Someone held open the tent entrance for them. They had arrived just in time. Sophie was already pushing. Jade covered her hands generously in antibacterial solution, slipped on some gloves and pulled the cord clamps from the birthing kit, along with the Syntocinon to assist with the afterbirth. She dropped to her knees for the delivery.

'Do you want me on my back?' Sophie managed to ask before the pain took her breath away.

'No, you're in a good position on all fours. It opens the pelvis right up, rather than being on your back. You're doing a wonderful job, Sophie,' Jade told her in a soft, calm voice. 'Just keeping breathing slowly…'

Jade's words were cut short by the next painful con-traction.

'Can you dampen the towel on her forehead a little?' Jade directed Jeremy. 'It's warm in here and it might help.'

Jeremy dipped the towel in a basin of water that had been brought to the makeshift birthing suite earlier and began gently mopping his wife's brow. 'I'm so sorry, darling, that I asked you to come here. It was a stupid idea but I thought you had another six weeks or more.'

'I'm not sorry we came on the camping trip,' she

muttered, between panting and pushing. 'But with this god-awful pain, I'm just sorry that I ever had sex with you. And, for the record, I'm never doing it again!'

Another powerful contraction came and the first baby's head emerged. A mass of black hair first, then a wrinkled forehead and tiny face.

'Just push slowly as you breathe,' Jade told her. 'We don't want to rush the baby.'

There were a few more contractions and Sophie's first baby was born into Jade's waiting hands. 'You have a little girl.'

Mitchell stepped closer and with sterile hands he reached for the tiny girl, who was not as small as he had imagined she would be for the gestational age. Given their surroundings, he was glad there must have been a discrepancy in dates, as a low birth weight baby might have struggled with a natural birth. Jade clamped and cut the cord quickly, and Mitchell wrapped her in sterile sheeting and took her aside to check her. Emma could not put the child to the mother's breast, as there was the second baby to deliver.

Another contraction began and the second baby was on its way quickly. A foot appeared and then with the next contraction it disappeared again inside Sophie.

'It appears that that we are looking at a breech birth after all,' Jade announced as Emma watched on, ready to collect the second baby so that Jade could look after Sophie during the third stage of delivery. 'I prefer "hands-off" breech births if possible so we will be taking this slowly.'

The next painful contraction came, and Sophie groaned loudly.

Both feet appeared this time and then with each

following contraction a little more of the second baby was exposed. With each breath Sophie pushed her second baby a little farther into the world. With concern on his face, her husband mopped her forehead as Jade coached her through the process. A little while later, with no intervention, the hips and stomach of the equally good-sized second baby girl emerged. Finally her little face and then her mop of thick black hair appeared.

'Another girl,' Jade announced.

Mitchell watched and saw that while her little heart was beating and the cord was still pulsing, she was not breathing on her own. He carefully handed the first baby to Emma, then placed an infant non-rebreather over the baby's nose and mouth and began resuscitation. He had been prepared as it was commonplace for breech babies.

'Breathe, baby girl,' Jeremy called to his tiny newborn daughter.

Jade could see the panic on his face and Sophie's. 'Don't worry,' she reassured them. 'It's not unusual and Dr Forrester knows exactly what to do.'

A few moments later the little girl began crying and so was Jeremy with joy and relief. Jade gave Sophie the prepared shot and the placentas arrived with a single contraction for each. Jade checked the placentas thoroughly to ensure they were complete and nothing had been retained in Sophie's uterus that could lead to haemorrhage, as she was already at increased risk of haemorrhage from delivering twins. Jade tended to Sophie as Mitchell and Emma tended to the two baby girls. Mitchell checked the second baby's vital signs and, like her twin, she was in good health with a good weight.

'You've been fortunate. Even with a breech birth you

won't be requiring any stitches,' Jade announced after the birth.

Mitchell had assessed both babies and noted that although they were small they were healthy and would need no additional support. Clearly there had been some mix-up with dates and for all concerned it was a welcome mistake.

'Although I have no concerns about the health of your daughters, we need to get mother and babies to hospital immediately,' Mitchell announced, as he gave the first-born to the father for a cuddle while he packed away his medical kit. 'Can you drive us back to the airstrip? I will need you to take it very slowly.'

Jeremy looked with joy at the tiny miracle in his arms, then at his second daughter, being held by Emma. He turned to look lovingly at his wife as a smile played at the corners of his mouth. 'They are perfect and beautiful, just like you.'

She stared in silence at the man who had given her the two most precious gifts in the world. 'They are beautiful, aren't they?' she said as she drew in a deep breath. Then, apparently forgetting the others still sharing the tent, she added, 'But we're still never having sex again!'

It was a bumpy ride to the makeshift airstrip where the pilot was waiting. They had travelled slowly in a convoy of four-wheel-drives with the assistance of the other campers.

'I won't get on the plane without Jeremy,' Sophie suddenly announced when the pilot explained that her husband could not fly back. There simply was insufficient room.

'We're at capacity as it is. Your husband will have to drive back to Adelaide.'

'I won't do it,' she said, clinging to her husband's T-shirt. 'I want him with me and our babies, or I won't take the flight.'

Mitchell considered Sophie's request. She had been through so much in the past few hours and her request was not unfair or irrational. The woman was in good health and both babies were healthy and he knew they would more than likely be discharged from the hospital in a week or so. They were both a good weight and had no obvious medical problems.

He crossed to Jade, hopeful that she would agree to take the later flight. Emma was the only choice to travel with Sophie and Jeremy. She was the flight nurse and knew the plane's equipment, and if turbulence occurred it would not be an issue to her. She could also more than adequately meet the three patients' medical needs.

Jade tentatively agreed. 'So we'll fly home later this afternoon, then?'

'Yes,' the pilot explained. 'Head back to the campsite in the four-wheel-drive for a couple of hours until I get back… Or you could hit the road but it would be about a six-hour drive.'

'We'll wait for you to return,' Mitchell said. 'There's been some bad weather and I don't know the condition of the road.'

The pilot nodded and, after loading the passengers, he took off.

Jade watched the plane disappear from sight. She was enormously relived that Sophie and her two beautiful babies were on their way back to the Eastern Memorial with Jeremy and Emma but she felt uneasy that she was on the ground with Mitchell.

One of the drivers from the campsite suggested they all head back to the campsite and have something to eat. Then they could return in two hours for the return flight. It was just before five in the evening and with daylight saving the sun wouldn't set for hours.

Mitchell and Jade agreed.

'I'll call home on the way and let them know you'll be late tonight,' Mitchell said as they climbed into the vehicle for the ten-minute trip back to the campsite. It was quicker going back as they didn't have to take it slowly for Sophie and the babies.

The early vegan dinner was lovely and much needed. Jeremy and Sophie's friends insisted on providing a healthy spread of food as a thank you for all that Jade and Mitchell had done in ensuring Sophie and the babies were fine. Mitchell and Jade didn't realise how hungry they were until they started eating. There was an abundance of everything and it was beautifully prepared and very tasty.

'As I said, Eastern suburbs hippies do the whole Woodstock thing in style,' he whispered in her ear. 'And they take their four-wheel drives to a campsite in the middle of nowhere so they're not exactly roughing it.'

Jade smiled as she took another bite of her salad. 'But maybe next time they shouldn't do it when one of them is heavily pregnant.'

The time was passing quickly and Jade was preparing to head back to the makeshift airstrip when a call came through.

'Dr Forrester, it's Doug from the RDFS base in Adelaide. I'm just calling to inform you that there's been an emergency on a sheep station just north of you and unfortunately the pilot has been redirected there and won't be able to collect you this evening. I can have a plane there in the morning.'

'I guess that will have to be okay. What time do you want us back at the airstrip?'

Jade was busy thanking her hosts for their hospitality.

'Fine,' she heard him say as she headed to the four-wheel-drive. 'We'll be there at nine a.m.'

Jade's jaw dropped. There had to be some mistake.

'Be where at nine in the morning?'

Mitchell drew a breath, well aware that Jade would not like his answer.

'The airstrip.'

'No, we can't be staying here tonight. Why? What happened?'

'An accident at a sheep station is more urgent than us, I'm afraid, so we're here till the morning.'

It was a disaster. Jade was upset and although she knew she had no right to be angry with Mitchell, she still felt that it was his fault in some way. She had never spent a night away from Amber and worried how the little girl would react.

Mitchell saw her stiffen and stare coolly at him. 'I'm not wanting to be here any more than you, believe me. I've done my fair share of camping over the years and I quite like the king-size bed and the air-conditioning I have back in Adelaide. But we need to make the best of it. I'll see if they have a spare tent so we can have one each and we'll get the bedding organised now.'

'But what about Amber? You promised me that I would be back to tuck her into bed.'

Mitchell ran his fingers through his hair. 'I know, and I'm sorry. I didn't plan for this to happen.'

'I never said you did, but I'm worried about Amber.'

'I'll call my mother and you can talk to her and to Amber while I organise our sleeping arrangements.'

Mitchell dialled and handed the telephone to Jade, who was quickly reassured by Maureen that Amber would be fine and that she would sleep in the room with her overnight. Jade felt better. Not great, but better.

Mitchell, however, wasn't feeling so great. He had been told they would have to share the tent that belonged to Jeremy and Sophie. It was a state-of-the-art tent and they did have spare clean sleeping bags and pillows to give them. He decided to deal with that problem later. He worried that if he raised that issue, Jade would start the three-hundred-mile trek home on her own.

'Let's walk around for a while,' Mitchell suggested as his footsteps cracked the fallen pieces of eucalyptus bark lying on the ground. 'Amber is under control back at home and my mother will call if there are any problems. There's nothing to do but make the most of the time here and I promise nothing daring or risky, just a nice bush walk.'

Jade still wasn't happy.

It was her worst nightmare. Stuck so far away from Amber. And with a man she had to admit she was growing fond of, despite her best efforts.

If it weren't for the joy she had seen on Amber's face when she had talked about spending her day with Maureen and Arthur, Jade would have regretted her trip to Adelaide immediately. But she couldn't turn back the clock and neither would she, as Amber, Maureen and Arthur deserved to spend time with each other.

She had to be logical. There was nothing anyone could do to change things. She reminded herself that Amber was settled with Maureen and Arthur and they would no doubt be making a fuss of her so she probably wouldn't be overly anxious. *She* was the anxious one. She told herself it would be just the one night and then she had four days off with Amber. They would celebrate her third birthday with a trip to the zoo. But not the one that Mitchell had suggested with the roaming lions. Jade liked the petting zoo, where they could walk among the goats, and chickens and ducks. She was slowly getting her anxiety under control. Looking for the positives was the best solution, she decided. It wasn't the end of the world. She would spend a few hours seeing some Australian bush wilderness up close before she crawled into her own tent, and then in the morning they would be back in Adelaide.

She just didn't want to get up close to Mitchell. But then she reminded herself that they had a group of campers with them. It wasn't as if anything could or would happen.

Jade looked down at her nursing uniform, now a little the worse for wear and stained with blood. 'I think it might be difficult to hike around in this. I mean, the white duty shoes are about the only bit that works. And you'll look a little silly in your outfit too, a little formal for a bush walk.'

Mitchell looked down at his clothes and realised his long grey slacks and white business shirt and the tie that was hanging loosely from the collar would not be the best outfit.

'Maybe someone can loan us some clothes,' he said, and headed over to the group about to begin their bush yoga class. 'Since we're here overnight, I was just wondering if you might have some clothes we could borrow until tomorrow.'

One of the older ladies in the group slowly undid her very awkward lotus pose with a grimace. 'I have some old things that belonged to my daughter and son-in-law. I meant to drop them at the mission but didn't have time. There's a bag in the car. I'll grab something for both of you,' she said as she stood up. 'And while you're off walking I'll fix up the tent with the new bedding since you'll be staying the night together. We don't have a spare tent.'

Jade felt her stomach fall and heart race. That was not how she had pictured the sleeping arrangements. Sleeping in the same tent with Mitchell had her close to panic.

Lying in the dark hearing him breathing. Knowing he was so close. Knowing he was stirring feelings that she should not be feeling.

Mitchell saw Jade flinch and he knew what he needed to do.

'I'll sleep under the stars and you can have the tent.'

She let a little breath escape with relief and her pulse returned to normal. She couldn't share a tent with Mitchell. It wasn't because she couldn't trust him, it was because she wasn't sure she could trust herself.

'Here you go,' the woman said, and handed Jade some denim shorts and a T-shirt and Mitchell a pair of cargo pants and a tank top. 'They might not be a perfect fit

but they'll be better than what you're wearing now for
out here in the bush.'

Jade smiled and took the clothes. 'Thanks so much.
I'll launder them and drop them off at the mission next
week.'

Jade disappeared into the tent and when she emerged,
Mitchell's jaw dropped. The tiny denim shorts fitted like
a second skin with her long bare legs pouring from them.
The tight T-shirt that bared her midriff was also the
perfect size, in Mitchell's opinion, but he was sure Jade
would not agree. He was certain her *prim and proper*
alarm would be ringing.

'I'll check if she has anything else for me to wear.
This is obviously for someone a few inches shorter,'
she said, tugging at the hem of the top, trying to hide
the bare skin.

'I think you look great…in fact, better than great.
There's no time to change, the sun will go down and
we won't see anything if you try on everything in the
mission bag. Let me throw on my hand-me-downs and
we can get out of here and take in some sights of the
Aussie scrub.'

Jade felt so self-conscious. It had been so long since
she had been out in public in revealing clothes and she
wanted to pull the denim fabric down to cover her legs
as well. But there wasn't any spare fabric and none was
about to magically appear. The shorts were so small and
the T-shirt was stretched very snugly over her breasts.
She was at least grateful she had worn a sports bra and
not a lacy number.

Mitchell emerged as if he had chosen the outfit. Jade
knew he couldn't have done better with a stylist. The
tank top showed off his perfectly sculpted arms and the

cargo shorts sat low on his hips, just the way he liked them and the way she had seen him wear them at the beach.

Remembering the fact that Mitchell had already seen her in her bikini, and the others were involved in an Outback yoga class, and the kookaburras definitely wouldn't care about her attire, she decided she had no choice but to let it go.

'Looks like you're about to get your first sighting of marsupials from the land Down Under,' Mitchell said with a smile.

He grabbed some bottled water from the campsite cooler and they headed off through the dry scrub with the leaves and bark snapping under their feet. The air was still dry and warm and Jade could smell the distinctive scent of the eucalyptus leaves. She was thrilled when half an hour into their walk she spied a lizard sunning itself on a hollow tree branch. The brown and black scales blended with the tones of the bush surroundings and it became almost invisible.

'Would poisonous snakes, like rattlesnakes, be around here?' she asked as she surveyed the tufts of dry grass dotted on the red dirt around her.

'There are poisonous snakes, but we don't have rattlesnakes, they're one of your countrymen. I'd say the deadly brown snakes would be the ones to watch out for around here.'

'That's a help.' She laughed as she jumped from one large boulder to another. 'That's the colour of most snakes!'

'Then maybe,' he called to her, 'don't try to pat any of them.'

Mitchell loved seeing that side of Jade. She was carefree and spirited. He wished they could stay here for a week and get to know one another. To see how much more he could uncover about the woman who was now standing atop a two-foot rock and smiling into the setting sun.

She was perfect and he was dangerously close to falling for her.

They were having such a great time that Jade even forgot how inappropriate her outfit was. The Outback and Mitchell were both captivating and distracting. The walk was wonderful with the scent of the warm summer night and the wildlife sounds all around them.

'So how do you like Outback Australia?'

'Well, it's definitely a far cry from LA,' she said as she climbed over some rocks to where he was standing. 'Can you tell me more about where we are?'

'As your personal tour guide—unpaid, I might add—I can.' His mouth curved into a ridiculously handsome smile. 'This is the Flinders Ranges National Park. We're about three hundred miles from Adelaide…' He paused as he realised immediately that it also meant from her niece.

'And Amber,' she added dryly. 'But I'm okay, really.' She decided the rock could be her makeshift seat in the sun as she dropped down onto the hard but warm boulder for a rest while she enjoyed the view. 'I'm sure Maureen and Arthur are spoiling her rotten and, to be honest, I couldn't be happier about it. She needs to know she has family who love her as much as I do.'

Mitchell was surprised. It was a huge step for Jade. He hoped he'd had something to do with her shift in demeanour. She was still far from the wild child that

David had spoken about, but she was even further from the governess in those shorts.

'We all do,' he said, and their eyes met for the longest time.

Jade pointed ahead and purposely broke the spell. 'So what's over there?'

Mitchell didn't want the moment or the feeling to end. For the first time in his life he loved the way he felt about a woman beside him.

Finally, he looked across the landscape and answered. 'Bunyeroo Gorge is about twenty miles from here. It's a great drive with spectacular views and a trip through the gorge itself. The last time I travelled through there, a few years ago, there was a fair amount of water, which added to the driving experience but we won't have time to do it today. Maybe if you want to see more of Australia we could come back.'

Jade was surprised by the invitation. She had not thought past this trip, and definitely not planned that they would spend additional time together, but it made her feel good that he had. She smiled at the thought of exploring the wilderness with Mitchell.

'Some of the rock formations are over six hundred million years old,' Mitchell continued. 'Then there's the Brachina Gorge, which is particularly awesome. It's rugged country but stunning up there.'

'So you've spent a great deal of time travelling around Australia?'

'I backpacked around when I was eighteen. I needed some space of my own and to not be responsible for anyone else so I took off and worked odd jobs to pay my way. I do love Outback Australia.'

'Tell me some of the history,' Jade said, then added, 'Your history, not the gorge's.'

Mitchell took Jade's cue and sat down on a rock not too far from her. 'Not much to say. I travelled a lot after graduating, I told you that in the plane. I worked overseas and I'm back in Adelaide for a while. That's about it.'

'What about your childhood?' she said, lying back a little on her rocky platform above the dirt. 'Did you want to study medicine because of your stepfather? Did he encourage you during your high-school years?'

Mitchell wished that Arthur had been there while he'd been in high school. That would have made his life much easier and particularly his mother's and brother's lives.

'No,' he replied as he waved a horse fly away from his brow. 'Arthur came into my mother's life when I was already in medical school. My father was long gone and she met Arthur when she was working as a dental receptionist. He needed an emergency appointment and she squeezed him in to see the dentist and that was it. Arthur asked her out to dinner after the dentist put in a temporary filling, and they've been together ever since. They say it was love at first sight.'

'What a romantic story,' Jade said as she stretched her legs out in front of her and instinctively curled her toes. 'It sounds like David and Ruby. Theirs was love at first sight too.'

Mitchell said nothing. He couldn't relate to the idea. Falling in love and settling down had always been the furthest thing from his mind. In his mind love didn't last and the collateral damage scared him to the core. But for some strange reason, sitting with Jade, it suddenly didn't seem so unnerving.

'I guess they're the lucky ones,' she said, looking up into the pink and purple striped sky that hung over them like a giant patterned canopy.

'Lucky perhaps the second time around, but not even close with the first,' he said without thinking.

'So her relationship with your father was very unhappy.' She turned to face him, her expression suddenly serious.

'Let's just say he let us all down, shattered the family, but we got through,' Mitchell said, climbing back to his feet. 'Not without some scars, mind you, but it's much too great an evening to waste it talking about my father.'

They walked in silence and enjoyed the sunset. While Jade was curious about Mitchell's father, she didn't bring it up again. He obviously didn't want to discuss it further and that was his prerogative. But it did make her think it might be an underlying reason for his behaviour over the years. His father's actions had definitely impacted on Mitchell.

They were both mindful they needed to be back before it was completely dark. Mitchell had a good sense of direction so he knew they would be safe. Jade realised how she once again she felt safe just being near him. And now knowing a little more about the man, feeling safe with Mitchell wasn't scaring her at all.

CHAPTER EIGHT

'SOMETHING TELLS ME Australian beer is not to Jade's liking,' Mitchell told the other campers. They had returned from their hike and had been invited to join them for a nice cold drink. It was the first time Jade had sampled the amber drink with the white froth and she quickly realised she would never ask for one again.

'It's so…bitter,' she said as her face contorted a little, and she quickly passed the small bottle to Mitchell. Without hesitation, he took a sip.

'It's cold and I'm off duty, so I'm not about to complain.

Suddenly they both realised how comfortable they had become in each other's company. They had a level of familiarity between them that made it natural for him to finish her drink.

The campsite hosts offered Jade a nice chardonnay instead and she quickly found that Australian wine was much more to her liking as they passed the evening with polite conversation. The men then pulled out some cards and suggested poker. Jade noticed Mitchell suddenly shift in his chair. She could see he clearly didn't like the idea, which suited her as she was getting tired. It had been a long day, but she couldn't help but notice there was more to Mitchell's reaction than just tiredness. There was a look of disapproval.

'It's getting late and the plane will be back in the morning, so I think we'll turn in for the night. Thank you all for your hospitality.' Mitchell stood up and with a look that Jade had trouble defining in her own mind he reached his hand down to help her up.

Without thinking, he kept holding Jade's hand long after he needed to and he led her to the other side of the camp and to their tent.

'You don't approve of cards?' she asked as they neared the tent.

'Let's just say I don't think much of anything related to gambling. No one should gamble money, lives…or people's feelings.'

'That sounds like it's coming from a place of experience,' she said softly. She wanted to know more about the man who was making her body and heart come alive.

Mitchell walked farther away from the others, still holding her hand. He sat down on a large fallen eucalyptus branch not too far from their tent and gently pulled her down beside him.

'My biological father gambled with our family and when he lost, we all lost.'

Without thinking, Jade stroked his arm as he looked into the distance and into his past.

'My father lost everything we owned, our home, savings, even my mother's jewellery was pawned before he took off with his mistress when I was only fourteen.'

'Mitchell, I'm so sorry.'

'Hey, we still had each other but in my infinite wisdom as a teenager I decided it was my job to make it up to my mother.'

Jade was confused. 'But it was your father who lost everything and walked out. You had nothing to do with it.'

Mitchell released her hand. His jaw tensed before he spoke. 'I saw him with the other woman. I was catching the tram home from school and I saw him leave the casino, holding hands with a woman I knew worked in his office. It was about six months before he left us. Looking back, I should have said something, maybe prepared my mother. Perhaps we could have secured the house, or at least the money and her jewellery. But I did nothing. I hoped it was a one-night stand, an affair that would blow over. I didn't tell anyone, not even my father.'

'Your mother may not have believed you, Mitchell. She may have thought you were mistaken, and more than likely your father would have lied his way out of it. A man who would do that is not going to admit it.'

'Who knows? But I couldn't change anything so I decided to make it up to my mother and brother and lied about my age, got a false ID and got work in a warehouse. I told my mother that I hated school and got home schooling, which allowed me to work all day and study at night. David was only nine and couldn't help. I just wanted him to stay on track and at school.'

Jade felt tears welling inside. Mitchell had made life choices at such a young age through misguided guilt and enormous reserves of compassion.

'My mother found employment too, but with little or no workplace skills her money was not enough to keep a roof over our heads and pay off the credit-card debt my father had also run up. So we both kept working and I missed out on a huge part of my teenage years. My mother hated that I had to work and she told me she'd work longer hours so I could return to school but we both knew she couldn't work any more hours. There weren't enough in the day for either of us.'

'Your father's selfish behaviour cost you your youth. No wonder you've spent the last few years having fun.'

'It was hardly the coal mines…'

'To a teenage boy, missing out on everything normal and natural and silly in those precious years would be life-changing and devastating,' Jade cut in, aware of her own carefree, rebellious youth.

'Arthur came into my mother's life when I was eighteen. He was a good man and I was very happy to see my mother happy, but I also was over it. I was over being responsible. I took off. It was as though I had handed my mother to Arthur and I was out of there.'

'That's being a little harsh on yourself. I'm sure Maureen was relieved that you no longer had to be the man of the house.'

'I worry that I would have bolted anyway, even if Arthur hadn't shown up. I was burnt out.'

Jade shook her head. 'I'm sure you would have stayed. If you managed to hold it together for three long years, working and studying, you would have seen it through. I'm sure of it.' Her hand reached up and brushed away a stray wattle flower that had landed on his shoulder.

'Nice of you to think so, but I guess I share my father's DNA. Maybe Arthur was a stroke of luck because I was done. That's why I've avoided family. I don't want to let anyone down. I felt trapped. Maybe that's how my father felt when he left.'

'Stop right there,' Jade demanded of the man she had so quickly come to know. 'You were fifteen when you took on the role your father abandoned, you held it down for three years and took care of your mother and brother, and finally, when you mother found love, you left to enjoy your life. How is that anything like a selfish middle-aged man gambling all the family's money, leaving them in debt and shooting through with his mistress? They are poles apart. You showed maturity beyond your years, love and loyalty, while your father's actions were despicable.'

'Maybe that's how you see it but I'm not that chivalrous. And I can't change now,' he admitted.

'I disagree. I think you cut your hair and shaved your beard to meet your niece. You wanted her to like you and not be scared away by the wild bushman. You cared about how she felt. It might seem a little thing but add that to the way you melt around Amber, and it shows the man you are. You have a wonderful heart and you're nothing like your father.'

Mitchell had told himself as he'd sat in the barber's chair the day after he'd arrived in Adelaide that it would be cooler to have shorter hair in the summer, and perhaps this way he wouldn't scare either Jade or Amber away. But he knew inside it was more than that. More than even Jade could see. A part of him wanted to be a little more like David. He wanted to be closer to the father Amber had lost, even if it was only for a few weeks.

But he doubted he could come close to being half the man his brother had been.

'I like to have no roots, I don't want to be in one place or responsible. I don't think that I ever will...'

Jade saw Mitchell in a different light and she cut short his words with a kiss.

He had been running from guilt that he shouldn't have

been carrying and she felt her last walls of resistance fall with his honesty. She now needed to be honest with herself. She wanted Mitchell Forrester.

Looking at Jade, comfortable in her skimpy outfit, enjoying the Outback, Mitchell also saw a different side of her and he couldn't hold back any longer either.

Their bodies only inches apart, her heart was pounding as she felt his breath on her cheek and smelt the scent of his woody cologne. Neither moved. Neither had the strength to walk away. The sincerity and warmth in his words drew her to him and she didn't know what to think any more. She was about to give in to feelings she had never thought she would feel again. The desire that he was stirring she had thought was buried completely under a sea of duty and guilt. With little effort he was resurrecting a side she had thought was lost for ever.

His hands cupped her face before passion took over and there was urgency as his mouth closed on hers. With no need for words, he pulled her close to him and, forgetting their bush surroundings, his hands roamed the curves of her body. Willingly, she pressed her body against the hardness of his and a little groan of pleasure escaped from her lips. She could hardly breathe.

His mouth moved slowly down her neck, trailing kisses across her skin. Her back arched as he gently tilted her head to take his kisses lower.

'Is there room in your tent for both of us?' His voice was low and husky.

She nodded her reply as his tongue teased her skin and he led her by the hand into the darkness of the tent, where he slowly removed every piece of her clothing. And then his own before he was consumed by passion for the woman lying naked on the ground.

* * *

Jade woke in the morning to the sounds of the kooka-burras in the treetops and some rustling in the leaves on the ground outside. She sat upright in surprise.

Then she felt a warm hand pull her back down to the softness of the thick sleeping bag for two.

'It's probably just a possum or koala. Lie back down with me and I'll protect you from ferocious marsupials.'

Her lips formed a soft smile before Mitchell's mouth claimed hers. His kiss held the same level of passion that they had enjoyed during the hours of lovemaking before they'd fallen asleep in each other's arms. It was very clear to Jade that the morning was beginning in the same wonderful way the night had ended. There would be no argument from her.

'Jade,' he began, realising that for the first time in his life he wanted more than a one-night stand. He wanted Jade in his life for ever. 'Last night was wonderful and I hope we can find a way to make this work…'

'Let's take it slow. I don't want you to feel pressured. I wanted you and you wanted me. I am so happy here with you right now. Let's see where this leads.' It was the Jade of old speaking and she was happy to hear that voice from the past. As they lay in each other's arms, they heard voices outside.

'Do possums talk?' she whispered with a smile in her voice.

He put his finger to her lips and softly said. 'Let's pretend we're asleep and they'll go away.'

The male voice drew closer. 'I can't hear you very well, the reception out here is terrible but I'll see if he's awake and get him to call you back.'

Jade drew the covers up as she heard the footsteps next to the zip door of the tent.

'Is anyone awake?' the man's voice called. 'It's quite urgent. There's a call from Adelaide.'

'Just a minute.' Mitchell struggled in a half-kneeling position to pull on his boxers and jeans before he bent down and tenderly kissed Jade again. 'Hold that thought and don't get dressed. I'll be back soon. I'm sure it's nothing. The plane's not due for another hour.'

He unzipped the tent, stepped into the warm morning air and stretched.

'Sorry to wake you but you left your phone out here on the chair and it was vibrating on and off for about ten minutes so I picked it up.'

Mitchell noticed the serious look on Jack's face.

'Who was it?' he asked with concern in his voice.

'Your mother…' he began.

'Is everything all right?' Mitchell could hear the man's voice was sombre. 'Did she say what it was about? Has there been an accident?'

'Not an accident but apparently your niece had a turn of sorts. She's in hospital, something about her kidney failing.'

'I mean, she has another one so I'm sure she'll be all right,' the man said with an inflection that made the statement become closer to a question.

'No, she won't, my niece only has one functioning kidney.'

Mitchell and Jade were driven back to the makeshift airstrip by one of the men from the camp. The plane would arrive half an hour earlier than originally planned to get them to Adelaide. Jade was back in her nursing uniform. Mitchell was had also changed back into his hospital clothes, and they stood under the shade of a giant eucalypt.

'I should never have come.' She scowled at herself. 'I should have insisted that you take another nurse. It just was another bad choice I've made in life. I can't believe what I've done, what *we've* done. I left Amber alone so far away from me. I was stupid and thinking about myself. Last night while we were…' She fumbled over her words, not wanting to admit to what had happened between them. 'Last night Amber needed me and I wasn't there.'

'You mean when I was making love to you.'

'While we were thinking about ourselves and forgetting the real world and our responsibilities,' she corrected him without referring to their lovemaking. 'I let Amber down, and I let Ruby down. It was wrong of me.'

'You didn't let anyone down. We spent the night together, and there was nothing wrong about it.'

'It shouldn't have happened. I came to Adelaide to let Amber meet her grandparents, not to hook up with her uncle.' She bit her lip angrily. Her breathing was laboured as she paced the dusty track and looked up at the sky impatiently.

'Call it whatever you want, but I'm not sorry it happened. I have feelings for you. I'm not sure where it will lead us but last night was not just a hook-up. It wasn't planned and it isn't why Amber is facing health issues right now. The two aren't related any more than the accident three years ago that you still carry around as if you personally caused it to happen.'

Jade shot him a look of contempt. 'You don't know anything about it. I booked the holiday for them. I told them to go and get away to Palm Springs. It's my fault they are both dead and now look what has happened to Amber because of me being away from her. She was probably fretting, I could have stopped it happening...'

'Don't do this,' he said firmly as he walked to where she was still pacing and pulled her to him. 'You couldn't change what happened. You're a nurse and you know that Amber's condition was present at birth and there was every chance this could happen without warning. The nephrologist would have explained that to you before you left Los Angeles to come here. You can't keep Amber in a glass room inside bubble wrap so she can't hurt herself and you can't watch over her twenty-four seven.'

Jade angrily pulled herself free from his embrace. 'I should have refused to come here.'

'You had no choice, you had to travel with me. You were the best nurse for the job. And if it wasn't for you, those two babies might not be alive today.'

'The plane is here,' she said, ignoring his remark about the birth and the positive outcome. It was still not enough to balance out what she had done wrong in her eyes.

There was an uncomfortable silence for the hour's flight. Mitchell did not want to add to Jade's stress or create a scene in front of the pilot. He was grateful that no bad weather was predicted and there was little chance of turbulence as he knew that Jade would never let him help her and he would hate to watch her suffer that anxiety along with the worry of Amber.

With clear skies, Mitchell's focus was on getting back to Adelaide to speak to the nephrologist at the Eastern Memorial. He knew that Adelaide had world-class renal facilities and he would turn every stone and make every call to ensure Amber had the best care.

Amber and Jade now meant so much more to him than he had ever thought possible. Even if Jade didn't want to pursue their relationship, he would always be there for the two of them, however that played out. He was certain it would be from a distance, but that didn't matter. What mattered was Amber.

Jade had caught a cab with Mitchell directly to the hospital as he had insisted on being present to discuss his niece's medical condition with the specialist.

'I can handle it,' she told him tersely when they arrived at the Eastern Memorial.

'I am fully aware that you can and do prefer to do things on your own. But I am here and I want to help if I can. I'm her uncle. I have a right to be there.'

'Just as you have been for the last three years?'

Mitchell ignored the remark. He knew it was deserved and he also knew that Jade was lashing out from fear. He refused to walk away and demanded to meet the renal specialist in his office before they saw Amber.

'What's the prognosis for Amber?' Jade asked as she tried to pretend that Mitchell was not in the room.

'Well, when the kidneys aren't working well, symptoms are varied and may be the same as many other conditions, but when her grandfather, Dr Forrester, Senior, accompanied Amber here last night, he quickly alerted the staff and A and E about her situation. After the initial examination, the senior consultant contacted me immediately and Amber was transferred to the renal unit.

'Amber, I note, has been feeling tired since arriving from the US, but I believe everyone put that down to jet-lag, which is understandable. She has also lost her appetite but, again, in a three-year-old that can be pickiness about food. But it was the swelling in the hands and the associated numbness that concerned Arthur so fortunately he drove her straight in to be seen and we immediately noted high blood pressure. We have tested her urine and it's positive for protein and the bloodwork shows creatinine. As you know, healthy kidneys usually filter both. Her only working kidney is failing. We have her on dialysis now.'

Jade gasped, and Mitchell instinctively moved towards her but she shot him a look that told him everything. His arm dropped away, and Jade moved away to stand alone and receive the remaining news.

'So are we looking at a transplant?' Mitchell asked.

'Yes, I'm checking the donor register now—' the doctor began.

'I want to be tested as soon as possible,' Jade announced. 'Family should prove a better match.'

The doctor nodded his head. 'Sometimes but not always.'

Mitchell found Jade pacing the corridor outside Amber's room a few hours later. She was back to the drab clothing again, which he suspected his mother had brought in for her.

'How's Amber?'

Jade looked in silence at Mitchell. She hated him for the choices she made when she was with him. First the motor bike ride and then…then making love in the tent when she should have been home with Amber. For the way he made her feel and the way she forgot her responsibilities in life. She couldn't be around him. Not now and not in the future. People she loved got hurt when she didn't think things through properly and that could never happen again.

'What is it? Are you still angry for what happened between us? Because I'm not. Together we can help Amber.'

'Amber and I don't need your help. We'll be fine on our own.'

'I know you can cope on your own. You're a strong woman, but you don't have to take on everything alone and think Amber's your sole responsibility. And you have this idea that everything bad that happens is your fault. And that if you behave in a certain way then everyone you love will be safe.'

'What's wrong with that? I love Amber and want what's best, and I know that if I don't watch out for her then something bad can happen. Look where we are today.'

'That has nothing to do with you not looking out for Amber. You left her in the care of my stepfather, who is a retired medic, and he saw the signs and brought her straight to hospital.'

'But I should have been there.'

'Why? What possible difference would it have made?'

'Because it's what Ruby would have wanted and what she would have done. She would have been there. She wouldn't have run off to the bush and slept with a man she barely knew.'

'Stop trying to live your life as if you were Ruby. She was a wonderful woman and my brother loved her. But you're not her. You're an amazing woman in your own right. You have to stop living your life in the shadow of someone else.'

'I'm not now, nor was I ever amazing,' she told him. 'I was shallow and didn't take life seriously. Hardly admirable qualities and definitely not good enough for Amber. She deserves so much more.'

'Having fun and loving life is not shallow in my book,' he told her as he ran his fingers through his hair in frustration. 'What Amber deserves is to know the real Jade. To see that the woman who willingly and selflessly put her life on hold to take care of her niece is not a serious, staid old spinster. Since when does having fun and living life make you less admirable? You didn't hesitate to take on the role of bringing up your niece so I think that makes you extraordinary and you need to stop judging yourself. No one else is. You're the judge and jury.'

'But Ruby was sensible and sweet and a warm and wonderful wife and homebody.'

'And you're not Ruby.'

'She was my sister and I can be like her. I owe it to Amber to be like her mother.' Jade knew even as she said it that it wasn't true. She was nothing like Ruby and that was what troubled her most. How could she be everything Amber needed if she wasn't like her sister?

'Were you ever looking for a man like David?'

'That question is so wrong,' she snapped. 'David was my sister's husband and he's dead. How can you ask that question?'

'It's not wrong. It goes to prove my point. Would you have ever seen a future with a man like my brother before the accident?'

'He was stable and considerate…'

'Was he your type before you became Amber's guardian?'

'No, he was Ruby's type.'

'Then stop trying to be Ruby. You're a wonderful person, Jade, and you should let Amber and the rest of the world see the woman who is hidden inside this shell.'

'But I was irresponsible and crazy and nothing close to what Amber needs.'

'No, you weren't, you aren't and you never could be,' he insisted. 'You stepped up and became the best parent that Amber could hope for while you were still the old Jade. The accident didn't give you time to reinvent yourself. You instantly and without hesitation did what you knew you had to do for your niece. And it was what you wanted to do. Nobody had to force you to do it. Dressing and behaving in a way that mimics your sister isn't going to bring her back or make you a better person.'

'But you didn't know me then, so you can't pass that judgement.'

'I know you now. I know the real you. The woman who was saving those babies then climbing rocks and then sharing a makeshift bed in that tent with me. That was the real Jade.'

'Amber loves me the way I am now…'

'Amber loves the woman who would give her life to make her happy, the woman who has that little girl in her heart so deeply that she is a part of her, but she would love you no matter what the packaging. You don't need to be someone else to have her love.'

'But her respect as she grows older is just as important.'

'Do you honestly think that a teenager is going to be able to relate to her maiden aunt looking and behaving like she stepped from a nineteenth-century novel?'

'I hardly dress or behave like that.'

'Jade,' he said as his fingers softly moved the stray

wisps of hair from her fringe, 'you are behaving exactly like that. I'm not asking you to be someone you're not, I'm asking you to be exactly who you are. A passionate, fun-loving woman who will raise Amber to be the best she can be and allow her to have fun and experience life at the same time. Not someone who will make her fear her own shadow.'

Jade flinched then moved her head away. 'But what if something happens to her along the way? What if she's hurt because I allow her to take a risk, to live life the way I did?'

Mitchell looked into the eyes of the woman he knew had crept into his heart. 'You are here, you are alive, despite the fun you had. Ruby and David were cautious and safe and they are not here to raise Amber. I'm not judging them, they lived life the way they wanted to, but it shows that you can't guarantee a long and healthy future by being pedestrian about life choices. Sure, you don't make ridiculous choices that will put you in harm's way but I don't think surfing or a spin on a motorbike or a Ferris wheel ride are called dangerous by definition.'

'But Amber was admitted to hospital while I was away…with you. Walking in the bush and then sleeping together.'

'Yes, *while* you were away with me, not *because* you were away.'

'That's the same thing,' she argued.

'Not even close,' he returned. 'You did nothing to cause Amber to be admitted. That was decided at conception. Genetics delivered her prognosis and now she needs a donor. It's earlier than her doctor had envisaged, and earlier than any of us imagined. But you can't take any blame for that, neither can I, or anyone in this world.

It's the hand that Amber was dealt and we will do our best to turn it around. And I want us to do it together.'

'But I need to behave in a way that will make Amber proud of me and look at me the way she would have looked at her mother. I took that away from her when I sent her parents on that holiday and now I need to make it up to her. Somehow I need to make sure that Amber doesn't miss out on the upbringing that Ruby and David would have provided if I hadn't...'

'Hadn't what?' he cut in angrily. 'Caused the accident? But you didn't, Jade. You weren't the cause, it was some idiot on the 101 who caused the pile-up and the deaths of innocent people but you were not that person. You generously paid for a holiday for my brother and your sister and they both died. But you were not responsible.'

'You're just trying to make me feel better, but I know the truth and I will spend my life making it up to Amber and trying to be as close as I can to the mother that she will never know.'

'So you'd rather be a poor impersonation of Ruby than a brilliant version of you?'

'It's not like that,' she retorted, tears spilling down her face. 'I know that if I hadn't suggested the trip they would still be here today to raise Amber a certain way, and that's just what I'm doing.'

'That argument doesn't hold any water for me,' he said, holding her shoulders with his hands and forcing her to look into his eyes. 'We don't know what might have happened and whether they would still be alive now or not. Perhaps it was not their destiny to raise Amber. Maybe that was always going to be your role. Perhaps even my role too. Who knows? But we can't change

the past. We can just build on what we have. Don't sell
Amber short. Let her see the awesome woman you are,
not some poor version of her mother.'

'I've managed so far and she seems to be doing okay,'
she retorted angrily. 'I know what I'm doing and I'm
doing a good job of raising her.'

'You won't be able to keep it up.'

'And you would know that because?'

'Because you will burn out. You are trying to fool
the most important person in your world—yourself. You
can't keep telling yourself it's okay to live a lie. It will
crush you because one day it will become too much. I
know that from experience.'

'Loving Amber would never be too much,' she spat
angrily. His words cut her like a knife.

'I'm not talking about Amber being too much. I mean
the lie you are living, trying to be half the woman you
really are. Suppressing how you feel, needing to live up
to an unreal image that no one but you wants.'

'One night sharing a bed doesn't mean you know me
or have any right to tell me how to live my life. You told
me yourself that you've spent the last decade running
from anything close to resembling ties or responsibility. Last night was fun but I know in my heart there's
the chance you won't stay around. I may be the only
one who will be here for Amber after the dust settles. I
can't lean on you and have you leave me. And I won't
risk putting Amber through that. Just go now before she
falls in love with you.'

Mitchell froze. His jaw clenched tightly. He hadn't expected that judgmental side of Jade and it disappointed
him. She knew what he had been through as a teenager.
The sacrifices he had made to ensure there had been

food on the table and the rent had been paid. He didn't want to argue. There was no point. Jade had summed him up before they had met and despite everything they had been through and how close they had grown, deep down her opinion hadn't changed. She didn't trust him.

But he had changed. He had fallen in love with the real Jade Grant. He wanted to see where it could lead. But he couldn't live with a woman not true to herself. Jade had no intention of letting Amber see the real woman who had raised her. She wanted to wrap her in cotton wool and let her grow up scared of her own shadow, and Mitchell didn't want to be part of a charade.

'You're right, Jade. I have no idea.' His chin fell to his chest as he drew a deep and resonating breath and prepared to walk away from the only woman he had ever loved. There was no point arguing. She had won. She could go on living a lie but he wouldn't and couldn't be a part of it.

He leaned in, and she closed her eyes as he tenderly kissed her cheek.

A tear escaped from her eye and ran down her face as she watched the love of her life walk away with nothing she could do to stop him leaving. They were both trapped by their pasts.

CHAPTER NINE

'MY DARLING AMBER, you are loved more than you will ever know and you *will* pull through, and grow into a beautiful young woman who can travel the world, climb the highest mountains and find adventure. We're all praying for you,' Maureen said softly to her grand-daughter, who lay sleeping peacefully in the hospital bed with the dialysis machine working through the night by her side.

Jade had fallen asleep in the chair and woke to hear Maureen speaking to her granddaughter. She sat up and rubbed her neck, which was stiff from the awkward po-sition she had been in when she'd dozed off. She was surprised to hear Maureen encouraging Amber to walk in her son's wanderlust footsteps but she didn't bother to set her straight. Amber would not be heading off for any adventures if she had anything to do with it. Espe-cially not with her medical condition.

Jade was angry with herself as much as Mitchell for the hard words they had spoken but they were all true. The night they had shared couldn't change their destiny. Mitchell wanted her to be someone she had left behind. Someone she knew wasn't good for Amber.

'The nephrologist left about two hours ago,' Jade said

while still blinking open her tired eyes. 'And Amber finally fell asleep about an hour ago. We were reading one of the books you brought in.'

It had been three days since Jade had slept in a proper bed. Although everyone had repeatedly suggested she take a break overnight, she'd refused. She didn't want Amber to open her eyes and find an empty room. She had returned home to shower and change while Arthur had kept vigil. And she had eaten a quick meal that Maureen had insisted on before she'd left for the hospital again.

'You really should let me stay tonight. I'm not past it, you know. I only just greeted my sixties.'

Jade knew Maureen's offer was genuine but she didn't want to be away from her niece at this critical time.

'I'm fine, really. You have already done too much for me.'

'Hardly,' Maureen returned, as she sat down next to Jade and patted her hand warmly. 'You're as stubborn as that son of mine. You two are so much alike. So ready to step up and try to fight battles on your own when there are people who want to help'

Jade didn't have the energy to argue. She knew that she and Mitchell were polar opposites except for those few hours they'd shared in the tent that night. A time that Jade would never forget but also a mistake. An error of judgement on her part but one driven by the need to be reminded she was a woman.

Maureen drew in a deep breath but kept her voice to little more than a whisper. 'I remember all those years ago, when his father left us.' Her face suddenly became quite serious as she began talking about the past. 'Mitchell was barely fifteen and David was only nine. Their father had been gambling for a long time without my knowledge. He'd kept up a façade for years and juggled money from one account to the other in an effort to keep up appearances when he lost, and then with a big win we would all head off on another extravagant holiday. One day he'd had enough of living two lives and juggling his gambling debts so he sent an email from his office that the marriage was over, he had someone else and he was moving on.'

Jade knew this was the more detailed version of what Mitchell had already told her. It didn't change anything as she listened to Maureen.

'But for us, there was more bad news to follow. Our family home was heavily mortgaged, the cars were repossessed by the finance company overnight, even my jewellery was missing when I thought at least I could sell that to help us make it through.'

'But wasn't your husband responsible for any of the debt?'

'When everything was sold, we broke even. I didn't have to file for bankruptcy but we walked away with very few possessions and I fell into a sad, dark place. Mitchell thought he had to be the strong one. He took everything on his shoulders as if he had to make it up to me and to his brother.'

Jade knew that was because he had seen his father with the other woman and had never told anyone. Except her.

'When he overheard the landlord demanding the rent I just didn't have one week,' Maureen continued, 'he decided that he would handle it all on his own. David was so young. He had no real concept of the damage that their father had done. He knew that I had to cancel his music lessons for a while, but Mitchell refused to let me cancel the maths tutor for his younger brother. Mitchell knew that David wanted to be a doctor and if his grades fell early in his schooling, Mitchell worried that David might not catch up so he paid the tutor from the money he earned working overtime.'

Suddenly David's admiration for his older brother made sense. It had been a deep-seated and long-held admiration for what Mitchell had done many years before. Mitchell had given so selflessly at an age when most teenagers thought only of themselves.

'Mitchell was gifted academically and didn't need additional tuition and said that he could easily work and fit in his own study load and help David with his other school subjects. He would work long hours in the warehouse after the store had closed, and as much as I argued he refused to cut back until we were on our feet and had money in the bank so the rent was never behind again. We pooled our funds and paid the bills. David worked very hard with his maths so he didn't let his brother down. They had so much love for each other.'

Jade felt a tear run down her face. Mitchell's devotion to his family was deeper than just paying bills. It had been ensuring his brother and mother had been taken care of over his own needs. Such sacrifice at such an early age was very rare. Mitchell had been a very special young man who had taken on an enormous responsibility at a young age.

'You must be proud of your sons.'

'Very, my dear, so very proud,' she said, with tears in her own eyes. 'And then I met Arthur.'

Jade's mouth curved into a smile. 'You deserved to be happy after what you had been through.'

'Thank you. Many women go through much worse than me, but there were a few lean years,' she admitted. 'Arthur asked me to marry him and by that time Mitchell was eighteen. He had finished school with an almost perfect score, and was a little battleworn so he took off on an adventure. I was happy for him but worried that what he had been through would affect him for a very long time. He headed off around Australia and spent many months in the Outback, then trekked through Indonesia and finally to Europe, where he backpacked for two years.'

'And grew a beard to look like a jungle hippy,' Jade added.

'Yes.' Maureen nodded. 'And he kept that beard for years, even when he came back to finish medical school and then specialise in neonatal. Arthur was a surgeon, so he encouraged Mitchell and helped where he could, but Mitchell was fiercely independent. He wanted to do it alone. I'm afraid after his father left he almost became an island. Learnt to depend on himself. I've been so worried that he would end up alone and that would be a waste of such a warm and generous heart.'

Jade nodded in silence. She knew he had a generous heart and she had experienced his warmth first-hand, but it didn't lessen the risk of him leaving without warning. Or change his inability to commit. His father had scarred him but she couldn't take a risk and be hurt. She felt sorry for him but she had to think about Amber.

'His father really destroyed his idea of family and as much as Arthur and I have tried it just hasn't made a difference. I'm not sure what it will take. Or *who* it will take to make him believe in love and family again.'

Maureen leant down and softly kissed her grand-daughter goodnight.

'Are you sure you won't let me stay? Arthur is down speaking with one of his former colleagues and he can run you home for a hot shower and some sleep. I can sit with Amber tonight.'

'Thank you, Maureen, but I'm fine, really. I can get a rollaway if I want but I prefer to sit up, to be honest. I can't really sleep anyway.'

Maureen patted her hand. 'I'll be back first thing in the morning, then. And I'll bring some fresh clothes for you.'

Jade watched her leave the room and then turned to Amber sleeping peacefully and thought back to everything that Maureen had told her. It all fell into place. She wondered if Mitchell was trying to finally look past the devastation his father had left behind and reach out to her. *Could she and Amber make him believe in love and family again?* She wasn't sure if he could. And she wasn't prepared to take that risk.

He might wake up one day and just decide it was too hard and leave. She fought sleep, her mind consumed with worry for Amber and the reality that she had pushed Mitchell away, probably for the last time. As her eyes finally closed she knew it was for the best. Mitchell didn't belong in her world any more than she belonged in his.

Morning finally came around and Jade woke just as Amber began to stir. Her eyelashes flickered and she made a little moan but quickly fell back to sleep again.

Jade stretched and then went out to the nurses' station to get some water. It was still early and the night shift nursing staff were finishing up paperwork.

'I can get you a coffee if you'd like,' one of the young nurses offered.

'No need,' came Maureen's voice. 'I picked up a long black for her on the way in.'

Jade saw the slightly tired, smiling face coming towards her with a coffee, something wrapped in a small white paper bag and an armful of clothing.

'And I picked up a ham and cheese croissant to go with it.'

The two women walked back to Amber's room, Jade sipping the hot drink.

'It breaks my heart to see her this way,' Maureen said, her expression turning to one of sadness. 'How long will she need to stay on dialysis?'

'I'm checking today if I'm a tissue match and can be Amber's donor. We're both blood type O so we're compatible on the first level so now we just need to undergo the HLA or tissue typing.' Jade put the fresh clothes on the seat beside her and began to unwrap the croissant.

'What does that mean?'

'Well, there are six antigens that have been shown to be the most important in organ transplantation. Of these six antigens, a child inherits three from each parent. It's extremely rare outside identical twins for a six-antigen match between two people, but I hope that we may have more than one matching since I'm a blood relative. Kidneys can be transplanted between two people with no matching antigens without a rejection episode but if by chance we had the six matching antigens then it would mean less anti-rejection drugs for Amber.'

'That's a little confusing but I guess it means if you match then you will have the surgery and Amber will receive your kidney?'

'There's another test called a cross-match test and it's a very important part of the living donor work-up and it's repeated again just before the transplant surgery. Some of my blood and some of Amber's blood will be mixed in the lab. If Amber's cells attack and kill the donor cells, the cross-match is considered positive. This means Amber has antibodies "against" my cells, but if they don't then the cross-match is negative and we're considered compatible.'

'I think you are very brave to donate a kidney to Amber and she's very lucky to have such a wonderful, generous aunt.'

Jade shook her head dismissively. 'No, I'm the lucky one.'

The nephrologist arrived about twenty minutes later. Jade had finished her much-needed breakfast and changed into another skirt and blouse in the bathroom while Maureen watched Amber.

Amber had woken and was able to be taken off the dialysis machine. She was uncomfortable and unsettled but happy that both Jade and Maureen were there.

'I just need you to sign the final consent forms for Amber's surgery.'

Jade was confused and she didn't try to mask it from the doctor. 'But I haven't undergone the tissue matching yet. My appointment is later today.'

'We have a match already. The patient is being prepped and that's why Amber was fasting overnight.'

Jade and Maureen both looked up to notice the sign by her bed. The nurse had come in while Jade had been asleep and put it up so the morning shift would not provide breakfast to the little girl.

'I don't understand. I thought family provided the best possible match.

The doctor approached Jade. 'As I said a few days ago, the likelihood of a perfect match other than an identical twin is about one in ten thousand. Well, it looks like we found our one in ten thousand so there is no need for you to be tested. We already have a perfect match for Amber. He's being wheeled into Theatre as we speak.'

'How did you find the match? Was the person on file already?'

'No.' The doctor hesitated. 'Mitchell underwent the tests two days ago.'

Jade rushed into the ward to find Mitchell being prepped.

'Why are you doing this?' she asked. 'I could have been a match and you wouldn't have to go through this.'

'You've done enough for Amber already. Now it's my turn.'

'This is ridiculous, Mitchell. I never expected you to be the donor. Regardless of the HLA results, if my cross-match is compatible then we can have the operation in the next few days.'

'I'm sure you could, but I'm compatible. End of story.'

Jade closed her eyes in disbelief and frustration. She didn't need Mitchell to offer a kidney from a misguided sense of duty. He was free to leave. Jade knew she would never forget what they had shared but she would survive a broken heart. She didn't want to trap Mitchell into staying. Or into taking on more than he wanted to or more than he could promise to do willingly.

'Mitchell, I finally know you well enough to see that you are trying to fulfil some role you think you should, but you don't. I'm a big girl and I can handle it. I've taken care of Amber since she was born. I can keep doing it.'

'But what if I don't want you to handle it on your own? What if I want to be part of the solution? Don't I get a say in it?'

Her voice was shaky. Amber was deteriorating by the day. They needed to find a donor but this could drastically change Mitchell's life. It was not a small ask to donate a perfectly healthy functioning kidney. He loved to lead the life of a nomad. This might change things. She loved him too much to see him like a bird in a cage.

'Let me get tested and if I'm a fail then maybe you can think about it, but don't rush in to this surgery,' she pleaded.

'You don't get it, do you? I'm doing this because I want Amber to have a long and happy life. I don't want her tied to a dialysis machine. I want her to go sky-diving, and windsurfing and anything else she wants to do. Just like you did and just like I did.'

'But she might not want to do those things.'

'That's true, but if I can give her my kidney I'm giving her the option to have fun and be a little wild, like her aunty was when she was young…and still can be, if she wants to.'

'But I'm not young any more. I have responsibilities and I won't let Amber down.'

'You could never let anyone down. It's not who you are. You would step up to the plate no matter where you were or what you were doing. Even a blind man could see your devotion to Amber but you shouldn't let it control and drive fear into every aspect of your own life. I've seen fun Jade, and I think it's a waste to put her away for even one moment longer.'

'But I don't want to be like that any more. Look what happened when I was irresponsible. Amber ended up in hospital.'

'Her genetic condition sent her to hospital. The fact we spent one amazing night together had no impact on Amber's health. If you had been tucked up in the bed next to hers, she would still have needed hospitalisation, and you know that's a fact. But it's a fact you don't want to face. Maybe because you think if you wrap her up in cotton wool and keep yourself near her, and behave more like her great-grandmother then nothing bad can befall her. It can, Jade. Good and bad things can happen to those we love and trying to control their lives won't change what is destined to happen by way of their genetic make-up.'

'Why are you trying so hard to make me see things your way?' she pleaded as she dropped her shaking head into her hands. 'And why do you want to put yourself through all this? It may change your life and not for the better.'

'Because I believe in my heart that you won't be happy without me and I won't be happy without the real you. Not some cardboard cut-out of another woman. And because Amber deserves to have two loving parents.'

'What do you mean, two loving parents?'

'The two of us. I'm not going anywhere, Jade.'

'But you hate feeling trapped, you said it.'

'That's true, and it still stands. I would never want to be trapped, but being with you and Amber is the opposite. It's the only place in the world I want to be. It's so far from being trapped…it's being wanted, and needed and loved, and it's a place I never want to leave. It's the true meaning of family. If you'll have me, I'll stay for ever.'

'For ever…in one place…with us?'

'I would take more than for ever if I could. I love you, Jade, and I'm here to stay, albeit down one kidney in a few hours. But if you don't want me minus a part, I'd understand.'

Jade didn't want to fight her feelings any more. She leaned down to the man being wheeled into Theatre and kissed him with all her heart.

'You're perfect any way you come.'

EPILOGUE

THE DATE MITCHELL and Amber chose to become husband and wife was one year to the day of the surgery to give Amber a healthy, happy life. With each passing minute Mitchell and Jade knew their love was growing stronger and would last for ever.

Australian immigration had granted extensions to Jade's and Amber's visas on compassionate grounds. Amber had needed time to heal after the surgery and after six months she and Jade had returned to Los Angeles briefly to say goodbye to the kind neighbours who had been like family to them. While it had been sad for everyone, it had been a new beginning for Jade and Amber, and the lovely older couple were happy that the little girl would be with her real grandparents.

Jade had packed up the house and put it up for lease. It was Amber's home and for that reason Jade had chosen not to sell it. She wanted it to be there in case, as an adult, Amber wanted to spend some time in the city where she'd been born. A lovely family who had relocated from Sacramento, with two small girls and a golden Labrador, had moved in, and Jade felt sure her neighbours would shower the little girls with attention, just as they had Amber since she was born.

Mitchell had proposed twice. Once to Jade with a solitaire diamond ring as they rode the Ferris wheel at Glenelg and then a week later he proposed that he and Jade adopt Amber. He didn't want them to be just her legal guardians as he wanted all their children in the future to have the same mother and father.

Amber was four and although she didn't really understand what adoption meant, she loved the idea of having a mummy and daddy like the other children at pre-school. Jade was so deliriously happy she thought she would burst. And so the very special wedding date was set and the adoption papers were filed. And Maureen stepped into one of her happiest roles of her life… and one she had never thought would be hers…the role of wedding planner.

The wedding guests chatted happily under the clear azure sky. They sat on white deck chairs in rows on the lawn, each chair decorated with a huge organza bow. The day was perfect, the guests had all arrived and the celebrant and solo violinist were both eagerly watching for movement from the small white marquee that held the bridal party.

Maureen, beautifully designer dressed and beaming, emerged from the marquee in a mint-coloured silk suit and signalled with a subtle wave of her lace handkerchief.

The solo violinist sat upright, adjusted his jacket and then began "Wedding March" by Felix Mendelssohn. All heads turned back to see Amber hug her grandmother before she took her first tentative step. She looked like a tiny angel in her ankle-length pastel pink silk dress. A circle of fresh rosebuds and gypsophila sat atop her blonde curls and a smile dressed her cherub-like face as she walked down the white carpet aisle, scattering rose petals with each tiny step.

Mitchell's mouth curved into an equally big smile as he caught sight of her. She was walking towards the jasmine-covered arbour where he stood with his groomsmen. His legs, hidden by the black designer suit, were shaking a little as the much-anticipated moment of his bride's entrance drew closer. Amber tried to stay in time to the strains of the violin but she gave up and happily skipped the last few feet.

'You look so pretty,' Mitchell told her as he bent down and kissed her forehead then took her tiny hand in his.

'You thould thee Mummy.' She beamed. 'She lookth like a printheth.'

'I bet she does.'

Alli and Laura appeared from the marquee in their floor-length pale pink silk bridesmaid's gowns and slowly made their way to the arbour. The shoestring straps of their dresses were embellished with tiny crystals, their hair was softly curled and falling around their shoulders, and they each held posies of roses and gypsophila. All eyes were on them until moments later Arthur escorted Jade onto the white carpet walkway.

Mitchell felt his heart stop for a moment. His wife-to-be was breathtakingly beautiful. Her cream silk dress clung to her body like a second skin. It was nothing close to a maiden aunt's attire. The halter neckline was trimmed in crystals and her shaking hands held a posy of pink rosebuds. A delicate short veil skimmed her bare shoulders but allowed Mitchell and the wedding guests to see her beautiful smiling face.

With short steps, she walked towards the man who

had shown her that it was okay to be herself. The man who would not let her live a life carrying guilt or regret. The man who had captured her heart and given her love in return was waiting for her and holding the hand of the most precious little flower girl. His daughter.

Each step brought her closer to the most important people in her universe.

They were all she would ever need.

Arthur finally released Jade's hand to the security of Mitchell's.

'You look beautiful,' Mitchell told her as he held her hand tightly.

Jade smiled at her soon-to-be husband. With one hand holding Amber and the other firmly clasping Jade's, the three of them stood before the celebrant.

'We do,' Amber suddenly called aloud.

The guests all laughed at the little girl's impromptu announcement, and Mitchell turned to face Jade with an overwhelming feeling of desire and love surging through his body.

'I guess if Amber can't wait…neither can I.'

Mitchell gently released Amber's hand. Throwing tradition to the wind, he lifted Jade's veil, swept her into his arms and just before his mouth met hers he whispered, 'I will love you for ever, Mrs Forrester.'

* * * * *

DOCTOR...
TO DUCHESS?

BY
ANNIE O'NEIL

MILLS
BOON

Published in Great Britain 2015
by Mills & Boon, an imprint of Harlequin (UK) Limited,
Eton House, 18-24 Paradise Road, Richmond, Surrey, TW9 1SR

© 2015 Annie O'Neil

ISBN: 978-0-263-24727-5

Harlequin (UK) Limited's policy is to use papers that are natural,
renewable and recyclable products and made from wood grown in
sustainable forests. The logging and manufacturing processes conform
to the legal environmental regulations of the country of origin.

Printed and bound in Spain
by CPI, Barcelona

Dear Reader,

This story was like completing a big circle for me, in that it is the tying up of the final 'loose end' for the women who didn't get their happily-ever-after in my first book, *The Surgeon's Christmas Wish*.

In good conscience I just wasn't able to let Julia wander around out there in my subconscious. Which is vast. Think bigger-than-the-Outback big—outer-space big would be getting closer. She deserves a happy ending as much as the next person, and I hope you agree that she's really met her match in Oliver. Ahem, excuse me…*Lord* Oliver Wyatt.

I'm sure you will be unsurprised to see there are lots of eating scenes. Guess what motivates me! It couldn't be the diet I'm on that made me write a deliciously tempting moment including chocolate-covered salted caramels, could it?

I really loved writing this, and found it particularly hard to finish because I just didn't want to say goodbye to Julia and Oliver at the end. I hope you enjoy it—and please do get in touch if you ever have any questions or want to let me know what you think. You can reach me at annie@annieoneilbooks or on my Facebook page (Annie O'Neil) or Twitter @annieoneilbooks.

Toodle-pip for now!

Annie O

Dedication

This book is dedicated, without reservation,
to my Happily Ever After guy—my husband.
He brings light into my life and infuses my heart with
an incredibly happy beat. Thank you. For everything.

Books by Annie O'Neil

Mills & Boon® Medical Romance™

The Surgeon's Christmas Wish
The Firefighter to Heal Her Heart

Visit the author profile page at
millsandboon.co.uk for more titles

Praise for Annie O'Neil

'A heartwarming tale of two opposites falling for each other. Annie O'Neil has done a fabulous job with her first offering. Highly recommended for readers of medical romance.'

—*GoodReads* on
The Surgeon's Christmas Wish

'A poignant and enjoyable romance that held me spellbound from start to finish. Annie O'Neil writes with plenty of humour, sensitivity and heart, and she has penned a compelling tale that will touch your heart and make you smile as well as shed a tear or two.'

—*CataRomance* on
The Surgeon's Christmas Wish

CHAPTER ONE

"C'MON, DOC! RACE you to the top!"

Clawing herself out of the mud was one thing, but clawing herself out of a mud-filled moat via a seven-meter mesh wall was another.

"I think I know who'll win." Julia panted, fairly certain the nineteen-year-old apprentice gardener had the advantage.

"You're the reason we're doing this. Show us how it's done!"

The words of encouragement gave her a new charge of determination. Julia grabbed ahold of the mesh and began to pull herself out of the waist-deep pool of mud and water, a trail of muck dripping down her legs. She felt and looked like a swamp creature. Big picture? This was fun!

Right?

Surely it was just like having an all-over body mask? Julia risked opening her mud-covered mouth to give a short bark of laughter. What did she know about fancy spas and mud masks?

Boarding school hadn't exactly been the stuff of luxury, and being a military wife from a young age? Let's just say the SAS boys weren't lining their coffers with gold pieces. Her foot found purchase on a mesh square as she blindly reached up to grab another handhold. A surge of adrenaline took over as she pulled herself up another meter.

The burst of energy was a reminder that her family's life was on a new track. After two dark years, this was all part of starting over. Thanks to a generous overload in the talent department, and a loving uncle, her children were enjoying an education she could only have dreamed of. And as for her? After military wife had morphed into military widow, she'd found herself on a different life path. One that had landed her in the middle of a mud-filled obstacle course! Matt would've laughed his socks off.

No. Check that. Matt would already have been at the finish line with the kids cheering her on. And laughing his socks off.

A quick squeeze of the eyes and Julia lifted her right knee again and found a foothold, arm reaching for another rung to pull herself even higher, as if the physical exertion would help push away the memories.

It was all right. Everything was going to be all right. She'd slogged through the grief-laden, crying-every-day thing and now it was time for the moving-on part. She had to do it. For herself and for her children. Here in St. Bryar she was slowly putting everything to rights, clearing the fug of heartache to make way for a new future. If only her feet weren't weighed down with fifty kilos of mud! The sensation reminded her of how she'd felt in the days after she'd opened the door to two uniformed officers handing her the official confirmation of her husband's death.

"Doc! I'm almost at the top!"

The quickfire scrabble of bodies jolted Julia back into the moment. There was laughter, shouting and cheering coming from everywhere. A group of villagers lined the stone wall circling the moat of Bryar Hall. Their shouts of encouragement rallied the unrecognizable runners as they scrabbled over the final hurdle before the finish line in front of the three-hundred-year-old hall.

"This should get you an extra fiver, Doc!" Julia peered through the mesh and watched as the assistant gardener flung himself from the other side of the mesh wall belly-flop style back into the moat. The crowd roared with delight.

Fingers crossed, the charity run would bring in some much-needed funds for the St. Bryar Country Hospital. Funds that would hopefully keep the rumors at bay about the heir apparent leaving the clinic—and the estate— to its own devices when a cash injection was what they needed. She didn't really know what to make of what she'd heard of Lord Oliver. Globetrotting do-gooder or playboy of the whole, entire world?

None of the stories she had heard added up to something—or someone—she could picture. For the villagers' sake, she hoped he saw the clinic as part of Bryar Estate's future. Right now, it was the only thing keeping the doors open to the public. Realistically, any funds gathered today would barely make an impact—but she couldn't think about that now. Not with a so-called fun run to finish.

She sucked in a deep breath, wiped the mud from her eyes and looked up. *A bit of training might not have gone amiss.* Only two more meters to go but she was knackered. Hanging in midair was not the optimal place to stop and have a peaceful break.

Logic was belatedly kicking in. So what if the run had been her idea? Surely, as GP of the clinic, she should have stayed on the sidelines in case anyone was injured?

Her gut? It was saying actions spoke louder than words—and it was time to get moving.

She flicked her mud-slicked ponytail out of her mouth, put a hand up to grab ahold of another rung and pulled up one step, then another, and another. Just a rung or two more and—

"Ouch! Foot! *Foot!* Foot on hand!" She looked up to see a desert-style military boot lift off her hand as the body attached to it vaulted over the top of the mesh wall, coming round soundly to land directly opposite her on the mesh.

Their bodies made impact with a gooey thwack. Mud-pie suction adhered their chests together then released and joined them together again as they each fought for breath and balance.

"I'm slipping!" Julia's feet struggled to find balance on the footholds. She wasn't winning. He-Man was.

She felt his arm slip round her waist, easily pulling her in tight to the mesh and what felt like a particularly nice man-chest. Muddy but nice. Her eyes lingered for a moment on the wet T-shirt outlining her captor's—or was it savior's?—shoulders. A lightning flash of response tugged her body closer into his. It was hardly the mile-high club, but tingles of excitement danced along her skin like an electric current.

"Are you on?"

What? Seventh heaven?

Oh, for goodness' sake. Don't say that.

"I just need to grab—"

"Put your feet in one of the squares. I've got you."

You sure do! Julia's bare legs slid along his as her feet finally slipped onto a rung. *Mmm...I could get used to this.* The cheering sounds around them shifted from distinct calls into a fuzzy hum. Was it possible to sustain a concussion from a couple of cracked fingers?

"What about your hand? Are you all right?" His voice kept pulling her back to reality.

I'm fitting a little too perfectly into your chest for me to answer that accurately.

"How's your hand?" he repeated. "Are you holding on? I can wrap my leg around you for support if necessary."

Please don't. That would definitely tip me over the edge. Who was this guy anyway? Tarzan? His hair was a bit shorter, but...

"I'm not going to let go of you until you tell me you're all right."

"I'm fine, I—"

Having finally dared to look directly at him, Julia felt the air being sucked out of her lungs for a second time. She was face-to-face with a pair of mossy-green eyes beaming out at her from the midst of a mud-slathered face. A face she was pretty certain sported a pair of very nice cheekbones, a broad mouth and, underneath the mud, jet-black hair. A gently furrowed brow...

The fingers of her left hand tightened on the rung. The physical connection reminded her of the ring she no longer wore. She glanced at the green eyes again and felt her knees wobble as her tummy did a heated whirly-hoop twirl. For the first time in a long time she felt an overwhelming urge to kiss. And it was very specific. She wanted to kiss He-Man.

No, she didn't!

Yes, she did.

What was she? Twelve?

Julia blew a controlled breath through her lips as she demanded her brain explain to her what a mature thirty-three-year-old widow with thirteen-year-old twins would do in these circumstances. There wasn't much room to escape the six-foot-something body pressing into hers. *She was a doctor, for heaven's sake.* She felt bodies all day long. Just not leanly muscled, mud-covered ones hanging five meters above a mud pit pressing a bit too sexy-style into hers. A surprise spree of spicy images sped up her heart rate.

"I'm really sorry if I've hurt you. May I have a look?"

Blimey, his voice was nice. Like hot chocolate. She could do with a cup of that about now. Direct delivery. *Oops! Remember to hold on!*

Julia felt his fingers tighten his grip on her waist, steadying her. She abruptly pulled her eyes away from his, certain she was blushing. *Wait a minute. You're covered in mud. He doesn't have a clue. Thank you, fun run!*

"Have I hurt you? Or are you up to making it to the finish line?"

Fine. If you're going to insist upon dealing with the matter at hand...

Julia put her left hand in front of her face. It wasn't bleeding—but two of the fingers were swelling fairly rapidly and had the telltale thudding pump of more to come. Prognosis? Most likely cracked, if not fully broken. Not really what a GP running a country hospital was hoping for.

"Don't worry. I'm a doctor."

"Don't worry. I'm a doctor."

Julia laughed as they spoke simultaneously then

shook her hand a bit as if to shake away the incident. *Youch.* Bad idea.

Hang on a second.

Doctor? She was the only doctor she knew of in St. Bryar. Was he from a neighboring village? Did that mean she'd see him again? *Stop it, Julia. Don't go there. Men are not part of the Get Your Career On Track scheme. Particularly men of the scrumptious-enough-to-eat variety.*

"Where do you practice?"

"Where do you practice?"

The laughter came again. Nervously now.

"St. Bryar."

She was the only one to answer this time and saw any warmth in his eyes cool.

Hmm. Had she stolen his job? Were there bad feelings about an 'outsider' coming into the small community? She'd not felt that from anyone else, so the reaction was a bit strange. Whatever it was, she didn't like the vibes coming off him.

"Not to worry." She wriggled out of his hold as best she could. "I'll sort it at the finish line. There wasn't much chance of me getting a red ribbon anyhow."

"Distinguished Service Medal would be more like it. I really am sorry about your hand. Do catch me up if there's anything I can do." A tight smile of apology broke through the man's mud-slathered face. Before a word could escape her lips, he grabbed ahold of the side of the mesh wall and slid down into the moat for the final stretch of the run.

Julia remained static, his words ringing in her ears. Hearing them had stung. Painfully so.

Matt had been given a Distinguished Service Medal

posthumously. Julia had been presented with it only a few months ago. As if it would change the fact her husband was dead.

"Better press on, then!" she called, hoping her voice sounded bright. A sharp blade of heat ran from her fingers through to her heart as she grabbed the top line of mesh and swung herself over. Her hand hurt like hell. Suppressed emotion was fueling her to finish the obstacle course now. Matt was gone and being here was the start of a whole new life. She had to remember that. It wasn't just her body's response to the sexy mud monster that was new. The past seven months here at St. Bryar had doled out moment after moment of proof she'd made the right decision. Pursuing her medical career had been a long time coming. Through the years her medical degree had fizzed and itched for action while she'd 'held the fort', as Matt had said each time he'd swung his duffel onto his shoulder and headed out the front door.

Well.

She couldn't stop a grin from forming as she took a one-handed, mud-slicked slide down the mesh wall into the history-rich confines of the moat. She was holding the fort, all right—a ruddy nice one—and this time it would be different. Even if she had to fund-raise her heart out to show the ever-absent future Lord of the Manor the clinic was worth its weight in gold.

Oliver scanned the crowd, wondering if he could pick out the blue eyes and mud-caked ponytail that had stayed with him since the obstacle course. The impact the woman—the new GP at St. Bryar Clinic—had made on him wasn't just physical. It was a hit-all-the-senses body-blow. Not something he was used to. Not by a long shot. Years of working as a volunteer surgeon in combat zones had helped him retain his emotional distance from just about everything.

Until now.

Since when had there been a new GP throwing fun runs in the moat? Where was Dr. Carney? The sixty-something doctor had been in charge of the estate's small country clinic since Oliver had been a boy. Surely his father wouldn't have replaced him without telling him? Then again, he hadn't imagined his father throwing an assault course, either.

"Lord Oliver! So nice to see you!"

Oliver turned to see a mud-encrusted man stretching out a hand.

"Hello there—ah…?"

"Max Fend. From down the village. I used to help my dad." He paused, waiting for a glimmer of recognition. "He sorts out all the Bryar Hall firewood. Done so for yonks." Max filled in the blank then withdrew his hand as he saw Oliver was freshly showered. "Best not muck you up, your lordship"

"Don't be ridiculous, Max." Oliver smiled, hoping it would cover the all too familiar fish-out-of-water feeling he was experiencing. "And, please, it's Oliver." He hated being called Lord Oliver. Served him right to get a big dose of it. He'd not recognized Max, someone he'd seen nearly every day throughout his childhood. It didn't sit well, being so out of the loop.

The one thing he'd always been able to count on at Bryar Hall was nothing changing. His title, the unwritten aristocratic code, the unnecessary kowtowing of locals who, like it or not, had livelihoods that depended upon what he did when he inherited the estate. He'd spent his entire adult life avoiding the confines of the role he'd be handed one day. And here he was, stepping right into the mold history had cast for him—an aloof aristocrat.

Kaboom! There goes ten years of plain old Dr. Ollie.

"Dr. MacKenzie sure knows how to throw one heck of a bash."

"Ah, the new GP?"

He received a nod and grin. Little wonder. Anyone could see the woman was a knockout, even covered in mud.

"So this was her brainchild, was it?"

"Oh, yes, sir. Like a whirlwind, she's been. Changing this, changing that. Sometimes you hardly recognize the place for all of her 'spring cleaning.'" Max held his fingers up in the air quotation-style but, instead of the frown of displeasure that usually accompanied change in St. Bryar, his lips held a broad smile.

"She seems to have bewitched the lot of you." Oliver wasn't sure if he was giving a compliment or castigating the locals for falling under the new GP's spell.

"Oh, that she has, Lord Oliver. That she has. High time someone with a bit of drive and commitment came round and gave the old carpets a fresh beating!"

"Indeed."

Call a spade a spade, why don't you?

"Not meaning you, Lord Oliver," Max quickly covered. "I know the Red Cross couldn't get by without you and all the help you must be giving all those poor people in war zones and whatnot."

"Not to worry. No offence taken."

Oliver smiled and gave Max a light clap on the shoulder to settle the matter but the remark niggled.

No. It had cut right through to the heart of the matter. The locals didn't see him as a stayer. And they were right. The last place he saw himself putting down roots—if he were to do such a thing at all—was here at Bryar Hall, the estate that time forgot.

A place bursting with life was the last thing he'd expected to see when his taxi pulled up in front of the house less than an hour ago. The kid in him had barely stopped to think before pulling on a pair of shorts and a scrubby T-shirt so he could join in—be the Oliver he was anywhere but here.

As a child, he'd always dreamed of an escapade in the moat, and here it was handed to him on a…not a silver platter, exactly…complete with a beautiful woman willing to risk her manicure for a charity combat exercise. Brilliant! Holding her against him had felt as natural as breathing.

Then he'd gone and stomped on it. With combat boots. Talk about a literary analogy! Crushing the very thing you'd been hoping for your entire life.

Just peachy.

If—or when—someone from the parish newsletter got ahold of the fact he'd just stepped on and possibly broken the new GP's fingers… The scandal!

He laughed and just as quickly felt his lips settle into a grimace. Had she really being fit enough to carry on? He should have insisted upon helping her off the climbing wall.

His mud-slicked introduction to the new doctor had perfectly foreshadowed what this whole palaver was turning into: messy and emotional, full of unexpected entanglements. All the top rankers on his "things to avoid" list.

This trip was about fulfilling a promise to his father

who had said long ago he would hang up his managerial hat when he turned seventy in exchange for seeing a bit more of the world. It was fair enough, but Oliver had been absolutely dreading it.

"Keep the estate, sell the estate, turn her into a National Trust property if you wish, son. Of course, I'd love it if you decided to keep the old family ship afloat, but the choice is yours."

His father's birthday was just a few months away, and Oliver could no longer put off the inevitable. Just buying the ticket home had made him feel as if millstones had been tied to his feet.

And what had he received instead? A good old-fashioned shock to the system.

What he had always pictured as a beleaguered old relic was now bursting with life. Life the place had been crying out for since—

"Oliver! Over here, please."

Oliver smiled in acknowledgement as his father beckoned him over to a bunting-decked table. Cane, silver goatee, a casual-smart outfit perfectly suited to an outdoor gentleman's catalogue. His father was pure class, elegant, charming, socially adroit. Everything becoming a landed gentleman. Everything he lacked.

As Oliver wove through the crowd, it struck him how much his father had aged in the ten months since his mother had died. A stab of remorse that he hadn't spent more time with his father over the past year tightened his stomach. He'd been on the end of the phone for their weekly update but it wasn't the same, was it? Being there—being *here*—made all the difference.

How would he ever fill his father's shoes when the time came? Just the thought of being the Duke of

Breckonshire actively stoked Oliver's adrenaline stores. Adrenaline he preferred to put to use in his work in conflict zones.

He loved being a doctor. Just a nameless doctor with a red cross on his back. Where he wasn't "m'lord." In the South Sudan or Syria—any outpost he found himself in—he was one of countless others in a sea of millions. He was jeans-wearing, red-dust-covered, on-call-round-the-clock Dr. Ollie.

"Oliver! There's someone I'd like you to meet." His father waved him over to a small group hovering over a table filled with ribbons and a trophy shaped like Bryar Hall. Before she'd even turned, he knew exactly who it was. He hadn't held her for long, but something told him he'd remember the sensation of his hands sliding along that particular pair of hips for some time.

"Dr. Julia MacKenzie—I'd like you to meet my son, Oliver. He's also a doctor, you know."

"We've already had the pleasure of meeting." He extended a hand, eyes locked with hers, unsure if there were sparks of pleasure or irritation flying between them. Did she recognize him without the mud?

"I would shake your hand," she replied with a slight lift to her brow, "but…"

He winced as Julia used her right hand to lift her freshly washed left hand to show him two obviously swollen fingers.

That answered that, then.

"Apologies. This generally isn't how I put my best foot forward." He pulled a hand through his wet hair and cringed, grateful she couldn't read his thoughts. *How cheesy was that? Fix it, you fool.*

"Is there anything I can tempt you with to ease the

pain? A scone, perhaps?" *Blimey.* Being suave had never been his forte. He ran a panicked eye over the other baked goods. "Some chocolate cake?"

"No, thank you." Her lips twitched into the hint of a grin. "I've already had some of Margaret's ginger cake when I was setting up the event, Dr. Wyatt. Or do you prefer Lord Oliver?"

"Oliver will do." He felt his own lips thin as hers curved into a broad smile. So they were playing the rank game? Time-worn territory. One turn of phrase and all the old familiar feelings thundered back into place. She'd judged him before she knew him and it irked him, more than he wanted to admit.

"So, you're the brains behind this little shindig? It's cute. The Big Day Out at Bryar Hall, was it?"

"I'm so pleased you think it's charming."

Julia's smile tightened as her blue eyes flitted from him to a large glass flagon on the prize table stuffed with bills and coins. A sign taped to the flagon read: *Coins for the Clinic!*

Terrific. A charity run—and he'd just belittled it. *Come on, Oliver. You're bigger than this. Don't spar with someone who's obviously been able to do what you deemed impossible.*

"It's better, in fact. Refreshing to see everyone having so much fun here."

He could see the tight smile on her lips soften. That was better. He might hate it here but there was no need to take the wind out of her sails. Getting this event together must've been like pulling teeth.

"Your father, of course, has been amazing in his support of the event," she continued.

Oliver couldn't hide his surprise.

"Oh, yes, it's been just wonderful, Oliver!" His father chimed in, clearly delighted with the day's event. "You know, more than anyone, the most we've ever done with the moat is feed the herons with some of your, ahem, less active goldfish. Dr. MacKenzie here seems to have an endless stream of ideas to breathe life back into the old place."

Julia flashed him a dimpled smile. "Perhaps *you'd* like to give a donation to the estate's valued clinic? Without it, of course, I'd have to drive all the way to Manchester to get an X-ray."

Ah. He knew which camp she stood in now: a fact finder.

That Oliver and Bryar Estate were not a match made in heaven was common knowledge. His looming take-over kept all the locals' minds spinning. In a small place like this, news of the estate's future—or lack thereof—was like gold dust. Or kryptonite. He felt himself being openly scrutinized by Julia's clear blue eyes. Kryptonite it was, then.

"I could do you better than that," he parried. "How about a free examination? On the house."

"That's very generous, but I think I'm fairly capable of diagnosing the injury myself." She pursed her lips as if daring him to contest her.

Or kiss her.

No, it definitely wasn't to kiss her, although it was not such an unappealing idea. He squared his feet again, aware his father was actively tuned into their conversation.

So she wanted to spar? *Fine by him.*

"You won't be able to X-ray yourself. I'm afraid

I'm going to have to insist you let me make up for my lead feet."

"The clinic won't be able to afford to take the X-ray if you don't put anything in the bottle." She returned his smile with a healthy dose of Cheshire cat.

Touché. She was good. Very good.

And distractingly attractive. Not your typical primped and preened heiress his mother had enjoyed trotting out in from of him—better. Natural. Not a speck of makeup needed on her milk-and-honey complexion. If he hadn't known better, he would've pegged her as a Scandinavian, but her accent was pure, unaffected English. An English rose with a particularly fiery spirit, from the looks of things. If circumstances had been different he'd...

No point in going there. Circumstances weren't different.

"Put it on my account. I'll see you at the clinic at, shall we say, three o'clock?" His words brought the conversation to an end but Oliver couldn't resist one last tip-to-toe scan. No doubt about it. Mud-slicked outdoor wear suited Julia MacKenzie. It'd be interesting to see how she scrubbed up.

Bubble bath? Shower? *Oliver! Stop it.*

He followed her eyes as she glanced up at the clock built into the stable's spire. It was just past two.

"Fine."

She didn't look happy. He didn't feel happy. A match made in heaven.

"Well, then. It's a date."

CHAPTER TWO

IF JULIA'S HAND hadn't been throbbing so much she would have had a proper go at washing that very annoying man right out of her hair. If only she could scrub the soap bubbles into her brain. As it was, she could just about handle a quick rinse and a slapdash effort to clean herself up before Dr. Oliver Wyatt—or was it just plain old Oliver?—met her in the clinic's exam room. She pulled on a sapphire-blue blouse she knew flattered her neckline and brought out the color of her eyes. Not that she was dressing up for him.

Maybe just a little.

Who knew Oliver Wyatt would be so good-looking? From the tangle of Chinese whispers she'd heard, the mental picture she'd formed of him would've matched the gargoyles leering over the roof of the gatehouse.

Now she was going all googly-eyed on herself, which was really irritating. Particularly considering that Oliver's presence here at St. Bryar could very well pull the very nice rug out from under her feet.

Then again, had the rug been all that permanent? No one had been able to tell her what would happen long-term with the country hospital. The Duke of Breckonshire had been very clear about the fact that when his son returned home the reins would be handed over.

The duke had stipulated she was free to fund-raise her heart out if she thought it would help the clinic. Help? The clinic was definitely...erm...*retro* would be putting it nicely. But it had spoken to her and she loved every worn linoleum inch of it. She had thought if she could somehow get the place free of needing funding from the estate before Lord Oliver—*Oliver*—returned from his posting in South Sudan, she could look toward a future here. Turned out seven months wasn't quite long enough to jack the place into the twenty-first century.

Her eyes moved to the lead-plated windows of her bedroom overlooking the tiny hospital's garden. If she was really going to go for accuracy, St. Bryar Hospital was little more than a patch-em-up service. Even so, thanks to a few beds and a twenty-four-hour rota of volunteers, it served as the only round-the-clock resource for the small village cut off from big city hospitals. There was a mid-sized NHS clinic about forty-odd minutes away if you didn't get stuck behind a tractor. Helicopter was the only quick way to get to a proper hospital in an emergency and, with the government cutting funds left, right and center, she worried about the day they wouldn't even have those. She'd searched on the internet for grants and extra funding and had already printed out an imposing stack of application forms waiting to be filled out. Soon. She'd get to them. Tonight.

She tugged on a skirt and ran her good hand along the soft fabric of the peasant-style blouse she'd chosen. A peasant blouse to meet the aristocrat? She snorted. Hilarious. Her stomach did a nervous flip, and she gave herself a get-a-grip shake.

What did she have to be nervous about? Being born into a great family didn't make you great. Actions made you great. Like finishing a fun run with a throbbing hand. She let herself give a smug little sniff before grabbing her keys and heading to the clinic. Hopefully, the brisk walk would focus her.

Julia was only seven months into her new job and it had already woven itself into her heart. Fat chance she was going to let Mr. Enigmatic Green Eyes with an unrelenting case of wanderlust take it all away. Never mind the minor fact he would one day be the rightful owner of it all—he clearly didn't have any staying power! South Sudan? Republic of Congo? Libya? Where else had he been over the previous year? Sure, he'd been helping people—but what about the people here in St. Bryar? What about his father? It was one heck of a big place to be knocking around in on your own.

She stopped short of harrumphing as she pulled open the clinic door, knowing full well she couldn't really point that particular finger. Her whole life had been a catalogue of packed bags, long-haul flights, change-of-address cards and now, finally, in this beautiful untouched village, she thought she'd found her place in the world.

"Anybody home?"

Julia felt a tremble of excitement play at her fingertips at the sound of Oliver's voice.

Don't let him rattle you! Put your best foot forward. Kill him with kindness.

"Just coming!" Julia called down the corridor as she flicked on the power switches in the small X-ray room. If she could just exhale all the mean thoughts she'd been thinking, she just might manage to greet Oliver with a winning smile.

One foot round the corner and her ambition flew out the window. The inscrutable look on Oliver's face as he took in the time-worn reception area made her heart sink. Scruffy or not, she loved it here—avocado-colored carpet and all.

"Looks like the old place is still in need of a facelift, eh? I don't think it's changed since I was a kid."

Julia met Oliver's sardonic smile with what she hoped was a steely gaze. In reality, she was sure he could see the question marks pinging across her face. Good thing he couldn't feel her pulse rate rising in exactly the way it shouldn't be. *Thanks a lot, blushing cheeks! You are relegated to the Turncoat Department!*

Oliver had the rugged, outdoorsy looks she'd always had a penchant for. Matt had been blond, buff and as "SAS poster boy" as they came. Of course, her husband had been attractive, but there was something almost primitive in the way she found herself responding to Oliver. No doubt about it, he was a top ranker on the masculinity scale. If anyone could make wire-rimmed glasses sexy, here was the guy. They leaned a studied air to his face, framed by that untamable black hair curling ever so slightly over his collar. His tweed jacket, complete with elbow patches, hung perfectly from his shoulders—the starting point of a lean physique. His long-fingered hands were obviously accustomed to hard graft. In short, he was not your typical la-de-dah heir apparent.

Pity.

It'd be easier to dislike him if he was a pale-faced, smarmy-eyed, snooty aristocrat. She turned on her heel and headed toward the X-ray room. Ogling him was going to get her nowhere.

"Funny you mention it." *Be brave, Julia.* "The clinic gets so much use from all of the villagers, it really would be a treat for them to have a cheerier reception center."

"Did you earn enough from your event today to cover the costs?"

Ah. She knew that tone. The "expressing idle curiosity with an agenda" thing. Apparently, those Indiana Jones looks were masking an inner reptilian nature. No problem. She could do cold-blooded as well as the next person.

"Probably." She opted for a bright and cheery tone. "Although I expect the money we raised would be better put to use on medical supplies." *Snap!*

"That's wise. People don't take much to change here."

Julia didn't risk a look back over her shoulder. Had he been patronizing her or complimenting her pragmatism? Maybe it was something deeper, something related to *his* childhood. There had to be something keeping him thousands of miles away from this beautiful nook in the world. Either way, she needed to stop taking things so personally. Each word he spoke was chinking away at her usually cool-as-a-cucumber exterior. Or was it those green eyes of his? The ones she wanted to stare into a bit more. See how the colors changed…

Blink them away, Julia! Eyes on the prize, not on Oliver Wyatt.

"You've switched things round. Shouldn't these be exam rooms?"

"Yes, they were. *Traditionally.*" She emphasized the word to let him know she was aware he, too, seemed to fall into the "people who don't like change" category.

"I've turned one into a... Well..." She faltered, wanting to choose the right turn of phrase.

"Dr. MacKenzie? Is that you?"

Julia gratefully slipped into the hospice room at the call.

"Hello there, Dr. Carney. Everything all right?"

"Yes, dear. Yes. I was just wondering how your Mud Day, or whatever you call it, went?" Julia's heart melted as she put a hand on Dr. Carney's wrist, taking a discreet check of his pulse. He was a dear man and just the reason the fund-raising was so important. Had it not been for a stage-four diagnosis of pancreatic cancer, she was sure he would've been out cheering at the finish line with the rest of the crowd. As things stood, she had a very quiet arrangement with the duke to handle the lifelong bachelor's care. She smiled at the memory of the duke making her cross her heart and promise never to tell Dr. Carney—or Oliver—of the supplementary funding. It wasn't a bottomless purse—but it helped.

"Dr. Carney? It's me—Oliver."

Julia stiffened as she felt Oliver approach then relaxed as Dr. Carney's eyes grew wide with delight.

"Oh, if it isn't little Jolly Ollie!"

Was that a grimace of embarrassment she saw? *Ooh, this was going to be fun.*

"Jolly Ollie, is it?" Julia smiled gleefully. "I say, Dr. Carney—pray do tell more."

She raised a protesting hand as the frail man tried to push himself up into a seated position and failed.

"Let me help." She reached for his mattress sheet then, remembering she only had one good hand, thought better of making the shift on her own. "Sorry, uh, Jolly Ollie? Would you mind grabbing the other side of the sheet, please?" She glanced up at Oliver's unreadable expression. *Too much?*

"It's my pleasure, Peculia' Julia."

Zap! And the man fights back! So he could be playful. Good to know. And a handy reminder to take a quick glance in the medicine-cabinet mirror. It sounded like her clean-up efforts hadn't been very successful.

As they repositioned Dr. Carney, Julia's brow furrowed. What exactly did she know about Oliver? Trauma surgeon. Residency at an inner-city hospital before he'd flown the coop entirely for some serious globetrotting with the Flying Doctors and the Red Cross. Rumored to want to be anywhere but here in St. Bryar. Not what you'd expect from a titled gentleman who would be inheriting a vast estate and a sprawling country pile.

Then again, none of the tearoom gossip told her what actually made him tick. A man in the army could be a general but that didn't describe who he really was at heart. She'd have to work her chit-chat magic to see what she could come up with.

"What brings you back from—Africa, was it, this time?"

Excellent. Dr. Carney was going to do her investigative work for her.

"Thought I'd help the old man keep his chess game up to par." Oliver said it jokingly but Julia could see there was true affection in his words.

"Good, for you, son." Dr. Carney patted Oliver's hand gently. "Mustn't let us old codgers waste away to nothing without a good round of chess to keep us in check—"

"Mate," Oliver finished, and the pair smiled at what was obviously an old ritual. Julia took a few steps back as Oliver sat himself down on the side of Dr. Carney's bed, holding the sick man's thin hand in his own. "May I take that as a challenge?"

"Of course you may, Ollie. But I'd get your date in the diary fairly sharpish."

Oliver shot an enquiring look at Julia. It told her he knew what the words meant as well as she did: Dr. Carney didn't have long to live. The last time they'd made the journey down to the hospital in Manchester, the prognosis had been dire: three months, maximum. That had been a month ago. From the look on Oliver's face, she already knew it would be difficult news to pass on.

"You can bet on it, Dr. Carney. It's time I showed my mentor how much I've learned."

"And the gauntlet is thrown!"

Julia felt the sting of tears tease at her nose as the two men continued to spar. Why did she always have to be so sentimental? Then again, it was plain to see the pair were extremely fond of each other. She hated that Dr. Carney was ill and hoped to heaven Oliver saw why being able to offer hospice care to lifelong residents like Dr. Carney was just one of the things she'd like to put in place to help the community.

The implications of Oliver being here hit her like a speeding truck. This man held their future in his hands. Whatever he decided to do with the estate would directly affect the clinic. They received a small but steady stipend from the duke but he'd made it clear, once Oliver took charge, any funding would be up to him. She was really going to have to kick things into another gear to get the clinic independent of the estate's money.

"Right." Oliver's voice briskly cut into her thoughts. "Shall we get you X-rayed?"

"I suppose we'd best." She laid a hand on Dr. Carney's

shoulder before leaving the room. "Are you sure you're comfortable? May I get you anything?"

"No, dear. I'm fine. You're just what the doctor ordered."

Was that a wink he just dropped in Oliver's direction? *Surely not?* From the flustered look on Oliver's face, maybe it had been. Julia gave her patient a quick wave and made a beeline for X-ray.

Everything was going topsy-turvy!

When she'd interviewed for the job, the duke and Dr. Carney had told her she could run the place as she saw fit. You'd hardly say that to someone if there was some big plan of Oliver's she was meant to have been following, right? There had been a lot of proverbial dust gathering in the corners of St. Bryar Clinic seven months ago and, Lord Oliver or not, she was determined to sort the place out and let it shine.

Oliver was reeling. Seeing his mentor in what was clearly a hospice room had been a genuine shock. Dr. Carney had not only been his inspiration as a teen but he'd been the physician to two generations of Wyatts and untold villagers for as long as Oliver could remember. The kindly doctor had cared for Oliver's mother through her losing battle with pneumonia and, whilst not a young man himself, he had not seemed ill in the slightest. What was it? Only ten months later and so much had changed. He knew he only had himself to blame. A life overseas had its ramifications and here they were—smack in the face. A virtual stranger was caring for his mentor. It didn't sit well.

He watched as Julia's wheatsheaf ponytail followed her curve-perfect body into the X-ray room at the far end of the clinic. He cleared his throat, beginning to feel uncomfortably aware of the effect this woman had, not just on him, but everyone she came in contact with. It sounded ridiculous but she seemed to bring out everyone's hidden sparkle. Quite a feat for what he'd always seen as a fusty little village mired in the past.

Staying detached was going to be harder than he thought. It was how he coped with the sprawling refugee camps; the never-ending queues outside the medical tent; the hunger, the disease, the deaths. Level-headed detachment worked wonders. Time to harness it up again. Cool. Calm. And distinctly collected. Doing the same with Dr. Carney was going to be tough.

"Right." He rounded the corner ready to get down to what he knew best—medicine.

"Are you ready for me, Doc?"

Was he imagining things or was that a come-hither voice? Surely not? Or was that him hoping...?

Being tongue-tied was not his usual modus operandi. But tongue-tied he was as he took in the sight of Julia leaning across the X-ray table with her hand laid out ready for the X-ray plate. Her blond hair fell in a damp coil over her shoulder, leading his eyes to travel downward toward her deep scoop-necked top. His gaze shifted as she peered up at him from beneath a swoop of stylish fringe, eyes twinkling. She had him off-balance and it had been some time since he—no, since his body—had responded so instinctively to someone. Not least of all when they'd been, well, breast to chest and slathered in a slick of mud just an hour or so ago.

"How do you want me?"

An urge to lift her up onto the X-ray table, slip his hands through her hair and along to the nape of her neck before teasing out some very deep kisses shot through him. *Cool and professional, Oliver!*

"Right! Let's see what we've got here." Oliver trained his eyes on Julia's hand. If he let them travel up her slender arm, farther up along the curve of her shoulder, which was just slipping out of the dark cotton fabric, exposing…

Stop it!

"What was that?" Julia looked up at him, a little smile playing on her lips.

"Sorry, what? I didn't say anything."

Did I? Going mad at the ripe age of thirty-five. Nice one. "Can I just get you to lift your hand for a moment? I'm going to slip a plate under…" His eyes zig-zagged round the tiny room.

"In the cupboard on your left."

"Right."

"No, left." She giggled then immediately clapped a hand over her mouth. Her nails were painted a bright purple. Were those daisies on her thumbnails?

"I know what you meant," he snapped, cross with himself for being so distracted.

One look in her direction and he knew he'd not just been rude. He'd hurt her feelings. Not a good move. Not one bit. The hurt in her eyes spoke of something deeper than just being snapped at—and hurling abuse at this completely innocent woman was the last thing he wanted to do. She wasn't to know she'd unleashed a wash of emotion in him when he needed now, more than ever, to remain level-headed.

Oliver quickly pulled out a plate and slipped it onto the table as he scrubbed a hand through his hair. Why did coming home always bring out the bad guy in him?

He exhaled heavily as a list of answers began jostling for pole position.

"Shall we get this X-ray wrapped up?"

"That sounds like an excellent idea." Her tone was curt. Any flirtation that had been cracking between them had evaporated entirely. He could've kicked himself. Not that he was planning on asking her out for a date or anything but surely he could've managed to be pleasant and professional?

Life in St. Bryar was normally so predictable. He arrived, saw his parents, attended the obligatory cocktail party his mother threw to see if she could tempt him with any women on that year's "available for marriage" list and stayed calm and neutral before flying off to another Red Cross camp. There he could be himself: passionate, caring, committed. Being that version of himself here? Impossible.

They remained silent until Oliver pulled out the used X-ray plate and slipped the results onto the light tray. "I hope you're not left-handed."

He didn't even try to sound chirpy. Fractured. Both her pinky and ring finger. A noticeably unencumbered ring finger.

"I'd normally tease you that I was a lefty but I daren't risk getting my head bitten off again." She said the words with a smile, but Julia saw they had hit their target. A microscopic green-eyed flinch.

Good.

She knew he must be hurting after seeing Dr. Carney so ill, but biting off the head of the person who was around day in, day out to care for him? Not a good move.

"I guess we'd better get you trussed up, then."

"Don't worry," Julia said grumpily. "I can buddy tape

and splint them myself. I will need as much dexterity as possible and don't want to be hassled with having my hand in plaster."

"Let me advise you, then," Oliver retorted without so much as a hint of a smile, "you are going directly against doctor's orders."

"That's rich, considering it's a *doctor* who put me in this predicament." Julia only just stopped her voice from rising.

"Are you going to realign them yourself? Perform the reduction? Give yourself the anesthetic jab?"

She glanced at the X-ray. It was doable. Sort of. Not completely advisable, but doable. Particularly since it meant the Ogre of St. Bryar would leave her alone. *A distractingly attractive ogre*—but an unwelcome beast nonetheless.

"Yes, thanks. I'm sure you've got plenty else to do."

"Fair enough." He turned to leave the X-ray room, his six-foot-something frame filling the doorway, before he stopped to speak over his shoulder, eyes fastidiously avoiding hers. "I'll be back in the morning. You'll need help."

"I'll be just fine, thank you. No help necessary," she called to his receding figure as she clapped her hand to the door frame. *Ouch!*

Julia forced herself to count to ten before stomping to the supplies cupboard where she crankily rooted around for a small splint and some medical tape. How dared he impose himself upon her and her clinic?

Hmm… Well, technically it was *his* clinic on *his* property. But apart from that she was the one responsible for running the place and there was little chance she was going to let him elbow in and reimpose the fuddy-duddy ways that had this place stuck in the mud.

Stuck in the mud... Like she had been. With Oliver. Face-to-face, their breath virtually intermingling. Their lips had been so close to each other's. And his eyes...just the most perfect, mossy green. Breathtaking. Her heart had thumped so wildly in response she'd been amazed he hadn't felt it. Perhaps he had.

Which made him all the more unpleasant for being such a curmudgeon! Julia sucked in a deep breath. She'd show him how to run a clinic—a clinic that kept a community afloat. Just because he swanned around the world with his flak jacket, looking gorgeous and aiding the masses, didn't mean helping the people of this beautiful village was a waste of time. Not one iota. Her chosen role was every bit as important as helping in war zones!

She rested her forehead on one of the shelves and forced her whirling thoughts to slow to a less heady speed. Was it Oliver she was battling or her guilt over Matt?

Matt. Soldier. Husband. The loyal man she had been best friends with since primary school. She'd learned to live with the niggling frustration that had cropped up every time he'd broken it to her she'd have to change her plans to kick-start her medical career *again* because they were moving. There was always "a bigger problem out there in the world" that needed fixing. How could you argue with that? War-torn nation versus small-town hemorrhoids?

You had to laugh.

Didn't you?

Not if, the last time you'd talked, you'd bickered about that very topic. Told him you had had it with packing boxes and following in his wake yet again as you sidelined your career for the umpteenth time. She'd wanted to be a family GP for so long and now, here she was, living the dream. If only it hadn't come about via her worst nightmare.

She swallowed hard. She'd been through this. Matt would've been happy for her. Happy to see her doing what she loved.

She resumed her search for supplies, doing her best to squelch down her feelings. She couldn't stop a grin from forming when she found some tape that had been donated by a big-city sports team. The company making the tape had spelled the name of the team incorrectly and it reeled an endless stream of Burnside *Tootball* Club.

Oops.

"Nice to see a smile on those lips."

Julia jumped at the sound of Oliver's voice.

"Sorry—I thought you'd gone."

"I have a feeling my bedside manner hasn't exactly been winning." He tilted his head at her and offered a smile complete with a couple of crooked teeth.

Good! He's not completely perfect! Or does his imperfection make him more *perfect?*

"It could be," Julia conceded after a thoughtful chew on her lower lip, "that you encountered my stubborn nature."

"Stubborn? You?" Oliver's smile broadened as he reached for the tape and small splint she was holding. "May I?"

Despite her resolve to complete the reduction herself, her logical side knew it was best to have it done properly. She was too young to worry about arthritis.

"All right, you win." She tipped her head in the direction of the exam room across the hall. It wasn't like she was going all weak-kneed or anything, but standing together in the tiny supplies cupboard was a bit too close for comfort.

Oliver took Julia's hand in his, suddenly very aware of how delicate her fingers were. They would have suited a surgeon—which would've made fracturing them doubly awful.

"Did you ever have any ambitions beyond being a village GP?"

Julia's eyes shot up defensively. If he could've swallowed the words right back he would've. There it was again—his "I'm better than you are" tone. His mother had always warned him against being a know-it-all and it looked like he still had some work to do.

Oliver quickly covered. "That came out all wrong. I just meant, are you happy with what you're doing?"

"Perfectly." The sharp look in her eyes dared him to challenge her. Then she sat back, visibly reconsidering, and continued openly, "The pace is obviously nothing like what you do, but I absolutely love what I'm doing here. You're looking at the child of parents in the Diplomatic Service. I went on to marry a military man. I'm not sure I've ever stayed anywhere longer than a couple of years." She pushed her lips into a deep red moue.

How did lips get that red without lipstick? Distracting. Very distracting. Oliver found himself quickly rewinding through everything she'd just said.

"You're married?" He made a stab at small talk, well aware he'd already clocked her ring-free hand.

"Yes. Well…" She was flustered. "Was."

What was she now? Divorced? Separated?

"Widowed." She filled in the unasked question for him. "Just over a year and a half now."

"I am sorry to hear that."

"It was always a possibility." Her voice was surprisingly even. Oliver looked up from taping her fingers with a questioning look.

"The military life is an uncertain one," she said without malice. "At least I've got the children."

Oliver felt his eyebrows raise another notch.

"Children?"

"Yes. Two."

"Did I see them today? I would've thought a fun day in a moat would be straight up a kid's alley." *Children?* She'd jammed a lot of living into her life. She didn't look as if she was over thirty years old.

"You're not wrong there!" She laughed, a bit of brightness returning to her eyes as she continued. "They love it here—absolutely love it. But their school—it's in Manchester—managed to lure them away from me for the weekend with the promise of a trip to London and a West End show."

"St. Bryar Primary not good enough?" The words were out before he could stop them. Oliver hadn't gone there, so why he was getting defensive about the tiny village school was a bit of a mystery.

"Not at all. You've got the wrong end of the stick." Julia waved away his words. "My two—thirteen-year-old twins—are at the Music Academy in Manchester. I don't know where they got it but they are unbelievably talented musicians. Cello for Henry and violin for Ella. Heaven knows they didn't get it from me or their father."

"He wasn't a musician?"

"Heavens, no!" Julia laughed. "Special forces through and through."

"Yes, of course. You mentioned the military." Oliver's mind raced to put all of the pieces together. Widowed military mother, a GP, with children a good hour away at boarding school. What on earth was she doing here? Hiding away from the world?

He watched as her blue eyes settled somewhere intangible. "His job was a different kind of creative. He saw his main mission as being a peacekeeper. Ironic, considering his job only existed because of war."

Oliver nodded for her to continue.

"It seems people are always busy trying to stake their claim on this town or that country, while others are desperately trying to cling to the tiny bolt-hole they have, no matter how insignificant. It's almost laughable, isn't it? The messes we humans get ourselves into."

If her words hadn't hit home so hard, Oliver would've immediately agreed.

Every day with the Red Cross he saw the ill effects of war. Huge swathes of humanity moving from one camp to another. Lives lost over what, exactly? Half the time it was hard to tell what the endgame was.

And now, sitting here in the tiny country hospital he had never imagined working in, it was next to impossible to divine what was significant in the world. The big picture? The small moments? The beautiful fingers resting on his palm? A torrent of emotion threatened his composure as he felt the heat of Julia's hand cross into his.

He looked up at Julia, unsurprised to see curiosity in her eyes.

"No, it's worse," he answered with feeling. "It's heartbreaking."

* * *

If Oliver hadn't left the small clinic when he did, Julia was certain her commitment to disliking him would have required some plasterwork. When she'd heard the first whisperings that the future heir of Bryar Estate had few to no plans to stick around once the place was his, she'd vowed to fight tooth and nail to keep the clinic open. If it could stand on its own two feet, there was no reason for it to be a factor in whatever he did with the rest of the estate.

To keep her focus, she'd vowed to see Oliver as her mortal enemy. Of course, she'd done this before clapping eyes on her globetrotting nemesis. Who would've thought he'd be all sexy-academic-looking? And smell nice? And have long black eyelashes surrounding some seriously divine green eyes? Her normal composed, calm and collected disposition was feeling distinctly volcanic.

Her laugh filled the empty exam room. Who was she kidding? Meeting Oliver had pulled the rug straight out from under her firmly planted feet. Up until now, life had been straightforward.

Well, not really. Okay, not at all.

Then when Matt had died everything had become an unknown. What did she know about being a thirty-something widow with two children and a general practice to build? Absolutely nothing.

And now, finally—after so much soul-searching and a huge burst of encouragement from her children, who were joyously pursuing their passion for music—she'd found something that was her own. Something solid. Safe.

Despite the clinic's retro vibe, she loved every square of the stone exterior. Every bud on the climbing roses just threatening to blossom in the soft spring air. Every patient they helped in this chocolate-box village brought a smile to her lips. Speaking of which, she owed Dr. Carney an update before she went back to her cottage. The overnight nurse would give him his meds later but Julia always like to check in on him around teatime. He'd dedicated his life to this place, and she wanted him to know he'd made the best choice when he'd selected her to take over.

She poked her head round the corner of his room and saw he was resting quietly. She placed a couple of fingers on his wrist and checked the heart-rate monitor. His obs looked good, considering. Truth of the matter was, she wasn't all that sure how much longer he had, but nothing would stop her from making sure he had the most comprehensive care and comfort he could enjoy in his final days.

"His heart's in the right place, you know."

Julia started, realizing Dr. Carney wasn't just talking in his sleep.

"Who?" Stupid question. *You both know who he's talking about, ninny.*

"Oliver." Dr. Carney opened his eyes to meet hers, and Julia was still amazed to see how clear and blue they were despite his rapidly declining health. "He's just never really recovered and it makes being here..." He hesitated. "It makes all this quite difficult to deal with."

Recovered from what? Being born into gentry, being handed an amazing estate on a plate and rejecting it? Or did Dr. Carney mean something more immediate?

"Do you mean seeing you here?" Julia sat down when he indicated she should perch on the side of the bed. She tugged at the corners of the handmade quilt one of the villagers had brought in.

"Oh, I'm sure that wasn't very nice for Oliver. We probably should have told him, but no. That wasn't what I meant. I'll leave him to tell you those things."

"Tell me *what*?" Julia felt the hairs prickle on the back of her neck.

"It's not my place to say, dear, but give him time. Patience."

"Dr. Carney, if you're trying to get me to understand a man who is set to inherit all of this and chooses to be anywhere but here…" She paused for a moment. Telling Dr. Carney she thought a man passing up the chance to run his very own family practice was bonkers might not go down well. Then again, if Oliver's plans didn't involve the clinic at all, she had to ramp up her fight to keep it alive. She needed to know where she stood. "You don't think he plans to sell the place, do you?"

"Now that's just idle gossip, my dear. Nothing's been set into motion, has it?"

Dr. Carney tutted as he gave Julia's hand an affectionate pat. "I've probably already said too much. Just give him a chance. The two of you are an awful lot alike, you know."

"Ha! I find that hard to believe. He seems to like the high-flying life and I'm quite happy here in good old-fashioned St. Bryar." Even as she said the words they didn't sit well. The little she did know about Oliver was that he was passionate about medicine. And that he cared for Dr. Carney. It must've hurt coming in here and seeing a man he'd known his whole life in this condition. "I'm sorry. You're right. I don't know the man at all. I guess his arrival just took me by surprise."

"It's all right, dear. No one takes easily to change."

"Isn't that the truth!" Julia quipped, meaning Oliver, then realized Dr. Carney had most likely meant her. Uh-oh. She thought she'd changed a lot since she'd come here. Maybe not. She peered at Dr. Carney, hoping for more answers, but he just smiled and looked toward the window. Just outside, a crab apple tree was in full blossom. Beautiful. If everything could stay exactly like this... *Screech! Wait a minute. Embrace the change. Embrace the change. And give Oliver a chance.* Maybe his plans for this place were for the better. Maybe he'd be sticking around for a while... An involuntary ribbon of excitement unfurled within her tummy.

Easy, tiger. Stop reading into things.

Julia gave Dr. Carney's hand a small squeeze. "Rest now, Doctor, it's been a long day."

Dr. Carney gave her a knowing smile. "Sweet dreams, Dr. MacKenzie."

Oliver vaulted over the centuries-old stable door. It was how he'd always entered the kitchen as a boy and suddenly—some fifteen years since he'd done it last—he felt a rush of impulse to do it again.

Sentimentality? Or just plain whimsy, because he'd met a beautiful woman? A beautiful woman who had tilted the world of St. Bryar on a whole new axis. He shrugged off the questions as a steaming stack of hot cross buns came into view.

"Mr. Toff! Hands off!"

The cry was familiar and so was the voice.

"Clara!"

"C'mere, you. I haven't seen hide nor hair of you since you've been back!" He was instantly surrounded with the same warm embrace he'd enjoyed as a boy and, after the shock of seeing Dr. Carney, he was grateful for the familiarity.

Clara Bates had been with the family for over forty years and showed few signs of releasing her iron grip on the Bryar Hall kitchens.

"It's only been a few hours!" He pulled out of the tight embrace and held her at arm's length. "Now. Tell me why I'm not allowed one of your delicious buns."

Pulling the platter of steaming baked goods out of his reach, she explained, "They're for the Cakes and Bakes stall at the church."

"Sorry?" There'd never been so much as a toast soldier at church services in his day.

"It's new," she continued with a broad smile. "One of our Dr. MacKenzie's ideas. We're raising money for one of those portable heart-attack machines."

"A portable AED?" he prompted. It was a good idea. In such a remote hamlet, they should have had one the second they'd come on the market. He should have thought of it. Then done something about it.

"That's it. If we make a certain amount, we can get a matching grant from the government or something like that. Dr. MacKenzie has all the bumph."

Oliver rocked back on his heels, finding purchase on the ancient cast-iron oven. Wait a minute: *our Dr. MacKenzie*? That was quick work. Making herself part of the woodwork here at St. Bryar was quite a feat, considering the villagers didn't consider you a local unless your family had tucked a good three hundred years under their collective belts. Impressive. And ruddy annoying. He'd come back to nail down how things ticked at Bryar Hall, but with Julia changing things left, right and center, it didn't seem anything would be still enough to get a proper perspective.

He felt his soft spot for her become less pliable.

"You don't know the half of it," the cook continued without noticing the creases beginning to form on Oliver's forehead. "She's just come along and blown a breath of fresh air into everything. Really made the place come alive again since your mother passed. Of course, it's all very different from when the duchess was with us. Your mother was very traditional, wasn't she? Liked things just so." She gave Oliver a wide-eyed look and a squeeze on the arm.

He knew what she meant. His mother had been renowned for living in the world of How Things Used To Be Done. If old-fashioned decorum was your thing, Bryar Hall was the place to be. One piece of cutlery out of place on a table laid for fifty, and his mother could've eagle-eyed it from the doorway. Oliver had always thought that was how everyone had liked things, as well. Surely he hadn't misread his entire childhood?

"Dr. MacKenzie's not so much a stickler for the details, but she sure likes a good commotion! Seems there's nothing she can't lay her hand to and make it better. You should meet her. Birds of a feather, you two!"

Birds of very different *feathers, is more like it.* He had always been hands-off when it came to the estate, and she was anything but.

He drummed his fingers along the stove top, rattling through options. When he'd come home, his remit had seemed so clear: start the long-put-off handover of the estate with his father and decide once and for all how he would take on the mantle of Duke of Breckonshire.

Home or away?

Sell up or stay put?

Suffocate under the aristocratic code or live freely as a conflict zone surgeon?

Bish, bash, bosh.

He knew he didn't want to be here and so did everyone else. All he had to do was find a way to make cutting ties permanently as painless as possible. And what had things been from the moment he'd arrived? The polar opposite.

How had Julia managed to get everyone here to don rose-tinted glasses? Even he'd been sucked in! Wild horses couldn't have kept him from joining in that fun run.

"Scooch. I have another batch of buns in the oven."

Oliver found himself being unceremoniously moved to the side as Clara bustled about the oven doors.

"Are you sure there isn't just one tiny bun free for me?"

"What? And rob the village of a heart attack machine? Oliver!" Clara's eyes went wide in mock horror before slipping one of the steaming currant buns onto the counter. "There you go, but I'll leave you to tell Dr. MacKenzie why we won't have hit our target if we're twenty-five pence short."

Add fuel to Julia's fire that he didn't give a monkey's about the locals? Hardly.

"I'll pay for it right now." Oliver dug into his pocket and pulled out a bit of lint with a sheepish grin. "Put it on my account?"

Perspective. That was what he needed to retain.

A Cakes and Bakes sale was hardly going to make a difference to his ultimate decision, but perhaps having Julia here would make things easier. He hardly wanted to leave the clinic hanging in the wind, and she obviously saw the need for the country hospital to stand on its own two feet. Maybe that was why his father and Dr. Carney had hired her. She was putting down roots. Something they suspected he wouldn't—couldn't—do. That had always been for Alexander.

He pushed away the thought. Some things weren't worth revisiting.

"What's for supper tonight, Clara?"

"Don't expect the usual setup, love. Your father tends to eat a small meal in the library now with a good book by the fire. I can make you up something more hearty if you fancy. The larder's always full."

Oliver raised his eyebrows in astonishment. His entire life, meals had been taken in the dining room. His parents had always insisted upon it. It was traditional. He tried to shrug off the surprise. He could hardly blame his father for not wanting to eat there alone. The formal dining room was *formal*. Not much fun if you were on your own.

"Not to worry, Clara. I'll eat with father." He gave her a quick peck on the cheek and jogged up the stone stairwell to the main floor, wondering what else might be in store for him.

The last thing he'd expected when he'd come home was to be the only thing about this place that hadn't changed. Who would have thought all it would take to shift centuries of tradition was one very beautiful English rose?

CHAPTER THREE

"HELLO?" OLIVER PUSHED on the clinic door a bit harder. It wasn't locked but the thing wouldn't budge. It probably just needed a good shove with his shoulder.

"Hang on! Stop! You can't come in." Julia's voice came through the curtained clinic door, clear as a bell.

"I'm sorry?" Oliver knew he and Julia hadn't gotten off to a particularly smooth start, but he didn't think he'd be barred entry to the clinic.

"You're not supposed to be here!" Her voice sounded strained.

"I didn't think there were prescribed visiting hours," Oliver snapped back. He'd been hoping to have a quiet visit with Dr. Carney—a game of chess, a bit of chat; perhaps a bit of fact-finding of his own. He guessed he didn't need more of that. He knew where he stood with Julia. Loud and clear.

"You'll have to come round the back if you want to come in."

Oliver shifted the large newspaper cone of daffodils from one arm to the other and picked up his chess set. He'd never expected special treatment for having been born "up at the big house"—but this was a bit rich.

He made his way around the small stone building,

noting how well the flower borders and baskets looked. Julia or the gardener? He wasn't sure, but he knew where he would lay his bets. At this point, he'd be surprised to hear a certain blond-haired, blue-eyed woman ever slept.

The back door opened without a problem and in an instant his grumbly thoughts disappeared. Julia was halfway up a stepladder at the front door rather fetchingly twisted in an unraveled roll of wallpaper. Things had quite obviously not gone to plan.

"Flowers!" Julia's eyes opened wide with delight. She swiveled round on the ladder, and Oliver automatically lurched forward, dropping the flowers so he could grab her with a steadying hand as she swayed on the top of the steps.

"Argh! Wrong hand!"

"Sorry, sorry."

Julia held her left hand aloft as he shifted his hands to her waist, her right hand grabbing ahold of his shoulder as she tried to regain her balance. "I love daffodils! You shouldn't have!"

Still holding her waist, Oliver looked down at the daffodils then back up at her beaming smile. Awkward moment!

"Ah—you didn't," she interjected before he could change his embarrassed expression. "They're not for me, are they?" A soft flush crept onto her cheeks as she shifted her hips to release his hold on her waist. Shame. He quite liked being here so close to her. Holding her.

Should he just lie and give the flowers to Julia? Her eyes had positively glittered at the sight of the spring bouquet. Then again, he was a terrible liar.

"I had intended them for Dr. Carney," Oliver confessed. "They're his favorite, and I thought they might brighten the place up a bit, but it seems you pipped me to the post."

"Hardly!" Julia tried to untangle herself from the soft green wallpaper speckled with daisies. "I don't know why I thought I'd be any good at DIY and now you're a witness to the fact that I'm a first-class disaster."

It was impossible not to smile along with her goofy grin but his gut was actively disagreeing with the "disaster" pronouncement. She looked like she'd stepped straight out of a nineteen-forties "Women Do It Well" war poster with blond hair caught up in a polka-dotted scarf, deep blue blouse knotted at the waist and pedal-pushers resting on her hips.

"See? You can't even speak, it's such a palaver. And this was meant to be your big surprise!"

"Surprise?" What on earth for? Stepping into—onto—her life and making about the worst series of impressions he could?

"Don't be coy, Oliver," Julia teased as she climbed down from the ladder, wallpaper crumpling to the floor as she went. "Your face spoke volumes when you saw that the waiting room hadn't changed since the queen's coronation. I have been planning on doing this for weeks, and this led to that… Then there was the fun run, and that took ages to organize, and all of the sudden you were here and everything's a big fat mess—and I'd so meant for it to look just perfect for you whenever it was you were meant to come back, which turned out to be now. I'd wanted everything to be perfect."

Just staring at her red-as-they-come lips as she spoke a mile a minute had Oliver in a daze. It was little wonder everyone had fallen under her spell. *Hurricane Julia?*

"Oliver?"

"Yes, sorry?" *Focus, man!*

"I'm doing it again, aren't I?"

"What's that?" Oliver forced himself to move his gaze from her lips to her eyes. Cornflower-blue—that was what they were. A very lovely shade of cornflower-blue.

"Talking and talking and talking until the other person gets brave enough to stop me because it turns out everything I'm saying is absolute rubbish." She put her hands on her hips and squared off with him as if daring him to interject.

I could lift you off that stepladder and kiss you. That would change the flow of conversation. Oliver forced himself to take a physical step back, incredibly grateful he hadn't said the words out loud. This was all going in a very different direction than he had intended.

Whoosh! There goes one quiet visit with Dr. Carney out the window.

"I know!" Julia zipped past him and headed down the corridor before he could stop her. "I'll just pop the kettle on and get you and Dr. Carney a nice cup of tea, then you can get on with your visit. I think we've got some biscuits from yesterday somewhere about the place. I'll find a vase for those flowers, too. Just forget that I'm here—I think that'd be for the best. Don't you?"

Sensibly? Yes. *Realistically?* Impossible. Oliver turned and watched as she disappeared into the clinic's tiny kitchen. He knew it was ridiculous but it seemed as if the very light of the waiting room had dimmed when she left.

He pulled a hand through his hair and gave his head a good shake. Hurricane or fresh spring breeze, he needed to keep his wits about him. This was the trip that was meant to serve as proof that a life at Bryar Hall was not his future. From the moment he'd arrived it had felt like an alternate universe. A Bryar Estate buzzing with life and possibility and Julia.

Must be sentiment playing tricks on him. It had been a while since his last visit. He gave his head another shake. Dr. Carney and a good game of chess. That would put him back in familiar territory.

Julia opened the tiny door to the freezer compartment and stuck as much of her face in as possible.

Could her cheeks have been burning any brighter? Talk about mortifying! She'd been hoping for a fresh start with Oliver—but this? Behaving like a complete and utter blithering idiot? Not really what she'd had in mind.

She pulled out an ice cube, closed the door and let herself slide to the floor. She ran the tiny cube along her face and let herself imagine the scene she'd actually hoped for. A cool, calm and collected Julia. One who had filled out all of the funding forms and had positive responses. One who ran a clinic that wouldn't need a single penny from the estate. Or, at the very least, one who'd crafted an immaculately refreshed waiting room. The walls were done up with the beautifully pale green paper she'd found for next to nothing on a trip into Manchester to see the kids on one of those days when she'd needed a dose of Mini MacKenzie hugs.

She could do with some of those now. The children came home most weekends and it was then that she felt she could really call this place home. The house would be filled with music and chatter and Dr. Carney would insist on one or both of the children playing for him in his room. Then the clinic would fill with music and

Julia would see drop-in patients, or garden, or pootle around the kitchen and forget for whole swathes of time that she was a widow and that all of this wonderfulness had come to pass because Matt was no longer here. Her hand curled into a fist around the melting remains of the ice cube.

The click of the kettle coming to a boil pulled her back into the room. She wiped her hands dry with a tea towel, pushed herself up and started making some tea. The ordinary, everyday action of swishing warm water into the brown pot, opening the dented canister for the tea bags and pouring milk into the small pitcher settled her. So much had been churning up inside her these past two days. She must be missing the children.

No. That wasn't it. She always missed the children. *Quit dodging the obvious, Julia!* There was one tall, dark-haired and very handsome reason she was feeling off-kilter and, from the click-clack of chess pieces coming from Dr. Carney's room, she had a premonition she would be feeling this way for a while.

Now, if only she could channel some of this energy into putting up wallpaper...

"Are you kidding me?"

Julia wailed the words in disbelief as she saw her Wellington boots float past the bottom of the stairs. Barely sleeping had been bad enough, but now this.

The late spring frost she'd enjoyed from her upstairs window had quite obviously not been entirely benign. If floating footwear was anything to go by, the pipes in her aging cottage had burst. Terrific! Her children would be home over the Easter break and that was only a fortnight away.

Sucking in a deep breath, she took a step into the water. Cold, cold, cold, cold! She stuffed her feet into the boots, not that they did any good, ran the handful of steps to the front door and opened it, feeling a rush of goose pimples shoot up her body as the shin-deep water eddied and gushed past her legs. The cottage would take ages to dry out. First-class disaster!

"That's an interesting way to start the week."

Julia looked up, startled to hear the resonant male voice. The voice that seemed to bring nothing but trouble with it.

"It's a tradition where I come from," she riposted, suddenly very aware she was only wearing a small nightdress. With tiny little straps. And not much disguising the fact her arms weren't the only bits of her body that had gone taut.

"Oh? And what tradition is that, exactly?" He lazily crossed his arms as he leaned against a beam in the small portico, water slipping past his booted feet and a smile playing across his lips. "Giving oneself pneumonia?"

He had a point. She was freezing.

"It's a spring cleansing," she retorted with what she hoped was a quirky smile and went to close the door. "Now, if you'll excuse me."

"I've actually come to help."

"What? How on earth did you know—?"

"With the clinic," he interjected, giving her a pointed look. With *those* eyes. "Remember? I said I'd help at the clinic?"

She stared at him as her brain played catch-up. Had she not said very specifically that he shouldn't come?

"Given our…mishap…I thought you might need an extra pair of hands. I'll also need a look at the books and, as things have obviously moved on from Dr. Carney's tried and true system, seeing how you run the place would be helpful."

Oliver pushed himself away from the beam and moved forward to take a look into her cottage. He was suddenly close. Very close. He took no notice of her personal space at all, which wasn't very considerate, given that he was barging into— *Mmm...* Julia's mind stilled, her senses caught in an intoxicating twist of Oliver's warmly spiced cologne. A fresh shiver of response reminded her she was really feeling the cold now. It would've been too easy to nestle into the crook of his neck, press into his chest and take another deep breath of...

"It looks as though I might have to play knight in shining armor to boot!"

"You forgot your white horse." Julia spoke before thinking, unsure if she was flirting or sniping. Common sense seemed to be taking a backseat to the flickers of attraction careening around her body on a race course to nowhere.

Flickers? Ha! Fully-fledged bonfire was more like it.

She chanced a look up into his eyes and saw the warm look had disappeared and been replaced by a cool efficiency at her comment.

Note to self: stop talking!

"You can't possibly stay here until the pipes are fixed. Go and get some things together. We'll stick you somewhere in the house. It's big enough. We shouldn't get under each other's feet."

Not really the most welcoming of invitations.

"No, that's not necessary. I'll be fine."

Stay in the same house as Oliver? Not a chance. How

she was going to clear out her house and run the clinic with one hand was beyond her but, if her gut was anything to go by, close proximity to a man whose moods flipped on the edge of a coin was definitely not something she needed. Not by a long shot. Especially since he seemed to want to put her and the clinic under the microscope. *Good luck finding any loose change. This is an efficient ship, Dr. Oliver Wyatt!*

"Don't be ridiculous." He walked back to the porch and pulled out his car keys, as if the matter was settled. "There isn't much chance of this place drying out in the next few days, let alone hours. I won't have you falling ill on top of everything else."

"It's not just me, remember?"

Oliver stopped, waiting for her to fill in the blank.

"My children. My children are coming home in a fortnight for the Easter holidays."

"As I said," Oliver repeated. "There's enough room that we shouldn't get under each other's feet."

"Thanks for the warm welcome," Julia whispered, her eyes following his receding figure. Hot and cold? Regal and relaxed? She wasn't sure which way the wind blew with this man but one thing was certain—her nice and cozy world looked set to be turned on its head. Again.

Oliver gripped the steering wheel tightly in the hopes his whitening knuckles would offer him some clarity. Banging his head against the dash might help. He briefly considered it as a viable option.

What on earth had he been thinking? Inviting Julia to stay at the house when her very existence barely gave him time to think? Out of sight she had already invaded his psyche. The past twenty-four hours away from the clinic—away from Julia—had been an exercise in self-control. A day apart was meant to have helped him get a clear head before tackling the clinic's future.

Seeing her in a tiny nightie… Talk about a near short circuit. Just the flick of a finger on one of those silky little shoulder straps and…

He cleared his throat roughly. This was going to have to be one of those "keep your friends close and enemies closer" situations. Regardless of the effect Dr. MacKenzie was having on his composure, she wasn't in the same camp. And things needed to stay that way.

"Start the car!"

Oliver's senses shot to high alert as a fully clothed Julia pulled open the back passenger door of his four-by-four and threw in what looked like a military medical trauma kit.

"What's going on?"

"Reggie Pryce. Do you know him?" She didn't wait for an answer. "He's trapped under his tractor in Shaw Field on the other side of the estate. They've called for an ambulance—but it could take well over an hour on these roads."

Oliver scowled as she spoke. Just like old times. No matter how many fun runs were held, you couldn't avoid the truth. This place was a deathtrap. Never enough time to get proper help.

He glanced at Julia, fully expecting her to give him a pointed look—a look that blamed him for their lack of resources. No. Quite the opposite.

"Let's get going, yeah?" Her tone wasn't accusatory. Just pragmatic. Wasted time cost lives. He cranked the engine.

"Do you know what the injuries are?"

"His son said he's conscious but not looking good. Complaining of chest pain, and apparently he's had quite a whack to the head. It's one of those open cabs with a metal roof hood. Like most farmers, he wasn't wearing his seat belt." Oliver gave her a nod to continue as he pulled away from the clinic. "He was muck-spreading the field, hit a fresh rabbit warren and the whole thing tipped."

"Right. I know a shortcut." Oliver sharply turned the four-by-four onto a woody track. "Should cut about ten minutes off of the journey."

"So there *are* advantages to being an insider."

Oliver glanced at Julia, looking for signs of sarcasm or malice, but simply saw a deeply focused woman, visibly on point for whatever awaited them.

"Done much field work before?"

"Not really, but an injury's an injury wherever it is. You know that more than most, I expect." Her left hand automatically flew forward onto the dash as they rounded a sharp curve. She cried out in pain then gave a quick laugh as if to cover it up.

"You all right?"

"Yes. Still not used to keeping the old left hand out of action."

"Trying to make me feel guilty?" It was a stab at light humor, but from the look on her face she was clearly unimpressed. A nice change from the sycophantic responses he usually received to his poor cocktail party banter.

Oliver stole another sidelong glance. He was fairly certain she didn't know pushing her red lips into a thoughtful pucker was the opposite of off-putting. Quite the reverse, in fact.

"Hardly. Just getting used to your rather, uh, dynamic driving."

Oliver gave an appreciative laugh. "This is my childhood turf! I know these woodland roads better than anything."

"And yet the rumor mill is saying you would rather be in a war zone than here."

There it was. The biting comment. He'd known it was coming and had to raise an impressed eyebrow. The woman didn't mince words.

"You didn't strike me as someone who took idle gossip for fact."

"Looks like we have bigger fish to fry at the moment." Julia ignored his parry as they drove through an open field gate. She was right to have blanked him. It wasn't her fault he hadn't been around to set the record straight.

The upturned tractor appeared beyond the gateway. Oliver felt his pulse steady, relieved to be back on safer turf. Medicine. It was his mast—the thing that had kept him strong throughout the years away from Bryar Hall.

Julia grabbed her medical kit from the backseat and flew out of the four-by-four as they reached the tipped tractor. Her eyes scanned the site as she approached, relieved to see the body of the tractor didn't appear to be bearing its full weight on Mr. Pryce's torso. The curve of the landscape bore some of the weight but, even so, his chest appeared to be trapped by the tractor's metal seat frame, while his torso had contorted so that his feet were lodged under the tractor's mainframe. She knelt on the ground, immediately checking his airways and pulse rate. There was air, only just, and an unsteady pulse.

As Mr. Pryce's son, Mike, hovered over her, Julia began to paw through the utility pouch of her trauma kit, well aware the field was covered in freshly spread manure. It was a minefield of bacteria—septicemia central. She had to get the seeping gash on Reg's forehead cleaned and fast. No point in adding a blood infection to the list of injuries he'd have to battle.

"He lost consciousness a couple of minutes ago. I tried everything I could think of to keep him awake."

"It's all right, Mike." Oliver appeared by her side, his voice full of reassuring calm. "We've got you covered. Julia?"

"I'm just going to clean up the blood and get some gauze on this head wound. It's bleeding heavily but isn't too deep." She chanced a glance up at Oliver. "He's not breathing as well as he should. Looks like flail chest." Julia kept her voice low. They both knew what that meant. A fifty percent survival rate. They had to work fast and hope there wasn't any internal bleeding to fight, as well.

"Good call." Oliver placed his fingers on Mr. Pryce's neck, trying to feel for a pulse as he spoke. "Rapid, shallow breathing. I'm guessing he passed out because of the pain, Mike. It's the body's way of coping." He put a hand on the young man's shoulder. "I'm going to need your help. We've got to lift the tractor. Who knows what's going on under there that we can't see?"

Oliver looked at Julia intently. Were his green eyes seeking trust or answers? He continued before she could respond.

"Looks like you have an oxygen kit in that pack of

yours, yes? As soon as that tractor is lifted, we can deal
with the full picture."

Julia shook her head. She knew Oliver was an experienced trauma doctor, and rapid response would be
something that came naturally, but something told her
they were better off waiting. "We should change that
ambulance to a helicopter and wait for it to arrive before doing anything beyond stabilization."

"There are only two choppers for this entire region,"
Oliver snapped. "Who's to say one's available?"

"We're hardly going to know if we don't try. I didn't
take you for a no-hoper."

Oliver quirked an eyebrow in response.

He was willing to listen. *Good.* Maybe some good
old-fashioned logic would get through that thick skull
of his.

She continued, "If any rib cage shards pierce his lungs
when the tractor moves, we won't have the equipment
to deal with it. Opening him up here would be as good
as killing him."

"Good point." Oliver pushed an arm under the por-
tion of the cab pinning Reg to the ground and felt his
extremities. "Nothing seems to be blocking blood flow.
His legs are still warm. Let's see what we can do."

She nodded and continued to swab away the blood
on Reg's forehead, hoping Oliver didn't see the slight
shake in her hand. He might be used to traumas like
this in Africa, but it was Julia's first. Volunteering at
military family clinics hadn't prepped her for this. The
fact there was even a semblance of calm steadying her
heart rate made her feel proud. And she was not a little
relieved Oliver was there. The man exuded control. He
was definitely in his element.

"Mike." Julia turned to Reg's son. "I don't want you to worry, but we may need to help your father breathe. We think he's fractured some ribs and it makes it very difficult for him to breathe on his own." *Or near impossible.* Flail chests led to a decrease in oxygen exchange at the site of the trauma and affected both lungs. Pendulum respiration was no joke. With the same air moving from one lung to the other, hypoxia or respiratory failure weren't far behind.

"Can you make a call to emergency services and say we need a helicopter right away? Tell them it's a flail chest. Got that?" He nodded, pupils wide with stress. She had to keep him focused. "Then can you help Oliver with the ropes, please? You're going to have to help pull the tractor off when the helicopter arrives."

"He's going to be all right, isn't he?"

"We're going to do everything we can. Maybe you could start by unhitching the muck spreader?" She knew better than most you couldn't make promises. Matt had never promised he'd come home safe—he'd only told her that his heart was always with her. She pulled a fresh swab out of her kit and got to work.

"You've got all the bells and whistles." Oliver nodded toward her kit, rising as he spoke. "You all right on your own for a bit?"

"Yeah. You two go ahead. I'll do what I can here."

Julia fine-tuned her focus and quickly went to work cleaning the wound on Reg's head before applying a bandage. Next, she lowered her cheek to his mouth to check on his breathing.

It was still strained, and Reg remained unresponsive. She needed to stabilize his chest wall before they moved him. If it wasn't secured now, just one misstep and he could die. It was as simple as that.

She popped her stethoscope on and forced a slow breath through her lips as she established his respiratory rate and pattern. The full minute she timed felt like a century. She checked for neck swelling, swollen veins along his cervical collar and hyper-expansion in his lungs. There didn't appear to be a pneumothorax but, from the cooling of his skin, things weren't looking good.

"Mike, how are we doing on the helicopter?

Mike appeared around the corner. "They say one can be here in ten minutes."

"Brilliant, thanks." It could've been an "I told you so" moment, but Oliver was nowhere to be seen, and smugness wasn't her style. "How are you holding up?"

"Muck spreader's unhitched. Just attaching the tow lines now."

Right. *Focus, focus, focus.* The number of things that could go wrong in ten minutes was mind-numbing: cardiac tamponade; pericardiocentesis; to chest drain or not to chest drain? Not to mention all the things they should be considering now that Reg was going to fly to hospital.

"Right, we're all hitched up. What do you need me to do?" Oliver's voice wrapped round her like a warm blanket. Oliver the doctor was a much nicer person to spend time with. He made her believe she could do this.

"We need to splint up his rib cage before the tractor is raised. Any ideas?"

"Obs?"

Julia rattled off what she knew while reaching into her kit for a trauma blanket.

"Maybe we could use this for splinting. If we can turn

him round to the flail side as we wrap him in the blanket, it should hold him steady and give him extra warmth while we wait." She pulled off her coat and bundled it up. "Use this as a support cushion to help."

He took the coat and placed it on the ground where they would roll Reg. "Do you have any morphine?"

"Some."

"Let's make use of it, shall we?" Oliver gave her a gentle smile before returning to his exacting placement of the blanket around Reg's ribs.

Julia handed over the vial and prepared a needle for him. She liked how he worked—steady. In control. Doing what he could in a bad situation. It was easy to picture him working in a conflict zone. Shame. As each moment passed, it was getting easier to picture him here. Julia shook her head. Not the time or place to daydream!

Ever so carefully, they managed to shift Reg's upper torso onto the left side, the high-flow oxygen mask attached to his mouth.

"How long is it before the helicopter arrives?"

Julia glanced at her watch, surprised to see five of the ten minutes had passed. It had felt like the blink of an eye. "About five more minutes."

"Why don't you hold Reg in place, and Mike and I will go ahead and pull the tractor off? It will take a couple of minutes and that way when the chopper arrives we won't be in the way. They can land in the center of the field no problem, put Reg on a board and get him to hospital."

"Are you sure the tow ropes can handle it?"

Oliver locked eyes with her, his voice rock solid. "I wouldn't try it—particularly with you looking after Reg—if I wasn't sure."

"Oh." She blinked away the desire to stay there, searching the depths of his eyes, exploring what he meant by "particularly with you." Was it a slight or was he looking after her as well as Reg? She blinked again and saw he needed a decision. "No, of course not. Let's get going."

Oliver double-checked the gears and eased his vehicle forward. It had a three-and-a-half-ton towing capacity. A quick check on the old-fashioned tractor had said it was just over two tons. This should be a no-brainer. He began to feel the strain of the tractor tug on his vehicle. Lifting it against the pull of the slope was going to make it tough. Tough—but not impossible. Slowly, he inched forward. With his eyes darting between the rear-view mirror and the field in front of him he began to feel his vehicle take on the full weight of the tractor. This would go well. The familiar sensation of success kicked in. This was the Oliver he knew. The one who made decisions and stuck with them. As the tractor came upright with a comfortable thud, Oliver gave himself a grin in the rear-view mirror. *See? Nothing to it.*

The familiar sound of a helicopter's rotors snapped him back into action. Mike was already untying the tow leads so Oliver could move the Land Rover out of the helicopter's way.

Within moments, the crew was on the ground, and Reg Pryce was boarded and on the way to hospital. He didn't know if the poor man would survive his injuries—they were serious—but at least they had done all they could. He looked over as Julia signed some paperwork before the flight took off. Scrubbing at his chin, he silently acknowledged that Reg stood a much higher chance because of her. He wouldn't even have tried to get a helicopter in and that bored straight through to his soul.

Had this place really made him that cold—that lacking in drive? He certainly wasn't like that anywhere else he worked. His brain worked well outside the box in the stark environs of a combat zone and it didn't feel good that he was as likely to fall into old patterns here at Bryar Estate as the next person. A smile crept onto his lips despite himself. Maybe Julia's arrival was a reminder of all that *was* possible in this hideaway hamlet. Just maybe.

CHAPTER FOUR

"Right." Oliver turned around decisively as the helicopter swept up and beyond their sightline. "It's time we jumped in the shower."

Julia stared at him in disbelief. She'd only just met the man and he wanted them to take a shower together? Images whirled through her mind kaleidoscope-style. Warm water cascading down her naked body, through the thick tangle of Oliver's black hair. Little streamlets weaving their way along the contours of his cheekbones, past those green eyes, along his jawline, as they took turns lathering…

"Earth to Julia. C'mon, jump in the car. We're going straight to the Hall. You're shaking."

Julia shook her head, not comprehending. She knew Oliver was hard to read, but this? This she wasn't ready for. "Sorry? No. No. I'm fine—you can just drop me at mine. I need to get to the clinic."

"You're not going anywhere near the clinic in the state you're in. You're lucky I'm not strapping you to the bonnet, you mucky pup."

Well, then. No room for misinterpretation on that one.

"Fine." She shot him a glare, as if it would change

anything. At least she'd stop thinking about soaping up his naked…

"No need to be churlish. We're on the same side here."

Unlikely.

Her eyes traveled up from his lips to the inky-black tumble of his hairline. What would it be like, she mused, just to tease her fingers through…?

Oliver tipped his head toward the four-by-four, an undisguised expression of exasperation playing across his face. "Are you getting in or am I going to have to lift you in?"

Ooh. Well, if you put it that way…

Shock. She must be suffering a minor case of shock after the accident. Never before had she been prone to the waves of saucy thoughts crashing through her systematically practical approach to life. "No Nonsense Julia," her friends had dubbed her. Blimey. It was more like Jitterbug Julia these days.

Shock. Definitely. Or she was going nuts.

Before she could climb into the car, Oliver was squaring her to him, a hand on each shoulder, the heat spreading like a warm balm along her neck and gently meandering down her spine. "Your pipes have burst, the place is filthy—*you're* filthy—and you need to get cleaned up. You're a head cold waiting to happen and that's the last thing your patients need."

Good point. She would've come to the same conclusion. Eventually. Particularly if he hadn't been standing a hand's breadth away from her, diverting her focus with all his man scent and rugged handsomeness. It was plain rude to be so distracting. Surely they'd taught him that in charm school or wherever it was dukes-in-waiting went?

"I think I can manage well enough, thank you," she primly announced.

He opened the door, pointedly ignoring her refusal as he put a supportive hand to her elbow while she climbed in. *Mmm...* That felt nice, too. She wondered how his hands would feel if they shifted from her elbow to her waist, a finger just tracing along the curve down to her hip and... She shook herself out of her reverie. This really had to stop.

The engine roared to life, and Julia grabbed ahold of the door handle as the vehicle surged forward under the thick green canopy of woodland.

She risked a glance over to the driver's side of the car. Oliver was stony-faced, staring dead ahead. *Uh-oh. Here they come.*

The giggles.

Her go-to nervous reaction. A hand flew to her mouth to stem the flow, only causing her to choke instead. A series of coughs overtook the giggles and before she knew it tears were streaming down her face. Without warning a sting of pain fought the whimsy of her laughter. She missed intimacy. Knowing someone would touch her. Desire her. Support her when she was feeling fragile. Matt would've known her giggles meant she was a bit overwhelmed and would've pulled her in for one of his reassuring bear hugs. A hiccupped laugh escaped the fingers clamped over her mouth. Were grief and joy natural bedfellows? Whether her tears were happy, sad or just a biological by-product of her coughing attack was suddenly beyond her. Perhaps Oliver had a point— she wasn't up to seeing the patients just yet.

She swiped at her face, hoping to heaven Oliver was

too focused on the rutted track flashing underneath them to notice her emotional tailspin.

"All right, there?"

"Of course!" Her high-pitched *I'm okay* voice filled the cab. "Just a little something stuck in my throat."

What was going on with her? With Matt she had never been this nervy. She could hardly bear what interacting with Oliver was reducing her to. A giggling wreck with a newfound panache for daydreaming. Seriously?

She had no illusions that Oliver was responding to her in the same way. He was too assured. Too no-nonsense. The man she'd seen out there working today had been one hundred percent focused. Not someone daydreaming about slipping his fingers through her hair. A latent twist of heat stirred within her. She pinned her legs tightly together and pressed her head against the car window, willing the cool glass to freeze away the tempest of thoughts teasing at her imagination.

She needed to see Oliver as the enemy. Frenemy? Whatever. He was the one person who could take away the life she'd built here. So. Enemy it was. Even if the enemy came in a to-die-for, six-foot-something, uber-assured, sexy-as-they-come package. Making St. Bryar her home and career base was the goal. Not soapy encounters in the shower with the man who had the power to take it all away.

"Right you are, madam. Let's get you scrubbed up."

Not helping!

Oliver watched as Julia skipped up the stone steps leading up and over the moat to Bryar Hall's formal entrance. He never used the front door. Using it was too close to ownership of the title that would inevitably fall to him.

Even so, something had made him bring her here. He had feigned ignorance when he'd seen Julia wiping away tears in the car and, despite all his well-constructed defenses, had physically ached to reach out to her, comfort her. There was something about this woman that spoke to him, told him they were on a similar emotional journey. Fighting demons from the past.

Bringing her here—to the cornerstone of his inheritance—was akin to admitting he wanted her to try and peel away the protective layers he'd built up through the years, see if the good man he knew he was still lay within. To having someone to confide in, to understand the pressure to fill his brother's shoes and take on the weight of history foisted upon him from that awful day when Alexander had died.

Who was he kidding? It was his burden alone. Julia had enough on her plate without him lumping his problems on, as well. Besides, one of her biggest problems was him. Whatever he chose to do with the estate wouldn't just affect him—it would directly affect her life in the form of the clinic.

He swung the car door shut with a satisfying clang.

"Is that a hint I've gone the wrong way? Are you sure you don't want me to go in the servants' entrance?" Julia teased, turning to him from atop the steps, her eyes bright with humor. She looked like a child about to go into a candy store.

"I'll make an exception, as you're a guest." He allowed his eyes slowly to scan up her skinny jeans and curve-hugging jumper as he carefully chose his words, his smile growing as he spoke. "It is *unusual* for someone covered in muck to enter through the front. My mother would have had a fit if she saw you like that in the entrance hall."

The thought felt simultaneously accurate and disloyal. She hadn't been a cruel woman by any means, just born and bred to an exceedingly strict set of guidelines. One he had always taken delight in stretching to the outer limits.

"I'm quite happy to go back to my—*your*—little cottage and change there." Julia's bright eyes darkened. "I've got patients to see, things to do. I didn't ask for any of this, Oliver."

"And you think I did? I wanted this about as much as you wanted—" He stopped, knowing he was heading toward being unfair. He'd nearly said she hadn't asked to be a widow. Surely a rage must be burning in her from the loss of her husband? God knew his brother's death seared his heart each time he thought of it. The subsequent battle to live up to the expectations of the title he'd never wanted... He would never be like Alexander. How could he?

"I didn't want what?" *Too late.* Julia's eyes were ice blue—and just as cold.

"You didn't ask for the pipes to burst in that tumbledown cottage of yours. Now come on. Let's get you sorted."

"I'm perfectly happy in that so-called tumble—"

Julia's voice stopped midprotest as Oliver swung open the doors to Bryar Hall. He knew they'd be unlocked. His father's voice rang through his head as the doors opened wide. "We've been given so much, son, we should always open our doors to others."

A trio of fingers played at Julia's lips as she scanned the grand hall. He envied them for a moment, the way her mouth pressed up against them as she intently took in the details of the opulent entry hall. He wondered how her lips would respond to his fingers touching her, tracing the lines of her mouth.

"I don't get it."

Oliver bristled at her tone. It was pretty clear she wasn't going to ask for an art history lecture.

"What?"

"Why you aren't here more. If this were mine, you'd have to tear me away from it." It was impossible to miss the delight and wonder in her voice. Exactly the type of reaction that made him want to get shot of the place as soon as possible. She didn't know the weight of memories that came with Bryar Hall. The loss. The grief. The millstone of responsibility his mother had weighted the title of Duke of Breckonshire with.

Wasn't being a good doctor enough? That was where his heart was. That was where his passion lay. Not in an old building. *This* old building.

"It's nothing particularly special—there are plenty of others with a much higher renown, if you're into that sort of thing," he replied briskly, reaching out to steer her away from the grand entrance hall after allowing himself a micromoment to scan their surroundings. They weren't opulent in an ostentatious way. The restrained elegance of the marble flooring, a dual twist of matching mahogany stairwells, enormous swathes of Persian rugs and walls covered in well-chosen artwork spoke of the centuries of care and craftsmanship that had brought a select renown to Bryar Hall. Too bad every beautiful nook and cranny also hid a private sorrow, a painful memory.

"Aha!" Her eyes sparkled with delight. "I knew it.

You *do* love it! How could you not? Are these portraits family members?"

"What?" Oliver turned to meet Julia's delighted expression. She wasn't to know there was a noticeable absence. Noticeable to him, anyway.

"A few. Most. Let's get on, then, shall we?"

"Feign to deny it, Oliver Wyatt. I saw love in your eyes when we walked in here. Or is it—?" She stopped speaking, her own eyes clouding as she looked at him intently, scrutinizing his face as if it would reveal his secrets. Her face was so open, honest—the antithesis of the unwritten codes of conduct for England's upper classes. Oliver felt another rush of desire to tell her everything. To bare it all and just see what happened.

"This can't be a burden to you, can it?" Julia put a hand on his arm as she unwittingly hit the emotional bull's eye. The first person ever to do so.

"Don't be ridiculous. It's just an old house, nothing more." Oliver cleared his throat, gave her hand a conciliatory pat and pointed her toward a staircase. "Come along, then, Dr. MacKenzie. Let's get you sorted."

Julia dutifully followed Oliver as he loped up the stairs two at a time in long-legged strides. She'd seen something in his eyes that had spoken to her very marrow. What was it that kept him away from such an amazing place? Surely there had been good times here? Many reasons to preserve the family home? The estate. *A community.* An interwoven support system of people. "Home is where the heart is!" Matt had always riposted whenever she'd daydreamed aloud of the "little house with a picket fence" scenario. "We'll have plenty of time to do that sort of thing!"

Perhaps it wasn't something they'd been meant to have together. She was so grateful to be able to give her children that solid base she'd always longed for. A home. But heartbroken at the price she'd had to pay. Looking around the beautiful surroundings, she had to stifle a laugh. This place was a far cry from her little cottage. A luxurious five-star setting with its arms flung wide-open.

Her children loved it here. She was loath to tell Oliver they'd all but moved in with his father over the Christmas holidays. He'd been planning on going to his gentleman's club in London but weather had snowed them in. They'd all been appalled at the idea of leaving him on his own and had made an enormous plate of gingerbread cookies for him on Christmas Eve, after which they'd ended up spending the rest of the holidays together. Reading by the fire, playing board games, playing music, chatting about the house and its history. It had been absolutely lovely.

Her cottage suited her to a T. But being here in the main house? She had to admit, it took her breath away. A true testament to the glories of yesteryear. If she'd been wearing crinolines she would've looked more at home. She mentally superimposed her face onto one of the portraits of a woman in a Victorian bonnet with ringlets just peeking out beneath the lace.

"What's so funny?" Oliver's tone implied he'd mistaken her burble of laughter for mockery.

"Cool it." Julia tried her best to placate him. "Just enjoying the view."

"It is quite special, isn't it?" Without her having noticed, Oliver had drifted back down the stairs to stand just behind her. His brisk demeanor seemed to have dissipated up and away into the sky-lit dome of the hall. His face visibly softened as he scanned the room. There was obviously much more to this man than she'd given him credit for. Her first impressions— Well, her first impressions had been downright physical, but as to his character? She was sure there was a kinder, gentler side to his periodically gruff demeanor. Was he seeking balance between the two? How else could you explain that the same man who had a clear passion for caring, healing, for helping people survive life's hardships, was so emotionally withdrawn from his own family?

"I don't understand it."

"What? The house?"

"No. How reserved you are about this place when everything about it represents your family."

A flash of pain—or was it fury?—shot through Oliver's eyes and drove directly into Julia's heart.

"Maybe forty-eight hours isn't quite long enough for you to read me as well as you think you can."

"It wasn't an accusation, Oliver. I am just trying to understand."

"Understand what, exactly?" Oliver countered.

"Why you stay away so much when you obviously love it." She let her words fill the space between them. He shot her another look, one intent on divining where her line of questioning was coming from. She felt herself straighten up under the scrutiny of his green eyes. There was nothing to fear in them, only questions to be answered.

"Simple. I love my job and I can't do it here." Oliver broke their eye contact and gave the hall a final, cursory scan before resuming a brisk assent up the stairs.

Interesting. It was an answer, but Julia was pretty

certain it wasn't *the* answer. Then again, maybe it was that simple. She'd not wanted a job in Manchester or London or Timbuktu. She'd wanted to be exactly where she was because the place spoke to her. Maybe that was what Oliver felt when he wasn't tethered anywhere. At home. Who was she to judge?

"Here we are." Oliver's voice sounded unexpectedly gruff as he opened a door just a short walk along the landing. "Everything you need should be in your room. I had one of the house staff pack up a few of your things while we were out. If you need anything else, ring me at the clinic and I can fetch it from your cottage."

"At the clinic?"

"I'm heading over. No doubt we'll catch up later in the afternoon."

Julia felt herself bristling. The clinic was her turf, at least for now. "Honestly, Oliver, don't worry. A quick shower will sort me out and I'll walk over to the clinic. If I need anything from the cottage, I can get the things myself."

"Don't be ridiculous."

She fought the impulse to fold her arms across herself as he scanned her blood- and mud-covered clothes. How could a pair of eyes have such a physical impact?

"You're soaking wet, filthy and most likely in need of a rest. You worked hard this morning. It was a tough job." He flashed her a smile. "Don't fret, Dr. MacKenzie. I am quite capable of looking in on Dr. Carney and seeing to anyone else who might pop by. I didn't get my degree via carrier pigeon."

"I wasn't doubting your abilities." She squeezed her eyes shut for a moment to try and regroup. Bickering with Oliver was hardly going to help her mission to prove she could run the clinic on her own. "I just—I just wanted to make sure you were all right, as well."

"Of course," He looked bewildered at her change of tack. "Why do you ask?"

She hesitated, wondering how far she dared tread into dangerous territory. *Safe.* Just play it safe. "It was a tough morning for me and I'm not used to receiving such royal treatment." She blushed at her own use of words and tried to wave them away before they settled. "You've been very generous. I'm a bit too used to fending for myself, so…thank you."

Without a moment's thought, Julia rose onto her tiptoes—pulled by an organic instinct—and kissed his cheek. In that instant, time took on an otherworldly pace. Her senses set alight as she felt her cheek moving against the soft stubble of an early five o'clock shadow. Heated tingles showered through her as Oliver's scent came to her—full, spicy, commingling with the morning's hard graft. Was it his breath or hers she heard caught in a throat? Had he leaned in toward her as she'd risen to kiss him? Was it his hand or hers that had caught the others for balance? She felt her pulse flare in her lips as she withdrew them from his cheek, just barely missing his lips, her mind a jumble of wayward thoughts.

Had she stood there, lips pressed to his cheek, for microseconds or the length of a sigh? She raised her eyes to his and saw they, too, were searching for answers— answers she couldn't give.

"Sorry, I—"

"Not to worry." His voice was light but the expression on his face told another story. Oliver had felt it, too. The connection. Something between them had shifted. Or fitted into place.

Oliver pointed to the sage-colored door. "Off you go, then. I'd best get a move on."

And for the second time that morning she watched as he retreated, her brain exploding with questions and sensory overload. *Could home be a person?*

Being with Matt had all come about as a happy fluke—they'd known the same childhood, the rhythms of how the other ticked. They'd been a good fit. They'd been great friends and lovers. But had she felt anything like this? *Honestly?* She closed the door behind her and leaned heavily against it.

Being with Oliver felt exhilarating and new.

She and Matt had known each other since they'd been kids—the only steady thing in each other's lives. The best of friends. A sudden overseas assignment for Matt on her twenty-first birthday—his first to a combat zone—had led to a tearful goodbye which, well, had led to two beautiful twins. Rather than let an early pregnancy stand in their way, they'd vowed to marry and support each other so they could each realize their dreams—hers as a doctor and his as a commander in the SAS. His had come to fruition almost straight away. Hers? She felt her teeth dig into her lower lip. Her professional dream did come true—just not in the way she'd imagined.

A door slammed shut below, jolting Julia out of her trip down memory lane. Was there any point in rehashing old dreams? Not really. Especially when, against the odds, it seemed as though other dreams were beginning to sneak into the old one's place.

An hour later, and smelling decidedly fresher, Julia walked into the clinic fully expecting a waiting room bursting with patients. Instead, she found the place quiet as can be. A small cinch of disappointment tightened in her stomach. Oliver had said he'd be there, but it seemed he'd reneged on his offer. She tried to shrug away the feeling. It wasn't like she had a hold over the guy or anything. Might as well sort out the clinic. There was nothing a good cleaning session couldn't fix.

She pulled open the door to one of the exam rooms, surprised to find Oliver in her chair preparing to lance what looked like a remarkably unpleasant boil on Nathan Tremblay's neck.

"Oh! So sorry, Mr. Tremblay." She found herself giving Oliver a shy smile. *What was that about?* She didn't do shy!

"Apologies, Dr. Wyatt, I didn't realize you were in here."

"It's first-class service here today, Dr. MacKenzie!" The grin on Mr. Tremblay's face was about as contagious as they came. "I only popped in to pick up my blood pressure pills. Lord Oliver took one look at my boil and insisted on having it out! Never knew his lordship was so handy with a needle and thread!"

"Dr. Wyatt will do, Mr. Tremblay," Oliver teasingly warned the local farmer. "Besides, we haven't done the hard part yet." He gave the man a knowing wink and lifted up a scalpel.

"I can take over if you prefer." Julia began to enter the room but stopped when Oliver put up a hand.

"Are you kidding, with only one good hand?" Then more seriously, "This is one of my specialties. I've done this a lot." He waved her out of the room. "We're quite happy here, aren't we, Mr. Tremblay? He was telling me about his switch over to organic cattle and how he keeps them clear of intestinal bugs with cider vinegar and garlic. Interesting stuff." He began to swab the awkwardly positioned boil with a local anesthetic. "I can bring some of this information to the farmers down in the Sudan. Inexpensive—and effective."

And there it was again. The uncomfortable tightening in her belly. She'd almost let herself forget he wasn't a "hang around" kind of guy.

"Guess I'll leave you two gents to it, then." Julia gave them both a mock salute and pulled the door shut behind her. Seeing patients was one thing, proactive treatment and taking an interest in their personal lives was something else entirely. Maybe he was interested in hanging around after all.

Stop it! He's only taking an interest as it relates to his work in Africa. Nothing long-term about chitchat. He's just showing good bedside manner.

Julia dawdled for a moment outside the room, enjoying a bit of earwigging. From the laughter and steady flow of conversation, it sounded as though everything was going well. She had to admit, it felt a bit peculiar to see Oliver looking so at home in the clinic. It was hers!

And we were back to square one. Anyway, if she didn't start filling out forms for grants it jolly well might not be hers for much longer. She was going to have to get used to that plain-as-day fact whether or not the man could charm the tail off a monkey.

"Whoops!" Julia fought to regain her balance as the door she'd been leaning on opened.

"Daydreaming, are we?"

"Hardly!" Julia righted herself and backed into the corridor as Mr. Tremblay came out of the exam room, a clean white bandage on his neck.

"Looking good!" Neck boils could be dangerous—
if they burst internally, the infection could cause blood
poisoning or sepsis to the brain. Oliver had done well
to take action. She walked and talked as they headed
toward the foyer, hoping she could cover over her obvious eavesdropping.

"That didn't seem to take long. How do you feel?"

"Right as rain." The farmer lowered his voice and
flicked a thumb toward the exam room where Julia
caught a glimpse of Oliver clearing things up. "He's
right good at this doctoring business, Lord Oliver."

"We're lucky to have him." *For a New York second.*
"Be sure to keep applying a warm, moist compress for
the rest of the day."

"I know, I know! Lord Oliver's already told me! Dr.
Wyatt, I mean." Mr. Tremblay waved a pamphlet in the
air as he departed, throwing the words casually behind
him, as if Oliver had been looking after him from the
day he was born.

Seriously? If Oliver hadn't been responsible for putting her hand in a splint, she was pretty sure the patients
here would've seen neither hide nor hair of their precious
heir apparent. And neither would she. She sighed. If their
moment on the stairs back at the hall was anything to go
by, she was the one who needed a healthy dose of reality.

Oliver materialized next to her with another one of
his stealth appearances. His hand brushed against her
hip. Another eddy of response from her tummy.

"Checking up on me, were you?"

"No!" *Yes.*

"You smell nice."

"I'm sorry?" Julia looked up at Oliver, feeling too
aware of the corridor not being built for two.

"Better than *eau de* cow-*logne*." Oliver grinned, waiting for her to catch up with his pun. If she hadn't been so busy trying to figure out whether he was flirting with her or trying to torture her, she would've gotten there faster. *Ha-ha. Very funny.*

Better stick to business. Safer terrain.

"You seem to have dealt with the patient list quickly."

"There wasn't too much to sort, but you already knew that." Oliver pulled the appointments clipboard from its nail on the wall. "Let's see, I saw Sarah Simms about a mole she wanted checked."

"Cancerous?"

"A beauty spot."

"Becky Watt's popped in for a well-baby check."

"Has the colic cleared up?"

"The little one was good as gold. Takes after her mother, apparently."

"Any word on Reg Pryce?"

"I called City Hospital and they say he's critical, but his chances of making it are looking good, pending any surprises. They wanted me to let you know the stabilizing you did really helped."

Oh! A compliment. *And a smile.* Nice. *Let's talk about us now and whether or not you're going to be straight with me about whether or not you're going to kiss the clinic open—I mean me. No—keep the clinic open.*

Oliver reached over her shoulder and hung the clipboard back on the wall. Did he do that just so she could take another deep inhalation of eau d'Oliver? Should she tell him how nice it was?

"Reg's not going to be back on the tractor for some time yet, though."

That would be a no.

"I hope you don't mind but I also did a couple of telephone consultations for patients you'd booked in for this afternoon who I thought might be happier staying at home."

"Right." Julia tapped her foot a bit, searching for anything else to ask him. Nope. No good. He'd thought of everything.

"This is fun! I don't think I've ever finished a day at work."

"Technically you've finished a day at *my* work."

"Isn't it great? My days are usually twelve hours plus." Oliver rubbed his hands together, as if revving himself up to say something big.

Oh, no. He's not going to let me go, is he? Say I overstepped the employer-employee line with the smooch on the cheek? Even though he'd appeared to like it, too? And didn't really seem to be making any moves to change the very teeny tiny distance between them? Julia's hackles started to go up and she was just about to launch into a grand defense of her role at the clinic when Oliver flashed her another one of those goofy grins of his.

"What say you and I go down to Elsie's tea shop for a cuppa and some cake?"

You are much *easier to hold at arm's length when you're cantankerous.*

"I don't know, Oliver—there's a lot to do."

"Rubbish. I've done it all, and don't bother arguing. Elsie makes a mean lemon drizzle cake. Just one slice drives me mad!" His eyes twinkled suggestively. "In a good way."

Well, in that case.

"I promise, you won't regret it."

Something tells me I will definitely regret it—but here goes nothing! And she flipped the Back In A Few sign on the clinic door.

Oliver was beginning to have second thoughts about his great idea. Every pair of eyes in the place had been firmly planted on him from the moment he'd walked in. He hadn't actually been in Elsie's tea shop for years and there didn't seem to be a chance in the world its proprietor was going to let him forget it. Oliver Wyatt getting a telling off from the local cake maven? This was better than television as far as the locals were concerned. So much for a quiet cuppa with Julia.

"Lord Oliver—"

"Oliver, please."

"Oliver," Elsie continued. "I know you're busy down in Africa and all, but I have to tell you, I've been making this lemon drizzle cake for well over a decade now, waiting for you to come in and have another slice." She set down two mismatched china plates weighted with enormous slices of cake and signaled for the teenaged girl behind her to place a teapot and creamer alongside them. Elsie's granddaughter, perhaps? Blimey. Had that much time passed?

Julia was doing a terrible job of disguising her amusement at his public berating. She was supposed to be sticking up for him, wasn't she? *Thanks for the backup!*

"Elsie, I will let you in on a secret." The woman leaned in toward him, obviously on tenterhooks.

"My mother used to send me one of your fabulous cakes once a month for years. You must never tell Clara." It had been the one chink in the heavy armor of aristocratic mothering. A cake care package from his mum with a small note in her meticulous hand keeping him updated on things in the village. He still had the notes.

"Well, you should have said! I could've carried on after your mother passed away. We all miss her, you know, Lord— Oliver."

"Thank you, Elsie, I'll hold you to that. She'd be pleased to know you're keeping me in cake!"

Elsie pressed a hand to the table and feigned a faint. "You make a woman blush with pleasure."

"I try my best." He dropped Julia a wink before noticing her expression had moved from mirthful to murderous. What had he done now?

"I'll let you get on, then. Enjoy your cake, you two."

He watched as Julia silently poked at the thick slice of yolk-yellow cake with her fork. She wasn't one of these women who preferred lettuce leaves to afternoon tea, was she?

"Lemon drizzle not to your liking?"

She pushed the plate across to his side of the table.

"You'd better have it."

"And would you mind telling me why?"

"Not at all." She lifted her blue eyes up to meet his. Bright as a cornflower. He liked them better when she smiled and that dimple of hers appeared high up on her right cheek.

No dimple.

"Why do you raise their hopes like that?"

"Like what?"

"Like you're going to stick around, be a part of their lives."

"Ah." He leaned back in his chair and studied her. "For an Englishwoman, you're very forthright."

"For an English gentleman, you're not behaving very honorably."

"And what, exactly, has led you to this conclusion?"

"From what I hear, you don't have many plans to stick around."

He didn't respond.

"You'll be letting down a lot of people if—*when*— you leave again. People who care about you."

Julia immediately regretted saying the words. It wasn't that she didn't believe them. It was that she didn't know what the villagers thought; she just knew what she thought—it was too soon for him to go!

"I'm sorry, Dr. Wyatt, that was uncalled for."

"Are you trying to pin the tail on the donkey?"

She blinked at him, not really certain where he was going with this.

"Are you trying to make an ass out of me, Dr. Mac-Kenzie?"

"No, not at all. I think you're doing a pretty good job of that yourself." She clapped her hands over her mouth, horrified she'd let more of her inner voice out than she'd planned, and was astonished to see Oliver's lips break into a broad smile.

"You're really not in the manner of mincing words, are you, Dr. MacKenzie?"

"What happened to Julia?"

"What happened to Oliver?"

"Good point."

Now what? Tell him you're sorry when you're not? Change the topic and pretend this never happened? Not likely to work.

She poured their tea, buying herself some more think-ing time before putting the eggshell-blue pot down with a quiet sigh. She may as well give peace a chance. Her parents had been diplomats, always advising the long game as the wisest move. Truth was, she didn't have a clue why he'd come home, and trying to rat him out as a fly-by-night before he'd announced his plans wasn't fair. She wanted him to be fair with her—so she owed him the same privilege. Private deal made, she offered her olive branch.

"What do you say we start over?"

He scrubbed at his chin and gave her a sideways look. She liked how he didn't agree immediately. That she could respect.

"Clean slate?"

"Erm…" She lifted up her splinted fingers. "Sort of."

At this, Oliver gave a full belly laugh, turning a few silver-haired heads in the small café in their direction. He lowered his voice and leaned forward on his elbows. "What do you say we negotiate an open-book policy?"

She quirked an eyebrow and nodded. "I'm listening." *Not to mention fighting the temptation to crook a finger and beckon you to lean in just a little bit closer. Julia! Stop it. The man's trying to reason with you, not lure you to into his gentleman's quarters.*

"I'm here for a month." Oliver pressed on despite her best "I'll believe it when I see it" look. "During which time, I promise I will answer everyone's questions as honestly and openly as I can—but I have to spend a lot of time with the estate ledgers."

"And?" She spread her palms in a "so what?" gesture.

"Let's just say Oliver and spreadsheets were never the best of friends. Until I have a real handle on all of the estate's enterprises, I can't decide—"

"Whether or not you are going to stay?" she finished

for him, not really wanting to hear the answer. A week in and the last thing she wanted was to see him leave.

Oliver fixed her with one of those "deep into your soul" gazes.

"Are you asking for yourself or for the good people of St. Bryar?"

"Both?"

Nice one. Oliver will never see through that answer.

"Honestly, Julia? I don't know."

She exhaled slowly, hoping he couldn't see the disappointment in her eyes. What had she expected? A declaration of love after one kiss on the cheek and a body-slam in a moat?

"It's not like I'm just going to leave the place to fall into ruin. It would kill my father, for one. And two, these people have meant a lot to my family."

"*Have* meant?"

"*Do mean.* A lot. To me." He gave her a pointed look and slid a hand over hers with a gentle squeeze. One that told her she'd been given a lot more access to the real Oliver Wyatt than most, but it was time to reel it in.

"Okay. That's fair." She nodded decisively then sat back in her chair with a playful grin, fingers crabwalking out from under his to pull the china plate of cake back to her side of the table.

"I thought that was mine!" Oliver protested, reaching for the plate, the glint of a chase in his eye.

Before he could reach it, Julia put a protective hand around the giant wedge of gooey cake, took a huge forkful and waved it in front of her lips. "Didn't I say?" She stuffed the bite into her mouth and mumbled through the crumbs, "Lemon drizzle is my favorite."

CHAPTER FIVE

"WITH A ROOK? How humiliating."

Oliver looked at the chessboard in disbelief. Nearly a week into his chess tournament with Dr. Carney and he was still getting trounced. The fact he also got to spend time with Julia might just have taken the edge off his daily humiliation. "I don't know how you do it!"

"Practice, dear boy. Practice." Dr. Carney smiled as he moved his rook across the board to take Oliver's king. Checkmate. Again. The piece suddenly fell from his hand with a sharp flinch.

Oliver jumped to his feet and pushed away the tray holding the chessboard. "Are you all right? Do you need more meds?"

"Not to worry, Ollie. Just a sore stomach is all. It comes with the territory."

"We can up the morphine." Oliver spoke seriously now, as a doctor.

"Honestly, Oliver. It is money best spent elsewhere."

"What are you talking about? You're going to get the best palliative care we can offer." As he said the words, reality dawned. Dr. Carney knew the place had limited funds and was trying to scrimp on his own treatment to save money for the other patients. Selfless to the end.

The realization was like a hammer blow to his conscience. Like it or not, he was part of this community and, like it or not, had a responsibility to be a better part of it.

"Look." Oliver laid a hand on Dr. Carney's painfully thin arm. "I am afraid, this time, you are going to have to obey doctor's orders. You're getting more meds. I'll sell Great-Aunt Myrtle's portrait if necessary. We should get a couple of hundred for the frame at least." He gave Dr. Carney his best teasing wink, hoping it covered his true feelings—utter grief. The sting of seeing him suffer was quadrupled by the knowledge his mentor was willing to forego meds to help others.

No longer able to fight the pain, Dr. Carney nodded his assent. "Thank you, Oliver." He took the proffered medication and his voice soon grew soft as it began to take effect. "It's so very nice to have you here. Better than all the medicine in the world."

Oliver stayed until Dr. Carney drifted off to sleep, keeping an eye on his obs, putting the pieces of the chessboard back in order and fighting the temptation to howl at the heavens for taking down a kind man in such a cruel way.

"Hey." Julia's whisper came from the doorway. "Everything all right?"

Oliver cleared his throat before answering. "Yes, he's just sleeping. Can I have a quick word?"

"Absolutely."

He followed her as she went to the waiting room and curled up in a corner of the sofa. It looked vaguely familiar. Had it been in his mother's sitting room? He hadn't been in there too often but something about the floral pattern struck a chord in his memory banks.

"What's up?" Julia prompted as he sank onto the other end of the sofa.

"It's about Dr. Carney's meds. He's concerned about the budget of the clinic and that's the last thing I want him to be worried about."

"I agree." Julia nodded a quick assent. This was a change in the right direction.

"I'm willing to pay for everything he needs. Money's not an object."

"Ah. You see. This is where it gets a bit tricky." Julia unfolded her legs and stretched them out as she struggled to find the best way to word things. She'd promised the duke she wouldn't tell anyone he was paying for Dr. Carney's care. But if he was refusing meds because he believed the resources would be better spent elsewhere... What a mess!

"What's tricky about me paying for some morphine?"

"It's already being paid for but Dr. Carney doesn't know it."

Oliver stared at her uncomprehendingly.

Talk about caught between a rock and an Oliver.

"Julia? What's going on? The man needs meds and he's refusing them." Oliver raised his hands with a "What gives?" expression and searched her face as if it would give him answers. Her cheeks flushed instantly, and she fought the urge to look away. She couldn't tell if she was blushing because Captain Adventure was staring deep into her eyes or because she knew something he should know. This was his future, after all—managing Bryar Estate, the clinic. One he was proactively avoiding. If you didn't count all the time he'd been spending in the clinic over the past week. Or was that just him hiding from the estate ledgers?

"Your father. He's been paying for everything." *There. She'd said it.* She'd have to apologize to the duke—but English decorum be damned! Her first loyalty was to her patient.

"My father? He didn't say anything to me. And Dr. Carney doesn't know?"

"We, your father and I, were pretty certain he would refuse it—would insist the money be put toward the clinic, other patients. I told him the bed and monitoring equipment had been donated by the City Hospital. Which was sort of true. Your father donated to the Wyatt Wing and in turn they gave us the equipment." Another uncomprehending look. "You know?" she pressed. "The one your great-grandmother put funding toward after World War I? They've now got a new serenity garden featuring the rose named after your mother. It's lovely. You should see it."

Julia watched as Oliver connected the dots and began to nod as the pieces came together. Her heart leaped to her throat. He obviously hadn't had a clue about any of this and it was affecting him deeply. Cold-hearted heir, he definitely was not.

"What have you told Dr. Carney about the fun run?" Oliver's energy level suddenly shot up a level, the cogs visibly whirling.

"Nothing yet. I've not really had a chance to tot it up." *You're not the only one who's been distracted lately.*

"Could we not tell him the villagers decided the money should go toward his care? A thank-you for the years of service?"

Julia felt the prick of tears at his words. "I think that's a perfect idea. We'll tell him tomorrow."

"No, no. You tell him."

She pushed herself up onto her and knees and crawled a little closer to him on the sofa. "Wouldn't it be nicer for him to hear the news from someone he really knows? Who really loves him?"

"No, you go ahead." He waved away her suggestion. "It was your idea."

"No, it wasn't—you just came up with it."

He laughed and gave her shoulder a gentle squeeze. And didn't remove his hand. "I would never, in my wildest dreams, have come up with the idea of holding a muddy fun run in the Bryar Hall moat."

Julia wanted to protest but one look at him was a giveaway that he spoke truthfully. "Fun" and "Bryar Hall" weren't things that went together in his book.

If Julia hadn't ached for him before, her heart was well and truly constricting with compassion for him now. She felt his thumb give a gentle rub along the base of her neck. Without stopping to check herself, she tipped her cheek toward her hand and closed her eyes, a smile tugging at her lips as she felt his hand move to her cheek. *Oh, my. This is nice.*

She forced herself to open her eyes again as Oliver slowly traced a finger along her jawline. His gaze had a softness to it she hadn't seen before. Had keeping everyone at arm's length—continent's length, more like it—made it easier not to care? What exactly was he trying to avoid? Feelings? Love? As she felt the gentle caresses of his fingers, all the thoughts in her mind blurred into one very clear desire. If she were to just lean over and—

The front door swung open and with it came Tina Staunton, one of the overnight volunteer relief nurses. Julia jumped up and made to close the door behind her as if she'd been standing there all along, heart thumping at full pelt. *That was close!*

"All right, Dr. MacKenzie?" She smiled at Julia then did a double take as she spotted Oliver on the sofa.

"Lord Oliver, so sorry. I didn't see you there." She shot him a bashful smile.

"Dr. Wyatt, you remember Tina Staunton? Her parents run the village shop," Julia prompted at turbo speed, seeing he was visibly struggling to remember who she was—maybe he was just at startled as she was.

"Of course!" Oliver got to his feet and extended a hand, clearly back in English gentleman mode. *He'd felt what she had, right?*

"How are they? I've not seen them for ages." He patted Tina's arm as he shook it.

"You should get down to the shop, then." Tina blushed as she shook hands. Little wonder; she was the right age to find him as attractive as Julia did. She glanced at the woman's ring finger. A gold band was firmly in place on it. Phew!

Uh-oh. Where had that come from? Had she been *jealous*?

Hardly.

Maybe?

Of what? A man you have no proprietary rights over who could demolish your long-awaited slice of dream-come-true? Or, more accurately, the man whose lips you can't keep your eyes off.

"Would you like to come along, Julia?" Oliver looked at her, a hint of furrow forming on his brow.

"Sorry, I was in cloud cuckoo land for a minute." She forced herself to tune back into their conversation. *Concentrate, Julia.*

"Tina's parents are highlighting some local artisan foods down in the village. There's a—" he looked to Tina "—what did you call it again?"

"A Bite of St. Bryar. That's what they're calling it," Tina enthused. "You should both go. Any money raised is for Dr. Carney and Reg Pryce. We all hate that Dr. Carney is so poorly and want to make sure he knows how much he means to us. And, of course," she continued, talking at a rate of knots now, "Reg's son is having to take on all of his dad's work with him in hospital and, with it being spring and all, he's going to need an extra pair of hands. A couple of the lads down the village have said they'd help, but if we can afford to get a contractor in for the day, it would make the world of a difference to the Pryces."

"Well, then." Oliver nodded decisively. "I guess you and I had best head down to the village."

"Have you tried this one?" Julia forgot herself entirely as the dark-chocolate-covered salted caramel began to melt on her tongue. Before she thought twice, she was lifting a piece to Oliver's lips. Her eyes connected with his and she stopped, midmovement, vividly aware of what a familiar gesture it was. Feeding someone. Her stomach began a mad carousel journey, her insides churning. Being with Oliver kept rousing the sensualist within her. She kept catching herself holding his gaze a bit longer than she would a friend's, flushing, looking away, then looking back to make sure the sensation had been real. Whenever their hands brushed, a whorl of heat curled up from her core to around her heart before she could squash it back down.

"Well, go on, then." His voice was low. Teasing.

Tempting her to move into that irresistible space where they weren't quite touching but might as well have been. "What are you waiting for?" His lips parted. Julia felt an electric response surge through her body. She felt ridiculously alive. He moved in closer. *Ooh...*

She barely stopped herself from blurting, "Open wide," throwing the chocolate in his mouth and scarpering.

Instead, the sensualist in her, a Julia she'd hardly known existed, slipped the chocolate between his lips, allowing her fingers to linger so that very, very briefly—and deliberately—she was able to feel his lips close upon them.

If someone had told her waves were crashing inside of her she wouldn't have disagreed. As she drew her fingers away she felt the space between them close. The connection was there again like a thick, humming band of energy. One look at his face was proof positive he felt it, too. As her hand dropped to her side, she felt his fingers slip through hers as he nonchalantly turned to scan the room. How could he do that? Probably wise. Snogging Oliver Wyatt in the middle of a village food fair probably wouldn't be the most discreet thing to do.

Nerves suddenly got the better of her. Who knew secret hand-holding could feel so sexy? Lucky chocolate. Swirling round behind those lips of his. She couldn't do this. *Play it cool.*

She would go find something she hated: beetroot. Someone had to have a beetroot something-or-other to help her get her feet back on planet Earth. Heaven did not and could not come in the form of Oliver Wyatt.

Oliver grinned broadly as the savory sweetness of the homemade chocolate trickled down his throat. It was delicious. But not as pleasant as the connection he'd just shared with Julia. She'd been visibly flustered and something told him, despite her feisty reactions to him, that she didn't see him as all bite. The idea that her feelings might blossom and grow as his had was appealing. About time something nice happened here. Then again, a fling with the GP whose future was in his hands was hardly a stellar move. Not to mention the fact that every moment he spent with her was a moment that would make it harder to leave. Who knew best-laid plans could suddenly grow flimsy? Pliable? He'd never even considered staying before now. Maybe…

He looked across the room as Julia spooned some bright purple chutney onto a cracker, laughing with the woman who had made it. If he didn't know she'd only been here some seven months, he would've sworn she was a local.

It had taken her half an hour to get past the front door when they'd arrived as person after person had greeted her. She certainly had the spirited tenacity of a GP committed to the long haul. He looked around the room, scanning the faces, trying to see things from her point of view.

Look at them all. Each and every one of these people was more than just a chart for her. She most likely imagined knowing them throughout their lives, the same as Dr. Carney had. She would see them through pregnancies, sickness, trifling matters, life-changers.

Totally different to the professional world he'd chosen. Of course, the odd patient stood out here or there, but mostly you only had time to do the best you could and move on to the next person the best you could. That was what everyone had told him he'd done when Alexander had fallen ill, but he'd never believed them. Had never let himself get close enough to anyone to explain how gut-wrenchingly sad he was that he'd not told someone about his brother's rash earlier. If only he'd known meningitis didn't take prisoners.

He was no different to anyone in this room yet he knew why he wasn't surrounded by the same chatting crowds Julia was. He came across as standoffish, wary—different. Absolutely rich, considering it was all of his own construct. Normalcy. He suddenly felt a craving for it.

Julia saw that in him. The regular guy. The Oliver behind the title. Or was it that he was a better man with her? A warmth spread through his chest. No guessing who inspired that, then.

Without Julia, he would've come and gone from the event in a matter of minutes. Or, more realistically, not come at all. As it was, he was enjoying being here with her, watching her, a fly on the wall.

"Lord Oliver, so good of you to come along!" Pamela Pryce, Reg's wife, made a beeline toward him through the ever-thickening crowd.

Perhaps not so much of a fly on the wall, then.

"I've not had a chance to thank you for all of your heroics down in Shaw Field, pulling off that tractor and all. Mike told me it was you who raised it and I refused to believe him until I heard it from the horse's mouth."

"Anyone would've done the same." He waved away the compliment, well aware it didn't sit right.

"Stuff and nonsense, Lord Oliver! You've come home for a nice rest and jumped right into the fray."

"Yes, but you know it was Dr. MacKenzie who did the real hard graft?"

"Oh?" Pamela's eyes widened.

"Without her quick thinking—calling the helicopter—I dare say things would've been a lot worse."

"But if you hadn't pulled the tractor off…" She smiled up at him, her voice trailing off as Oliver stiffened. This was precisely the type of thing that gnawed at him. Undue credit just because of his title.

Be gracious.

His mother's words echoed through him. And maybe the poor woman just wanted to talk to him. It wasn't that strange a thing, after all. Talking to a neighbor who'd just helped your husband. *Get a grip, man. Don't read so much into things—and, yes, be gracious.*

"It wasn't any trouble, Mrs. Pryce. I assure you. But it really is Dr. MacKenzie you should be thanking."

"Oh, yes, I know. Of course, the village is ever so happy to have her here." Mrs. Pryce carried on talking as Oliver looked over her shoulder toward Julia, now deep in discussion with a flat-capped gentleman giving out samples of hard cheese. She looked up at Oliver, lifted an eyebrow and smiled. Something in him tightened. In a good way. Over here was too far away. He was hardly the hovering type, but…

"So, anyway, the hospital says it should be another week and he can come home—so long as Dr. MacKenzie can do his checkups, of course. Or you? I hear you're taking appointments while Dr. MacKenzie's hand is all trussed up."

Oliver looked at Mrs. Pryce blankly for a moment then shook his head. He'd been away with the fairies—the blond-haired, blue-eyed variety.

"Absolutely. Yes. Do bring him in. Now, if you'll excuse me, I think there's some cheese over there I need to get a taste of."

* * *

"What a good night!" Julia enthused. She risked a glance over at Oliver, who had turned from amiable to visibly brooding halfway through the event. "Did you find anything you liked?"

"Sort of."

"Sort of?" She guffawed but kept her eyes trained on the wooded path they were following back to the Hall. "What kind of response it that?"

"It means there were a lot of nice things, but nothing that really spoke to me."

Julia stopped, astonished he hadn't found one thing to his taste. "Are you kidding me? I could give you a shopping list as long as my arm! I can't wait to get back into my little cottage and fill up the larder. I had some amazing crisps made with heritage potatoes and just a hint of paprika. Delicious!"

"Is Clara's cooking not to your taste, then?"

Touchy.

"She's a wonderful cook. Don't be ridiculous. I'm just surprised you're so lackluster about it all. Some of these kitchen table projects could turn into a real boon for St. Bryar. The villagers could certainly do with the income."

"There's no point in getting attached to things you can't have."

Julia stopped, feeling physically struck by his words. She was pretty sure they weren't on the topic of paprika crisps anymore.

"What exactly are we talking about here?"

"Nothing." Oliver shook his head and picked up the pace. He was hardly going to tell her virtually every thought of his managed to touch on her in some way or other.

"Hang on a second." Julia jogged a few steps to catch up with him and caught ahold of his sleeve. "What are you talking about, Oliver? Is there something I need to know?"

It would be so easy to take her in his arms. Hold her, take in that soft scent of hers, grab ahold of her hand and run through the woods like a couple of young lovers. But it would hardly be fair.

How could he explain that tonight—and every other St. Bryar-centric thing she'd gotten him involved in since he'd returned—was exactly what he'd been hoping to avoid when he'd come home? Being attached, caring for people, loving people then losing them was precisely what he'd spent his entire adult life avoiding. Each and every moment he spent with her made the place feel more like—home.

"Oliver, are you sure you're all right?" Julia's blue eyes appealed to him to open up.

He ached to let her in. Anywhere else in the world, he knew he would've pulled her into his arms and savored the sensation of holding her and being held. Here? Where everything turned to poison?

Not a chance.

"Right as rain." He flashed a practiced aristocratic smile and turned her toward Bryar Hall, just visible through the trees. "Shall we get you back before dark, then?"

Julia scrunched up her pillow. Nope. No good. Maybe fluffing it would do the trick. There. Perhaps now that she'd rearranged it about fifty thousand times she could get to sleep.

She tossed. Then turned. Then flung herself into a

snow angel position and stared at the ceiling, willing her mind to slow down.

If only she could hoover the thoughts away, stick a tube to her ear and suck every single thought about Oliver Wyatt right out of her brain.

Oliver Wyatt.

It seemed every dark-haired, green-eyed morsel of the man was threatening to eat her brain alive. And her body. Her hands slipped onto her belly as yet another wash of warmth set her body alight. For heaven's sake! She was responding to him like a giddy teen and he wasn't even in the room! Yet again her body was playing traitor to her pragmatism.

Hadn't she made a deal with herself? Play it cool while Oliver went through the books. Which, she noted with a wry grin, he hadn't really seemed to do much of. She frowned. *Get on with it!*

On the other hand, with him helping out at the clinic so much, there was every chance his love for Bryar Estate and the village would be reignited. It was the perfect match. Medicine and making a difference. Those seemed to be the things that made him tick.

Her heart sank a bit.

Just not here. His dark mood on their walk home from the village hall was proof positive he had little to no time for the place.

What was it that he hated so much? Being a duke didn't have to be all that horrible if decorum wasn't his thing. His father hardly looked taxed by his position. Look at the King of Spain! He was always roaring around Madrid on a motorcycle. Hardly restrained behavior. Then again, they were English. Firm-jawed in the face of adversity and all that.

She had to get to the heart of it. Find out what really made him hate it here so much. Then she would—what, exactly? Solve all his problems with a winning smile and a bit of emotional elbow grease? Unlikely.

Her hands slipped to her hips and ran along her thighs as she rolled onto her side. For the fifty-thousandth time.

Her thoughts flitted about before landing back at the moment when she slipped the chocolate in Oliver's mouth. If she hadn't run away, would they have carried on holding hands as if it had been a perfectly natural thing to do?

Would she have gone up on tiptoe to taste the salted caramel a second time? Pressed into him to feel if his appetite, like hers, wasn't for food but for the other's touch?

Aargh! She turned flat on her belly and pulled a pillow over her head. Enough!

He didn't want the same things—and the sooner she got that through her head the better.

CHAPTER SIX

OLIVER DREW A finger down the list of the day's remaining patients. Between the two of them, they'd make quick work of it. He could've sworn the clinic of days gone by had been one of well-intentioned but hapless disorder.

Hats off to Julia. Yet another tick in "the woman is a star" book. The clinic was a world away from how he remembered it. She was efficient, professional and obviously very dedicated. Oh—and beautiful. Did he mention beautiful? And funny? And had the softest skin. He'd barely had a moment to trace the soft outline of her cheek—but by God he wouldn't mind doing that again. Not that he'd had a moment alone with her since the Bite of St. Bryar.

She was always at the clinic before him, beavering away at some paperwork or cleaning, and she'd never left until well after he'd hung up his stethoscope. She wouldn't be avoiding him, would she? Had she seen through his veneer of charm and realized he was a man who couldn't commit? Or maybe it was simpler: she loved her work here at the clinic. And who could blame her? He'd enjoyed the past few days immensely.

Word had quickly spread that there was an extra pair of hands in St. Bryar Hospital—and not just any old hands. After an initial surge of patients, who all seemed to be suffering from hypochondria more than anything else, the appointments list had settled back to a steady trickle. He grinned as he pictured Julia re-enacting the disappointed faces of patients who'd drawn the short straw and been seen by her.

"Ooh—I was just hoping Lord Oliver might have a listen with his stethoscope, you see. I'm sure you're very good, but this condition might call for a specialist."

"What have you done to my practice?" she'd wailed. "Everyone's out for their heartbeat to be listened to by the future Duke of Breckonshire."

How she managed to push all his buttons and make him grin instead of growl was beyond him. Perhaps because she had one heck of a gift for mimicry, he could forgive it.

Realistically? His soft spot for the cheeky blonde was growing despite his resolve to push it into the back of a wardrobe somewhere and forget about it. That in and of itself was steadily sanding away the sheen of his well-laid plans.

Apart from feeling like a bit of a tourist attraction, he was genuinely beginning to enjoy this whole country-living thing much more than he'd bargained for. He'd been an idiot to think springtime, when the estate was virtually exploding with new life, was the best time to wipe his hands of St. Bryar. There were lambs bouncing around the fields and gorgeous, fluffy calves gorging themselves on their mother's milk—not to mention every shrub, hedgerow and fruit tree bursting into spectacular life. And—of course—Julia. The place was a rural idyll. Anyone would be a fool not to want to be a part of it.

He rapped a pen on the desk. That was just the point,

wasn't it? Did he or didn't he want to be a part of it? He'd been doing a fairly terrific job of avoiding the real reason for coming home—and he'd be hard pressed to eke out this "lending a helping hand" ruse for much longer. A couple of more weeks and Julia's hand would be right as rain, the cottage would be fixed and he would have all the time in the world to focus on the estate's books. He rapped the pen on the desk again. He wasn't behind a pile of ledgers yet!

"Let's see," he said aloud. "What have we got here? Post-op hernia check for Arthur 'The Knife' Potts. Mole removal for Elaine Duncan. Blood pressure check for Mrs. Winters."

A smile crept to his lips. The butcher, the baker...and the schoolgirl who'd come to ride at the stables once a week when he'd been a boy. St. Bryar had never had a candlestick maker, so far as he knew. Pity.

The names all pinged with images of encounters he'd had with each of them over the course of growing up. Part of him was astonished all of these people from his childhood were still here.

He hadn't appreciated how few tabs he'd kept on everyone here and it bridled. What he'd seen as the frippery and excess of the Bryar Hall tea parties and village shoots unexpectedly made sense: they were ways for his parents to see and be with the villagers on a level other than that of employer, landowner, duke and duchess. He could've easily held open clinics during his annual trip home and given Dr. Carney a much-needed holiday. Caught up with folk. Made a difference. He sat back in the chair and sighed. Truth be told, he could've done a lot of things.

"I know it's not what you're used to, but it keeps us busy enough!" Julia's soft voice broke into his thoughts.

"Looks more than enough for a clinic running on little more than loose change!"

Her expression told him in an instant he'd said the wrong thing. Again. He'd meant it as a compliment but his words had definitely cast a shadow across those blue eyes of hers. *Blue eyes he'd grown awfully fond of seeing brighten when they rested on him.*

"I can assure you, Oliver, that the people of St. Bryar are happy to have what little we can offer. The alternative would cost them a lot more than loose change."

"Go on."

From the look on her face, she was hardly asking for his permission to continue. His mouth twitched with the hint of a smile. It was almost worth annoying her just to enjoy the myriad expressions that lovely face of hers could morph into. All of them, no matter how cross, featured those lovely, deep red lips of hers. *Zwerp! Focus.* The woman was trying to make a point.

"For starters, just think of the fuel it costs them to get to the nearest town. That's a forty-mile-odd round trip. Or if they have to go all the way to the city—that's over ninety miles' round trip on quite a few single-track lanes. There and back for a pensioner is a lot of time and money."

"Good point, but what about the flipside? An estate without an obvious income supporting a cottage hospital? Where's the return in that?"

"Are you kidding me?" Julia stared at him incredulously.

"Wait. That didn't come out exactly how I meant it."

"Or maybe it did."

"No. Be reasonable, Julia. I'd hardly have donated the last ten years of my life to helping people in conflict zones if I didn't see the value of medicine."

"But you don't seem to see the value of it here."

"That's not fair. What about the people overseas?"

"What about the people here? Right here in your hometown?" She tamped a finger down on the desk.

"I'm not saying they shouldn't have medical care."

"Then what exactly are you saying? That Dr. Carney should spend his final days in a hospice too far away for his friends to visit regularly? That Elaine Duncan lose a day's wages to get a simple mole removed when she's got two children to care for? That Arthur close up his shop for half a day or more?"

"I don't know the answer. Not off the top of my head."

"Then why are you hiding out down here doing checkups with me when you could be going through the books with your father like you said you would?"

Because I like it here. With you.

The screech of the iron gate at the front of the clinic put an abrupt halt to his thoughts.

"This isn't the time or place to discuss it."

"When *is* a more appropriate time?" Julia's stance was solid. For a woman a good head shorter than him, she sure had presence.

"Tonight." He held her gaze steadily, waiting for her to waver.

"Great."

No wavering.

"Time?"

"Seven. I'll cook."

Julia's eyebrows shot up in amazement. "You don't fancy Clara's cooking, then?"

"Yes, but we have this odd custom called a day off."
He tipped his chin to the side and teased a smile out of
her.

"So we'll be eating lemon drizzle cake then?" She
giggled.

"Thanks for the vote of confidence, Julia."

The front door opened and a patient walked in.

"Go on—get out of here and let me do good." She
shooed him down the corridor as she ushered her patient
into the exam room.

Oliver felt a smile forming. She was already good.

Very good. He slipped out the back of the clinic after
a quick farewell wave to Dr. Carney. Yet another person who was lucky to have her in his life. Something
told him that, no matter how many times he went over
the books, he'd come up with the same conclusion: Julia
was the one who added value to things here, not the pal-
try stipend the estate had the clinic on. She was an intelligent, fun, spirited, life-charged, passionate doctor
who ticked all of his boxes—including "wrong place"
and "wrong time."

"I can't believe you did all of this in an hour!" Julia
ogled the plate Oliver placed in front of her, stopping
just short of clapping her hands. Steamed coconut rice,
a white-miso eggplant dish with a sprinkle of black ses-
ame seeds, glossy bok-choi and thick slices of soy-glazed
pork tenderloin. It looked amazing.

"We don't exactly have a Chinese takeaway round
here and this is how I sate my desire. Chopsticks?" Oliver brandished a pair of silver-tipped bamboo chopsticks
for her to inspect.

"Easier than a fork and knife!" Julia quipped, waving

her bad hand in the air, hoping it hid the fact she abruptly crossed her legs at the mention of "desire." How could eyes be so green? Or cooking skills so sexy? Too bad her brain was in direct conflict with her body's response to Oliver. This was, after all, meant to be a meeting of the minds in regards to the clinic. She needed to be steeling herself, not melting at his prowess with a wok. *Neutral territory, please. Keep it neutral!*

"Will your father not be joining us?"

"Sorry, no. He sends his apologies. The spiced delights of the Far East aren't really up his alley." Oliver sat opposite her at the large wooden kitchen table. "He had a bowl of soup and some of Clara's bread earlier and thought he'd turn in early. He'll join us tomorrow if you're happy with that."

"Delighted." Julia replied honestly. "Your father is fascinating. I've had such a great time hearing all of his stories about this place. The 'olden days' when the house was transformed into a hospital for soldiers in World War II..." She knew it was a leading statement but she might as well grab the bull by the horns.

"It's a shame the 'olden days' aren't like modern times," Oliver parried.

"In what way?"

"Pragmatic. Sensible. Forward-thinking."

"That's interesting. Those are words I'd easily apply to the olden days. Add to that list *generous, community-minded, caring...*" Julia retorted sharply. She stabbed a bit of eggplant with her chopstick and popped it in her mouth. Just as quickly the piece came flying out again.

"Hot, hot, hot, hot!"

"What a relief," Oliver replied drily. "I thought it might have been my cooking."

"Apologies," Julia muttered into her serviette. "That wasn't very ladylike of me." *Understatement of the year!*

"Not to worry," Oliver said with a smile. "Plenty else is."

Julia felt her cheeks flush. If catching her off-guard with compliments was his method of disarming her, it was definitely working.

Taking care to blow on her food before taking another bite, and then another, Julia began to eat with true relish. "This is really delicious. You know your stuff."

"I spent a bit of time in China."

"Cooking school?" She guffawed at the thought— Oliver in an apron. Then again...*just* an apron...

"Hardly." He gave her a "you should know better" look. "Working."

Of course. What else did Oliver Wyatt do but work on other people's causes? Anywhere But Here. That seemed to be his motto.

"There are a lot of isolated communities out there and when an epidemic hits—SARS, for example—they are the ones to suffer most. We fly out and bring medical supplies and extra pairs of hands in exchange for training."

"Training for what?"

"Acupuncture, herbal remedies—that sort of thing. The Chinese are great with preventative medicine in the form of what they eat—the exercise they take. A lot of the communities I've worked in just don't have the resources to pay for Western medicines. Any techniques we can bring to their practitioners that help keep costs down help enormously."

"So what would you recommend for me?"

"You?" It was Oliver's time to look surprised.

"Sure. I work in a clinic with limited means and a community to serve. Anything you would recommend I could do to keep costs down?"

Oliver put down his chopsticks and folded his serviette on the table in a definitive gesture. *Whoops.* Looked like she'd brought the chatty atmosphere to a close.

Oliver looked her directly in the eye. "What you're doing here is amazing, but there's no chance one or a hundred muddy fun runs could raise the money to buy the building from the estate, if that's what you're aiming for."

Gulp!

"How'd you know?"

"Am I wrong?"

"Not in the strictest sense of the word." Her stomach clenched in a tight ball.

"I saw your grant application forms," he explained. "And I don't think you've got the right angle for what most of those groups are looking to fund."

He cleared his throat as if to continue, but Julia dove in. It was "now or never" time.

"I get it, Oliver. You've seen the big wide world out there and want to solve all of its problems. But have you stopped—for a moment—to think about all of the people right here in St. Bryar who you'll be letting down? People who've lived here and worked here for generations? I can't believe how selfish a decision you're making!"

"Selfish? Seriously? You think I'm *selfish* for wanting to help women and children caught up in a war they having nothing to do with?"

Julia felt as though a plug had been pulled out of her. No. She shook her head; she didn't think that at all.

"I'm sorry, Oliver." Tears began to form a queue in

her eyes. The first few fell in an orderly fashion, then there was a sudden scramble for the front and she felt her cheeks burn with a flood of grief.

"This is the exact same fight I had with my husband the day he was killed and I promised never to do it again."

"Do what?" Oliver reached across the table, gently taking hold of her hand.

"Ask someone to give up their dream for mine."

Their eyes met and, in an instant, any anger Julia had felt toward Oliver disappeared. At the end of the day he was exactly the same as her—someone struggling to find their place in the world.

He released her hand and drew a finger along the curve of her cheek. More than anything she wanted to press into his hand as she had the other day. Feel his touch.

"Do you want to know why I don't—can't—stay here?"

She nodded, hoping it would conceal the bitter taste rising in her throat. At last. At last she was getting to the heart of the matter—*his* heart.

"This place, this house, these grounds—all of it—they're stuck in a time and place that doesn't exist anymore. It won't take to the change you're so eager to impose on it. No matter what anyone thinks or dreams or tries to do, this place is stuck in the past. A past I have no interest in living."

Julia sighed in frustration. This was hardly the truth she'd been promised. "That sounds like claptrap to me. Your father hardly seems to cling to the past. He approved the race in the moat, for one. Not to mention the fact he hired me! I can't imagine he would've done that if his whole plan was to keep things as is."

"My father was filling a void."

The words cut straight through her. Was that how he saw her? As a void-filler?

She fought the sour taste of bile rising again. His words didn't sit right. This was a man lashing out against something much bigger than her.

A low moan escaped his lips as he scrubbed his hands across his face. "Do you see what being here does to me? I'm not a man who says things like that! Please believe me. Things would've been so different for me—for you as well—if—"

"If what?" She could hardly breathe. What could have hurt him so deeply?

"If I had been different."

What? Now he was driving her round the bend.

"Different how? When you're not being a jerk you seem like a wonderful man to me."

Oliver laughed and shook his head. "What I'm trying to say—very badly—is that Bryar Estate needs some-one at its helm. Someone who wants to be the Duke of Breckonshire. Or the Duchess, for that matter. You'd be great at it—but it's never been the job for me."

"It's true." Julia nodded sagely. "You'd be a terrible duchess."

Oliver laughed again, the atmosphere between them softening to something more familiar, more relaxed. "You know what I mean. I'm not duke material."

"Says who?" Julia couldn't keep the incredulity out of her voice. "You're smart, obviously passionate about medicine, which easily translates into people. Despite your very valiant efforts to appear aloof, I can tell you are genuinely interested in the people of St. Bryar and their welfare. What more does a duke need to be?"

"Some people are born to fulfill a destiny, Julia. Mine simply isn't here."

"What exactly do you think will happen to you when you inherit your title, Oliver? That you'll turn into some sort of dimwitted fop or a miserly ogre? Look around you! Your father is a wonderfully kind man. I don't think the apple fell too far from the tree on that front."

Oliver's ramrod-straight posture softened a smidgen.

"My father was never the problem."

Ah.

"So who was?"

"My mother."

"But she sent you all those cakes!"

Oliver gave a hollow laugh and nodded.

"Yes. She sent me cake." Oliver looked her in the eye and for the first time she saw a hollowness in them, as if he'd frozen any feeling for his mother straight out of his heart.

"You two didn't see eye to eye?"

Oliver's sharp laugh reverberated off the stone walls of the kitchen. "That's one way to put it. Suffice it to say, once Alexander was gone I was never going to be able to put a foot right."

"Who was Alexander?"

"My older brother."

"You have an older brother?"

"Had."

"Oh, Oliver. I didn't know." Julia felt a flash of understanding snap through her. Had his mother been so consumed by grief at the loss of one son, she'd lost sight of the one she still had? A son who was also grieving for his older brother? It was heartbreaking. She knew as well as anyone, no matter how old you were, you always wanted to please your parents. And Oliver was no different.

She could have protested. Could have told him dukes and earls and even kings came in all shapes and sizes. It was about leadership. And a vision. Both things he obviously had in spades.

She twiddled her chopsticks through the remains of her supper, trying to think of the right thing to say.

One look at the storm clouds in his eyes told her she should back off. Oliver was obviously wrestling with his past. But it seemed at odds with the story he'd told her. His mother had hardly tethered him here, so she couldn't have been that intent on pinning him to a lifestyle he didn't want.

After Matt had died she'd wanted her children close—so very close. When they had come to her and said they'd like to go to music school, she'd realized she was the only thing standing in the way of their dreams. Stifling her children so she could immerse herself in grief? It just wasn't an option. Had Oliver's mother come to the same conclusion?

She watched Oliver play with the few grains of rice remaining on his plate and suddenly saw her own situation a bit more clearly. Maybe she hadn't been as "freewheeling" as she'd given herself credit for. By choosing an isolated village, perhaps she had shut herself off from fully healing—from participating in the wider world, as her children were. Was this whole discussion they were having just a case of the pot and the kettle calling each other out?

Where she was proactively hiding from her grief, he

was running away at high speed. Each of them misguidedly hoping for some sort of peace.

"I'm sorry, Oliver."

"For what?" He looked up, as if surprised to see her there at all.

"For your loss. I am truly sorry."

"Not to worry." He answered shortly. "It was a long time ago."

"I know—but time doesn't always change things, does it? Look." She pushed herself away from the table. "I am going to go to bed. Thank you very much for the lovely dinner—I'm sorry if I spoiled it by probing too much. I always was too nosy."

"Not to worry," Oliver repeated, suddenly fighting the urge to share everything. To share how lonely being at Bryar Estate made him feel. How the weight of expectation suffocated him. How it seemed, no matter how much good he'd done in the world, he would never achieve what his mother wanted. How could he? He could never bring Alexander back and that was the only thing that would have made her happy.

"Whatever you decide to do here—with the estate— I'm sure it will be for the best."

"I doubt reverse psychology is going to work on me, Dr. MacKenzie."

Her lips pulled back into a brilliant smile and she laughed. "You give me too much credit. I was just trying to see things from your perspective and, the truth is, no one likes change. Few people are brave enough to see it through. Maybe this is one of those scenarios where you are the only one who can see the wood for the trees."

Had kismet put her here to have it out with his demons? Was he wrong to want to shut the door on the past instead of taking a fresh look at things? He shook away the thought. Mumbo-jumbo. Facts were facts. He didn't want to live here. That was what it boiled down to.

"You're right, Julia."

"About change?"

"About bedtime." He nodded toward the flagstone stairwell. "I'll see you in the morning." Oliver felt as if all the life was being sucked out of the room as she left.

He'd just summarily dismissed the one person he had ever come close to opening his heart to. The one person who saw nothing but hope and possibility in a place he saw nothing but dead ends. A dull ache thumped through his veins. Would his mother have been proud? At long last, he was beginning to behave like an aristocrat.

"Julia!" He called after her receding figure as he took the steps two at a time.

"Yes?" She turned to him, cheeks flushed with emotion, eyes alight with curiosity. Expectation?

A rush of desire washed through him. Every pore in his body wanted her. Before he could stop himself, he slid his fingers along her jawline and into her hair. His lips met hers in a heated, fiery explosion of desire. By the way she responded to him, to his touch, he could tell she wanted him, too. He moved a hand to the base of her neck as the other slid down her spine to the small of her back. A small moan of pleasure left her lips as he rained kisses along her neck. He physically ached to be closer, more intimate.

"Stop. Please." He felt Julia push at his chest, her words completely at odds with the sensations he was experiencing.

He pulled back, still holding her, not wanting to let go. "Why?"

"I can't. Not with things so— Not until you decide what you want to do."

"Don't you want to be together? Tell me you don't want me."

Her hands slid down his chest and she shook her head sadly.

"I can't." She looked up into his eyes. "Not unless you're going to stay."

Oliver let his hands drop from her hips. He couldn't promise that. Not now. Not yet. She must've seen the answer in his eyes as, before he could protest further, she turned and ran the rest of the way up the stairs to her room and very solidly closed the door.

A good run. That was what Julia needed after another night of feeling like the princess with the pea. Or was it the commoner with the coconut? The latter, judging by the cricks in her neck.

A run and a hot shower and then on to the clinic where she knew a full day's work awaited her. The perfect way to avoid the real reasons she'd spent most of the night awake. Lord Oliver Wyatt equaled insomnia central.

She hadn't seen him since The Incident on the Stairs which she supposed spoke volumes. He didn't have plans to stay. Never had. She was right to have stopped things from going further. Even if it made her skin ache to think of his touch.

Realistically? She needed to face the future head-on. Oliver hadn't said what she was filling a gap for—but, whatever it was, she obviously wasn't the endgame. So, time for another new beginning? Perhaps a job a bit closer to the twins? Or by the ocean? Sunsets on the

Atlantic could be nice. Or an inner-city appointment? Heaven knew it would be a sea change from the life she'd lived so far.

A leaden feeling began to creep through her. None of the options fit. She'd found the perfect place to live and work and she was just going to let it go? Just thinking about the woods filled to the violet-colored brim with bluebells made her want to weep. Or was it the thought of losing Oliver? Hard to tell at this point.

She had to fight. She just had to! If it meant filling out application form after application form, she would find the funding to buy the clinic from Oliver. Then she could stand on her own two feet and never think about him again. An image of his green eyes flashed through her mind—green eyes locking into hers before closing and kissing her more purely and deeply than she thought she could bear. Her stomach clenched. Maybe the "not ever thinking about him again" part wouldn't come quite as easily.

A good run; that's what she needed. A full-speeder through the woods would clear out the cobwebs and then she'd be ready for action.

Julia popped in her earphones and selected an intense track as she headed off down her favorite woodland track. It was a full five kilometers and she was hoping to give it some good old-fashioned welly this morning.

"Fancy meeting you here."

"Ack!" Julia pulled out her earphones, properly startled to discover Oliver running alongside her. All her nerves gathered up in a tight coil then began to pinball through her nervous system.

"I thought I'd see you at breakfast."

"I thought I'd be on my own out here." Julia couldn't keep the bite out of her voice.

Oliver smiled and made a "fair enough" face, his eyes trained on the track ahead of them.

Julie grimaced. Did he have to wear such form-fitting exercise gear? It was just plain bad mannered when a girl was trying her best to maintain a professional distance from someone. Not watch the way his T-shirt hitched up over his shoulders, or see how she now had proof positive his legs were well-defined and really nice to ogle. *Rude!*

"Did you say something?"

Uh-oh. Out-loud voice?

"No, just trying to sort out how to tackle the day."

"A lot of patients?"

Like you care.

"No—that's fine. I just wanted to see if I could prove you wrong."

"What do you mean?" Oliver kept his gaze straight ahead as they ran.

"There are still a few grants I could apply for that could push the clinic in the direction of standing on its own—but I'd have to think outside the box."

"Julia, you're looking at a couple of hundred thousand if the estate is to get market value for the place."

"What would you use it for?"

"I'm sorry?"

"Apologies." Julia put her hands up. "None of my business."

"No, it's a fair question." Oliver glanced over at her but she couldn't meet his eyes. Not yet. "I'd probably donate it to the Flying Doctors or the Red Cross."

"Oh, I see."

"You disapprove?" Oliver was getting a bit too good at reading between the lines.

"It's just a bit weird to me that you'd give such a huge amount of money to an overseas charity—who, granted, do good in the world—when, if you're in the mood for giving, you could just give the building to the village."

"That's a fair comment."

Julia's heart skipped a beat. *Would he be part of the deal?* "So you'd consider donating the building to the village?"

"I didn't say that."

"Right."

"But I didn't say no, either, did I, Miss Frowny-Face?" He gave her a playful kick on the bum with his foot.

"Hey! Don't kick a girl while she's down." She chanced a glance up at him. Maybe those green eyes of his were actually frog-colored. The frog-faced prince-duke.

"I should be kicking myself, really. It's a good idea."

"You think?" It took a lot of willpower to keep her tone light.

"I do." His tone turned serious. "I'll put it into the mix."

"Right. In with the rest of the hoi polloi."

"For heaven's sake, Julia! I'm not going to just up and give away part of the estate without considering all of the ramifications, am I? Don't go all pouty on me— you're bigger than that."

"You, of all people, should know I didn't mean it that way." Julia pouted then pulled her lips into a thin line.

Oliver stopped running, hands on hips, and stared at her. "Why me 'of all people'?"

Blimey! What do you want? My heart on a platter?

"I'm just saying I care! And there's no one else I can talk to who understands what it is to believe so strongly in something. I care!"

"About the clinic?"

Oh, so very much more than the clinic.

"Yes, about the clinic…"

"And?"

What did he want? A confession of her true feelings? To know that having him around made a perfect place to live and work even better than she ever could have imagined?

"It's just nice to have—you know—" She faltered. This was tough. She hadn't found someone to be her sounding board since she'd moved here. And everyone needed someone to have a good rant with who would dole out some solid advice, right? She looked up into Oliver's eyes—steady, unwavering. "To have a someone…to talk to," she finished softly.

"So, I'm your 'someone'?"

"You'll do 'til I find someone proper…" Julia affected a teasing tone, pressing her lips forward into a cheeky pout, then thought better of it and pressed them together. How on earth she'd gone from bickering to flirting in a matter of a millisecond was beyond her.

"Shall we?" Oliver nodded toward the path, indicating they should carry on running. "You're actually right, you know." He flashed her a smile. "I don't admit that very often, so you should take this moment to bask in the limelight."

"Ha! I think I'll take a rain check on that one. What am I right about, anyway?"

"I was a bit rash in thinking I could just fly in, sort out my future and fly back out without leaving a mark."

You got that right!

"I need a proper sit down with my father and the ledgers." He gave her a sidelong glance. "The truth?"

"Uh—yes, please."

"I haven't really got the foggiest about what to do with the estate. Up until now, it's mostly been a case of out of sight, out of mind."

"Up until now?"

"Julia, don't be coy. You know more than most the estate hasn't been the only thing that's been on my mind."

"He doesn't seem to mind."

"I suppose he wants you to be happy." *You dodged it! Why, you ninny?*

"And what about you?" Oliver refused to be distracted.

"Do *I* want you to be happy?"

"No, silly. I mean, that'd be nice, but do you want a look at the books?"

Yes. Of course. The books. What else would we be talking about? Not beating my heart to a pulp or anything.

"You want me to look at your family's accounts?"

"Well, it's hardly akin to opening up the vaults of MI5."

"I know, but it's your private business."

"I'd like you to see them."

"Really? Why?"

"Let's just say it'd be nice, on this occasion, to have a someone."

His someone? The telltale swirl of warmth began to ribbon through her. Was this his way of showing her he would take a serious look at staying? She grinned. So did Oliver. And then he play-kicked her on the bum again for good measure.

CHAPTER SEVEN

"THERE'S A BIT of improvement, but not much." Julia gave Margaret Simms's arm a quick squeeze as she took off the blood-pressure cuff. "Have you made any of those lifestyle changes we discussed?"

The sixty-seven-year-old woman sent a sharp look over her shoulder as if someone might overhear them in the private consultation room.

"Oh, yes! *Diligently*, Dr. MacKenzie, but let me tell you I'm struggling to fit it all in. On top of which, it all makes me so hungry!"

"Really? What exactly have you been doing?" Julia asked. She had previously diagnosed Margaret's high blood pressure as a classic "lose a bit of weight, do a bit of exercise and things should improve" scenario. A bit less salt and sugar and a splash of exercise should have made an impact by now. Had Margaret initially presented with a sudden rise in her blood pressure and her lifestyle been a bit more active, she would've had more concern. Blocked arteries were often to blame and they generally required stents to be fitted. Margaret hadn't complained of any chest pain—so she had ruled out that option.

"The list…" Margaret began to dig through her handbag. "The list you gave me when I wasn't feeling right."

"You mean the list of ways to lower your blood pressure?" Julia kept the smile twitching at her lips at bay. Margaret was a regular visitor, but it was rare for her actually to listen to any of her advice. Her husband had passed away about a year ago and Julia was fairly certain the visits were more for a bit of company than any true ailment.

"That's right. That's the one." Margaret triumphantly held up a folded pink printout. "Here, look. It took me all of Sunday to get through them! I'd no time to sit and take my afternoon sherry. My knitting needles didn't know what to do with themselves, but I couldn't half have murdered a shepherd's pie!"

Julia took a moment to scan the pamphlet. "Hang on, Margaret. Have you been doing *all* of these exercise suggestions in one day?"

"Well, of course. Twenty minutes each. I was inspired by watching the fun run and you said very clearly to try these suggestions. I take everything you say very seriously, Doctor." Margaret gave her an appropriately pious expression.

Julia laughed good-naturedly. "I didn't mean all at once! When you take on exercise, you want to do it gradually. Particularly if you haven't been doing very much. No wonder you're tired." She sat back in her chair and thought for a moment. "Did you say you haven't been taking your sherry any longer?"

"Yes, that's right. Well, just the once, really."

"And do you do your knitting when you take your sherry?"

"Yes, that's right. To make a hat is three glasses, a scarf is four…" She petered off as Julia's eyes widened.

"And is this an everyday thing, your knitting?"

"Oh, yes. Although, with Harold gone," she reluctantly admitted, "there might be a bit more sherry than knitting. I made all of his sweaters, you see. Always getting holes in the elbows, he was. The man kept me ever so busy."

Julia considered Margaret's chart for a moment before continuing. Moving from the physical to the personal was always a delicate trick—particularly with the older, more private generation. "Margaret, since your husband passed, have you been getting out much? To see your friends?"

"No, not so much. It's hard to get back into action after these winter months, isn't it? They keep you in."

"Mmm, yes." She nodded. "I've got an idea for you, Margaret. I bet there are a few women round the village who might be suffering from a bit of cabin fever. Rather than working your way through this exercise list, why don't you walk into town a couple of times a week— what's that, a fifteen minute walk?—and start a knitting club down at Elsie's tea shop? Send your hats and scarves to—" Julia stopped as she heard Oliver greeting Dr. Carney in the room across from them. "You could send them to Africa."

Margaret cackled delightedly. "Africa? Dr. MacKenzie, have you gone mad?"

Very, very possibly.

"Not at all." Julia covered with what she hoped was calm bravura. Could Oliver's presence really have made such an impression on her subconscious or was the answer to that blaringly obvious? "There are all sorts of things you could knit for charities down there. Blankets for the orphans, little infant caps—that sort of thing."

She slipped her hand under the desk, crossing her fingers that such a charity existed. If not, maybe she could get her computer whiz of a son to start one up on the internet. "I think you'd be helping a lot of the ladies to get out for a bit of fresh air and a cup of tea if you were to start a knitting club."

Margaret stifled her laughter then visibly considered the suggestion. "Perhaps Elsie's shop could do with a bit more local business. I would be helping St. Bryar by doing that, wouldn't I? And, of course," she continued, giving Julia's knee a pat, "Lord Oliver would most likely appreciate it, what with all of the work he does for those poor orphans."

"Good thinking." *Whatever it takes.*

"You know, Dr. MacKenzie..." Margaret leaned in as if to share a secret. "Most of the girls call me Peggy. I could call the club 'Knit & Purl with Peggy'!"

Julia clapped her hands in delight. "That sounds great."

"I could also teach some of the younger girls!" Margaret enthused. "I hear on the television knitting has become trendy again!"

There was a quick knock on the door, and Oliver's head popped round the corner. "So sorry to interrupt. Dr. MacKenzie, could I borrow you?"

"Yes, of course, we're just wrapping up here." Julia rose quickly to her feet. She wouldn't normally rush a patient out the door, but she trusted Oliver enough to know he wouldn't interrupt a consultation if it wasn't urgent. "Margaret—Peggy—I think we're onto a winner here. You'll keep me updated?"

"Of course, dear. Of course."

Julia gave the woman's shoulder a quick squeeze and

nipped across the corridor to Dr. Carney's room. Oliver had already disappeared behind the curtain masking the bed from the door.

"Dr. Carney, how is everything?" Julia stopped in her tracks. Initial but obvious signs of jaundice were evident in his eyes and skin tone.

"Not looking my best today, I'm afraid, my dear."

"I wouldn't say yellow is your color." Julia made a feeble stab at humor before glancing across the room at Oliver.

"Most likely a bile blockage. We were discussing surgery and *someone*—" Oliver pointedly looked at Dr. Carney "—claims he isn't keen. I was hoping another doctor's viewpoint might help this stubborn old bugger to see sense."

Julia felt as though someone was physically reaching in and constricting her heart into a taut rope. Oliver was obviously struggling with his mentor's illness and it was going to be tough to be as blunt with him as her predecessor had been with her.

Dr. Carney didn't want surgery. He had a "do not resuscitate" request on his medical file, and she knew better than to fight him. The prognosis had never been good and the best she could get him to agree to was to let her keep his pain in check.

"I think the old bugger knows as well as we do what lack of treatment will lead to." Julia tried to lighten the mood in the room, hoping Oliver would take the hint and discuss the situation with her outside.

Dr. Carney tried to push himself up and failed, but managed a weak smile. "Of course I do, dear boy! It's not as if this cancer nonsense has gone to my brain." He rattled off an impressive definition of bile duct blockage, possible treatments and prognoses. When he went on to clarify the fact that long-term blockages could lead to cancer, he gave the pair a wry smile. "I think I've already got the cancer part covered."

Oliver signaled to Julia they should pull Dr. Carney's sheets up a bit to make him more comfortable. As they did, he gently pressed, "I'm not going to teach you to suck eggs, Dr. Carney, but you know an infection from this can lead to a dangerous build-up of bilirubin. You hardly want to add sepsis to your symptoms."

"No. That's fair." Dr. Carney patted Oliver's hand. "But I wouldn't have really put pancreatic cancer on my list of life ambitions, either. Come now, Oliver. Didn't I teach you anything about bedside manner? Looking horrified is hardly in the best interest of the patient."

"I have an idea that might appeal to you," Julia interjected. "I just read about this in an article from a German medical study." She knew she was taking a stab in the dark here but one thing she was sure of—Dr. Carney would refuse any sort of invasive treatment. "Artichoke tablets or milk thistle can help stimulate bile flow, which could decrease the blockage." She continued quickly as Oliver made a move to interrupt. "The downside to the treatment is, if the blockage is really bad, the increase of flow could make the condition worse."

"Which is precisely why a percutaneous biliary drainage is the best option," Oliver countered.

Wow. So much for homeopathic remedies helping those in poor clinics. Julia had to stop her jaw from dropping as Oliver continued.

"Dr. Carney, it's hardly surgery. We just place a fine needle through your skin, after numbing it, then guide it to the correct location and inject some removal fluid. Easy-peasy."

Julia had to turn away from Oliver. *What was wrong with him?* How could he offer procedures they didn't have the equipment to perform? X-ray cameras, ultrasound machines, X-ray contrast dye… All easy to come by in the trauma ward of a state-funded hospital—not so much out here in St. Bryar's humble country clinic. Apart from which, if the removal fluid didn't work, inserting a balloon catheter would be the follow-on option—precisely the type of invasive procedure they didn't have the wherewithal to perform. And exactly the type of procedure Dr. Carney would refuse. The patient had to come first. Biting her tongue was no longer an option.

"A PBD could lead to a bile leak causing peritonitis. I doubt we want to risk an abdominal infection."

"An antibiotic drip is the easy solution to that," Oliver parried.

Julia felt her sympathy flick into frustration.

"I think you've both given me plenty to think about." Dr. Carney waved his hands weakly at the pair of them. "It's not as if I haven't done my own research. One of the lads down the village loaned me his tablet thingy and I feel quite *au fait* with what my choices are." He made a shooing gesture. "Give me a few moments to think and I'll press this nice buzzer Julia's rigged up here when I've made my decision."

Barely containing her anger at Oliver, and embarrassed that Dr. Carney had been caught in the middle of a pair of bickering doctors, Julia strode to the clinic's back door, desperate for a calming breath, or a hundred, of spring air.

"What was that all about?" Oliver pressed, following her into the garden.

"I could ask you the same thing!" Julia whirled around, not caring that her cheeks were flaming with emotion.

"I'm trying to do best by the patient."

"And I'm trying to do best by the patient's *wishes*!"

"By offering him artichoke tablets? Are you kidding me?" Oliver's eyes widened to the point she doubted his eyebrows could've gone much higher.

Slow breath, Julia. He's upset. No one likes to see a loved one dying.

"I'm in a tricky place here, Oliver. Of course I want to do everything I can to prolong Dr. Carney's life, but he's fully aware we don't have most of the equipment required for these treatments. On top of which, the future owner doesn't really know where he stands as regards the clinic, so I hardly think putting in an order for an X-ray camera is going to meet with any success."

Oliver scanned the garden as if it would give him answers. A shocked expression played across his features. Had she been too direct?

"You could've asked me for the equipment." His eyes settled on hers.

"Really? While you were out there in South Sudan, saving the masses, you would've been sympathetic to the cause of one?"

No answer. Just one pair of angry green eyes and a very set jaw.

"If I'd told you it was for Dr. Carney I don't doubt for a moment you would've helped, that we would've been able to buy the equipment in. You obviously love him and want the best for him. But if I'd kept the patient anonymous I'm not so sure you would've pushed as hard for treatment, Oliver."

"How coldhearted do you think I am? 'Hippocratic Oath' mean anything to you, Dr. MacKenzie?"

Julia had to stop herself from feeling the effects of verbal whiplash. She'd struck a nerve. A deep one.

"I don't think you're coldhearted at all. But I think you're confused about what you want in this particular case."

"I'm a surgeon. I fix things. This is an easy procedure and I am trying to do what is best for the patient."

"Against his wishes?"

It was all Oliver could do not to physically vent his frustration—kick a fence, punch a wall. Something to relieve the pressure. Everything Julia said was hitting home. Up until now he'd avoided situations like this by simply not being around. So much easier not to get involved if you couldn't see it happening in front of you.

"This place is a shambles."

"I'm sorry?" Julia looked as if he'd slapped her and he hated himself for it. He was heading for a dark place. The one he'd been hoping to rid himself of forever by putting the past behind him. He pulled a hand through his hair, willing the gesture to give him some clarity. Hurting Julia wasn't part of the plan. Hell, *Julia* wasn't part of the plan, yet here she was, well and truly under his skin.

"You've got to understand, this place has been a noose around my neck from the moment my brother died. He is dead because I didn't tell anyone about his rash and by the time I did this so-called hospital lacked the resources to help." He couldn't believe he was saying these things. They'd always been his silent torture. But for the first time he needed someone to understand. *No. Quit avoiding the truth.* He needed *her* to understand.

Julia gave a tight-lipped nod of encouragement to continue. She didn't look happy and he could hardly blame her.

"Don't think I'm apportioning blame. I know my lot in life has hardly been tragic—quite the opposite. But seeing Dr. Carney like this and not being able to do anything..." He paused, searching for the right words. "It's my fault we lost my brother. Don't you see? It's because I didn't do anything and losing him was the most painful thing my family has ever gone through. Pure heartbreak. I know it's nothing other people haven't endured."

He chanced a glance at Julia and was immediately glad he had. Her eyes spoke volumes, assuring him he wasn't alone. He leaned against the clinic wall, pressing a foot up against the ivy-covered stone with a noisy exhalation. This was really out of character. All of this confessing. What was it about this woman that brought all of his neatly filed away issues tumbling out? He'd lashed out at her, and she'd stood her ground. She was still here, trying her best to understand. Trying her best to be his someone. *In for a penny...*

"You know the burdens of grief as well as I do, but living up to my brother's unfulfilled legacy when I was to blame? Impossible. In my mother's eyes, Alexander could do no wrong, and I can't say I disagreed with her. He was truly born into the right life. He relished the idea of running the estate, maintaining the status quo, ensuring the Wyatt name stayed high on the social register of the nation's elite. He loved all of this—the estate, the village, the tea parties, the shoots, the humdrum everyday life of St. Bryar."

"You think it's humdrum?" Julia asked. "Being here?"

"What do you think?"

She shrugged noncommittally, and he couldn't say he blamed her.

"No. No, I don't. Not anymore." Of course he didn't. Hurricane Julia had whirled into his life and changed everything. But she couldn't change the past. He scrubbed his hands across his face, as if willing the memories away, then looked directly into Julia's eyes. "Until now, I never envied Alexander's passion for the estate because it let me get on with my life. Being a duke? It's just not me. Never has been. I wasn't made for a life of ribbon cuttings and fox hunts. I was made to practice medicine, pure and simple."

A crease formed on her forehead. If she hadn't thought he would hang around before, she was suffering no illusions now.

"How old were you both when this happened?"

Her question caught him by surprise.

"I was fourteen and he was eighteen. Why?"

"You're blaming yourself for not diagnosing teenaged meningitis when you were a teen yourself?"

"The symptoms were textbook. I should have known."

"Of course they're textbook to you *now*—you're an experienced doctor. But then? Oliver—how could you have known?"

"Because nothing was normal in how he was behaving. He was irritable and complaining about muscle pains and a headache. That wasn't Alexander. He was the poster boy for 'good-natured.'"

"And it's natural for a little brother to go tell his parents his brother is being irritable?" Julia raised her hands in disbelief. "I think you've been too hard on yourself."

Oliver shook his head, not wanting to let himself believe her words even though they rang true. "I'm not so sure. Regardless, none of this is helping Dr. Carney. I'm not going to stand by and do nothing this time."

"You know as well as I do, practicing medicine involves a lot of listening." Julia crossed over to him and laid a hand on his arm, her thumb soothingly sliding back and forth across his wrist. "Go in there." She inclined her head toward the door. "Go in there and *talk* with him."

She was close. Not more than a few inches away. He could smell the scent of her freshly washed hair; read the appeal for peace in her eyes, as if it had been handwritten. He tucked a stray wisp of her hair behind her ear, his fingers slipping along her arm, before reluctantly returning to his side.

It was all he could do not to pull Julia in toward him and kiss her promise of a mouth with unchecked passion. Pull her in tighter and begin to physically explore her—with his hands, his lips, his tongue, as he had the other night. He wanted to tug her hair out of the tight ponytail she wore and slip his fingers through the flax-colored waves. He wanted Julia to be his someone. The someone he knew more intimately than anyone else in the world. Every pore in his body ached for it.

And every cell in his brain was saying no. For that to happen he would have to let go of years of cemented beliefs. Rage. Grief. He couldn't forgive himself. Not yet.

"Good idea. I'll do that." He nodded toward the clinic door. "Shall we get on, then? Busy day ahead."

"Dr. MacKenzie!" Clara called from the stove as Julia stepped into the huge old kitchen. "I was just bringing some soup up to Oliver and His Grace. Shall I fetch you some?"

Julia closed the kitchen door behind her, already feeling revived by the savory scent of fresh soup. Her gut instinct was to say yes. Clara's soup and some freshly baked bread in the library? Just what she needed after a tense afternoon in the clinic. Dr. Carney had elected to try out the artichoke and milk thistle tablets in lieu of surgery. Oliver's tightened jaw at the news had spoken volumes. Not happy. Giving him a wide berth was probably for the best.

"Would it be all right to eat down here or in my room?"

"Rubbish! I won't hear of it—you'll join us in the library." Oliver's voice filled the kitchen before Julia had noticed him entering.

"I'm sorry, Dr. Wyatt," Julia replied evenly. "I am fairly certain I hadn't chosen that as an option."

"Clara, tell Dr. MacKenzie she's being silly. Besides," he countered with a soft smile, "Father's been asking after you. If you won't accept an invitation from me, surely you wouldn't refuse The Most Noble Duke of Breckonshire?"

"Ooh! Listen to you, Mr. Toff! Since when have you gone all traditional?" Clara guffawed openly as she ladled some soup into a third bowl.

"Mr. Toff?" Julia couldn't help but clap her hands gleefully at Oliver's mortified expression. "I think there's a story there."

He'd been an old grump all day. It was nice to see his obvious emotional turmoil regroup into a bit of good old-fashioned embarrassment. She plonked her elbows on the long expanse of a wooden counter and cupped her chin in her hands. "Pray, do tell Clara."

"Oh, now, I wouldn't betray a confidence, dear. Nothing to hurt my Ollie." Clara gave her a broad wink. "Let's just say a certain ten-year-old needed a trip to the dentist after a particularly greedy toffee apple episode."

"Clara, I don't really think we need to delve into the past," Oliver sternly protested, but his obvious affection for the woman turned his words from terse to loving. "Here, hand us the tray, you old minx—*with* an extra bowl of soup for Dr. MacKenzie. Everything smells delicious, as usual. Why don't you knock off and I'll sort out the washing up after?"

"Don't be ridiculous, Ollie. You'd do it all wrong. Besides, you'll be doing me out of a job if you keep hanging round the place like this!"

"Clara! You're irreplaceable!"

Julia's heart leaped at the words. Had he reconsidered? Was he going to stay? She immediately checked herself. *He's talking about dishes, you fool. Now, c'mon. Be a big girl and play nice. Have a bowl of soup with the man.*

"You know, I *was* being silly." Julia picked up the chopping board laden with steaming bread. "I will join you. I could do with a good game of backgammon after, if you're willing?"

"We'd best get on, then, before this gets cold." Oliver smiled and headed for the stairs.

"Don't worry. I'm right behind you."

Julia leaned back in the deep cushioned armchair and sighed contentedly. "That was delicious."

"I'm so glad you joined us. An unexpected surprise!" the Duke of Breckonshire quipped.

Julia shot Oliver a sharp look. Hadn't he lured her here under the premise his father had been asking after her? He gave her a noncommittal raise of the eyebrows as his father continued, "It's nice to have a young woman round the house again."

Julia laughed. "I'm hardly a young woman, but thank you for saying so."

"To me, my dear, *everyone* is young." The kindly gentleman reached across to pat her hand before moving to push himself up and out of his chair. "Which brings me to the point of the evening where I must make my excuses. It's time for me to turn in. Oliver?"

Oliver rose to give his father a bit of support as he got to his feet. "Sure you don't want to stick around for a battle of the champions, Father?" He nodded toward the backgammon board he'd been setting up.

"Oh, heavens, no. Not tonight, anyway. I'm sure you'll give each other a run for your money—or whatever it is you're going to play for." The twinkle in his eye was undeniable, and Julia felt, for just a moment, she was being set up on a not-very-blind date.

"Good night, all."

"Good night, Duke." Julia made a move to get up but was stopped as Oliver's father waved her back down to her seat.

"Please, dear. Do call me Stephen. It's my given name and I'm not so caught up in all the formalities these days. With Lorna gone, there's no one round to say my given name. It could be our little secret." He patted his son's arm as he spoke. "Doesn't do a body good to be averse to change, does it, son?"

"Have a good night, Father," Oliver replied noncommittally.

"That I will, son." He tossed a quick wink over his shoulder at Julia. "Give him a run for his money, dearie. The boy's a shark!"

Oliver gave his father a loving clap on the back before pulling the library doors shut after him.

"He's great. I just love your father."

"It's rich, hearing him talk about throwing tradition to the wind!" There was a tight bite to Oliver's words.

"He's hardly sitting in the cobwebs praying for time to stand still," Julia shot back, feeling defensive on the duke's behalf. "He's always been open to all of my suggestions."

"And how do you think he's going to take to me shrugging off hundreds of years of tradition and becoming the daredevil doctoring Duke in Absentia?"

"Is that what you want to do? Work in conflict zones for the rest of your life?" Was she holding her breath while she waited for his answer—or holding her breath because she already knew it?

"Honestly?"

She nodded. "I think we've moved beyond light chitchat, don't you?"

Oliver laughed good-naturedly then took up a studied position by the impressive stone fireplace. "Honestly, Julia—if it were two or three weeks ago, I would've told you I'd put Bryar Estate on the market in an instant and donate the lot to the Red Cross or Flying Doctors—or both. But now?" He ran a hand along the mantelpiece and turned to her, green eyes focused so intently on her she had to fight the urge to squirm. "Right now, I couldn't even begin to tell you what I want."

"Why's that? Are the books more complicated than you thought?" Playing dumb didn't come naturally, but they were treading on territory where Julia felt anything but safe.

"Don't be daft. You know as well as I that I've been doing anything but looking at the ledgers from the very moment I arrived at Bryar Hall." He began to rattle off a list. "I've been eating cake that reminds me of my mother, seeing people I haven't spoken to in years, learning about the merits of a long-term family practice and dredging up memories I had hoped to never think of again."

"Why?" She knew the answer, knew it in her heart right that very instant, but wanted—needed—to hear it anyway.

"Because they're painful. Horribly, horribly painful. And I wanted more than anything to keep them locked up forever. Then one very blue-eyed lady I've come to know, someone I've grown very fond of, suggested it just might be possible to forgive myself."

"And what would you do if you did—if you forgave yourself?" She held her breath again, the room so silent she was sure she could both hear the blood rushing between her ears.

"That's a loaded question." He quirked an eyebrow but didn't break eye contact.

Julia's mind positively reeled with questions.

Would you stay? Would you stay here with me?

Could she live with the answer? Could she even believe it was fair to ask? What would she say if he asked her the same thing? *Think, think, think! Do you love him? He quizzed you about your feelings—now it's your turn.*

"I suppose it's not your usual garden party question, but you've been more than clear that's not your sort of thing."

"Are you suggesting, Dr. MacKenzie, that I lack social dexterity?"

"Oh…" She mused, a smile playing on her lips. "I hardly think your social skills are substandard." She glanced down at her fingers, still lightly splinted, and laughed. "Then again…"

Oliver collapsed onto the sofa, swinging his long legs up onto the overstuffed cushions. "See?" He was grinning now. "If that's the kind of first impression I make here at home, I don't think the House of Lords is quite ready for this Most Honourable Marquess of St. Bryar."

"Pah!" She hadn't meant to bark with laughter, but… too late now. "You made quite a first impression, all right." And a second. And a third. Julia's belly felt a warm eddy of desire as their eyes connected.

"Really?" Oliver propped up his head on an elbow and pushed himself up onto his side. "What sort of impression was that?"

"A favorable one." She tried for an air of nonchalance but knew her body language was betraying her. A shift of the hips. A finger winding up a strand of hair. Thank goodness Oliver didn't know about the fiery tingles working their slow and leisurely way through her body. As if she could be any easier to read.

"Are you still up for that game of backgammon?" Oliver pushed himself up from the sofa and offered her his hand.

Don't take it. If you take it you might kiss him again. If you kiss him again you won't be able to stop...

"Come here, you."

Was he thinking what she was thinking?

Her lips parted.

He tipped his head down toward her.

He was thinking what she was thinking.

As Oliver pulled her into his arms, all the problems of the world, all of their sparring, the unanswered questions, the unknown of the future, just faded away. All that existed in the world was Oliver and the most languorous, deeply intentioned kisses she'd ever known. Her body responded intuitively to Oliver's touch, barely giving her mind a moment to keep pace. She felt her arms slip up his chest and across his shoulders, tangling together in the soft, dark curls at the nape of his neck. Her back arched as she pressed into his chest, the slightest of shudders running down her spine as he spread his fingers along the small of her back.

His breath played along her neck as he gave her small, exploratory kisses along her jawline. A small "ooh," escaped her lips as his mouth began to travel down her neck and farther down along to her collarbone, which he was exposing one delicious inch at a time. She wanted him. She had from the moment they'd met.

Without having noticed how they got there, Julia became aware of being in front of the fireplace. Oliver pulled back a bit, his hands holding her face so that it was impossible not to lose herself in his eyes.

"Do you want this to go further?"

She didn't trust herself to speak. Her body was aching for Oliver's, for more of his touch. Could she put aside the fact he'd made her no promises?

She physically desired him as she had no other man. If he decided to leave she knew in her soul she would never see him again. Never know the intimacy of his touch. If life had taught her anything, it was to seize the moment, and this could be one of her last with Oliver. They were adults, after all. Surely, one night wouldn't change anything? Much. Would a nod suffice?

Oliver's fingers teased at the buttons of her blouse as Julia stretched out on the silky Persian carpet, decision made. She wanted him. By the languorously slow caresses of his lips and fingertips, she could tell he too was fueled with the same powerful force of desire. It obliterated everything else. One by one the buttons of her top came undone, a finger straying here or there against her breasts, then her midriff, as he teasingly went about undressing her. He shifted a lock of hair away from her eyes and smiled softly before he began to kiss her again. Deeply, this time. Urgently.

Oh, this is nice.

No, it's not! It's naughty, the "lingerie catalog shoot" type of naughty. A mother of thirteen-year-old twins shouldn't be— Ooh.

Then again, what's so wrong with naughty?

Oliver stroked a hand up along Julia's leg and under the hem of her skirt in one fluid motion, fingers playing along the lacy edges of her panties while he planted decidedly sensuous kisses along her belly. Her body arched into his caresses. He was obviously no stranger to a woman's body, but each and every touch felt indescribably personal. Waves of desire surged through her as clothes were dispensed with, their movements becoming more fluid, almost synchronized in the instinctive hunger to please the other. She buried her head in the crook of his neck, stifling her moans of pleasure as they joined together, her body alive and blazing with desire for him. Never before had she wanted someone so badly.

Conflicting thoughts flittered out of her mind as Oliver's touch became more pressing. She wanted him. She'd desired him on a primal level from the moment she'd seen him. That wasn't quite right.

Felt him.

And feeling him now, as she slipped her fingers along the bare skin of his back, skimming lightly along his waistline onto his hips—warm, responsive, impassioned—she wanted nothing more than to be with Oliver, no matter what tomorrow might bring.

CHAPTER EIGHT

"I THOUGHT I'D find you here." Oliver's crooked grin crept round the corner of her small clinic office. "You just disappeared this morning."

"You know what they say," Julia tried to chirp back. "Up with the lark and all that!"

"I hate to leave you on your own here, but I told my father I would meet up with the accountants today. Stop putting off the inevitable."

"Oh, that's great!" she lied. Julia's mind was still a muddle of fireside love-making, king-size bed passion and about the sexiest bubble bath she'd ever taken before drifting off to sleep in Oliver's arms. A handful of hours later, her eyes had snapped wide-open—all too aware she had just taken a swan dive into a world of unknowns.

Jumping into the arms of the one man who held your fate in his hands? Talk about the number one no-no in the bad decisions department.

Oh, but it had been good. Better than good. An involuntary shiver slipped along her spine, irritatingly spooling into a warm pool below her belly.

"So, I'll see you up there later?"

"Where?" *He doesn't think we're going to make love again, does he?* Not that she'd mind… *No! Stop that, Julia.*

"You said you'd go over the books with me after the clinic shuts. Help me figure out which way the land lies for ol' Bryar Estate."

He must've read the poorly disguised dismay on her face. "You're not going back on it, are you?"

"Of course not!" Julia plastered a smile onto her face as her stomach clenched, sending a sour ache through her body. Last night had been about the most sensually bewitching blunder she'd ever made. For Oliver? Obviously a passing fancy to fill the time while he was wrapping things up at Bryar Hall. What an idiot! Brainy and no-nonsense were the last things she was feeling.

What did you do when you'd just slept with the one man standing in the way of your personal and professional goals? Particularly when he was standing right in front of you looking all deliciously tousle-haired and green-eyed. Didn't he know looking this sexy was outrageously inconsiderate?

"I wouldn't dream of letting you down. A deal's a deal."

"You're sure?" He didn't look like he was buying it.

Stiff upper lip? Check. Smile in the face of adversity? Check. Comment about the weather?

"It's a perfect day for it."

"April showers…" he began to riposte then petered out, visibly aware Julia's words weren't ringing true with her demeanor.

Julia felt perilously off-balance, as though she was walking a conversational tightrope.

"Bring on those May flowers!" *There.* Was that bright-eyed and bushy-tailed enough?

"I'll catch you later up at the house, all right? I'll just pop in on Dr. Carney before I go."

She kept her focus on the chart she'd been updating. "He's sleeping. Probably best to leave him be. I'll let him know you asked after him." *Oops.* There went the "Miss Congeniality" prize.

"What's going on, Julia?"

"Nothing, just a lot to do today."

Oliver stepped into the office and turned her, chair and all, toward him. "Spill it, MacKenzie."

"What's the point?"

"I beg your pardon?"

"Oh, don't get all upper-crusty on me. You know what's going on as well as I do."

Oliver raised his eyebrows in surprise. *Oh.* Maybe he didn't.

"I saw the estate appraiser's car pull up to the house this morning." She let the words sink in. "So, I know this—this thing between us—is just a time-filler for you. You'd never planned to stay, so it doesn't matter what I think of the books."

His eyes opened wide and any warmth she'd seen in them vanished. "I think you know me a little better than to be a love 'em and leave 'em type, Julia."

She stared at him, suddenly feeling as though she was looking at a stranger. A stranger she could have loved if only absolutely everything about their lives had been different.

"Do I?"

"Yes," he answered solidly. "You do. But you know as well as I do, the last thing I've been paying attention to these past few weeks is the estate. If I'm going to get a true understanding of the place, I have to have solid facts and figures. What if it's a money pit? There's no point in hanging on to something that isn't sustainable."

Julia looked at him, wide-eyed with disbelief. Did he mean her or the estate?

Oliver straightened, but his voice had softened. "You know we're not talking about you and me here, right?"

"Of course I do." The burning in her cheeks began to flush her throat.

He tried to give her shoulders a rub, but it was impossible not to stiffen under his touch. "Hey," he continued softly. "I wouldn't have asked for your help if your opinion didn't matter, but we can't ignore reality, can we?"

She shook her head. Talking would've betrayed the tremble she felt building in her throat.

"C'mon, Julia. This is a big decision for me. I thought you were my sensible someone."

"Maybe not so sensible after all." Her eyes darted away from his. It felt as though her heart would break.

She dropped her head into her hands and pulled her hair into a taut ponytail, as if the tightness on her scalp would help her think more clearly. She'd been an idiot to think she could sleep with him then just carry on as if nothing had happened. Everything had changed. She was in love with Oliver. Sensible and pragmatic were the last things she was feeling.

"Apologies." Julia shook her head and tried to flush the emotion from her voice. "I must've woken up on the wrong side of the bed or something. Catch you later?"

Oliver let go of the door frame after unsuccessfully trying to catch Julia's eye one last time. This was not how he'd envisioned "the morning after." Not even close.

"See you later, then." He left the clinic and jumped into his car, his jaw tightening as he pushed the car into gear. It didn't sit well. Leaving things like this with Julia

He slapped at the steering wheel in frustration. If this wasn't just another piece of proof nothing could go right at Bryar Hall, he didn't know what it was.

Julia was the best thing to have happened to him in he didn't know how long. They made a genuinely good team on so many fronts. Working, talking, laughing. She was someone he could be *silly* with, for heaven's sake.

Love-making. There was no comparison.

Why had he met her here of all places? They were a natural fit. *In more ways than one.*

Was he falling for her? No; too late for that sort of reflection. He'd already taken the final steps off the cliff edge. He'd well and truly fallen. His fingers did an agitated dance on the steering wheel.

Think, Oliver. Think.

There were ways around this. Life wasn't static.

She could join him in South Sudan. They always needed new doctors. Together they would make an impressive team.

No. He shook his head. The children. She wouldn't think for a minute of leaving the children.

What else could he do to be with her? He couldn't bear the thought of proving her right—being so intimate, so perfectly in body and spirit, then leaving her. He knew they'd only just begun to scratch the surface of something truly beautiful. Beautiful. That was what a life with Julia could be.

The obvious solution began to prod and goad him as he drove past the large washes of daffodils, the espaliered avenue of blossoming fruit trees, and pulled up in front of the house where he had only recently known so much joy was possible. He stared at the house, willing it to give him the answer he wanted.

Could he forgive himself for Alexander's death? That was at the heart of it. Without doing so, Bryar Hall could never be his home.

The scent of freshly baked shortbread drew Julia into the library. Oliver was already in there, head bent over a pile of ledgers and looking...what was that expression, exactly? She tilted her head to get a glimpse of his expression. "Not very happy" would've been a pretty big understatement.

Perhaps she'd been too brusque with him this morning. They had flown straight into the intimacy stratosphere the night before and coming down off a high like that had been one heck of jolt. If he'd had any idea of the jumble of thoughts she'd been trying to put into order today, he would've placed her on Burke's peerage— directly under Right Old Royal Mess.

"Shortbread?" Oliver looked up as she approached.

Yup. He still took her breath away.

"You've been hard at work." Her fingers played along the edges of the wooden table, unsure of what sort of mood he was in.

"No more than usual."

Oh. His manner was short, miles away from the man who had flowed with mischievous whispers and throaty groans the night before.

"Oliver, I wanted to apologize for this morning, I—"

"No need," Oliver interrupted, his tone curt, officious. "We're all busy. Can I get you a chair?" He pointedly laid down his pen and looked directly into her eyes. If she hadn't been so hurt by the absence of affection in them she would've laughed. Bitterly. *What a difference a day makes, eh?*

"I'll get one myself." She pulled a straight-backed chair over from the other side of the long mahogany table where he was working and set it beside him. The slight twitch he gave as she sat down told her he was as aware of her as she was of him. It was as though the energy from their bodies couldn't resist joining together with a magnetic pull. Chemistry united them. Fate seemed determined to intervene.

She pulled her chair back a few inches. That was better. Just.

Now, if she could just get her head to reason with the dance floor full of jitterbugs making their way round her tummy, she'd be a content woman.

Ha-ha ha-ha! Good one.

She snuck another peek at him. She was a doctor, for heaven's sake. Surely she could be objective about this perfect mix of sexy, smart and rakish adventurer? He was made of the same stuff everybody else was, right?

Her heart refused to agree. It skipped a bit. Then cinched.

Nope.

No chance of being objective. He was perfect. Even if he was actively ignoring her. She stopped a building sigh from escaping her lips. It looked like he was revving up to give her some bad news. She better get in with her news before he told her his.

"Oliver—"

"Julia—"

"After you."

"Please." Oliver gave her a look. An "I'm not in the mood" look. "Go ahead."

How on earth do I do this?

You just breathe. Then you exhale. Then you do it.

"I've just had a call from my children's school." *Uh-oh! There go the raised eyebrows. Keep talking, keep talking!* "I'm afraid I muddled up their holiday dates and I need to collect them from the train station."

"Oh, yes?" He gave her an inscrutable look. "When's that, then?"

"Tonight."

"What's on tonight?"

Julia turned to see the duke had just entered the library, a book tucked under his arm, his aging chocolate Labrador at his knee.

"Julia's children are going to be joining us for the spring holidays a bit earlier than expected." Oliver answered for her, rising to greet his father.

"Oh, splendid. I did have such a lovely time with the twins over the Christmas holidays." He turned to Julia, openly delighted. "What good news!"

"Oh, really?" Oliver gave her a bemused glance. "You all had Christmas together, then?"

Julia's eyes ping-ponged between the pair, her teeth pressing so hard into her lip it was in danger of being bitten clean off. If Oliver had caught her off-guard with his estate business, she'd opened a cupboard full of info he didn't have.

"Yes, didn't I say?" Oliver's father clapped a hand on his son's shoulder with an apologetic grimace. "Sorry, old chap. I thought I'd put it in a letter to you. Your mother was always much better at that sort of thing. You know what they say about short-term memory for us old fellows." He turned back to Julia with a warm smile. "They'll be staying here in the house, then, this time?"

"I—I'm not—"

"Of course they will," Oliver finished smoothly. "Dr. MacKenzie's children are most welcome at Bryar Hall."

She swallowed. Hard. He'd been hurt. Life had gone on at Bryar Hall and left a grieving Oliver in its wake.

"Thank you."

"Nothing to thank me for," Oliver replied, moving to the desk as he did. He pointedly closed an open ledger and turned to her. "Bryar Hall has always opened her doors to visitors."

Youch. So that was what she was, then. A visitor.

It seemed as though Oliver was taking the news of her children coming a few days early a lot worse than she thought he would. Or was she taking everything personally again? He had looked far from cheery when she'd come into the library. Were the ledgers full of doom and gloom? Had he been on the brink of telling her the place had to go? She tried to catch his eye, desperate to find out what was going on.

"Sorry to have interrupted." The duke placed his book on a side table. "Just dropping this by then Barney and I are going for a walk."

"I think I'll join you, Father." Oliver didn't even bother to give Julia a second glance. "I could do with a change of scene."

Julia closed the door to her bedroom, no longer fighting the temptation to cry. She loved her children dearly and needed to clear her clutter of mixed emotions before they arrived. Ella and Henry had had enough to deal with over the past year and a half—losing Matt, moving schools, having to make new friends. The last thing she wanted was for them to feel unwelcome in the place she had hoped they could call home.

She looked around the spacious bedroom she'd spent the past couple of weeks in and gave a hiccuping laugh as she wiped away the last of her tears. The children weren't so silly they would look at Bryar Hall as their home, but her little cottage? They'd adored it when she had first come along for her job interview and had put dibs on their rooms within moments of arriving.

On a recce to St. Bryar High Street, the twins had pronounced the job hunt over. Together with the clinic and her ivy-laced cottage, they'd pronounced St. Bryar home. If only Oliver could see the place through their eyes. Maybe it was just too late for all that. Oliver's vision was well and truly stained by the past. He might never be able to see the Bryar Estate they did.

She was tempted to go have a nosy and see how work was coming on at the cottage. Surely it was ready now?

Then again, things did take forever to happen out here in the country. Perhaps that was what drove Oliver mad. He obviously preferred life to move at a high-octane pace, not the steady clip-clop of Bryar Estate.

Julia huffed out a loud breath. What was a bit of damp when the other option was staying with a man who wasn't in love with her? She hardly wanted to be skulking around the large house with the children if Oliver was going to be itching to slap for sale signs up the whole time.

Julia opened up the room's French windows and took a step out onto the small balcony overlooking the gardens. She took a restorative breath of the cooling early evening air. They were properly into spring now, but the light still held that faintly watery quality of winter sun, glazing the gardens in the ephemeral sheen of the golden hour.

Her heart skipped a beat as first Barney then Oliver and his father appeared from the thick foliage of the small maze at the far end of the garden.

How could one man have made such an imprint on her life in such a short time?

Matt had been a steady Eddie—he'd always been there—and, except her surprise pregnancy, everything about their relationship had been familiar. Like a favorite jumper. Something she could rely on.

The most she could rely on Oliver for was to be *un*reliable.

That wasn't fair. She shook her head, unable to stop watching as Oliver and his father held what looked to be an intense conversation. No. Oliver wasn't unreliable. He was hurting. He blamed himself for his brother's death and seemed to be serving a never-ending penance in the form of his work overseas. It was as if he really did believe that turning his back on everything here would make it better. A classic British response to gut-wrenching sorrow: just close the doors and leave it all behind as if nothing had happened.

Except a lot had happened. Too much to ignore. He had turned her world on its head and now her cozy little hideaway from the big, bad world was not so safe.

She walked back into the bedroom, firmly closing the doors behind her. You had to laugh, didn't you?

She lifted her arms up and turned in a circle as she tried to stretch away the worry. The warm yellow wallpaper flecked with miniature poppies smiled out at her. She grinned back. It was good for the soul. Especially when dark and brooding distractions were wandering round the garden outside her bedroom window.

Who knew? Maybe a brief encounter with Oliver was

what she had needed to bring some clarity to her life—make her really think about what she was doing here. Was she hiding or living the life she'd always dreamed of?

Right. Get a grip, girl. Your children are due in half an hour. Tear-stained and hangdog was never your look. Time to focus.

Julia pulled out the stool to the art deco dressing table and stared at herself in the mirror. First and foremost, she was a single parent. A fierce, loving mama bear. She'd do everything in her power to protect her children. That was what really mattered. Not Bryar Hall, not Oliver.

Her heart seized for a moment. Okay. Not really a lie that would fly, but whatever. She needed to brainwash herself and fast.

Julia tipped her head toward the fading rays of sunlight, pulled the hairband away from her ponytail and watched her hair fall across her shoulders.

Yeah. Why not admit it? She was pretty. Not in a supermodel way but she would do in a pinch. She grinned at her reflection, giving a little prayer of thanks for her parents' good genes. If she wanted to meet someone again, have a relationship on equal terms, she was hardly past her prime.

A sigh huffed out of her chest and made a small cloud on the mirror. Ha! Was this the part where the thought process got a bit murky?

So. She'd had sex with Oliver. It wasn't the worst thing to have done, was it? She squeezed her eyes shut as a series of flame-lit images of his body moving in fluid synchronicity with her own flickered past her closed lids.

Had it been great? Her stomach flipped at the thought.

Okay. That's that answered, then. Better than great. Their bodies were made for each other.

Had it been a one-off? Her belly tightened. Maybe so, but falling in love with him was going to be a lot harder to shake off than one steamy night by the fire. The prickly heat of tears teased at her eyes again. She'd have to find a way to make nice for the next few weeks and then chances were he'd be gone again.

She glanced at her watch. Eek! She needed a fast and refreshing shower before she picked up the children.

Ella and Henry. They were her true north, what had gotten her up every morning after Matt had been killed. They would keep the "almost had a shot at love" blues at bay. She squeezed her eyes shut, forcing herself to picture the twins coming off the train and running toward her for a huge family hug. Just the three of them. That was real. That was lasting. Even a bit of heartbreak over Lord Oliver Wyatt wouldn't take that away.

CHAPTER NINE

"TAKE A RIGHT HERE, SON. I've been giving the stables a miss these days."

"What about Star? Surely it's snack time?" Oliver gave his father a knowing smile. The duke's "tour of duty" round the estate had always finished at the stables where he would give his favorite horse the carrot or two always tucked away in the deep pockets of his waxed jacket.

"Ah, I'm afraid Star is no longer. We lost him in February."

"I can't believe it! Why didn't you tell me?" Oliver felt the hollowness of shock obliterate anything else he'd been feeling. Star had been around since he'd been a gangly teenager. He and Alexander had always begged their father to let them race him round the fields. If ever you couldn't find the duke, you looked for the chestnut stallion. It had always been that easy.

"I didn't want to burden you with my troubles, son. It's been a couple of months now. I'm getting used to the change."

It sickened him to think his father hadn't felt comfortable telling him about this. Or the funding for Dr. Carney's treatment. Realistically? The list could go on.

He pulled a hand through his hair and shook his head. Had he made himself that inaccessible? Here was a wonderfully, loving and aging father still looking after him when it was high time to turn the tables. Particularly now that it was just the two of them.

"Are you thinking of getting a replacement, Dad?"

"Oh, I've toyed with hiring out the stables or bringing back in one of his progeny and starting a new line, but…" He stopped to admire a broad wash of cherry blossom running along the edge of the orchard. "Those sorts of decisions are largely up to you now, son."

"Don't be ridiculous, Father. I've never known you not to ride."

"You haven't seen me riding these past few weeks and haven't said a word." The words weren't unkind, just observant—and Oliver felt a torrent of guilt pour through him.

In his frustration and sorrow over Alexander's death and his mother's everlasting grief he'd put too much focus on putting everything behind him. To the extent he hadn't been able to see what was right in front of his face. A living, breathing, caring parent. Options. Possibilities. Love. All of the things Julia saw. His eyes flicked up to the room where she was staying. The lights were out. She must've left already. Little wonder, considering his anticharm offensive.

His eyes moved across to his father. A light smile was playing across his lips as he bent over to examine a spring rose. How could he be so forgiving of his son when Oliver had been so—absent?

Resolve charged through him. He might not have an inbuilt sense of duty to the landed gentry, but Oliver would do anything for his father, and it hurt to the core that he could have been there for him and hadn't been.

In closing his heart to the estate, he had cut himself off from the people he loved. And had begun to love. Was that what Julia was trying to get him to see? He had a lot of work to do—emotional hurdles he didn't know if he could leap but he'd be a fool not to try.

"An entire lemon drizzle cake?" Elsie blinked at Julia and stared as if she was asking her for forty cakes instead of just the one.

"Yes, please, Elsie."

"Are you sure you and the children wouldn't just like to share a slice now? I've got one left here."

Julia could feel her children move in closer, interest rising. Immediate satisfaction? That was a kid's dream come true.

"No thanks, Elsie. Just the one cake to take away, please."

"Are you sure I couldn't interest you in another? The carrot cake is always lovely."

Oliver hated carrot cake and this was a peace offering. Carrot cake would definitely send the wrong message. Her brow furrowed as she looked at Elsie. If Julia wasn't mistaken, there was a hint of panic in the poor woman's eyes. What on earth was going on?

The bell above the door tinkled. Julia watched wide-eyed as Elsie snatched up the lemon drizzle cake she'd been trying to buy and held it out as if it was the Hope Diamond. She might as well have been invisible for all the notice Elsie was taking of her now.

"Will this one do, m'lord?"

"Gorgeous."

Julia stiffened. She knew that voice and was already feeling her body's response to the person attached to it as he approached. His tone was all warm and chummy. What a sea change from just an hour ago. She watched, openmouthed, as he lavished his natural charisma on Elsie.

"When will I be able to convince you to call me Oliver?"

"Probably never, your lordship." Elsie barely stifled a schoolgirlish giggle. "I'm too stuck in my ways." Elsie sent an apologetic wince in Julia's direction as she expertly packed up the cake in a white box and wrapped it with the shop's telltale green ribbon.

Julia had had just about enough. Stealing cake from children? Was that what he'd been reduced to? Particularly after she and the children had devised a plan to surprise him with it as a peace offering for their unexpected arrival. Any goodwill Julia had planned to extend to him was now out of the question. Suave, debonair and a cake thief? The outrage!

"Madam, may I be so bold?"

Julia looked up at Oliver, not comprehending why he was standing with the cake outstretched toward her.

"I'm sorry, I don't—"

"Mum." Henry was tugging at her sleeve. "The man's giving you the cake!" *Humph! It takes a thirteen-year-old, does it?*

"Henry, hush." Julia jutted out her chin proudly and looked back toward the cake display feeling anything but calm inside. Here she was again—back on Oliver's emotional yo-yo ride. Well, no thank you very much indeed. She'd had enough swinging to and fro.

"What was it you were saying about the carrot cake, Elsie?" He could take that for his ruddy peace offering.

"Julia, I was hoping to surprise you at home. You're making a scene out of nothing." Oliver's voice was low and moving from charmingly persuasive to peeved. Or was that just her imagination? She refused to make eye contact with the green knee-weakeners and could only just see him holding out the box from the corner of her eye.

No way. She simply wasn't going to give him the satisfaction of winning this one, particularly with her children in tow. It was time to set an example.

"Ella? It's Ella, isn't it? And Henry?" Her children nodded as Oliver solemnly shook hands with them. "I'm Oliver, from up at Bryar Estate. I understand your mum is an awfully big fan of lemon drizzle."

"Yes, it's her favorite. Yours, too! She told us!"

Julia shot her children a horrified look. Hadn't she spoken to them about speaking to strangers? Sure, it wasn't strictly accurate that Oliver was a total stranger...

She knew him.

Her insides did a melting, fluttery thing, reminding her just how well she knew him. But her children didn't know him from Adam and that was the point. She shot Oliver a look she hoped said *steer clear, Mama Bear is in the house and someone has just stolen her...his... lemon drizzle cake.*

She jutted out her chin, prepared to stare him down, just in time to see her internal monologue was having zero effect on her children who were quite merrily chatting away with Oliver. It was hardly a Shakespearean betrayal, but honestly! Oliver should know better than to try to get to her through her children. On the other hand, was he being sneaky smart? Whose good opinion would he have to gain to win her over?

She looked down at her kids, beaming away as they carried on with Oliver.

The man was good. She felt her heart soften—a little bit. A crumb-sized bit.

"Well, after your mum left to collect you at the train station, I decided you all deserved a nice welcome treat. You've probably heard the cottage is a bit damp and your mum's been staying with me at Bryar Hall?"

He gave Julia a pointed look. *Danger! Green Eyes Alert!*

"So," he continued, oblivious to the tummy fairies doing the two-step inside her, "I rang ahead and asked Elsie to set a cake aside for me because I wanted to surprise your mummy with something she loved."

Julia stared openmouthed as her children laughed along with Oliver at the mix-up. Oh, ha-bloody-ha! So they'd all been trying to do a good deed for the other. So what? It wasn't like it meant Oliver had suddenly realized he was madly in love with her and planned to stay at Bryar Hall so they could all live happily ever after.

Did it?

Something she loved?

That something was a someone and he was standing right in front of her, pulling open a corner of the cake box for the children to take a peek.

"Do you think we should just eat it right now?"

She ground her teeth together and forced a stiff grin onto her lips at his suggestion. She'd fallen for his sweet talk before. Cake right before supper? Ridiculous suggestion.

Her children looked up at her, clearly delighted with

the idea, Ella clasping her hands together in a "pretty please" formation for added emphasis while Henry gave a little jumpy "can we can we?" jig. She felt herself give a little. It had been too long since she'd seen them last. Surely a little treat wouldn't go amiss?

No. She couldn't give in this easily. Oliver needed to know she wasn't a pushover, didn't he? Buying her children's affections with cake? *Shameless.*

"Shall I get some plates, then?" Elsie began to move from the counter, her eyes anxiously trained on Julia.

"Oh, go on, then." Julia threw up her hands in surrender as her children cheered and made a beeline for the table Elsie was already setting.

"Thank you." Oliver's voice stopped her before she went to the table.

"For what, exactly?" Julia couldn't keep the wary edge out of her voice. She loved him, and a life together was the stuff dreams were made of—impossible dreams. Why did he have to make coming to terms with it so difficult?

"For giving me a chance."

Her heart quickened. "A chance to what?"

"Be a more gracious host." He took her hand in his, unleashing a spray of goose bumps up her arm. "You know your children are welcome. Very welcome."

"Are they?" She knew her voice was sharp and she didn't care. The she-bear in her needed assurance. She could sort out her own mashed up heart later, but her children? No one was going to toy with their emotions.

"Of course," he said with a rueful shrug. "It will be lovely to have children in the house—along with their mother, of course."

She glanced over her shoulder at her children, a swell

of motherly pride overriding the sensations accompanying Oliver's close proximity. Wait a minute! Did that mean...? Julia gave herself a mental shake. *Get a grip. He's not proposing or starting a family with you, he just likes children. And you?*

"They seem like great kids."

See?

"They are." She retrieved her hand and fixed him with a steely eye. "You best be careful, Oliver. They have fragile hearts and need to be treated carefully."

Just like me.

"Don't worry." He let go of her hand, and she felt its absence instantly. "I can do careful." He gave her an unreadable wink. "Piece of cake."

Oliver closed the door to his room, feeling a bit like a character in an episode of *The Waltons*. The halls were echoing with "good nights" and "sleep tights." Sweet dreams were probably the last thing that would come to him as he wasn't the tiniest bit sleepy.

Julia hadn't seen the least bit taken with his attempts to win her over with Elsie's finest, nor had she taken up his invitation to share a quiet drink by the fire. He wasn't expecting an immediate repeat of the unforgettable love-making they had shared—but surely she knew it wasn't something he had done casually? Far from it. How could he tell her he'd fallen for her but that he needed some time to sort out his head?

He'd already been processing a lot as he'd gone through the estate's accounts. They'd unveiled a lot of surprises. Black inky-type surprises he hadn't had a chance to wrap his head around. And, when she'd thrown the children's arrival into the fray, well; it wasn't his proudest moment.

He sank into a chair and let the cold, hard truth sink in. He and Julia weren't meant to be together. It was as simple as that. One plus one equaled zero.

"Mummy, look what I found."

Julia swiveled round in her office chair as Ella carefully laid a large scrapbook stuffed to the hilt with photos and clippings, complete with a family crest, onto her desk. A twist of anxiety went through her. The fortnight had been going so smoothly, she didn't want to rock the boat so close to the children going back to school.

She put on her best warning voice. "You've not been snooping, have you?"

"No, not at all." Ella looked shocked her mother would even have thought such a thing and hurriedly explained. "His Grace said I could go into Her Grace's dressing room and look at her ballgowns, and when I opened one of the cupboards I found this."

"Why did you take it out of the dressing room?"

"It's all about Oliver, and I thought you'd like to see it."

Julia gave a mortified laugh. "Why would I want to see it?" Was she that transparent?

Ella rolled her eyes as if it were a no-brainer.

Guess so.

"Mu-um..." her daughter continued as if speaking to a five-year-old. "You've only been making googly eyes at him ever since we arrived."

"Don't be ridiculous." Julia closed the book shut without looking at the contents. "I've been doing no such thing. Now, you'd best put that back where you found it."

"Whatever you say, Mum." Ella drew the book along the desk then picked it up. "I just wanted you to know, Henry and I wouldn't mind if you—you know..."

"What?" She asked the question but knew instantly what her daughter was saying. She was giving her permission to love again.

"If you want to get married again, Henry and I are cool with that. We just love it here!"

This was definitely not a topic she wanted to discuss. Marriage was the last thing on Oliver's mind and should most definitely be well out of her own. A picture of her in a wedding dress walking through the rose garden popped up in her head. *No!* Not allowed.

Ella started idly flipping through the pages of the scrapbook. Julia chanced a discreet peek. Or seven. Images of Oliver at work in war zones covered many of the pages. Oliver holding a baby girl. Oliver standing proudly amongst a gaggle of gangly-limbed teens. Oliver getting cornrows put in his thick hair from a group of laughing ladies. A beautiful script gave detailed descriptions of each photograph or dated an article. His mother's hand, no doubt. She scrunched her eyes shut. His mother had obviously been incredibly proud. And Oliver very obviously loved his work. Work she could never ask him to give up.

Waves of feeling shunted through her as her heart constricted.

She pulled her daughter into her arms and gave her a hug. Ella began wriggling for freedom before Julia had had enough.

"Mum! I've got to put the book back, all right?"

She reluctantly let go of her daughter after tucking a stray blond curl behind her ear.

"Go on, get out of here." She made a shooing gesture to cover the fact she really wanted her to stay. "See
you at dinner."

Her daughter popped a kiss on her cheek and began
to run out of the door. "Why don't you leave the book
out for Oliver?" Julia called after her. He might enjoy
seeing how proud his mother had been of him and all
he'd achieved. Maybe it would help him lay some old
ghosts to rest.

She turned back to the piles of paperwork on her desk.

She had at least a dozen new application forms for
grants—private funding, public funding, lottery funding; you named it, she'd researched it and printed it.
Now, to start filling them in.

Oliver might find it easy to abandon everyone here
but, newcomer or not, she felt part of this community
and, even if she had to work out of Elsie's teashop, she
would continue to serve the people of St. Bryar—with
or without the green-eyed love monster.

Gales of laughter traveled from the kitchen to the library. They taunted Oliver who had thought it wise to
try to give the MacKenzie clan a wide birth. It was one
thing to be graciously welcoming, but a whole other
beast to let himself be woven into the "happy family"
web. It wouldn't be based on anything sustainable and
it wouldn't be fair to raise Julia's hopes.

Another peal of laughter curled up the stairs. Against
his better judgment, Oliver found himself tugged by the
merry voices to join Julia and the children all huddled
round a board game on the kitchen table.

Mugs of hot chocolate were strewn about the table
and what appeared to be a smear of marshmallow was

waiting to be licked from the top of Julia's lip. Distracting. Very distracting. And they hadn't even noticed him. He was a ghost in his own home.

"What's all this noise about, then, eh?"

Silence.

Talk about being a killjoy. *C'mon, Oliver. Social skills!*

"There's a big fire up in the library, should you so desire." They all looked at him as if he'd just spoken in Swahili.

No. That wasn't it. French? No. It suddenly came to him—he'd spoken English aristocrat. Even worse.

"Biscuit tin is down here," Julia explained. "We didn't want to make a mess."

Oliver was tempted to reach over and thumb away the bit of gooey sugar on her lip—or, better yet, kiss it away—but Julia's tone was clear: *back off.*

"Mum! Your face." Ella made a scrubbing movement and Julia's tongue made quick work of the smudge.

That settled that, then.

"There's better lighting upstairs." He tried again, though it wasn't strictly true.

"Honestly, we're fine here. We make a mess wherever we go."

Terrific. What a great host. Making your guests feel they had to hide away for fear of leaving biscuit crumbs on an antique rug. Precisely the sort of reason he'd never in a million years imagined having a family of his own here.

Another peal of laughter erupted from the table as Henry started drawing a melting snowman after Ella had flipped over a tiny hourglass. The children, at least, didn't seem constrained by the environment. He'd never seen such a relaxed family scene in the house. It was nice. Something he would love to see more of. Something he'd love to be part of.

"There's a much bigger hourglass up in the drawing room." Oliver tried again. "Shall I fetch it for you?" *Blimey.* This was just getting worse. Now he sounded like a stuffy butler!

"No thanks, Dr. Wyatt." Ella looked up at him with a smile. "This is loads funnier when you only have thirty seconds."

"You can call me Oliver, if you like."

"Springtime!" Julia shouted, clearly more interested in the game than his awkward stab at chitchat. "Would you care to join us?"

She hadn't looked up, but could obviously see he was hovering. Hoping to stay.

"Yeah, that's a great idea!" Henry chimed in with a grin. "Kids versus adults."

This time Julia did look up, her sapphire-blue eyes connecting with his. "Well, then. I guess that makes us a team."

Julia's heartrate accelerated as Oliver slid along the kitchen bench next to her. Despite her best efforts, she couldn't squelch any of the sensations she'd lectured her body to appreciate were no longer appropriate. His thigh grazed hers as he shifted into place. *Zing! Pow! Pop!* There went the internal fireworks display!

She grabbed an extra pencil and pad from the game box and handed it to him. Their fingers brushed. *Sizzle!* Good grief!

Little wonder her children had noticed her response to Oliver. She might as well have a large blinking neon sign over her head with Unrequited Love written on it and a big arrow pointing down at her for all of the non-subtle reactions she was having.

Come to think of it—she could do with a whole host of signs. What would be perfect for Oliver? She gave him a sidelong glance. Dreamboat or Dream-Destroyer? Her fingers played along her lips as she considered which was best. Lips that would have been ridiculously happy to kiss him again. And again. And...

"Mum!" Julia looked across at Ella's exasperated face. "Your turn!"

"Right." She grabbed a card, eyes widening as she read the item she'd have to draw for Oliver. Just great.

Cupid.

It was going to be a long night.

CHAPTER TEN

OLIVER HEARD JULIA'S voice in the entry hall and rose from his chair. The timing—as usual—was awful. She'd just dropped the children at the station, holidays having raced to an end. She'd be feeling low. And she wouldn't be alone. He was surprised how empty the house already felt without them. Despite his best efforts to be a bystander with Julia and the children, he just hadn't been able to stop himself from joining in. It didn't seem to matter what they did, it was just fun.

And here he was, ready to play number one rain-maker. A year ago—hell, a few weeks ago—the news he was about to impart would've been the answer to his prayers. Now, it all sat wrong, but he'd be a fool to ignore a gift horse. Best get it over with.

"Julia?" Oliver called out from the open library door as she began heading up the stairs.

"Yes?" She stiffened but didn't turn around.

"Can you come down, please?"

The instant Julia reluctantly turned around, he was struck by how much she suited the place in completely the opposite way from his mother had. His mother had been authentic—Julia seemed *real*. "Real" was what he had been searching for by working in conflict zones.

You couldn't get more real than that and yet, there she was, cheeks flushed, deep blue eyes a bit red-rimmed, as if she might have been crying—heart-on-her-sleeve real. His gut clenched.

"Everything go well at the station?"

"Yes, fine, thanks." She turned to go up the stairs.

"Would you mind joining me in the library? I need a word."

Seriously?

This was the last thing she needed. What Julia really wanted was to close her bedroom door behind her and have a quiet little blub in her room. With her children on their way back to school, the empty feeling in her heart was threatening to grow. Holding on to the idea that she could build a rich, fulfilling life in St. Bryar had been keeping her chin above water these past eight or so months but everything about the past few weeks had put her on unsteady ground again. No, that wasn't right.

Oliver had put her on unsteady ground and it was breaking her heart.

"Can't it wait?"

"Not really, no."

Fine. Have it your way. She didn't move.

"Shall we get on, then?"

No mistaking that tone. Short and not at all sweet.

"Fine." *Not.* "Ready when you are." She did her best to flounce into the library where Oliver proceeded to take her through a painstaking, blow-by-blow tour of the previous three years' accounts, all of which led her to one mind-blowing conclusion.

"Are you telling me the estate is in the black with money to spare?"

"It's happy news, isn't it?" Oliver replied.

He looked anything but pleased.

"I don't understand. I thought you—"

"The point is—" he spoke pointedly, slowly, as if she were a small child "—we've actually got quite a valuable asset. To sell." He let the words sink in.

Julia's hands began to shake.

"I don't understand. You've just shown me in triplicate all the reasons why you should keep the place and you're still planning on selling? On leaving?"

"There is a buyer ready to move quickly." Oliver pushed away from the desk and strode over to the picture windows facing out to the manicured gardens.

Julia was hardly going to let him off this easily. She was by his side in an instant, pulling him round to face her. Oliver was going to have to look her in the eye if he was going back on their deal.

"So what? There have probably been willing buyers for hundreds of years and your family hasn't sold."

"And they probably hadn't received the offer I have. It's a lot of money, my dear."

Julia cringed at the term of endearment. It was the last thing he meant, and she couldn't bear false charm.

"Since when were you concerned about money? The guy I met in the moat wouldn't have given two beans about a fat check."

"It would solve a lot of problems."

She nodded, clearly struggling with her emotions. He felt like he was ripping both of their hearts in two. He hadn't expected a business decision to hurt so much. But it wasn't really a business decision, was it? It was a very poorly disguised way of dodging his demons.

"I can't stay, Julia. I've tried to picture it—believe me

I have tried. And meeting you? It made so much seem possible. So much that I couldn't have imagined. But this place has done well because my father has been incredibly hands-on—and that's what is needed. Someone to turn kitchen table projects like the ones we saw the other night into profitable ventures. Someone to shout above the rooftops about St. Bryar's cheese and damson wine and salted caramels. Someone should be doing that— but it's not me. I'm not that guy."

"And what type of guy are you, then?" Julia's arms were tightly crossed over her chest as if she were protecting herself from his answer.

Oliver's heart was in his throat. He wasn't the kind of man to break a woman's heart and that was what he felt like he was doing.

"A medicine type of guy. Medicine is my thing—you know that." He exhaled heavily. "Which is why this sale is so important. It means I can gift the clinic to the village with you in charge. You'll be looked after."

"You're selling the place so I can stay at the clinic?"

Tears swam in Julia's eyes, her face a portrait of incredulity. It was all Oliver could do not to pull her into his arms, but he simply couldn't risk it. Staying here, loving her, her children—he hadn't earned the right to be so happy. Hadn't—*couldn't*—forgive himself for the loss of his brother.

He gave the ledgers a solid rap. "We're sensible folk, aren't we? The most good I can do in the world is to sell this place when it is riding a financial high. Far better than trying to offload the old money pit I thought it was. Think of how much good the money can do out there in the world."

"What about love?"

The air between them hummed with taut emotion. Julia had said the words before she'd thought them. She suddenly, urgently, needed to know if Oliver loved her. Loved her as she loved him.

"One can't love a house, Julia." His eyes were darker than she'd ever seen them.

Her heart contracted. There was her answer. He didn't love her. Plain and simple.

A heavy weight settled in her stomach. It was well and truly over. The dream of a life in St. Bryar—a life with Oliver—*poof.* Gone.

A phone rang in the corridor. A muffled voice answered and footsteps approached the library door.

"Excuse me, m'lord?" A maid cracked open the library door. "I'm very sorry but it's the clinic. They say it's urgent."

Julia knew in an instant it was Dr. Carney. It was after office hours and only the volunteer hospice nurse was there. She tugged her jacket tightly round her, pulled open the doors to the garden and began to run.

Oliver held Dr. Carney's frail hand in his, still hardly able to believe it was real. He'd seen this a hundred—no, a thousand—times before. But this time it was as if the sorrow would eat him alive.

Dr. Carney was gone.

He felt a hand slip onto his shoulder and, without turning, knew it was Julia. Her scent filled the air around him—the most beautiful thing left in his life and he was letting her go. She loved him and he was letting her go. He wished she could see it as he did. Being with him would be like tying a millstone round her neck. He brought nothing but pain to St. Bryar, and she was all joyous, brilliant light.

"Would you like to stay with him awhile longer?"

"No. No, that's fine." Oliver pushed himself up from his chair, grateful only for the fact he had arrived in time to say goodbye. To say thank-you.

Julia had been there first, ensuring Dr. Carney felt no pain. Then, when Oliver had arrived, she'd smoothed his mentor's brow, kissed him goodbye and left the two of them alone. A generous act if ever there was one. He knew she'd cared for Dr. Carney as much as he had yet she'd respected their history. The shared past.

Oliver had sat with him in that timeless space filled only with deep, unfettered emotion. He'd talked and talked and then, as he'd seen Dr. Carney begin to slip away, they sat in silence. He'd been too weak to reply, but Oliver knew his message had gotten through. He owed his mentor an unpayable debt of gratitude, owed him for being everything he had not been. Someone who'd stayed.

Despite the pain, the grief, the heartache, Dr. Carney had remained in St. Bryar not just for the Wyatt family but for the community. He'd seen them all through sickness, health, beginnings, endings—he'd been a part of their lives, an inextricably linked part of St. Bryar. Everything Oliver had fought to keep at arm's length, Dr. Carney had had the fortitude to face every single day of his life.

"The men from Tryvens Funeral Home are here." Julia's soft voice brought him back into the room.

"Ah. Well, then. I guess I better push off."

"Oliver, you don't have to leave. We all understand."

"We?"

"Quite a few people from the village are here. Outside."

He looked at her uncomprehendingly. It was well past midnight.

"To pay their respects," she explained.

"Of course!" He raked a hand through his hair, as if it would clear the fug of grief. "You go ahead. I'll just get back to the house, make sure Father's all right."

"He's here, Oliver. In the waiting room. We're all here." Julia reached out to him, her fingers making contact with his hand. Gratefully, he wove his fingers through hers and, before he could check himself, he pulled her in tight to his chest urgently, as if his life depended on it. He felt her hands slip around his waist, up along his back, pressing into him as if she knew it would help lessen the pain he was feeling.

"He was so proud of you, you know. All you've achieved."

Oliver pulled back and looked at her, eyes wide with disbelief. "Which was what, exactly? A drop in the pond compared to what he did."

"What you've done with your career is different, Oliver—but it still makes a *difference*. Surely you can see that?"

"I was meant to follow a very particular path and only succeeded in making a compete hash of it. I *had* to leave, had to do something else so I didn't ruin anything else here."

Coming from someone else, the words would have sounded plaintive. From Oliver they were the cry of a soul in torment. He just couldn't see all of the good he'd done in the world, and Julia's heart ached for him.

"I hardly think the countless patients you've seen and helped would agree."

"I think my mother would agree with me. The things I was supposed to do—the shoes I was supposed to fill—they're still empty, Julia. Can't you see? My life is a catalog of letting the people I love down, and the longer I stay here the more obvious it is—I will never be my brother. I will never earn the title."

"You were never meant to be anything other than who you are, son," Oliver's father interjected from the doorway.

Oliver was at the door in two long-legged strides. "I didn't mean it that way, Dad—this isn't about you."

"Ah, but that's where you're wrong. There is an awful lot of this that has to do with me. I saw how your mother's grief affected you and I did nothing. I let you leave us without making sure you knew how much we loved you."

"I always knew you loved me, Dad." It was easy to see in his eyes that much was true.

"And your mother loved you too, son. Very much."

Oliver shook his head as if trying to keep his father's words at bay. Julia could see he couldn't believe them.

"How could she have? I was a terrible son—never facing up to what I'd done. I ran away, away from all of my responsibilities, as soon as I could."

Oliver's eyes lit on Julia, and clear as day she understood: Oliver didn't feel he'd earned the right to stay.

She physically ached to go back to him, hold him, assure him he could start afresh. Everyone's heart in St. Bryar was wide-open to him. But you couldn't hold someone somewhere against their will. Not if their heart wasn't in it.

His father laid a reassuring hand on Oliver's arm, steadying his son's gaze. "It's a terrible night and we're all very sad. But you mustn't throw the baby out with the bathwater. You have always been loved, just as you are."

Julia's heart leaped to see a small glimmer of light return to Oliver's eyes. He may never find peace here in St. Bryar but perhaps one day, he could find peace. She'd find solace in that one day, too—knowing he was happy.

The duke gave Julia a small nod and smile then continued, "Oliver, why don't we give everyone else a chance to say goodbye? I think you and I could do with raising a glass to Dr. Carney back at the house."

"You know—there's something you could do for me if you're heading back up to the house."

Oliver looked at her with a baffled expression.

Julia deftly ran from the room to her office and picked up the scrapbook her daughter had never put back.

"Here you go. I'm afraid Ellie didn't put this back when I asked her." She handed it to him without having the nerve to look into his eyes. "Kids!" She gave a nervous laugh. "You might want to have a look. It's a good read."

"Are you sure there's enough, Dr. MacKenzie?" Clara, hand on hips, was dubiously eyeing the long trestle table laden with just about every canapé and finger food imaginable.

"I think you've done him proud, Clara. Dr. Carney would be impressed." Julia gave Clara a quick squeeze round the shoulders. The poor woman must've been up for days from the looks of the vast spread that lay before them.

They both started at the sound of the entry bell then looked at each other and quietly laughed. "And so it begins!" Julia scanned the large library, her arms curled around herself as mixed feelings washed through her. Wakes were funny things. Happy and sad. It was a shame this was most likely the last time the villagers would come together at Bryar Hall. A farewell to the hall, as well as to Dr. Carney. And, much more painfully, to Oliver.

She gave herself a shake. At least today was a celebration of someone's life.

Footsteps clipped down the stairwell.

Oliver.

Black tousled hair, clean shaven and bespoke-suited, the Marquess of St. Bryar looked every bit the future heir to a grand estate. Life could really be ironic sometimes.

It was probably just as well she'd hardly seen him in the days since Dr. Carney had passed. He'd been holed up in the library with his father and the estate accounts, the pair of them inseparable. It was hard to believe the laughter and steady flow of chat she heard coming from the room would ultimately lead to his departure.

She gave her head a quick shake and held her chin high. Oliver didn't need to know she'd spilled more than her share of private tears over the past few days. He'd found peace with his father and would leave without the burden of regret. That should be enough.

Who was she kidding? Her mind knew the facts, but her heart was finding it impossible to say goodbye.

Bryar Estate wouldn't be the same without him, and for the first time she was beginning to question the wisdom of staying on once he was gone. Everything would irrevocably change. St. Bryar would no longer be the colorful palette of the duke, the villagers, the flower contests and lemon drizzle cakes that made up her adopted home. St. Bryar had changed for her. It was Oliver. And he would soon be gone.

He stopped midway down the stairs, those green eyes of his locking with hers, his expression unreadable. Her gut clenched and an explosion of heat detonated in her very foundation. *C'mon, Julia. It's all over now. Act English. You can do this.*

A maid opened the main door for the villagers who had begun to arrive in droves. Oliver knew he should be down among them, meeting and greeting, but he couldn't move for the effect Julia had on him. Seeing her standing at the entrance with his father, a simple navy dress lightly outlining her figure, blond hair brushing on and off her shoulders as she turned, took his breath away. Shaking hands, smiling, touching a shoulder, laughing quietly with someone, consoling someone else, *connecting*, she looked every bit the lady of the house.

He thought he'd already known it in his heart—but it well and truly hit him like a bolt of lightning now. He'd made the right decision. Julia belonged here. He couldn't believe he'd spent the past weeks being about as thickheaded as they came. He should've realized long ago that love at first sight was a very real thing. Even if you needed to clear a bit of the mud away to see the whole picture.

Julia personified everything he had imagined Bryar Hall should be. Could be. If he hadn't been so mired in the past, he might have seen straight away that a life with Julia was exactly what his mother would have loved for him.

He saw that now—clear as day. Saw the pride in the careful notations his mother had made in her scrapbook. And no matter how awful it had been when Alexander had died, it hadn't been his fault. No one had been to blame.

And life was about right now. Not drowning in a sea of regret.

And right now, watching Julia command the grand hallway of his family home, Oliver knew the work he'd done, the late nights he'd pulled over the past three days, had been worth it. They had to be if he was going to win back Julia's respect. Her approval. She alone knew he was capable of more than he had ever given—professionally and personally. Because of her, he would spend the rest of his days striving to be a better man.

His gaze softened as he continued to watch her. The ease and grace with which she handled herself was simultaneously compassionate and genuine. If he'd thought he'd loved her before, Oliver knew now that Julia fully claimed his heart.

Adrenaline flooded through him. Before he could change his mind, he was by her side, joining in welcoming the people of St. Bryar with Julia alongside him. It felt right. It felt real.

"I can't believe you were going to do this at the clinic," he muttered sotto voce.

She stiffened. *Not the best opening gambit, then.*

"It was his home away from home. But your father insisted we have it here when it became clear everyone was going to come along."

"You've done a brilliant job organizing all of this." Oliver put a hand on her elbow and turned her toward the library as the last of the guests arrived. She kept her eyes trained on the crowd and ever so slightly turned her shoulder away from him. He'd hurt her badly and it stung. He wanted her to know everything in his heart but was now the right time?

"You should say a few words before you go. Everyone would appreciate hearing from you."

Oliver hesitated. Of course he would say something about Dr. Carney but so much else needed to be said. Could he explain it all? Tell everyone—Julia—what a fool he'd been?

"Don't worry, Oliver," she encouraged, mistaking his hesitancy. "I've seen you cast your spell over dozens, scores, of people at a time. I have zero doubt in your ability to say something about Dr. Carney as long as you speak from the heart."

The energy between them began to build. He felt a surge of pure connection—one so complete he could never have imagined it possible. The dart of pain he saw flash across her eyes was like a shot of poison through his bloodstream.

Yet, here she was, offering him good advice. Non-judgmental. Caring. It was proof that she loved him—and he'd done so very little to deserve it.

The tips of his fingers tingled as a physical ache to touch her took hold of him. He wanted to tell her how he felt, put words into action. Make her dreams come true.

"Oliver! Over here." The vicar waved Oliver over to a small group standing by the fireplace where his father was midway through a story.

Brilliant timing—as usual.

Stop it, Oliver. New beginnings.

He gave Julia's hand a quick squeeze. "I'll put something together. Trust me."

Julia watched as Oliver joined the group, her body still responding to his touch. How that man had turned her life topsy-turvy, crushed her dreams of a quiet little life in the country to a pulp and still laid claim to her heart was well and truly beyond the confines of logic. The sooner he sold up and moved away, the better. Right?

What was that saying? Better to have loved and lost...?

Humph.

That saying was pants.

"Dr. MacKenzie, can I get you some carrot cake?"

Elsie and her carrot cake appeared from the crowd.

Perfect.

Oliver hated it. And she needed to hate him. If by some strange turn of events he tried to kiss her—which would be weird, considering he'd made his intentions to leave particularly clear—he would be repulsed. And maybe even break out in a rash. Which would be satisfying for about half a second.

His laughter floated across to her from where he appeared to be holding court with a fireside clutch of villagers. She tried to create an Oliver-free force-field around her.

Nope. No good. He still gave her tummy flutters.

"Any lemon drizzle on offer?"

"Are you all right, Dr. MacKenzie?" Elsie was peering at her as if mushrooms had suddenly started sprouting out of her ears.

"Of course, just—you know—" She halfheartedly turned toward the crowd. "It's just hard to take it in."

"I know, dear. We're all going to miss Dr. Carney dreadfully. All the villagers feel so lucky to have you here. We're all ever so grateful you're staying put."

Julia swallowed a bit of cake and forced a smile onto her lips. This was going to be a long day.

* * *

"Could I have everyone's attention, please?" Oliver pinged a fork on the side of his wineglass and took a step or two up one of the library's short ladders.

As the crowd settled, he eagle-eyed Julia. She was tucking herself behind a gaggle of women over by the French windows as if hoping for a quick escape. He'd taken over two hours to "come up with a few words." He hoped to heaven they were the right ones. Oliver threw his traditionally private self to the wind and began to address the crowd. This wasn't about him, after all.

"Dr. Carney would be the first to be humbled by the incredible show of affection and community here today. He played a role in all of our lives. Some of us, he brought into the world. Most of us, he saw through life's usual aches and pains. And for those of us who lost loved ones, he was always there to provide comfort in the wake of their loss. He was, in short, always there. For that we owe him a debt of gratitude and a well-deserved toast."

He sought Julia's blue eyes as he raised his glass and, as she met his direct gaze, drew strength from their clarity. "What all of this has taught me is to be a bit more honest with myself. Many of you have heard—or even started rumors—that I myself will be moving on." A murmur of nervous laughter and hushed conversation confirmed what he knew to be true. He'd been unfair to hold the villagers on edge. Over the past two hours he'd spoken with everyone whose livelihood was tied in with the estate; he hoped that they could finally rest easy. Today he was decided. Today he knew which way his destiny lay.

"Which is why," he continued, "I would like to announce today, in order to make a clean slate of it—a fresh start—all of the changes that will be coming to Bryar Estate."

Julia dug her fingernails into her hands, wishing she could clamp her ears shut—or better yet run from the room. *Talk about torture!* She knew it wasn't personal but watching Oliver up there, preparing to tell everyone about the sale, felt like being dumped in front of her nearest and dearest. Fleeing would be easy—but it was the coward's way out. If he was going to bail on her publicly, she was going to take it without one single tear spilled. *Chin up!*

"A while ago, my father was telling some of you about the days when he first moved to Bryar Hall."

Another murmur of interest rose from the crowd. Julia tuned in more closely. Where was this going?

"Not all of you will know, he and his family stayed in the Gate House while the main house was used as a hospital during World War II—as it had been in World War I. Dr. Carney, in fact, was the son of the midwife who delivered my father."

"Hear, hear!" shouted one of the older villagers. There was laughter and another round of clinking glasses. It was a great story, but Julia was now impatiently rapt. Where exactly was all this leading?

Oliver adjusted his stance on the ladder and continued, eyes firmly fixed on Julia. "As some of you might know, Dr. MacKenzie has been working night and day trying to secure funding to move our little country hospital out of the dark ages and into the modern world. It was with great sadness that I came upon all of her applications for grants and saw that they were unsuccessful."

The collective hush of the crowd began to physically press in on Julia. She could hardly breathe. Was he really going to humiliate her in front of everyone? Right here in front of all these people on the very day they were meant to be celebrating Dr. Carney? Of all the selfish...

"Which is why my father and I would like to put forward the proposal that we follow in the footsteps of my forebears and turn Bryar Estate back into a rehabilitation hospital for the wounded veterans who serve our country and—when able—open the doors further to those affected by war in other countries."

Julia's heart swooped up her throat and began flying round the room on fairy wings. She watched, open-mouthed, as Oliver shushed the crowd for more. "We will, of course, keep the clinic open for your day-to-day needs and hope some—many—of you will consider job offers here at the main house once it is up and running. I've spoken with a few of you already—and I hope the village as a whole will be pleased to hear the Bite of St. Bryar inspired us to seek agreements from the estate's farmers to supply food for the hospital's kitchens."

Julia's hands flew to her mouth. It was a wonderful idea. But what about him? He still hadn't mentioned what he would be doing in all of this.

"You ladies who hold court at Elsie's with your knitting needles?" Oliver scanned the room and stopped at a group of women by the buffet. "We'll be needing some of your lovely jumpers and blankets if you're up to the challenge."

"Just try and stop us!" cheered one of the women.

Oliver's smile turned sober. "All of this, of course, will take a lot of work and a lot of change but, if you're up for it, this is the path I would like Bryar Estate to follow. It is inspired in large part by Dr. Carney and Dr. Julia MacKenzie. For their selfless contribution to our lives, we should all raise a glass."

A stunned silence followed, quickly broken by Reg Pryce.

"Hip-hip hooray!"

The crowd began to mark out the cheers, Oliver looking increasingly delighted as each "hooray" did its best to lift the roof.

Julia couldn't move. She felt absolutely stunned. Did this mean he was staying? Her eyes darted around the room, searching for a glimpse of him as he was absorbed into the crowd.

Was he staying? Her body felt all floaty and light, her fears of losing him reordering in her mind. A rush of emotion threatened to overwhelm her as Oliver unexpectedly appeared before her. All she felt capable of was staring at him with a happy, dazed grin on her face.

"What do you think, then?"

About a thousand million things! Speech eluded her as he continued, "I think it's a plan that could really work, for the patients and the village." He put a finger to her lips before she could respond. "There is only one condition."

"Which is?" A thump of nerves weighted her stomach. Here it was. The other side of the coin. She knew it had to be too good to be true. *Come on, Julia. Be a grown-up.* "And what, pray tell, is that, Jolly Ollie?" *Oops. Not so grown-up.*

Oliver took her hands in his and brought them to his lips, planting a kiss on each one. His dark lashes lifted and her heart gave another pirouette as their eyes met.

"Marry me, Julia. Let's do this. Let's make Bryar Hall come alive again. Together."

Oliver's heart felt near to bursting as Julia rose up on tiptoe and gave him a soft kiss. A kiss that held a thousand promises.

"Ask me again in a year."

Ah. Not quite what he'd had in mind for a "yes." Cue English aristocratic response.

"Is this your way of saying no thank you?"

Julia unleashed a giddy laugh. "Not at all. I'd marry you this very moment if it was just a question of us running off into the sunset."

She slipped her hand down along his arm and wove her fingers through his. "It's my way of saying make sure this is truly where you want to be. I'm not going anywhere—but you need to make sure you feel the same way. And don't forget—I've got a couple of teenagers who come along with the package."

Oliver could easily imagine the children's laughter filling the empty spaces of Bryar Hall. They were as much a part of his plans for the future as Julia.

"They are a very welcome part of an awfully, awfully nice package."

"Good." She gave his hand another squeeze, tears glistening in her eyes. "It's an amazing idea, Oliver. I just love it. Just think of everything we have to do! I bet I could apply for more grants… Now that we've got a focus, there are bound to be all sorts of organizations that would contribute and—"

"Should we enjoy the rest of the party first?" Oliver interrupted, giving her a kiss on her forehead and wrapping an arm around the woman whom he couldn't wait to call his wife. He was already feeling more settled at Bryar Hall than he had in a lifetime. He'd wait a year. He'd wait forever as long as she was here by his side.

One year later

"I don't think I can even fit through the door."

"Of course you can, Mum. Just turn sideways!" Julia's children went into fits of giggles as they watched her negotiate the entrance to the Gatehouse.

Getting married was one thing. Getting married in an enormous meringue of a wedding dress she'd let her daughter talk her into was another.

"Mum, hurry up! Oliver's waiting!"

"Honestly, you'd think he was the King of England for all the fuss you two are making."

"Would you rather I were?" Oliver appeared at the doorway, a hand extended to take hers in his. It was impossible to wipe the smile from her face. He looked absolutely gorgeous in his fawn-colored linen suit, a sky-blue kerchief just peeking out of his breast pocket.

"Are you kidding me? Think of all the things we could do with Buckingham Palace!" Julia teased, still overwhelmed with all the changes that were well underway as Bryar Hall was transformed from a stately home into a beautiful rehabilitation hospital. None of the character of the hall house had been detracted from—and, thanks to some clever thinking from Oliver's father and a local architect, the changes to make it accessible for all of the veterans were truly breathtaking. She couldn't believe the support they'd received locally, and from national charitable institutions now clamoring to help.

"We'd better get along to the courthouse, you old

fusspot. Father and Clara are already on their way, the kids are in the car…" Oliver gave her hand a little tug. "We've only got an hour booked. I, for one, intend to use most of that time kissing the bride."

Julia grinned, enjoying a slow inhalation of his scent as he tilted his head toward her. "You don't think anyone will mind that we're not having a big shindig, do you?"

"Mind? I should think they'd be terrified to do anything against your wishes to make sure you stay!"

"Make sure *you* stay, is more like it." Julia slipped her fingers through his.

"Both of us, my love. You know as well as I do everyone's over the moon that Bryar Hall is bursting with life. I couldn't imagine being anywhere but here—with you." He gently tapped a finger on her nose then gave it a kiss. "Ready to become a proper local?"

"Ready as I'll ever be!"

"Well, then, m'lady…" Oliver planted a kiss on her cheek and took her hand. "Your chariot awaits!"

* * * * *

MILLS & BOON®

THE ULTIMATE IN ROMANTIC MEDICAL DRAMA

A sneak peek at next month's titles...

In stores from 4th September 2015:

- **Falling at the Surgeon's Feet** – Lucy Ryder *and*
  One Night in New York – Amy Ruttan

- **Daredevil, Doctor...Husband?** – Alison Roberts *and*
  The Doctor She'd Never Forget – Annie Claydon

- **Reunited...in Paris!** – Sue MacKay
- **French Fling to Forever** – Karin Baine

0815/03